Creator of brilliant quadriplegic criminalist Lincoln Rhyme and investigator Kathryn Dance, Jeffery Deaver is a number one bestselling author.

THE BURNING WIRE

A killer is crippling New York City with fear.
His weapon — the electrical grid. The killer
harnesses huge arc flashes with voltage so
high that steel melts and his victims are set
afire, or he reconnects the wires in buildings,
so that sinks, lamps, or computer keyboards,
can kill. The first attack reduces a city bus to
a pile of molten metal, and officials fear
terrorism. Rhyme, a world-class forensic
criminologist, is tapped for the investigation.
Long a quadriplegic, he assembles NYPD
detective Amelia Sachs and officer Ron
Pulaski as his eyes, ears and legs on crime
sites, along with FBI agent Fred Dellray. The
attacks continue — the team work desperately against time. And whilst Rhyme's health
falters — his determination could drive away
his closest allies . . .

Books by Jeffery Deaver
Published by The House of Ulverscroft:

THE DEVIL'S TEARDROP
THE STONE MONKEY
THE EMPTY CHAIR
THE VANISHED MAN
GARDEN OF BEASTS
THE TWELFTH CARD
THE COLD MOON
THE SLEEPING DOLL

JEFFERY DEAVER

THE
BURNING
WIRE

Complete and Unabridged

CHARNWOOD
Leicester

First published in Great Britain in 2010 by
Hodder & Stoughton, London

First Charnwood Edition
published 2011
by arrangement with
Hodder & Stoughton
An Hachette UK Company, London

British Library CIP Data

Deaver, Jeffery.
The burning wire.
1. Rhyme, Lincoln (Fictitious character)- -
Fiction. 2. Sachs, Amelia (Fictitious character)- -
Fiction. 3. Forensic pathologists- -Fiction.
4. Quadriplegics- -Fiction. 5. Electric utilities- -
New York (State)- -New York- -Fiction.
6. Suspense fiction. 7. Large type books.
I. Title
813.5′4–dc22

ISBN 978–1–44480–615–1

Published by
F. A. Thorpe (Publishing)
Anstey, Leicestershire

Set by Words & Graphics Ltd.
Anstey, Leicestershire
Printed and bound in Great Britain by
T. J. International Ltd., Padstow, Cornwall

This book is printed on acid-free paper

For editor extraordinaire, Marysue Rucci

'*Hell, there are no rules here.
We're trying to accomplish something.*'

— THOMAS ALVA EDISON,
on creating the first electric grid

I

THE TROUBLEMAN

THIRTY-SEVEN HOURS UNTIL EARTH DAY

'*From his neck down a man is worth a couple of dollars a day, from his neck up he is worth anything that his brain can produce.*'

— THOMAS ALVA EDISON

1

Sitting in the control center of Algonquin Consolidated Power and Light's sprawling complex on the East River in Queens, New York, the morning supervisor frowned at the pulsing red words on his computer screen.

Critical failure.

Below them was frozen the exact time: 11:20:20:003 a.m.

He lowered his cardboard coffee cup, blue and white with stiff depictions of Greek athletes on it, and sat up in his creaky swivel chair.

The power company control center employees sat in front of individual workstations, like air traffic controllers. The large room was brightly lit and dominated by a massive flat-screen monitor, reporting on the flow of electricity throughout the power grid known as the Northeastern Interconnection, which provided electrical service in New York, Pennsylvania, New Jersey and Connecticut. The architecture and decor of the control center were quite modern — if the year were 1960.

The supervisor squinted up at the board, which showed the juice arriving from generating plants around the country: steam turbines, reactors and the hydroelectric dam at Niagara Falls. In one tiny portion of the spaghetti depicting these electrical lines, something was wrong. A red circle was flashing.

3

Critical failure . . .

'What's up?' the supervisor asked. A gray-haired man with a taut belly under his short-sleeved white shirt and thirty years' experience in the electricity business, he was mostly curious. While critical-incident indicator lights came on from time to time, actual critical incidents were very rare.

A young technician replied, 'Says we have total breaker separation. MH-Twelve.'

Dark, unmanned and grimy, Algonquin Consolidated Substation 12, located in Harlem — the 'MH' for Manhattan — was a major area substation. It received 138,000 volts and fed the juice through transformers, which stepped it down to 10 percent of that level, divided it up and sent it on its way.

Additional words now popped onto the big screen, glowing red beneath the time and the stark report of the critical failure.

MH-12 OFFLINE.

The supervisor typed on his computer, recalling the days when this work was done with radio and telephone and insulated switches, amid a smell of oil and brass and hot Bakelite. He read the dense, complicated scroll of text. He spoke softly, as if to himself, 'The breakers opened? Why? The load's normal.'

Another message appeared.

MH-12 OFFLINE. RR TO AFFECTED SERVICE AREA FROMMH-17, MH-10, MH-13, NJ-18.

4

'We've got load rerouting,' somebody called unnecessarily.

In the suburbs and countryside the grid is clearly visible — those bare overhead high-tension wires and power poles and service lines running into your house. When a line goes down, there's little difficulty finding and fixing the problem. In many cities, though, like New York, the electricity flows underground, in insulated cables. Because the insulation degrades after time and suffers groundwater damage, resulting in shorts and loss of service, power companies rely on double or even triple redundancy in the grid. When substation MH-12 went down, the computer automatically began filling customer demand by rerouting the juice from other locations.

'No dropouts, no brownouts,' another tech called.

Electricity in the grid is like water coming into a house from a single main pipe and flowing out through many open faucets. When one is closed, the pressure in the others increases. Electricity's the same, though it moves a lot more quickly than water — nearly 700 million miles an hour. And because New York City demanded a lot of power, the voltages — the electrical equivalent of water pressure — in the substations doing the extra work were running high.

But the system was built to handle this and the voltage indicators were still in the green.

What was troubling the supervisor, though, was why the circuit breakers in MH-12 had separated in the first place. The most common reason for a substation's breakers to pop is either a short circuit or unusually high demand at peak times — early morning, both rush hours and early evening, or when the temperature soars and greedy air conditioners demand their juice.

None of those was the case at 11:20:20:003 a.m. on this comfortable April day.

'Get a troubleman over to MH-Twelve. Could be a bum cable. Or a short in the — '

Just then a second red light began to flash.

CRITICAL FAILURE.
NJ-18 OFFLINE.

Another area substation, located near Paramus, New Jersey, had gone down. It was one of those taking up the slack in Manhattan-12's absence.

The supervisor made a sound, half laugh, half cough. A perplexed frown screwed into his face. 'What the hell's going on? The load's within tolerances.'

'Sensors and indicators all functioning,' one technician called.

'SCADA problem?' the supervisor called. Algonquin's power empire was overseen by a sophisticated Supervisory Control and Data Acquisition program, running on huge Unix computers. The legendary 2003 Northeast Blackout, the largest ever in North America, was caused in part by a series of computer software errors. Today's systems wouldn't let that disaster happen again but that wasn't to say a different computer screw up couldn't occur.

'I don't know,' one of his assistants said slowly. 'But I'd think it'd have to be. Diagnostics say there's no physical problem with the lines or switchgear.'

The supervisor stared at the screen, waited for the next logical step: letting them know which new substation — or stations — would kick in to fill the gap created by the loss of NJ-18.

But no such message appeared.

The three Manhattan substations, 17, 10 and 13, continued alone in providing power to two service areas of the city that would otherwise be dark. The SCADA program wasn't doing what it should have: bringing in juice from other stations to help. Now the amount of electricity flowing into and out of each of those three stations was growing dramatically.

The supervisor rubbed his beard and, after waiting, futilely, for another substation to come online, ordered his senior assistant, 'Manually move supply from Q-Fourteen into the eastern service area of MH-Twelve.'

'Yessir.'

After a moment the supervisor snapped, 'No, now.'

'Hm. I'm trying.'

'Trying. What do you mean, *trying*?' The task involved simple keyboard strokes.

'The switchgear's not responding.'

'Impossible!' The supervisor walked down several short steps to the technician's computer. He typed commands he knew in his sleep.

Nothing.

The voltage indicators were at the end of the

green. Yellow loomed.

'This isn't good,' somebody muttered. 'This's a problem.'

The supervisor ran back to his desk and dropped into his chair. His granola bar and Greek athlete cup fell to the floor. He ignored them.

And then another domino fell. A third red dot, like a bull's-eye on a target, began to throb, and in its aloof manner the SCADA computer reported:

CRITICAL FAILURE.
MH-17 OFFLINE.

'No, not another one!' somebody whispered.

And, as before, no other substation stepped up to help satisfy the voracious demands of New Yorkers for energy. Two substations were doing the work of five. The temperature of the electric wires into and out of those stations was growing, and the voltage level bars on the big screen were well into the yellow.

MH-12 OFFLINE. NJ-18 OFFLINE. MH-17 OFFLINE. RR TO AFFECTED SERVICE AREAS FROM MH-10, MH-13.

The supervisor snapped, 'Get more supply into those areas. I don't care how you do it. Anywhere.'

A woman at a nearby control booth sat up fast. 'I've got forty K I'm running through feeder lines down from the Bronx.'

Forty thousand volts wasn't much and it would be tricky to move it through feeder lines, which were meant for about a third that much voltage.

Somebody else was able to bring some juice down from Connecticut.

The voltage indicator bars continued to rise but more slowly now.

Maybe they had this under control. 'More!'

But then the woman stealing power from the Bronx said in a choking voice, 'Wait, the transmission's reduced itself to twenty thousand. I don't know why.'

This was happening throughout the region. As soon as a tech was able to bring in a bit more current to relieve the pressure, the supply from another location dried up.

And all of this drama was unfolding at breathtaking speeds.

700 million miles an hour . . .

And yet another red circle, another bullet wound.

CRITICAL FAILURE.
MH-13 OFFLINE.

A whisper: 'This can't be happening.'

MH-12 OFFLINE. NJ-18 OFFLINE.
MH-17 OFFLINE. MH-13 OFFLINE. RR TO AFFECTED SERVICE AREAS FROM MH-10.

This was the equivalent of a huge reservoir of water trying to shoot through a single tiny spigot, like the kind that squirts cold water out of a refrigerator door. The voltage surging into MH-10, located in an old building on West Fifty-seventh Street in the Clinton neighborhood of Manhattan, was four or five times normal load and growing. The circuit breakers would pop at any moment, averting an explosion and a fire, but returning a good portion of Midtown to colonial times.

'North seems to be working better. Try the north, get some juice from the north. Try Massachusetts.'

'I've got some: fifty, sixty K. From Putnam.'

'Good.'

And then: 'Oh, Jesus, Lord,' somebody cried.

The supervisor didn't know who it was; everybody was staring at their screens, heads down, transfixed. 'What?' he raged. 'I don't want to keep hearing that kind of thing. Tell me!'

'The breaker settings in Manhattan-Ten! Look! The breakers!'

Oh, no. No . . .

The circuit breakers in MH-10 had been reset. They would now allow through their portal ten times the safe load.

If the Algonquin control center couldn't reduce the pressure of the voltage assaulting the substation soon, the lines and switchgear inside the place would allow through a lethally high flood of electricity. The substation would explode. But before that happened the juice would race through the distribution feeder lines into below ground transformer boxes throughout the blocks south of Lincoln Center and into the spot networks in office buildings and big high-rises. Some breakers would cut the circuit but some older transformers and service panels would just melt into a lump of conductive metal and let the current continue on its way, setting fires and exploding in arc flashes that could burn to death anybody near an appliance or wall outlet.

For the first time the supervisor thought: Terrorists. It's a terror attack. He shouted, 'Call Homeland Security and the NYPD. And reset them, goddamn it. Reset the breakers.'

'They're not responding. I'm locked out of MH-Ten.'

'How can you be fucking locked out?'

'I don't — '

'Is anybody inside? Jesus, if they are, get them out now!' Substations were unmanned, but workers occasionally went inside for routine maintenance and repairs.

'Sure, okay.'

The indicator bars were now into the red.

'Sir? Should we shed load?'

Grinding his teeth, the supervisor was considering this. Also known as a rolling blackout, shedding load was an extreme measure in the power business. 'Load' was the amount of juice that customers were using. Shedding was a manual, controlled shutdown of certain parts of the grid to prevent a larger crash of the system.

It was a power company's last resort in the battle to keep the grid up and would have disastrous consequences in the densely populated portion of Manhattan that was at risk. The damage to computers alone would be in the tens of millions, and it was possible that people would be injured or even lose their lives. Nine-one-one calls wouldn't get through. Ambulances and police cars would be stuck in traffic, with stoplights out. Elevators would be frozen. There'd be panic. Muggings and looting and rapes invariably rose during a blackout, even in daylight.

Electricity kept people honest.

'Sir?' the technician asked desperately.

The supervisor stared at the moving voltage indicator bars. He grabbed his own phone and called *his* superior, a senior vice president at Algonquin. 'Herb, we have a situation.' He briefed the man.

'How'd this happen?'

'We don't know. I'm thinking terrorists.'

'God. You called Homeland Security?'

'Yeah, just now. Mostly we're trying to get more power into the affected areas. We're not having much luck.'

He watched the indicator bars continue to rise through the red.

The vice president asked, 'Okay. Recommendations?'

'We don't have much choice. Shed load.'

'A good chunk of the city'll go black for at least a day.'

'But I don't see any other options. With that much juice flowing in, the station'll blow if we don't do something.'

His boss thought for a moment. 'There's a second transmission line running through

Manhattan-Ten, right?'

The supervisor looked up at the board. A high-voltage cable went through the substation and headed west to deliver juice to parts of New Jersey. 'Yes, but it's not online. It's just running through a duct there.'

'But could you splice into it and use that for supply to the diverted lines?'

'Manually? . . . I suppose, but . . . but that would mean getting people inside MH-Ten. And if we can't hold the juice back until they're finished, it'll flash. That'll kill 'em all. Or give 'em third-degrees over their entire bodies.'

A pause. 'Hold on. I'm calling Jessen.'

Algonquin Consolidated's CEO. Also known, privately, as 'The All-Powerful.'

As he waited, the supervisor stared at the techs surrounding him.

He kept staring at the board too. The glowing red dots.

Critical failure . . .

Finally the supervisor's boss came back on. His voice cracked. He cleared his throat and after a moment said, 'You're supposed to send some people in. Manually splice into the line.'

'That's what Jessen said?'

Another pause. 'Yes.'

The supervisor whispered, 'I can't order anybody in there. It's suicide.'

'Then find some volunteers. Jessen said you are not, understand me, not to shed load under any circumstances.'

2

The driver eased the M70 bus through traffic toward the stop on Fifty-seventh near where Tenth Avenue blended into Amsterdam. He was in a pretty good mood. The new bus was a kneeling model, which lowered to the sidewalk to make stepping aboard easier, and featured a handicapped ramp, great steering and, most important, a rump-friendly driver's seat.

Lord knew he needed that, spending eight hours a day in it.

No interest in subways, the Long Island Railroad or Metro North. No, he loved buses, despite the crazy traffic, the hostility, attitudes and anger. He liked how democratic it was to travel by bus; you saw everybody from lawyers to struggling musicians to delivery boys. Cabs were expensive and stank; subways didn't always go where you wanted to. And walking? Well, this was Manhattan. Great if you had the time but who did? Besides, he liked people and he liked the fact that he could nod or smile or say hello to every single person who got on his vehicle. New Yorkers weren't, like some people said, unfriendly at all. Just sometimes shy, insecure, cautious, preoccupied.

But often all it took was a grin, a nod, a single word . . . and they were your new friend.

And he was happy to be one.

If only for six or seven blocks.

14

The personal greeting also gave him a chance to spot the wackos, the drunks, the cluck-heads and tweakers and decide if he needed to hit the distress button.

This *was*, after all, Manhattan.

Today was beautiful, clear and cool. April. One of his favorite months. It was about 11:30 a.m. and the bus was crowded as people were heading east for lunch dates or errands on their hour off. Traffic was moving slowly as he nosed the huge vehicle closer to the stop, where four or five people stood beside a bus stop sign pole.

He was approaching the stop and happened to look past the people waiting to get on board, his eyes taking in the old brown building behind the stop. An early twentieth century structure, it had several gridded windows but was always dark inside; he'd never seen anybody going in or out. A spooky place, like a prison. On the front was a flaking sign in white paint on a blue background.

ALGONQUIN CONSOLIDATED POWER AND LIGHT COMPANY SUBSTATION MH-10 PRIVATE PROPERTY DANGER, HIGH VOLTAGE, TRESPASS PROHIBITED.

He rarely paid attention to the place but today something had caught his eye, something, he believed, out of the ordinary. Dangling from the window, about ten feet off the ground, was a wire, about a half inch in diameter. It was

15

covered with dark insulation up to the end. There, the plastic or rubber was stripped away, revealing silvery metal strands bolted to a fitting of some kind, a flat piece of brass. Damn big hunk of wire, he thought.

And just hanging out the window. Was that safe?

He braked the bus to a complete stop and hit the door release. The kneeling mechanism engaged and the big vehicle dipped toward the sidewalk, the bottom metal stair inches from the ground.

The driver turned his broad, ruddy face toward the door, which eased open with a satisfying hydraulic hiss. The folks began to climb on board. 'Morning,' the driver said cheerfully.

A woman in her eighties, clutching an old shabby Henri Bendel shopping bag, nodded back and, using a cane, staggered to the rear, ignoring the empty seats in the front reserved for the elderly and disabled.

How could you not just *love* New Yorkers?

Then sudden motion in the rearview mirror. Flashing yellow lights. A truck was speeding up behind him. Algonquin Consolidated. Three workers stepped out and stood in a close group, talking among themselves. They held boxes of tools and thick gloves and jackets. They didn't seem happy as they walked slowly toward the building, staring at it, heads close together as they debated something. One of those heads was shaking ominously.

Then the driver turned to the last passenger

about to board, a young Latino clutching his MetroCard and pausing outside the bus. He was gazing at the substation. Frowning. The driver noticed his head was raised, as if he was sniffing the air.

An acrid scent. Something was burning. The smell reminded him of the time that an electric motor in the wife's washing machine had shorted out and the insulation burned. Nauseating. A wisp of smoke was coming from the doorway of the substation.

So that's what the Algonquin people were doing here.

That'd be a mess. The driver wondered if it would mean a power outage and the stoplights would go out. That'd be it for him. The crosstown trip, normally twenty minutes, would be hours. Well, in any event, he'd better clear the area for the fire department. He gestured the passenger on board. 'Hey, mister, I gotta go. Come on. Get on — '

As the passenger, still frowning at the smell, turned around and stepped onto the bus, the driver heard what sounded like pops coming from inside the substation. Sharp, almost like gunshots. Then a flash of light, light like a dozen suns, filled the entire sidewalk between the bus and the cable dangling from the window.

The passenger simply disappeared into a cloud of white fire.

The driver's vision collapsed to gray afterimages. The sound was like a ripping crackle and shotgun blast at the same time, stunning his ears. Though belted into his seat, his upper body was

17

slammed backward against the side window.

Through numb ears, he heard the echoes of his passengers' screams.

Through half-blinded eyes, he saw flames.

As he began to pass out, the driver wondered if he himself might very well be the source of the fire.

3

'I have to tell you. He got out of the airport. He was spotted an hour ago in downtown Mexico City.'

'No,' Lincoln Rhyme said with a sigh, closing his eyes briefly. 'No . . . '

Amelia Sachs, sitting beside Rhyme's candy apple red Storm Arrow wheelchair, leaned forward and spoke into the black box of the speaker-phone. 'What happened?' She tugged at her long red hair and twined the strands into a severe ponytail.

'By the time we got the flight information from London, the plane had landed.' The woman's voice blossomed crisply from the speaker-phone. 'Seems he hid on a supply truck, snuck out through a service entrance. I'll show you the security tape we got from the Mexican police. I've got a link. Hold on a minute.' Her voice faded as she spoke to her associate, giving him instructions about the video.

The time was just past noon and Rhyme and Sachs were in the ground-floor parlor turned forensic laboratory of his townhouse on Central Park West, what had been a gothic Victorian structure in which had possibly resided — Rhyme liked to think — some very unquaint Victorians. Tough businessmen, dodgy politicians, high-class crooks. Maybe an incorruptible police commissioner who liked to bang heads.

Rhyme had written a classic book on old-time crime in New York and had used his sources to try to track the genealogy of his building. But he could find no pedigree.

The woman they were speaking with was in a more modern structure, Rhyme had to assume, three thousand miles away: the Monterey office of the California Bureau of Investigation. CBI Agent Kathryn Dance had worked with Rhyme and Sachs several years ago, on a case involving the very man they were now closing in on. Richard Logan was, they believed, his real name. Though Lincoln Rhyme thought of him mostly by his nickname: the Watchmaker.

He was a professional criminal, one who planned his crimes with the precision he devoted to his hobby and passion — constructing timepieces. Rhyme and the killer had clashed several times; Rhyme had foiled one of his plans but failed to stop another. Still, Lincoln Rhyme considered the overall score a loss for himself since the Watchmaker wasn't in custody.

Rhyme leaned his head back in his wheelchair, picturing Logan. He'd seen the man in person, up close. Body lean, hair a dark boyish mop, eyes gently amused at being questioned by the police, never revealing a clue to the mass murder he was planning. His serenity seemed to be innate, and it was what Rhyme found to be perhaps the most disturbing quality of the man. Emotion breeds mistake and carelessness, and no one could ever accuse Richard Logan of being emotional.

He could be hired for larceny or illegal arms or any other scheme that needed elaborate planning and ruthless execution, but was generally hired for murder — killing witnesses or whistleblowers or political or corporate figures. Recent intelligence revealed he'd taken a murder assignment in Mexico somewhere. Rhyme had called Dance, who had many contacts south of the border — and who had herself nearly been killed by the Watchmaker's associate a few years earlier. Given that connection, Dance was representing the Americans in the operation to arrest and extradite him, working with a senior investigator of the Ministerial Federal Police, a young, hardworking officer named Arturo Diaz.

Early that morning they'd learned the Watchmaker would be landing in Mexico City. Dance had called Diaz, who scrambled to put extra officers in place to intercept Logan. But, from Dance's latest communication, they hadn't been in time.

'You ready for the video?' Dance asked.

'Go ahead.' Rhyme shifted one of his few working fingers — the index finger of his right hand — and moved the electric wheelchair closer to the screen. He was a C4 quadriplegic, largely paralyzed from the shoulders down.

On one of the several flat-screen monitors in the lab came a grainy night-vision image of an airport. Trash and discarded cartons, cans and drums littered the ground on both sides of the fence in the foreground. A private cargo jet taxied into view and just as it stopped a rear hatch opened and a man dropped out.

'That's him,' Dance said softly.

'I can't see clearly,' Rhyme said.

21

'It's definitely Logan,' Dance reassured. 'They got a partial print — you'll see in a minute.'

The man stretched and then oriented himself. He slung a bag over his shoulder and, crouching, ran toward and hid behind a shed. A few minutes later a worker came by, carrying a package the size of two shoeboxes. Logan greeted him, swapped the box for a letter-size envelope. The worker looked around and walked away quickly. A maintenance truck pulled up. Logan climbed into the back and hid under some tarps. The truck disappeared from view.

'The plane?' he asked.

'Continued on to South America on a corporate charter. The pilot and copilot claim they don't know anything about a stowaway. Of course they're lying. But we don't have jurisdiction to question them.'

'And the worker?' Sachs asked.

'Federal police picked him up. He was just a minimum-wage airport employee. He claims somebody he didn't know told him he'd be paid a couple of hundred U.S. to deliver the box. The money was in the envelope. That's what they lifted the print from.'

'What was in the package?' Rhyme asked.

'He says he doesn't know but he's lying too — I saw the interview video. Our DEA people're interrogating him. I wanted to try to tease some information out of him myself but it'll take too long for me to get the okay.'

Rhyme and Sachs shared a look. The 'teasing' reference was a bit of modesty on Dance's part. She was a kinesics expert — body language

22

— and one of the top interrogators in the country. But the testy relationship between the sovereign states in question was such that a California cop would have plenty of paperwork to negotiate before she could slip into Mexico for a formal interrogation, whereas the U.S. Drug Enforcement Agency already had a sanctioned presence there.

Rhyme asked, 'Where was Logan spotted in the capital?'

'A business district. He was trailed to a hotel, but he wasn't staying there. It was for a meeting, Diaz's men think. By the time they'd set up surveillance he was gone. But all the law enforcement agencies and hotels have his picture now.' Dance added that Diaz's boss, a very senior police official, would be taking over the investigation. 'It's encouraging that they're serious about the case.'

Yes, encouraging, Rhyme thought. But he felt frustrated too. To be on the verge of finding the prey and yet to have so little control over the case . . . He found himself breathing more quickly. He was considering the last time he and the Watchmaker had been up against each other; Logan had out-thought everybody. And easily killed the man he'd been hired to murder. Rhyme had had all the facts at hand to figure out what Logan was up to. Yet he'd misread the strategy completely.

'By the way,' he heard Sachs ask Kathryn Dance, 'how was that romantic weekend away?' This had to do, it seemed, with Dance's love interest. The single mother of two had been a widow for several years.

'We had a great time,' the agent reported.

'Where did you go?'

Rhyme wondered why on earth Sachs was asking about Dance's social life. She ignored his impatient glance.

'Santa Barbara. Stopped at the Hearst Castle . . . Listen, I'm still waiting for you two to come out here. The children really want to meet you. Wes wrote a paper about forensics for school and mentioned you, Lincoln. His teacher used to live in New York and had read all about you.'

'Yes, that'd be nice,' Rhyme said, thinking exclusively about Mexico City.

Sachs smiled at the impatience in his voice and told Dance they had to go.

After disconnecting, she wiped some sweat from Rhyme's forehead — he hadn't been aware of the moisture — and they sat silent for a moment, looking out the window at the blur of a peregrine falcon sweeping into view. It veered up to its nest on Rhyme's second floor. Though not uncommon in major cities — plenty of fat, tasty pigeons for meals — these birds of prey usually nested higher. But for some reason several generations of the birds had called Rhyme's townhouse home. He liked their presence. They were smart, fascinating to watch and the perfect visitors, not demanding anything from him.

A male voice intruded, 'Well, did you get him?'

'Who?' Rhyme snapped. 'And how artful a verb is 'get'?'

Thom Reston, Lincoln Rhyme's caregiver, said, 'The Watchmaker.'

'No,' grumbled Rhyme.

'But you're close, aren't you?' asked the trim man, wearing dark slacks, a businessman's starched yellow shirt and a floral tie.

'Oh, close,' Rhyme muttered. '*Close*. That's very helpful. Next time you're being attacked by a mountain lion, Thom, how would you feel if the park ranger shot really *close* to it? As opposed to, oh, say, actually *hitting* it?'

'Aren't mountain lions endangered?' Thom asked, not even bothering with an ironic inflection. He was impervious to Rhyme's edge. He'd worked for the forensic detective for years, longer than many married couples had been together. And the aide was as seasoned as the toughest spouse.

'Ha. Very funny. Endangered.'

Sachs walked around behind Rhyme's wheelchair and gripped his shoulders, began an impromptu massage. Sachs was tall and in better shape than most NYPD detectives her age and, though arthritis often plagued her knees and lower extremities, her arms and hands were strong and largely pain-free.

They wore their working clothes: Rhyme was in sweatpants, black, and a knit shirt of dark green. She had shed her navy blue jacket but was wearing matching slacks and a white cotton blouse, one button open at the collar, pearls present. Her Glock was high on her hip in a fast-draw polymer holster, and two magazines sat side by side in holsters of their own, along with a Taser.

Rhyme could feel the pulsing of her fingers; he

had perfect sensation above where he'd sustained a nearly fatal spinal cord fracture some years ago, the fourth cervical vertebra. Although at one point, he'd considered risky surgery to improve his condition, he'd opted for a different rehabilitative approach. Through an exhausting regimen of exercise and therapy he'd managed to regain some use of his fingers and hand. He could also use his left ring finger, which had for some reason remained intact after the subway beam broke his neck.

He enjoyed the fingers digging into his flesh. It was as if the small percentage of remaining sensation in his body was enhanced. He glanced down at his useless legs. He closed his eyes.

Thom now looked him over carefully. 'You all right, Lincoln?'

'All right? Aside from the fact that the perp I've been searching for for years slipped out of our grasp and is now hiding out in the second-largest metropolitan area in this hemisphere, I'm just peachy.'

'That's not what I'm talking about. You're not looking too good.'

'You're right. Actually I need some medicine.'

'Medicine?'

'Whisky. I'd feel better with some whisky.'

'No, you wouldn't.'

'Well, why don't we try an experiment. Science. Cartesian. Rational. Who can argue with that? I know how I feel now. Then I'll have some whisky and I'll report back to you.'

'No. It's too early,' Thom said matter of factly.

'It's afternoon.'

'By a few minutes.'

'Goddamn it.' Rhyme sounded gruff, as often, but in fact he was losing himself in Sachs's massage. A few strings of red hair had escaped from her ponytail and hung tickling against his cheek. He didn't move away. Since he'd apparently lost the single-malt battle, he was ignoring Thom, but the aide brought his attention around quickly by saying, 'When you were on the phone, Lon called.'

'He did? Why didn't you tell me?'

'You said you didn't want to be disturbed while you were talking with Kathryn.'

'Well, tell me now.'

'He'll call back. Something about a case. A problem.'

'Really?' The Watchmaker case receded somewhat at this news. Rhyme understood that there was another source of his bad mood: boredom. He'd just finished analyzing the evidence for a complicated organized crime case and was facing several weeks with little to do. So he was buoyed by the thought of another job. Like Sachs's craving for speed, Rhyme needed problems, challenges, input. One of the difficulties with a severe disability that few people focus on is the absence of anything new. The same settings, the same people, the same activities . . . and the same platitudes, the same empty reassurances, the same reports from unemotional doctors.

What had saved his life after his injury — literally, since he'd been considering assisted suicide — was his tentative steps back into his prior passion: using science to solve crimes.

You could never be bored when you confronted mystery.

Thom persisted, 'Are you sure you're up for it? You're looking a little pale.'

'Haven't been to the beach lately, you know.'

'All right. Just checking. Oh, and Arlen Kopeski is coming by later. When do you want to see him?'

The name sounded familiar but it left a vaguely troubling flavor in his mouth. 'Who?'

'He's with that disability rights group. It's about that award you're being given.'

'Today?' Rhyme had a fuzzy recollection of some phone calls. If it wasn't about a case, he rarely paid much attention to the noise around him.

'You said today. You said you'd meet with him.'

'Oh, I *really* need an award. What am I going to do with it? Paperweight? Does anybody you know ever use paperweights? Have *you* ever used a paperweight?'

'Lincoln, it's being given to you for inspiring young people with disabilities.'

'Nobody inspired me when I was young. And I turned out all right.' Which wasn't completely true — the inspiration part — but Rhyme grew petty whenever distractions loomed, especially distractions involving visitors.

'A half hour.'

'Is a half hour I don't have.'

'Too late. He's already in town.'

Sometimes it was impossible to win against the aide.

28

'We'll see.'

'Kopeski's not going to come here and cool his heels like some courtier waiting for an audience with the king.'

Rhyme liked that metaphor.

But then all thoughts of awards, and royalty, vanished as Rhyme's phone blared and Detective Lieutenant Lon Sellitto's number showed up on caller ID.

Rhyme used a working finger on his right hand to answer. 'Lon.'

'Linc, listen, here's the thing.' He was harried and, to judge from the surround-sound acoustics piping through the speaker, apparently driving somewhere quickly. 'We may have a terrorist situation going on.'

'Situation? That's not very specific.'

'Okay, how's this? Somebody fucked with the power company, shot a five-thousand-degree spark at a Metro bus and shut down the electric grid for six square blocks south of Lincoln Center. That specific enough for you?'

4

The entourage arrived from downtown.

Homeland Security's representative was a typically young but senior officer, probably born and bred among the country clubs of Connecticut or Long Island, though that was, for Rhyme, merely a demographic observation and not, necessarily, a fault. The man's shine and sharp eyes belied the fact that he probably wouldn't quite know where he fit in the hierarchy of law enforcement, but that was true of nearly everybody who worked for HS. His name was Gary Noble.

The Bureau was here too, of course, in the incarnation of a special agent whom Rhyme and Sellitto worked with frequently: Fred Dellray. FBI founder J. Edgar Hoover would have been dismayed at the African-American agent, only partly because his roots were clearly *not* in New England; rather, the consternation would come from the agent's lack of 'Ninth Street Style,' a reference to FBI headquarters in Washington, D.C. Dellray donned a white shirt and tie only when his undercover assignments called for such an outfit and he treated the garb like any other costume in his player's wardrobe. Today, he was wearing authentic Dellray: a dark green plaid suit, the pink shirt of a devil-may-care Wall Street CEO and an orange tie that Rhyme couldn't have thrown out fast enough.

Dellray was accompanied by his newly named boss — assistant special agent in charge of the New York office of the FBI, Tucker McDaniel, who'd begun his career in Washington, then taken assignments in the Middle East and South Asia. The ASAC was compact of build and thick of dark hair, swarthy of complexion, though with bright blue eyes that focused on you as if you were lying when you said, 'Hi.'

It was a helpful expression for a law enforcement agent and one that Rhyme affected himself as the occasion merited.

The NYPD's chief presence was stout Lon Sellitto, in a gray suit and, unusual for him, powder blue shirt. The tie — splotchy by design, not spillage — was the only unwrinkled article of clothing swathing the man. Probably a birthday present from live-in girlfriend Rachel or his son. The Major Cases detective was backed up by Sachs and Ron Pulaski, a blond, eternally youthful officer from Patrol, who was officially attached to Sellitto, but who unofficially worked mostly with Rhyme and Sachs on the crime scene side of investigations. Pulaski was in a standard dark blue NYPD uniform, T-shirt visible in the V at his throat.

Both of the feds, McDaniel and Noble, had heard about Rhyme, of course, but neither had met him and they exuded various degrees of surprise, sympathy and discomfort seeing the paralyzed forensic consultant, who tooled around the lab deftly in his wheelchair. The novelty and uneasiness soon wore off, though, as they usually did with all but the most ingratiating guests, and soon they were struck by the more bizarre presence here: a wainscoted, crown-molded parlor chockablock with equipment that a crime scene unit in a medium-sized town might envy.

After introductions, Noble took the point position, Homeland Security carting the bigger umbrella.

'Mr. Rhyme — '

'Lincoln,' he corrected. Rhyme grew irritated when anyone deferred to him, and he considered the use of his surname a subtle way of patting him on the head and saying, Poor thing; sorry you're confined to a wheelchair for the rest of your life. So we'll be extra special polite.

Sachs caught the weight behind his correction and rolled her eyes in a gentle arc. Rhyme tried not to smile.

'Sure, Lincoln, then.' Noble cleared his throat. 'Here's the scenario. What do you know about the grid — the electricity grid?'

'Not much,' Rhyme admitted. He'd studied science in college but never paid much attention to electricity, other than electromagnetics' appearance in physics as one of the four fundamental forces in nature, along with gravity and the weak and the strong nuclear forces. But that was academic. On a practical level Rhyme's main interest in electricity involved making sure enough of it got pumped into the townhouse to power the equipment in his lab here. It was extremely thirsty and he'd twice had to have the place rewired to bring in additional amperage to support the load.

Rhyme was very aware too that he was alive

and functioning now solely because of electricity: the ventilator that had kept oxygen pumping through his lungs right after the accident and now the batteries in his wheelchair and the current controlled by the touchpad and voice-activated ECU, his environmental control unit. The computer too, of course.

He wouldn't have had much of a life without wires. Probably no life at all.

Noble continued, 'The basic scenario is our UNSUB got into one of the power company's substations and ran a wire outside the building.'

' 'Unknown subject' singular?' Rhyme asked.

'We don't know yet.'

'Wire outside. Okay.'

'And then got into the computer that controls the grid. He manipulated it to send more voltage through the substation than it was meant to handle.' Noble fiddled with cuff links in the shape of animals.

'And the electricity jumped,' the FBI's McDaniel put in. 'It was basically trying to get into the ground. It's called an arc flash. An explosion. Like a lightning bolt.'

A 5,000-degree spark . . .

The ASAC added, 'It's so powerful it creates plasma. That's a state of matter — '

' — that isn't gas, liquid or solid,' Rhyme said impatiently.

'Exactly. A fairly small arc flash has the explosive power of a pound of TNT and this one wasn't small.'

'And the bus was his target?' Rhyme asked.

'Seems so.'

Sellitto said, 'But they have rubber tires. Vehicles are the safest place to be in a lightning storm. I saw that someplace, some show.'

'True,' McDaniel said. 'But the UNSUB had it all figured out. It was a kneeling bus. Either he was counting that the lowered step would touch the sidewalk or hoping somebody'd have one foot on the ground and one on the bus. That'd be enough for the arc to hit it.'

Noble again twisted a tiny silver mammal on his cuff. 'But the timing was off. Or his aim or something. The spark hit the sign pole next to the bus. Killed one passenger, deafened some people nearby, and dinged a few with glass, started a fire. If it'd hit the bus directly, the casualties would've been a lot worse. Half of them dead, I'd guess. Or with third-degree burns.'

'Lon mentioned a blackout,' Rhyme said.

McDaniel eased back into the conversation. 'The UNSUB used the computer to shut down four other substations in the area, so all the juice was flowing through the one on Fifty-seven Street. As soon as the arc happened, that substation went offline, but Algonquin got the others up and running again. Right now about six blocks in Clinton are out. Didn't you see it on the news?'

'I don't watch much news,' Rhyme said.

Sachs asked McDaniel, 'The driver or anybody see anything?'

'Nothing helpful. There were some workers there. They'd gotten orders from the CEO of Algonquin to go inside and try to reroute the

34

lines or something. Thank God they didn't go in before the arc happened.'

'There was nobody inside?' Fred Dellray asked. The agent seemed a bit out of the loop and Rhyme guessed there hadn't been time for McDaniel to fully brief his team.

'No. Substations're mostly just equipment, nobody inside except for routine maintenance or repairs.'

'How was the computer hacked?' Lon Sellitto asked, sitting noisily in a wicker chair.

Gary Noble said, 'We aren't sure. We're running the scenarios now. Our white hat hackers've tried to run a mock terrorist scenario, and they can't get inside. But you know how it works; the bad guys're always one step ahead of us — techwise.'

Ron Pulaski asked, 'Anybody take credit?'

'Not yet,' Noble replied.

Rhyme asked, 'Then why terrorism? I'm thinking it's a good way to shut down alarms and security systems. Any murders or burglaries reported?'

'Not so far,' Sellitto pointed out.

'A couple of reasons we think it's terrorists,' McDaniel said. 'Our obscure-pattern-and-relationship-profile software suggests so, for one thing. And right after it happened I had our people go through signals from Maryland.' He paused, as if warning that nobody here should repeat what he was about to say. Rhyme deduced the FBI man was referring to the netherworld of intelligence — government snooping agencies that might not technically have jurisdiction in the country but

35

who can maneuver through loopholes to keep on top of possible malfeasance within the borders. The National Security Agency — the world's best eavesdroppers — happened to be in Maryland. 'A new SIGINT system came up with some interesting hits.'

SIGINT. Signal intelligence. Monitoring cell phones, satellite phones, email . . . seemed an appropriate approach when confronted with somebody using electricity to stage an attack.

'Picked up references to what we think is a new terror group operating in the area. Never cataloged before.'

'Who?' Sellitto asked.

'The name starts with 'Justice' and has the word 'for' in it,' McDaniel explained.

Justice For . . .

Sachs asked, 'Nothing else?'

'No. Maybe 'Justice For Allah.' 'Just For the Oppressed.' Anything. We don't have a clue.'

'The words in English, though?' Rhyme asked. 'Not Arabic. Or Somali or Indonesian.'

'Right,' McDaniel said. 'But I'm running multi-language and -dialect monitoring programs on all communications we can pick up.'

'Legally,' Noble added quickly. 'That we can pick up *legally*.'

'But most of their communications take place in the cloud zone,' McDaniel said. He didn't explain this.

'Uhm, what's that, sir?' Ron Pulaski asked, a variation of what Rhyme was about to, though in a much less deferential manner.

'Cloud zone?' the ASAC responded. 'The

phrase comes from the latest approach to computing — where your data and programs are stored on servers elsewhere, not on your own computer. I wrote an analysis paper on it. I'm using the term to mean new communications protocols. There's very little standard cell phone and email use among the negative players. People of interest are exploiting new techniques, like blogs and Twitter and Facebook, to send messages. Also embedding codes in music and video uploads and downloads. And personally I think they've got some new systems altogether, different types of modified phones, radios with alternative frequencies.'

The cloud zone, negative players . . .

'Why do you think Justice For is behind the attack?' Sachs asked.

'We don't necessarily,' Noble said.

McDaniel filled in, 'Just, there were some SIGINT hits about monetary dispersals over the past few days and about some movement of personnel and the sentence 'It's going to be big.' So when the attack happened today, we thought, maybe.'

'And Earth Day's coming up,' Noble pointed out.

Rhyme wasn't exactly sure what Earth Day was — and didn't have an opinion about it one way or the other, except recognizing with some petulance that it was like other holidays and events: crowds and protesters clogging the streets and depleting the resources of the NYPD, which he might otherwise need to run cases.

Noble said, 'Might be more than a coincidence. Attack on the grid the day before Earth Day? The President's taking an interest.'

'*The* President?' Sellitto asked.

'Right. He's at some renewable energy summit outside of D.C.'

Sellitto mused, 'Somebody making a point. Ecoterror.'

You didn't see much of that in New York City; logging and strip-mining weren't big industries here.

' 'Justice For the Environment' maybe,' Sachs suggested.

'But,' McDaniel said, 'there's another wrinkle. One of the SIGINT hits correlated 'Justice For' with the name 'Rahman.' No family name. We've got eight unaccounted-for Rahmans on our Islamist terror watch list. Could be one of them, we're thinking, but we don't know which one.'

Noble had abandoned the bears or manatees on his cuffs and was now playing with a nice pen. 'We were thinking, at Homeland, that Rahman could be part of a sleeper cell that's been here for years, maybe from around the time of Nine-Eleven. Staying clear of an Islamist lifestyle. Sticking with moderate mosques, avoiding Arabic.'

McDaniel added, 'I've got one of my T and C teams up from Quantico.'

'T and C?' Rhyme asked, peeved.

'Tech and Communications. To run the surveillance. And warrant specialists to get taps if we need them. Two DOJ lawyers. And we're getting two hundred extra agents.'

38

Rhyme and Sellitto glanced each other's way. This was a surprisingly substantial task force for a single incident that wasn't part of an ongoing investigation. And mobilized with incredible speed. The attack had happened less than two hours ago.

The Bureau man noticed their reaction. 'We're convinced there's a new profile to terrorism. So we've got a new approach to fighting it. Like the drones in the Middle East and Afghanistan? You know the pilots are next to a strip mall in Colorado Springs or Omaha.'

The cloud zone . . .

'Now, T and C's in place, so we'll be able to hook more signals soon. But we'll still need traditional approaches.' A look around the lab. Meaning forensics, Rhyme supposed. And then the ASAC looked toward Dellray. 'And street-level work. Though Fred tells me he hasn't had much luck.'

Dellray's talent as an undercover op was exceeded only by his skills as a handler of confidential informants. Since 9/11 he'd curried favor with a large group of CIs in the Islamic community and taught himself Arabic, Indonesian and Farsi. He worked regularly with the NYPD's impressive anti-terror unit. But the agent confirmed his boss's comment. Grim-faced, he said, 'Haven't heard anything about Justice For or Rahman. Ran it past my boys in Brooklyn, Jersey, Queens, Manhattan.'

'Just happened,' Sellitto reminded.

'Right,' McDaniel said slowly. 'Of course something like this would've been planned for,

39

what would you guess? A month?'

Noble said, 'I'd imagine. At least.'

'See, that's this damn cloud zone.'

Rhyme could also hear McDaniel's criticism of Dellray: the point of informants was to learn about things *before* they happened.

'Well, keep at it, Fred,' McDaniel said. 'You're doing a good job.'

'Sure, Tucker.'

Noble had given up fidgeting with the pen. He was consulting his watch. 'So Homeland'll coordinate with Washington and the State Department, embassies too, if we need to. But the police and the Bureau'll run the case like any other. Now, Lincoln, everybody knows your expertise with crime scene work, so we're hoping you'll work point on analysis of the trace. We're assembling a CS team now. They should be on location at the substation in twenty minutes. Thirty, tops.'

'Sure, we'll help,' Rhyme said. 'But we run the entire scene. Entrance to exit. And all secondary scenes. Not just trace. The whole ball of string.' He glanced at Sellitto, who nodded firmly, meaning, I'm backing you up.

In the ensuing awkward moment of silence, everybody was aware of the subtext: who would ultimately be in charge of the investigation. The nature of police work nowadays was such that whoever controlled the forensics basically ran the case. This was a practical consequence of the advancements in crime scene investigative techniques in the past ten years. Simply by searching the scenes and analyzing what was found, forensic investigators had the best insights into the nature of the crime and possible suspects and were the first to develop leads.

The triumvirate — Noble and McDaniel on the federal side and Sellitto for the NYPD — would be making strategic decisions. But, if they accepted Rhyme as key in the crime scene operation, he would be in effect the lead investigator. This made sense. He'd solved crimes in the city longer than any of them had, and since there were no other suspects or significant leads at this point, other than evidence, a forensic specialist was the way to go.

Most important, Rhyme wanted the case bad. The boredom factor . . .

Okay, some ego too.

So he offered the best argument he could: He said nothing. Just settled his eyes on the face of the Homeland Security man, Gary Noble.

McDaniel fidgeted a bit — it was his crime scene people who would be demoted — and Noble lobbed a glance toward him, asking, 'What do you think, Tucker?'

'I know Mr. Rhyme's . . . I know Lincoln's work. I don't have a problem with him running the scene. Provided there's one hundred percent coordination with us.'

'Of course.'

'And we've got somebody present. *And* we get the findings as soon as possible.' He looked into Rhyme's eyes, not at his body. 'The most important thing is fast response time.'

Meaning, Rhyme suspected, can somebody in your condition deliver? Sellitto stirred, but this wasn't a crip put-down. It was a legitimate question. One that Rhyme himself would have asked.

He answered, 'Understood.'

'Good. I'll tell my Evidence Response people to help however you want,' the ASAC assured him.

Noble said, 'Now, for the press, we're trying to downplay the terror angle at this point. We'll be making it sound like an accident. But the news leaked that it may be more than that. People are freaked out.'

'I'll say they are.' McDaniel nodded. 'I've got monitors in my office checking Internet traffic. Huge increases in hits in search engines for 'electrocution,' 'arc flash' and 'blackouts.' You Tube viewings of arc flash videos are through the roof. I went online myself. They're scary as hell. One minute there're two guys working on an electric panel, then all of a sudden there's a flash that fills the whole screen and a guy's on his back, with half his body on fire.'

'And,' Noble said, 'people're real nervous that arc flashes might happen someplace other than a substation. Like their houses and offices.'

Sachs asked, 'Can they?'

McDaniel apparently had not learned all there was to know about arc flashes. He admitted, 'I think so, but I'm not sure how big the current has to be.' His eyes strayed to a 220v outlet nearby.

'Well, I think we better get moving,' Rhyme said, with a glance at Sachs.

She headed for the door. 'Ron, come with me.'

Pulaski joined her. A moment later the door closed, and he soon heard the big engine of her car fire up.

'Now, one thing to keep in mind, one scenario we ran on the computers,' McDaniel added, 'was that the UNSUB was just testing the waters, checking out the grid as a *possible* terror target. It was pretty clumsy and only one person died. We fed that into the system and the algorithms are suggesting that they might try something different next. There's even a potential that this was a singularity.'

'A . . . ?' Rhyme asked, exasperated at the language.

'Singularity — a onetime occurrence. Our threat analysis software assigned a fifty-five percent nonrepeatability factor to the incident. That's not the worst in the world.'

Rhyme replied, 'But isn't that just another way of saying there's a *forty-five* percent chance that somebody else somewhere in New York City's going to get electrocuted? . . . And it could be happening right now.'

5

Algonquin Consolidated Power substation MH-10 was a miniature medieval castle in a quiet area south of Lincoln Center. It was made of unevenly cut limestone, dingy and pitted from decades of New York City pollution and grime. The cornerstone was worn but you could easily read, *1928*.

It was just before 2 p.m. when Amelia Sachs skidded her maroon Ford Torino Cobra up to the curb in front of the place, behind the ruined bus. The car and its bubbling exhaust drew glances of curiosity or admiration from bystanders, cops and firemen. She climbed out of the driver's seat, tossed an NYPD placard on the dash and stood with hands on hips, surveying the scene. Ron Pulaski exited from the passenger door and slammed it with a solid clunk.

Sachs regarded the incongruity of the setting. Modern buildings, at least twenty or so stories high, bracketed the substation, which for some reason had been designed with turrets. The stone was streaked with white, thanks to the resident pigeons, a number of which had returned after the excitement. The windows were of jaundiced glass and covered with bars painted black.

The thick metal door was open and the room inside was dark.

With a bleat of an electronic siren a rapid response vehicle from the NYPD Crime Scene Unit eased into the area. The RRV parked, and three technicians from the main operation in Queens climbed out. Sachs had worked with them on a number of occasions and she nodded to the Latino man and the Asian woman under the direction of a senior officer, Detective Gretchen Sahloff. Sachs nodded to the detective, who waved a greeting and with a somber look at the front of the substation walked to the rear of the large van, where the newly arrived officers began to unload equipment.

Sachs's attention then moved to the sidewalk and street, cordoned off with yellow tape, beyond which a crowd of fifty or so watched the action. The bus that had been the object of the attack sat in front of the substation, empty, lopsided; the right tires were deflated. Near the front the paint was scorched. Half the windows were gray and opaque.

An EMS medic approached, a stocky African-American woman, and nodded. Sachs said, 'Hi.'

The woman gave a tentative nod of greeting. Med techs had witnessed just about all the carnage you could see but she was still shaken. 'Detective, you better take a look.'

Sachs followed her to the ambulance, where a body lay on a gurney, waiting transport to the morgue. It was covered with a dark green waxy tarp.

'Was the last passenger, looks like. We thought we could save him. But . . . we only got him this far.'

'Electrocuted?'

'You better see,' she whispered. And lifted the covering.

45

Sachs froze at the smell of burned skin and hair and she gazed at the victim, a Latino in a business suit — or what was left of one. His back and much of the right side of his body was a mix of skin and cloth from the burn. She guessed second and third degree. But that wasn't what unsettled her so much; she'd seen bad burns, accidental and intentional, in her line of work. The most horrifying sight was in his flesh, exposed when the EMS team had cut away the cloth of his suit. She was looking at dozens of smooth puncture wounds, which covered his body. It was as if he'd been hit by a blast from a huge shotgun.

'Most of them,' the medic said, 'entrance and exit.'

They went all the way through?

'What'd cause that?'

'Don't know. Never seen anything like it, all my years.'

And Sachs realized something else. The wounds were all distinct and clearly visible. 'There's no blood.'

'Whatever it was cauterized the wounds. That's why . . . ' Her voice went soft. 'That's why he stayed conscious for as long as he did.'

Sachs couldn't imagine the pain. 'How?' she asked, half to herself.

And then she got the answer.

'Amelia,' Ron Pulaski called.

She glanced toward him.

'The bus sign pole. Take a look. Brother . . . '

'Jesus,' she muttered. And walked closer to the edge of the crime scene tape. About six feet from

46

the ground a hole had been blasted clean through the metal pole, five inches wide. The metal had melted like plastic under a blowtorch. She then focused on the windows of the bus and a delivery truck parked nearby. She'd thought the glass was frosted from the fire. But, no, small bits of shrapnel — the same that had killed the passenger — had hit the vehicles. The sheet-metal skins were also punctured.

'Look,' she whispered, pointing at the sidewalk and the façade of the substation. A hundred tiny craters had been dug into the stone.

'Was it a bomb?' Pulaski asked. 'Maybe the respondings missed it.'

Sachs opened a plastic bag and removed blue latex gloves. Pulling them on, she bent down and collected a small disk of metal shaped like a teardrop at the base of the post. It was so hot it softened the glove.

When she realized what it was, she shivered.

'What's that?' Pulaski asked.

'The arc flash melted the pole.' She looked around and saw a hundred or more drops on the ground or sticking to the side of the bus, buildings and nearby cars.

That's what had killed the young passenger. A shower of molten metal drops flying through the air at a thousand feet a second.

The young officer exhaled slowly. 'Getting hit by something like that . . . burning right through you.'

Sachs shivered again — at the thought of the pain. And at the thought of how devastating the results of the attack might have been. This

47

portion of street was relatively empty. Had the substation been closer to the center of Manhattan, easily ten or fifteen passersby would have died.

Sachs looked up and found herself staring at the UNSUB's weapon: From one of the windows overlooking Fifty-seventh Street about two feet of thick wire dangled. It was covered in black insulation but the end was stripped away and the bare cable was bolted to a scorched brass plate. It looked industrial and mundane and not at all the sort of thing that could have produced such a terrible explosion.

Sachs and Pulaski joined the cluster of two dozen Homeland Security, FBI and NYPD agents and officers at the FBI's command post van. Some were in tactical gear, some in crime scene coveralls. Others, just suits or regulation uniforms. They were dividing up the labor. They'd be canvassing for witnesses and checking for post-incident bombs or other booby traps, a popular terrorist technique.

A solemn, lean-faced man in his fifties stood with his arms crossed, staring at the substation. He wore an Algonquin Consolidated badge on a chain around his neck. He was the senior company representative here: a field supervisor in charge of this portion of the grid. Sachs asked him to describe what Algonquin had learned about the event in detail, and he gave her an account, which she jotted into her notebook.

'Security cameras?'

The skinny man replied, 'Sorry, no. We don't bother. The doors are multiple locked. And there's nothing inside to steal, really. Anyways, all that juice, it's sort of like a guard dog. A big one.'

Sachs asked, 'How do you think he got in?'

'The door was locked when we got here. They're on number-pad locks.'

'Who has the codes?'

'All the employees. But he didn't get in that way. The locks have a chip that keeps records of when they're opened. These haven't been accessed for two days. And that — ' He pointed to the wire dangling from the window. ' — wasn't there then. He had to break in some other way.'

She turned to Pulaski. 'When you're finished out here check around back, the windows and roof.' She asked the Algonquin worker, 'Underground access?'

The field supervisor said, 'Not that I know of. The electric lines into and out of this station come through ducts nobody could fit in. But there could be other tunnels I don't know about.'

'Check it out anyway, Ron.' Sachs then interviewed the driver of the bus, who'd been treated for glass cuts and a concussion. His vision and hearing had been temporarily damaged but he'd insisted on staying to help the police however he could. Which wasn't very much. The round man described being curious about the wire protruding from the window; he'd never seen it before. Smelling smoke, hearing pops from inside. Then the terrifying spark.

'So fast,' he whispered. 'Never seen anything

that fast in my life.'

He'd been slammed against the window and woke up ten minutes later. He fell silent, gazing at his destroyed bus, his expression reflecting betrayal and mourning.

Sachs then turned to the agents and officers present and said she and Pulaski were going to run the scene. She wondered if word really had come down from the FBI's Tucker McDaniel that this was kosher. It wasn't unheard of for senior people in law enforcement to smilingly agree with you and then intentionally forget the conversation had ever taken place. But the federal agents had indeed been told. Some seemed irritated that the NYPD was taking this pivotal role, but others — the FBI's Evidence Response Team mostly — didn't seem to mind and indeed regarded Sachs with admiring curiosity; she was, after all, part of the team headed up by the legendary Lincoln Rhyme.

Turning toward Pulaski, she said, 'Let's get to work.' Sachs walked toward the RRV, binding her crimson hair into a bun, to suit up.

Pulaski hesitated and glanced at the hundred dots of cooling metal disks on the sidewalk and lodged against the front of the building, then at the stiff wire hanging from the window. 'They *did* shut the power off in there, didn't they?'

Sachs just motioned him to follow her.

6

Wearing the drab, dark blue Algonquin Consolidated Power overalls, a baseball-style cap without logo and safety glasses, the man busied himself at the service panel in the back of the health club in the Chelsea district of Manhattan.

As he did his work — mounting equipment and stripping, connecting and snipping wires, he was thinking about the attack that morning. The incident was all over the news.

One man was killed and several injured this morning when an overload in a power company substation in Manhattan produced a huge spark that jumped from the station to a bus sign pole, narrowly missing an MTA bus.

'It was like, you know, a lightning bolt,' one witness, a passenger on the bus, reported. 'Just filled the whole sidewalk. It blinded me. And that sound. I can't describe it. It was like this loud growl, then it exploded. I'm afraid to go near anything that's got electricity in it. I'm really freaked out. I mean, anybody who saw that thing is freaked out.'

You're not alone, the man thought. People had been conscious of — and awed and frightened by — electricity for more than five thousand years. The word itself came from the Greek for 'amber,' a reference to the solidified tree resin that the ancients would rub to create static charges. The numbing effects of electricity created by eels and fish in the rivers and off the coasts of Egypt, Greece and Rome were described at length in scientific writings well before the Christian era.

His thoughts turned to water creatures at the moment since, as he worked, he furtively watched five people swimming slow laps in the club's pool. Three women and two men, all of retirement age.

One particular fish he'd come to be fascinated with was the torpedo ray, which gave its name to the weapons fired by submarines. The Latin word *torpore* — to stiffen or paralyze — was the source of the name. The ray had, in effect, two batteries in its body made up of hundreds of thousands of gelatinous plates. These generated electricity, which a complicated array of nerves transported through its body like wires. The current was used for defense but also offensively, for hunting. Rays would lie in wait and then use a charge to numb their next meal or sometimes kill it outright — larger rays could generate up to two hundred volts and deliver more amps than an electric drill.

Pretty fascinating . . .

He finished rigging the panel and regarded his job. Like linemen and master electricians all over the world, he felt a certain pride at the neatness. He'd come to feel that working with electricity was more than a trade; it was a science and an art. Closing the door, he walked to the far side of the club — near the men's locker room. And, out of sight, he waited.

Like a torpedo ray.

This neighborhood — the far West Side — was residential; no workers were getting their jogs or swims or squash games in now, early afternoon, though the place would fill up after working hours with hundreds of locals, eager to sweat away the tensions of the day.

But he didn't need a large crowd. Not at the moment. That would come later.

So people would think he was simply another worker and ignore him, he turned his attention to a fire control panel and took the cover off, examining the guts without much interest. Thinking again about electric rays. Those that lived in salt water were wired in parallel circuits and produced lower voltage because seawater was a better conductor than fresh and the jolt didn't need to be so powerful to kill their prey. Electric rays that inhabited rivers and lakes, on the other hand, were wired in *series* and produced higher voltage to compensate for the lower conductivity of freshwater.

This, to him, was not only fascinating but was relevant at the moment — for this test about the conductivity of water. He wondered if he'd made the calculations right.

He had to wait only for ten minutes before he heard footsteps and saw one of the lap swimmers, a balding man in his sixties, padding by on slippers. He entered the showers.

The man in the overalls snuck a peek at the swimmer, turning the faucet on and stepping under the stream of steaming water, unaware that he was being studied.

Three minutes, five. Lathering, washing . . .

Growing impatient, because of the risk of detection, gripping the remote control — similar to a large car-key fob — the man in the overalls felt his shoulder muscles stiffening.

Torpore. He laughed silently. And relaxed.

Finally the club member stepped out of the shower and toweled off. He pulled his robe on and then stepped back into the slippers. He walked to the door leading to the locker room and took the handle.

The overalls man pressed two buttons on the remote simultaneously.

The elderly man gave a gasp and froze.

Then stepped back, staring at the handle. Looking at his fingers and quickly touching the handle once more.

Foolish, of course. You're never faster than electricity.

But there was no shock this time and the man was left to consider if maybe it was a burr of sharp metal or maybe even a painful jolt of arthritis in his fingers that he'd felt.

In fact, the trap had contained only a few milliamps of juice. He wasn't here to kill anyone. This was simply an experiment to tell two things: First, would the remote control switchgear he'd created work at this distance, through concrete and steel? It had, fine. And, second, what exactly was the effect of water on conductivity? This was the sort of thing that safety engineers talked and wrote about all the time but that no one had ever quantified in any practical sense — practical, meaning how little juice did one need to stun somebody wearing damp leather footgear into fibrillation and death.

The answer was pretty damn little.

Good.

Freaked me out . . .

The man in the overalls headed down the stairwell and out the back door.

He thought again about fish and electricity. This time, though, not the creation of juice but the detection of it. Sharks, in particular. They had, literally, a sixth sense: the astonishing ability to perceive the bioelectrical activity within the body of prey miles away, long before they could see it.

He glanced at his watch and supposed the investigation at the substation was well under way. It was unfortunate for whoever was looking into the incident there that human beings didn't have a shark's sixth sense.

Just as it would soon be unfortunate for many other people in the poor city of New York.

7

Sachs and Pulaski dressed in hooded baby blue Tyvek jumpsuits, masks, booties and safety glasses. As Rhyme had always instructed, they each wrapped a rubber band around the feet, to make easier differentiating their footprints from those inside. Then, encircling her waist with a belt, to which were attached her radio/video transmitter and weapon, Sachs stepped over the yellow tape, the maneuver sending some jolts of pain through her arthritic joints. On humid days or after a bout of running a tough scene or a foot pursuit, her knees or hips screaming, she harbored secret envy of Lincoln Rhyme's numbness. She'd never utter the thought aloud, of course, never even gave the crazy idea more than a second or two in her mind, but there it was. Advantages in all conditions.

She paused on the sidewalk, all by herself within the deadly perimeter. When Rhyme had been head of Investigation Resources — the outfit at NYPD in charge of crime scenes — he ordered his forensic people to search alone, unless the scene was particularly large. He did this because you tended psychologically to be less conscientious with other searchers present, since you were aware there was always a backup to find something you missed. The other problem was that just as criminals left behind evidence, crime scene searchers, however swaddled in protective gear, did too. This contamination could ruin the case. The more searchers, the greater that risk.

She looked into the gaping black doorway, smoke still escaping, and then considered the gun on her hip. Metal.

The lines're dead . . .

Well, get going, she told herself. The sooner you walk the grid after a crime, the better the quality of the evidence. Dots of sweat, full of helpful DNA, evaporated and became impossible to spot. Valuable fibers and hairs blew away, and irrelevant ones floated into the scene to confuse and mislead.

She slipped the microphone into her ear, inside the hood, and adjusted the stalk mike. She clicked the transmitter at her side and heard Rhyme's voice through the headset. ' . . . you there, Sachs? Are . . . okay, you're online. Was wondering. What's that?' he asked.

He was seeing the same things she was, thanks to a small, high-definition video camera on a headband. She realized she was unintentionally looking at the hole burned into the pole. She explained to him what had happened: the spark, the molten raindrops.

Rhyme was silent for a moment. Then he said, 'That's quite a weapon. Well, let's get going. Walk the grid.'

There were several ways to search crime scenes. One popular approach was to begin in the outside corner and walk in an increasingly smaller concentric circle until you reached the center.

But Lincoln Rhyme preferred the grid pattern. He sometimes told students to think of walking the grid as if mowing a lawn — only doing so twice. You walked along a straight line down one side of the scene to the other, then turned around, stepped a foot or so to the left or right and went back in the direction you'd just come. Then, once you'd finished, you turned perpendicular to the lines you first walked and started all over again, doing the same back-and-forth.

Rhyme insisted on this redundancy because the first search of a scene was crucial. If you did a cursory examination initially you subtly convinced yourself that there was nothing to be found. Subsequent searches were largely useless.

Sachs reflected on the irony: She was about to walk the grid in part of a very different grid. She'd have to share that with Rhyme — but later. Now she needed to concentrate.

Crime scene work was a scavenger hunt. The goal was simple: to find something, *anything* left behind by the perp — and something *would* have been left behind. The French criminalist Edmond Locard nearly a hundred years earlier had said that whenever a crime occurred there was a transfer of some evidence between the perpetrator and the crime scene or the victim. It might be virtually impossible to see, but it was there to find if you knew how to look and if you were patient and diligent.

Amelia Sachs now began this search, starting outside the substation, with the weapon: the dangling cable.

'Looks like he — '

'Or *they*,' Rhyme corrected through the headset. 'If Justice For is behind this, they might have a sizeable membership.'

'Good point, Rhyme.' He was making sure she didn't fall into the number-one problem crime scene searchers suffered from: failure to keep an open mind. A body, blood and a hot pistol suggested that the victim was shot to death. But if you got into your head that that was the case, you might miss the knife that was actually used.

She continued, 'Well, he or *they* rigged it from inside. But I'd think he had to be outside here on the sidewalk at some point to check distances and angles.'

'To aim it at the bus?'

'Exactly.'

'Okay, keep going — the sidewalk, then.'

She did, staring at the ground. 'Cigarette butts, beer caps. Nothing near the door or the window with the cable, though.'

'Don't bother with them. He's not going to be smoking or drinking on the job. He's too smart — considering how he put this whole thing together. But there'd be some trace where he stood. Close to the building.'

'There's a ledge, see it?' She was looking down at a low stone shelf about three feet above the sidewalk. The top was set with spikes to keep pigeons, and humans, from perching there, but you could use it as a step if you wanted to reach something in the window. 'Got some footprints, on the ledge. Not enough for electrostatic.'

'Let's see.'

She bent her head down and leaned forward.

He was looking at what she was: shapes that could be toe marks of shoes close to the building.

'You can't get prints?'

'No. Not clear enough. But looking at them I'd say they're probably men's. Wide, square toes, but that's all I can see. No soles or heels. But it tells us that if there's a 'they' involved, it was probably just a 'he' rigging the trap outside.'

She continued to examine the sidewalk and found no items of physical evidence that seemed relevant.

'Get trace, Sachs, and then search inside the substation.'

At her instruction, the other two techs from Queens set up powerful halogen lights just inside the door. She took pictures and then collected trace on the sidewalk and the ledge near the cable.

'And don't forget — ' Rhyme began.

'Substrata.'

'Ah, one step ahead of me, Sachs.'

Not really, she reflected, since he'd been her mentor for years and if she hadn't picked up his procedures for walking the grid by now, she had no business in crime scene work. She now moved to an area just outside the perimeter and took a second rolling — substrata, control samples to compare to the first. Any difference between what was collected at some distance from the scene and at the spot where the UNSUB was known to have stood might be unique to him or his dwelling.

Might not, of course . . . but that was the

nature of crime scene work. Nothing was ever certain, but you did what you could, you did what you had to.

Sachs handed off the bagged evidence to the technicians. She waved to the Algonquin supervisor she'd spoken to earlier.

The field supervisor, just as solemn as before, hurried over. 'Yes, Detective?'

'I'm going to search inside now. Can you tell me exactly what to look for — how he rigged the cable? I need to find where he stood, what he touched.'

'Let me find somebody who does regular maintenance here.' He looked over the workers. Then he called to another man, in dark blue Algonquin Consolidated Power overalls. A yellow hardhat. The worker tossed aside his cigarette and joined them. The field supervisor introduced them and told him Sachs's request.

'Yes, ma'am,' he said, his eyes leaving the substation for an excursion across Sachs's chest, even though her figure was largely hidden by her billowy blue Tyvek jumpsuit. She thought about glancing down at his excessive belly but of course she didn't. Dogs pee where you don't want them to; you can't correct them all the time.

She asked, 'I'll be able to see where he attached the cable to the power source?'

'Everything'll be in the open, yeah,' the man told her. 'I'd think he'd connect close to the breakers. They're on the main floor. That'll be on the right side when you get in there.'

'Ask him if the line was live when the UNSUB

rigged it,' Rhyme said into her ear. 'That'll tell us something about the perp's skill.' She did.

'Oh, yeah. He tapped into a hot line.'

Sachs was shocked. 'How could he do that?'

'Wore PPE — personal protective equipment. And made sure he was insulated pretty damn good on top of that.'

Rhyme added, 'I've got another question for him. Ask him how he gets any work done if he spends so much time staring at women's breasts.'

She stifled a smile.

But as she walked toward the entrance, traipsing along the sidewalk over the molten dots, all humor vanished. She paused, turned back to the supervisor. 'Just confirming one last time. No power, right?' She nodded at the substation. 'The lines are dead.'

'Oh, yeah.'

Sachs turned.

Then he added, 'Except for the batteries.'

'Batteries?' She stopped and looked back.

The supervisor explained, 'That's what operates the circuit breakers. But they're not part of the grid. They won't be connected to the cable.'

'Okay. Those batteries. Could they be dangerous?' The image of the polka-dot wounds covering the passenger's body kept surfacing.

'Well, sure.' This was apparently a naive question. He added, 'But the terminals're covered with insulated caps.'

Sachs turned and walked back to the substation. 'I'm going inside, Rhyme.'

She approached, noting that, for some reason, the powerful lights made the interior even more ominous than when it was dark.

The door to hell, she was thinking.

'I'm getting seasick, Sachs. What're you doing?'

What she was doing, she realized, was hesitating, looking around, focusing on the gaping doorway. She realized that, though Rhyme couldn't see it, she was also rubbing her finger compulsively against the quick of her thumb. Sometimes she broke the skin doing this and surprised herself by finding dots or streaks of blood. That was bad enough, but she sure didn't want to break through the latex glove now and contaminate the scene with her own trace. She straightened her fingers and said, 'Just checking it out.'

But they'd known each other too long for any bullshit. He asked, 'What's wrong?'

Sachs took a deep breath. Finally she answered: 'Little spooked, got to say. That arc thing. The way the vic died. It was pretty bad.'

'You want to wait? Call in some experts from Algonquin? They can walk you through it.'

She could tell from his voice, a tone, a pacing of his words, that he didn't want her to. It was one of the things she loved about him — the respect he showed by not coddling her. At home, at dinner, in bed, they were one thing. Here they were criminalist and crime scene cop.

She thought of her personal mantra, inherited from her father: 'When you move they can't getcha.'

So move.

'No, I'm fine.' Amelia Sachs stepped into hell.

8

'Can you see okay?'

'Yes,' Rhyme responded.

Sachs had clicked on the halogen lamp affixed to her headband. Small but powerful, it shined a fierce beam throughout the dim space. Even with the halogens, there were many shadowy crevices. The substation was cavernous inside, though from the sidewalk it had seemed smaller, narrow and dwarfed by the buildings on either side.

Her eyes burned and nose stung from the smoke residue. Rhyme insisted that anyone searching scenes sniff the air; scents could tell you a great deal about the perp and the nature of the crime. Here, though, the only odor was a sour perfume: a burned-rubber, metallic, oily smell, reminding her of car engines. She flashed on memories of herself and her father, spending Sunday afternoons, backs aching, hunched over the open hood of a Chevy or Dodge muscle car, coaxing the mechanical nervous and vascular systems back to life. More recent memories too: Sachs and Pammy, the teenager who'd become a surrogate niece, together tuning the Torino Cobra, as Pammy's small dog, Jackson, sat patiently on the tool bench and watched the surgeons at work.

Swinging her head to train her miner's light around the hazy area, she noticed large banks of equipment, some beige or gray and relatively new-looking, some dating back to the last century: dark green and labeled with metal plaques offering the manufacturer and city of origin. Some, she noted, had addresses with no ZIP codes, revealing the distant era of their birth.

The main floor of the station was circular, overlooking the open basement, twenty feet below, visible over a pipe railing. Up here the floor was concrete but some of the platforms and the stairs were steel.

Metal.

One thing she knew about electricity was that metal was a good conductor.

She located the UNSUB's cable, running from the window about ten feet to a piece of equipment that the worker had described. She could see where the suspect'd had to stand to string the wire. She began walking the grid at that spot.

Rhyme asked, 'What's that on the floor? Shiny.'

'Looks like grease or oil,' she said, her voice falling. 'Some of the equipment ruptured in the fire. Or maybe there was a second arc here.' She noted burned circles, a dozen of them, which seemed to be where sparks had slammed into the walls and surrounding equipment.

'Good.'

'What?'

'His footprints'll come through nice and clear.'

This was true. But, as she looked down at the greasy residue on the floor, she was thinking: was oil, like metal and water, a good conductor too?

65

And where are the fucking batteries?

She did indeed find some good footprints near the window in which the perp had knocked a hole to feed the deadly wire outside and near where he'd bolted it to the Algonquin line.

'Could've been left by the workers,' she said of the prints, 'when they came in after the spark.'

'We'll just have to find out, won't we?'

She or Ron Pulaski would take prints of the workers' footgear to compare with these, to eliminate them as suspects. Even if Justice For was ultimately responsible, there was no reason why they couldn't recruit an insider for their terrorist plans.

Though as she laid down numbers and photographed the sole marks, she said, 'I think they're our UNSUB's, Rhyme. They're all the same. And the toe's similar to what was on the ledge.'

'Excellent,' Rhyme breathed.

Sachs then took electrostatic impressions of them and put the sheets near the door. She looked over the cable itself, which was thinner than she expected, only about a half inch in diameter. It was covered with black insulation of some kind and was made of silver-colored strands, woven together. It wasn't, she was surprised to see, copper. About fifteen feet long, in total. It was joined to the Algonquin main line by two wide brass or copper bolts with three-quarter inch holes in them.

'So that's our weapon?' Rhyme asked.

'This's it.'

'Heavy?'

She hefted it, gripping the rubbery insulation. 'No. It's aluminum.' It was troubling to her that, like a bomb, something so small and light could cause such mayhem. Sachs looked over the hardware and judged what she'd need from her tool kit to dismantle it. She stepped outside to retrieve the bag from her car's trunk. Her own tools, which she used on her car and for home repair, were more familiar to her than the ones in the Crime Scene Unit RRV; they were like old friends.

'How's it going?' Pulaski asked.

'It's going,' she muttered. 'You find how he got in?'

'I checked the roof. No access. Whatever the Algonquin people said, I'm thinking it has to be underground. I'm going to check out nearby manholes and basements. There're no obvious routes but that's the good news, I guess. He might've been feeling pretty cocky. If we're lucky we might find something good.'

Rhyme constantly urged officers under him to remember that one crime always had multiple scenes associated with it. There was, yes, perhaps just one location where the actual offense had occurred. But there're always entrance and exit routes to consider — and those might be two different paths, or more if multiple perps were involved. There could be staging areas. There could be rendezvous locations. And there could be the motel where they got together to gloat and share the loot afterward. And nine times out of ten, it's *those* scenes — the secondary or tertiary — where the perps forgot to wear gloves and clean up trace. Sometimes they even left their names and addresses lying around.

Through Sachs's microphone Rhyme had heard the comment and said, 'Good call, Rookie. Only lose the 'luck.''

'Yessir.'

'And lose the smug grin too. I saw that.'

Pulaski's face went still. He'd forgotten Rhyme was using Amelia Sachs for his eyes as well as ears and legs. He turned and walked off to continue his search for the perp's access to the substation.

Returning inside with her tools, Sachs wiped them down with adhesive pads to remove any contaminating trace. She walked up to the circuit breaker, the spot where the attacker's cable was mounted with the bolts. She started to reach for the metal portion of the wire. Involuntarily her gloved hand stopped before she touched it. She stared at the raw metal gleaming under the beam of her helmet light.

'Sachs?' Rhyme's voice startled her.

She didn't answer. Saw in her mind the hole in the pole, the deadly bits of molten steel, the holes in the young victim.

The lines are dead . . .

But what if she got her hand on the metal and somebody two or three miles away in a comfy little control room decided to make it undead? Hit a switch, not knowing about the search?

And where the fuck are those damn batteries?

'We need the evidence back here,' Rhyme said.

'Right.' She slipped a nylon cover over the end of her wrench so that any distinctive marks on her tools wouldn't transfer to the nuts or bolts and be confused with marks left by the perp's. She leaned forward and with only a moment of hesitation fitted the wrench onto the first bolt. With some effort she loosened it, working as quickly as she could, expecting to feel a searing burn at any moment, though she supposed with that much voltage she wouldn't feel anything at all as she was electrocuted.

The second fixture was undone a moment later and she pulled the cable free. Coiling it, she wrapped the wire in plastic sheeting. The bolts and nuts went into an evidence bag. She set these outside the substation door for Pulaski or the technicians to collect and returned to continue her search. Looking at the floor, she saw more footsteps that seemed to match what she thought were the UNSUB's.

Cocking her head.

'You're making me dizzy, Sachs.'

She asked herself as much as Rhyme, 'What was that?'

'You hear something?'

'Yes, can't you?'

'If I could hear it, I wouldn't be asking.'

It seemed to be a tapping of some sort. She walked to the center of the substation and looked over the railing into darkness below.

Her imagination?

No, the sound was unmistakable.

'I *do* hear it,' Rhyme said.

'It's coming from downstairs, the basement.'

A regular beat. Not like a human sound.

A timed detonator? she wondered. And

thought again about a booby trap. The perp was smart. He'd know that a crime scene team would spare no effort to search the substation. He'd want to stop them. She shared these thoughts with Rhyme.

He replied, 'But if he'd put together a trap why hadn't he done it near the wire?'

They came to the same conclusion simultaneously but he voiced the thought: 'Because there's some greater threat to him in the basement.' Rhyme then pointed out, 'If the power's off what's making the noise?'

'It doesn't sound like one-second intervals, Rhyme. It might not be a timer.' She was gazing over the railing, careful not to touch the metal.

He said, 'It's dark, I can't see much.'

'I'm going to find out.' And then she started down the spiral staircase.

The *metal* staircase.

Ten feet, fifteen, twenty. Random shafts of light from the halogens hit portions of the walls down here, but only the upper portions. Below that everything was murky, the smoke residue thick. Her breaths were shallow and she struggled not to choke. As she approached the bottom, two full stories below the main floor, it was hard to see anything; the miner's light reflected back into her eyes. Still, it was the only illumination she had; she swung her head, with the light, from side to side, taking in the myriad boxes and machinery and wires and panels covering the walls.

She hesitated, tapped her weapon. And stepped off the bottom of the stairs.

And gasped as a jolt pierced her body.

'Sachs! What?'

Sachs had missed the fact that the floor was covered in two feet of freezing brackish water. She couldn't see it with the smoke.

'Water, Rhyme. I wasn't expecting it. And look.' She focused ten feet or so over her head at a pipe that was leaking.

That was the sound. Not a click, but dripping water. The idea of water in an electrical substation was so incongruous — and so dangerous — that it hadn't occurred to her that this could be the source of the noise.

'Because of the blast?'

'No. He drilled a hole, Rhyme. I can see it. *Two* holes. Water's also flowing down the wall — that's what's filling up the room.'

Wasn't water as good an electrical conductor as metal? Sachs wondered.

And she was standing in a pool of it, right next to an array of wires and switches and connections above a sign:

DANGER: 138,000 VOLTS.

Rhyme's voice startled her. 'He's flooding the basement to destroy evidence.'

'Right.'

'Sachs, what's that? I can't see it clearly. That box. The big one. Look to the right . . . Yes, there. What is it?'

Ah, finally.

'It's the battery, Rhyme. The backup battery.'

'Is it charged?'

'They said it was. But I don't . . . '

She waded closer and looked down. A gauge on the battery showed that it was indeed charged. In fact, to Sachs, it looked like it was over-charged. The needle was past 100 percent Then she remembered something else the Algonquin workers had said: not to worry because it was sealed with insulated caps.

Except that it wasn't. She knew what battery caps looked like and this unit had none. Two metal terminals, connected to thick cables, were exposed.

'The water's rising. It'll hit the terminals in a few minutes.'

'Is there enough current to make one of those arc flashes?'

'I don't know, Rhyme.'

'There has to be,' he whispered. 'He's using an arc to destroy something that'll lead us to him. Something he couldn't take with him or destroy when he was there. Can you shut the water off?'

She looked quickly. 'No faucets that I can see . . . Hold on a minute.'

Sachs continued to study the basement. 'I don't see what he wants to destroy, though.' But then she spotted it: Right behind the battery, about four feet off the ground, was an access door. It wasn't large — about eighteen inches square.

'That's it, Rhyme. That's how he got in.'

'Must be a sewer or utility tunnel on the other side. But leave it. Pulaski can trace it from the street. Just get out.'

'No, Rhyme, look at it — it's really tight. He'd

have to squeeze through. It's got some good trace on it, has to. Fibers, hair, maybe DNA. Why else would he want to destroy it?'

Rhyme was hesitating. He knew she was right about preserving the evidence but didn't want her caught in another arc flash explosion.

She waded closer to the access door. But as she approached, a tiny wake rose from the disturbance of her legs and the waves nearly crested the battery.

She froze.

'Sachs!'

'Shhh.' She had to concentrate. By moving a few inches at a time she was able to keep the waves below the top of the power source. But she could see she had no more than one or two minutes until the water hit the leads.

With a straight-bladed screwdriver she began to remove the frame holding the access door.

The water was now nearly to the top of the battery. Every time she leaned forward to get leverage to unscrew the paint-stuck hardware, another small tide rose and the murky water sloshed up onto the top of the battery before receding.

The battery's voltage was certainly smaller than the hundred thousand volt line that had produced the arc flash outside, but the UNSUB probably didn't need to cause that much damage. His point was to create a big enough explosion to destroy the access door and whatever evidence it contained.

She wanted the damn door.

'Sachs?' Rhyme whispered.

Ignoring him. And ignoring the image of the cauterized holes in the smooth flesh of the victim, the molten teardrops.

Finally the last screw came out. Old paint held the door frame in place. She jammed the tip of the screwdriver into the edge and slammed her hand onto the butt of the tool. With a crack, the metal came away in her hands. The door and frame were heavier than she'd thought and she nearly dropped it. But then she steadied herself, without sending a tsunami over the battery.

In the opening she saw the narrow utility tunnel that the suspect would have used to sneak into the substation.

Rhyme whispered urgently, 'Into the tunnel. It'll protect you. Hurry!'

'I'm trying.'

Except the access door wouldn't fit through the opening, even diagonally, because the frame was attached. 'Can't do it,' she said, explaining the problem. 'I'll go back up the stairs.'

'No, Sachs. Just leave the door. Get out through the tunnel.'

'It's too good a piece of evidence.'

Clutching the access door, she began her escape, wading toward the stairs, glancing back from time to time to keep an eye on the battery. She moved agonizingly slowly. Even so, every step sent another wave cresting to the edge of the battery terminals.

'What's going on, Sachs?'

'I'm nearly there,' she whispered, as if too loud a voice would create more turbulence in the water.

She was halfway to the steps when the water rose in tiny eddies and swirled around first one terminal, then the next.

No arc flash.

Nothing.

Her shoulders sagged, heart thumping.

'It's a dud, Rhyme. We didn't have to worr — '

A burst of white light filled her vision, accompanied by a huge cracking roar, and Amelia Sachs was flung backward, under the surface of the grim ocean.

9

'Thom!'

The aide hurried into the room, looking Rhyme over carefully. 'What's wrong? How're you feeling?'

'It's not *me*,' his boss snapped, eyes wide, nodding his head at the blank screen. 'Amelia. She was at a scene. A battery . . . another arc flash. The audio and video are out. Call Pulaski! Call somebody!'

Thom Reston's eyes narrowed with concern but he had practiced the art of caregiving for a long time; no matter what the crisis, he would coolly go about his necessary tasks. He calmly picked up a landline phone, regarded the number pad nearby and hit a speed-dial button.

Panic isn't centered in the gut, and it doesn't trickle down the spine like, well, electricity in an energized wire. Panic rattles the body and soul everywhere, even if you're numb otherwise. Rhyme was furious with himself. He should have ordered Sachs out the instant they saw the battery, the rising tide. He *always* did this, got so focused on the case, the goal, finding the tiny fiber, the fragment of friction ridge print, anything that moved him closer to the perp, that he forgot the implications: He was playing with human lives.

Why, look at his own injury. He'd been a captain in the NYPD, the head of Investigation

Resources, and was searching a crime scene himself, crouching to pick up a fiber from a body when the beam tumbled from above and changed his life forever.

And now that same attitude — which he'd instilled in Amelia Sachs — might have done even worse: she could now be dead.

Thom had gotten through on the line.

'Who?' Rhyme demanded, glaring at the aide. 'Who're you talking to? Is she all right?'

Thom held up a hand.

'What does that mean? What could that *possibly* mean?' Rhyme felt a trickle of sweat down his forehead. He was aware his breath was coming faster. His heart was pounding, though he sensed this in his jaw and neck, not his chest, of course.

Thom said, 'It's Ron. He's at the substation.'

'I know where the fuck he is. What's going on?'

'There's been . . . an incident. That's what they're saying.'

Incident . . .

'Where's Amelia?'

'They're checking. There're some people inside. They heard an explosion.'

'I know there was an explosion. I fucking saw it!'

The aide's eyes swiveled toward Rhyme. 'Are you . . . how are you feeling?'

'Quit asking that. What's going on at the scene?'

Thom continued to scan Rhyme's face. 'You're flushed.'

'I'm fine,' the criminalist said calmly — to get the young man to focus on his phone call. 'Really.'

Then the aide's head tilted sideways and to Rhyme's horror he stiffened. His shoulders rose slightly.

No . . .

'Okay,' Thom said into the phone.

'Okay *what?*' the criminalist snapped.

Thom ignored his boss. 'Give me the information.' And, cradling the phone between neck and shoulder, he began to type on the keyboard of the lab's main computer.

The screen popped to life.

Rhyme had lost the pretense of calm and was about to lose his temper when, on the screen, up came the image of an apparently uninjured, though very wet, Amelia Sachs. Strands of her red hair were plastered around her face like seaweed on a surfacing scuba diver.

'Sorry, Rhyme, lost the main camera when I went under.' She coughed hard and wiped at her forehead, examined her fingers with a look of distaste. The motion was jerky.

Relief immediately replaced panic, though the anger — at himself — remained.

Sachs was staring back, somewhat eerily, her eyes focused only in his general direction. 'I'm on one of the Algonquin worker's laptops. It's got a camera set up on it. Can you see me okay?'

'Yes, yes. But you're all right?'

'Just took in some pretty disgusting water through my nose. But I'm okay.'

Rhyme was asking, 'What happened? The arc flash?'

'It wasn't an arc. The battery wasn't rigged for that. The Algonquin guy told me there wasn't enough voltage. What the UNSUB did was make a bomb. Apparently you can do that with batteries. You seal the vents and overcharge it. That produces hydrogen gas. When water hits the terminals, it short-circuits and the spark ignites the hydrogen. That's what happened.'

'And have the medics looked you over?'

'No, no need. The bang was loud but it wasn't that big. I got hit by some bits of plastic from the housing. Didn't even bruise me. The impact knocked me down but I kept the access door above the water. I don't think it's contaminated too bad.'

'Good, Ame — ' His voice braked to a halt. For some reason, years ago they'd settled on an unspoken superstition: They never used their first names. He was troubled that he nearly had. 'Good. So that's how he got in.'

'Had to be.'

It was then that he was aware of Thom walking toward the wall. The aide grabbed the blood pressure monitor and wrapped it around Rhyme's arm.

'Don't do that — '

'Quiet,' Thom barked, silencing Rhyme. 'You're flushed and you're sweating.'

'Because we just had a fucking *incident* at a crime scene, Thom.'

'You have a headache?'

He did. He said, 'No.'

'Don't lie.'

'A little one. It's nothing.'

Thom slapped the stethoscope against his arm. 'Sorry, Amelia. I need him quiet for thirty seconds.'

'Sure.'

Rhyme started to protest again, but then he decided that the sooner his blood pressure was taken the sooner he could get back to work.

Without sensation he watched the cuff inflate and Thom listened as he let the air out of the sphygmomanometer. He ripped off the Velcro noisily. 'It's high. I want to make sure it doesn't get any higher. I'm going to take care of some things now.'

A polite euphemism for what Rhyme bluntly called the 'piss and shit' detail.

Sachs asked, 'What's going on there, Thom? Everything okay?'

'Yes.' Rhyme was struggling to keep his voice calm. And to obscure the fact that he felt oddly vulnerable, though whether it was her near miss or his troubled condition he couldn't say.

He was embarrassed too.

Thom said, 'He's had a spike in blood pressure. I want him off the phone now.'

'We'll bring back the evidence, Rhyme. Be there in a half hour.'

Thom was starting forward to disconnect the call when Rhyme felt a tap in his head — it was cognitive, not physical. And he instinctively barked, 'Wait,' meaning the command to both Thom and Sachs.

'Lincoln,' his aide protested.

'Please, Thom. Just two minutes. It's important.'

Though clearly suspicious of the polite appeal, Thom nodded reluctantly.

'Ron was searching for the place the perp got into the tunnel, right?'

'Yes.'

'Is he there?'

Her jerky, grain-filled image looked around. 'Yes.'

'Get him on camera.'

He heard Sachs call the officer over. A moment later he was seated, staring out of the monitor. 'Yessir?'

'You find where he got into the tunnel behind the substation?'

'Yep.'

'Yep? You sound like a dog, Rookie. Yip, yip.'

'Sorry. Yes, I did.'

'Where?'

'There's a manhole in an alley up the street. Algonquin Power. It was for access to steam pipes. It didn't lead to the substation itself. But about twenty feet inside, maybe thirty, I found a grating. Somebody'd cut an opening into it. Big enough to climb through. They'd stuck it back up but I could see it'd been cut.'

'Recently?'

'Right.'

'Because there was no rust on the cut edges.'

'Yeah, I mean yes. It led to this tunnel. It was really old. Might've been for delivering coal or something a long time ago. That's what went to the access door that Amelia got. I was at the end

81

of the tunnel and I saw the light when she took the door off. And I heard the battery blow and her scream. I got to her right away, through the tunnel.'

The gruffness fell away. 'Thanks, Pulaski.'

An awkward moment. Rhyme's compliments were so rare he'd found that people didn't quite know what to do with them.

'I was careful not to contaminate the scene too much, though.'

'To save lives, contaminate to your heart's content. Remember that.'

'Sure.'

The criminalist continued, 'You walked the grid at the manhole — and where he cut through the grating? And the tunnel?'

'Yessir.'

'Anything jump out?'

'Just footprints. But I've got trace.'

'We'll see what it says.'

Thom whispered firmly, 'Lincoln?'

'Just a minute more. Now, I need you to do something else, Rookie. You see that restaurant or coffee shop across the street from the power station?'

The officer looked to his right. 'I've got it . . . Wait, how'd you know there was one there?'

'Oh, from one of my neighborhood strolls,' Rhyme said, chuckling.

'I . . . ' The young man was flustered.

'I know because there *has* to be one. Our UNSUB wanted to be able to see the substation for the attack. He couldn't watch from a hotel room because he'd have to register, or an office building because it would be too suspicious. He'd be someplace where he could sit at his leisure.'

'Oh, I get it. You mean psychologically, he gets off on watching the fireworks.'

The time for compliments was over. 'Jesus Christ, Rookie, that's profiling. How do I feel about profiling?'

'Uhm. You're not exactly a big fan, Lincoln.'

Rhyme caught Sachs, in the background, smiling.

'He needed to see how the device was working. He'd created something unique. His arc flash gun isn't the sort of thing he could test-fire at a rifle range. He had to make adjustments to the voltage and the circuit breakers as he went along. He had to make sure it discharged at the exact moment when the bus was there. He started manipulating the grid computer at eleven-twenty and in ten minutes it was all over. Go talk to the manager at the restaurant — '

'Coffee shop.'

' — of the coffee shop and see if anybody was inside, near a window, for a while before the explosion. He would've left right after, before police and fire got there. Oh, and find out if they have broadband and who's the provider.'

Thom, now in rubber gloves, was gesturing impatiently.

The piss and shit detail . . .

Pulaski said, 'Sure, Lincoln.'

'And then — '

The young officer interrupted, 'Seal off the

restaurant and walk the grid where he was sitting.'

'Exactly right, Rookie. Then both of you, get the hell back here ASAP.'

With a flick of one of his working fingers Rhyme ended the call, beating Thom's own digit to the button by a millisecond.

10

The cloud zone, Fred Dellray was thinking.

Recalling when Assistant Special Agent in Charge Tucker McDaniel, newly on board in the FBI's New York office, had gathered the troops and given, in lecture form, a talk similar to what he'd just delivered at Rhyme's a few hours earlier. About the new methods of communication the bad guys were using, about how the acceleration of technology was making it easier for them and harder for us.

The cloud zone . . .

Dellray understood the concept, of course. You couldn't be in law enforcement now and not be aware of McDaniel's high-tech approach to finding and collaring perps. But that didn't mean he liked it. Not one bit. Largely because of what the phrase stood for; it was an emblem for fundamental, maybe cataclysmic, changes in everyone's life.

Changes in *his* life too.

Heading downtown on a subway on this clear afternoon, Dellray was thinking about his father, a professor at Manhattan Marymount College, and a writer of several books about African-American philosophers and cultural critics. The man had eased into academia at the age of thirty, and he'd never left. He died at the same desk he'd called home for decades, slumping forward on proofs of the journal he'd founded when

Martin Luther King's assassination was still fresh in the world's mind.

The politics had changed drastically during his father's lifetime — the death of communism, the wounding of racial segregation, the birth of nonstate enemies. Computers replaced typewriters and the library. Cars had airbags. TV channels propagated from four — plus UHF — to hundreds. But very little about the man's lifestyle had altered in a core way. The elder Dellray thrived in his enclosed world of academia, specifically philosophy, and oh, how he had wanted his son to settle there too, examining the nature of existence and the human condition. He'd tried to fill his son with a love of the same.

To some extent he was successful. Questioning, brilliant, discerning young Fred did indeed develop a fascination with humankind in all its incarnations: metaphysics, psychology, theology, epistemology, ethics, and politics. He loved it all. But it took only one month as a graduate assistant to realize he'd go mad if he didn't put his talents to practical use.

And never one to pull back, he sought out the rawest and most intense practical application of philosophy he could think of.

He joined the FBI.

Change . . .

His father reconciled himself to his son's apostasy and they enjoyed coffee and long walks in Prospect Park, during which they came to understand that, although their laboratories and techniques were different, their outlooks and insights were not.

The human condition . . . observed and written about by the father and experienced firsthand by the son.

In the unlikely form of undercover work. Fred's intense curiosity about and insights into the nature of life made him a natural Everyman. Unlike most undercover cops, with their limited acting skills and repertoires, Dellray could truly become the people he played.

Once, when Dellray was in disguise as a homeless man on the streets of New York, not far from the Federal Building, the then Assistant Special Agent in Charge of the Manhattan office of the FBI — Dellray's boss, in effect — walked right past and dropped a quarter into his cup, never recognizing him.

One of the best compliments Dellray ever received.

A chameleon. One week, a scorched-brain tweaker desperate for meth. The next a South African envoy with nuclear secrets to sell. Then a Somalian imam's lieutenant, lugging around a hatred of America and a hundred quotations from the Koran.

He owned dozens of outfits, purchased or hacked together by himself, which now clogged the basement of the townhouse he and Serena had bought a few years ago in BK — Brooklyn. He'd advanced in his career, which was inevitable for someone with his drive, skill and absolute lack of desire to stab fellow workers in the back. Now Dellray primarily ran other undercover FBI agents and civilian confidential informants — AKA snitches — though he still got into the field occasionally. And loved it just as much as he ever had.

But then came the change.

Cloud zone . . .

Dellray didn't deny that both the good guys and the bad guys were getting smarter and more tech-savvy. The shift was obvious: HUMINT — the fruits of intelligence gathering from human-to-human contact — was giving way to SIGINT.

But it was a phenomenon that Dellray simply wasn't comfortable with. In her youth Serena had tried to be a torch singer. She was a natural at all forms of dance, from ballet to jazz to modern, but she just didn't have the skill to sing. Dellray was the same with the new law enforcement of data, numbers, technology.

He kept running his snitches and he kept going undercover himself, and getting results. But with McDaniel and his T and A team — oh, 'scuse me, Tucker — his *Tech and Com* team, old-school Dellray was feeling, well, old. The ASAC was sharp, a hard worker — putting in sixty-hour work weeks — and an infighter; he'd stand up for his agents against the President if he needed to. And his techniques had worked; last month McDaniel's people had picked up sufficient details from encrypted satellite phone calls to pinpoint a fundamentalist cell outside Milwaukee.

The message to Dellray and the older agents was clear: your time's passing.

He still stung from the dig, possibly inadvertent, delivered at the meeting in Rhyme's lab.

Well, keep at it, Fred. You're doing a good job . . .

Meaning, I didn't even expect *you* to come up with any leads to Justice For and Rahman.

Maybe McDaniel was right to criticize. After all, Dellray had as good a network of CIs in place as you could hope for to track terrorist activities. He met with them regularly. He worked them all hard, doling out protection to the fearful, Kleenex to the wet-eyed guilty, cash to the ones who informed as a livelihood and painful squeezes to the shoulders and psyches of those who'd gotten, as Dellray's grandmother said, too big for their britches.

But of all the information he'd gathered about terrorist plots, even embryonic ones, there'd been nothing about Rahman's Justice For or about a big fucking spark.

And here McDaniel's people had made an ID and defined a real threat by sitting on their asses.

Like the drones in the Middle East and Afghanistan? You know the pilots are next to a strip mall in Colorado Springs or Omaha . . .

Dellray had another concern too, one that had arisen around the same time as youthful McDaniel appeared: Maybe he just wasn't as good as he used to be.

Rahman might've been right under his nose. Cell members in Justice For might've been studying electrical engineering in BK or New

Jersey the same way the 9/11 hijackers had studied flying.

Then something else: He had to admit he'd been distracted lately. Something from his Other Life, he called it, his life with Serena, which he kept as separate from the street as you'd keep flame from gasoline. And that something was pretty significant: Fred Dellray was now a father. Serena had had a baby boy a year ago. They'd talked about it beforehand, and she'd insisted that even after their child was born Dellray wouldn't change his job one bit. Even if it involved running dangerous undercover sets. She understood that his work defined him the way dancing defined her; it would be more dangerous to him, ultimately, to move behind a desk.

But was being a father altering him as an agent? Dellray looked forward to taking Preston to the park or a store, feeding the boy, reading to him. (Serena had come by the nursery, laughed and gently taken Kierkegaard's existentialist manifesto *Fear and Trembling* from Dellray's lengthy hand and replaced it with *Goodnight Moon*. Dellray hadn't realized that even at that young age, words count.)

The subway now stopped in the Village, and passengers rustled aboard.

Instinctively the undercover operative within him immediately spotted four people of note: two almost-guaranteed-to-be pickpockets, one kid who was carrying a knife or box cutter and a young, sweaty businessman pressing a protective hand against a pocket so hard that he'd split open the bag of coke if he wasn't careful.

The street . . . how Fred Dellray loved the street.

But these four had nothing to do with his mission and he let them fade from his consciousness, as he told himself: Okay, you fucked up. You missed Rahman, and you missed Justice For. But the casualties and damage were minimal. McDaniel was condescending but hasn't made you a scapegoat, not yet. Which somebody else might've done in a heartbeat.

Dellray could still find a lead to their UNSUB and stop him before another of those terrible attacks happened. Dellray could still redeem himself.

At the next subway stop, he climbed out and began his trek east. Eventually he came to bodegas and tenements and old, dark social clubs, rancid-smelling diners, radio taxi operations whose signs were in Spanish or Arabic or Farsi. No fast-moving professionals like in the West Village; here people weren't moving around much at all, but merely sitting — men mostly — on rickety chairs or on doorsteps, the young ones slim, the old round. They all watched you with cautious eyes.

This was where the serious work of the Street got done. This was Fred Dellray's office.

He strode up to a coffee shop window and looked inside — with some difficulty since the glass hadn't been cleaned for months.

Ah, yeah, there. He spotted what would either

be his salvation or his downfall.

His last chance.

Tapping one ankle against the other just to make sure the pistol strapped there hadn't shifted, he opened the door and stepped inside.

11

'How are you feeling?' Sachs asked, walking into the lab.

Rhyme said stiffly, 'I'm fine. Where's the evidence?' Sentences spoken without discernible punctuation.

'The techs and Ron are bringing it. I took the Cobra by myself.'

Meaning, he supposed, she'd sped home like a NASCAR driver.

'And how are *you*?' Thom asked.

'Wet.'

Which went without saying. Her hair was drying but the clothes were still drenched. Her condition wasn't an issue. They knew she was fine. They'd established that earlier. Rhyme had been shaken at the time but now she was all right and he wanted to get on with the evidence.

But isn't that just another way of saying there's a forty-five percent chance that somebody else somewhere in New York City's going to get electrocuted? ... And it could be happening right now.'

'Well, where are — ?'

'What happened?' she asked Thom, a glance toward Rhyme.

'I said I was fine.'

'I'm asking *him*.' Sachs's own temper flared a bit.

'Blood pressure was high. Spiking.'

'And now it's not high, Thom, is it?' Lincoln Rhyme said testily. 'It's nice and normal. That's sort of like saying the Russians sent missiles to Cuba. That *was* tense for a while. But since Miami isn't a radioactive crater, I guess that problem sorted itself out, now, didn't it? It's. In. The. Past. Call Pulaski, call the techs from Queens. I want the evidence.'

His aide ignored him and said to Sachs, 'Didn't need medicine. But I'm keeping an eye on it.'

She gave Rhyme another visual examination. Then said she was going upstairs to change.

'There a problem?' asked Lon Sellitto, who'd arrived from downtown a few minutes before. 'Aren't you feeling good, Linc?'

'Oh, Jesus Christ,' Rhyme spat out. 'Is everybody deaf? Is everybody ignoring me?' Then he glanced into the doorway. 'Ah, at last. Another country heard from. Goddamn, Pulaski, at least *you're* being productive. What do we have?'

The young cop, back in uniform, was carting in milk crates that the crime scene officers usually used for transporting evidence bags.

A moment later two techs from the Queens Crime Scene HQ brought in a bulky plastic-wrapped object: the wire. The strangest weapon Rhyme had ever seen in a case. And one of the deadliest. They also had the access door from the substation basement, similarly wrapped in plastic.

'Pulaski? The coffee shop?'

'You were right. I've got some things here, sir.'

A lifted eyebrow from the criminalist reminded the officer the appellation wasn't necessary. The criminalist was a *retired* captain of the NYPD. He didn't have any more right to a formal title or 'sir' than anybody else on the street. And he'd been trying to break Pulaski of his wispy insecurities — they were due to youth, of course, but there was more to it: he'd sustained a serious head injury on the first case they'd worked together. It had nearly ended his career in law enforcement, but he'd stayed on the force, despite the injury and the resulting bouts of confusion and disorientation that occasionally still plagued him. (His determination to remain a cop had been inspired largely by Rhyme's decision to do the same.)

In furthering his cause to make Pulaski a top crime scene officer, one of the most important things Rhyme needed to instill was a bullet-proof ego. You could have all the skills in the world but they were useless if you didn't have the balls to back them up. Before he died, he wanted to see Pulaski move up high in the ranks of Crime Scene in New York City. He knew it could happen. He had a brief image of a hope of his: Pulaski and Sachs running the unit together. Lincoln Rhyme's legacy.

He thanked the CS technicians as they left with respectful nods and expressions that suggested they were memorizing what the lab looked like. Not many people made it over here from headquarters to see Rhyme in person. He occupied a special place in the hierarchy of the NYPD; there'd been a recent turnover and the head of forensics had gone to Miami-Dade County. Several senior detectives were now running the operation until a permanent head could be appointed. There was even some talk of hiring Rhyme back to run Crime Scene once more.

When the deputy commissioner had called about this, Rhyme had pointed out that he might have a few problems with the JST — the NYPD job standard test portion of the requirements. The physical fitness exam required candidates to complete a timed obstacle course: sprint to a six-foot-high barrier and jump over it, restrain a fake bad guy, race up stairs, drag a 176-pound mannequin to safety and pull the trigger of a weapon sixteen times with one's dominant hand, fifteen with the other.

Rhyme demurred, explaining to the NYPD official who came to see him that he could never pass the test. He could probably clear only a five-foot barrier. But he was flattered by the interest.

Sachs returned downstairs, wearing jeans and a light blue sweater, tucked in, her hair washed and lightly damp, pulled back into a ponytail once more, bound with a black rubber band.

At that moment Thom went to answer the doorbell and another figure stepped into the doorway.

The slim man, whose retiring demeanor suggested he was a middle-aged accountant or shoe salesman, was Mel Cooper, in Rhyme's opinion one of the best forensic lab people in the country. With degrees in math, physics and organic chemistry, and a senior official in both the International Association for Identification and International Association of Blood Pattern Analysis, he was constantly in demand at Crime Scene headquarters. But, since Rhyme was responsible for kidnapping the tech from a job in upstate New York years ago and getting him to the NYPD, it was understood that Cooper would drop what he was doing and head to Manhattan if Rhyme and Sellitto were running a case and they wanted him.

'Mel, glad you were available.'

'Hm. "Available." Didn't you call my lieutenant and threaten him with all sorts of terrible things if he didn't release me from the Hanover-Sterns case?'

'I did it for you, Mel. You were being wasted on insider trading.'

'And I thank you for the reprieve.'

Cooper nodded a greeting to those in the room, knuckled his Harry Potter glasses up on his nose and walked across the lab to the examination table on silent, brown Hush Puppies. Though by appearances the least athletic man Rhyme had ever seen, apart from himself, of course, Mel Cooper nonetheless moved with the grace of a soccer player, and Rhyme was reminded that he was a champion ballroom dancer.

'Let's hear the details,' Rhyme said, turning to Sachs.

She flipped through her notes and explained what the power company field executive had told her.

97

'Algonquin Consolidated Power provides electricity — they call it 'juice' — for most of the area. Pennsylvania, New York, Connecticut, New Jersey.'

'That's the smokestacks on the East River?'

'That's right,' she said to Cooper. 'Their headquarters is there and they have a steam and electricity generation plant. Now, what the Algonquin supervisor said was that the UNSUB could've broken into the substation at any time in the last thirty-six hours to rig the wire. The substations are generally unmanned. A little after eleven this morning he, or they, got into the Algonquin computers, kept shutting down substations around the area and rerouted all that electricity through the substation on Fifty-seven. When voltage builds up to a certain point, it has to complete a circuit. You can't stop it. It either jumps to another wire or to something that's grounded. Normally the circuit breakers in the substation would pop but the perp had reset them to take ten times the load, so it was sitting in that — ' she pointed to the cable, ' — waiting to burst. Like a dam. The pressure built up and the juice had to go someplace.

'Here's how the grid works in New York. One of the workers drew this for me, and it was helpful.' Sachs pulled out a piece of paper on which was a diagram. She stepped to a whiteboard and, with a dark blue marker, transferred the writing.

Power Generation Plant or Incoming Supply (345,000v)

↓ *(through high tension cables)*

Transmission Substation (steps 345,000v down to 138,000v)

↓ *(through area transmission lines)*

Area Substation (steps 138,000v down to 13,800v)

↓ *(through distribution feeder lines)*

1. *Spot Networks in major commercial buildings (steps 13,800v down to 120/208v), or*
2. *Street-level transformers (steps 13,800v down to 120/208v)*

↓ *(through incoming service lines)*

Households and offices (120/208v)

Sachs continued, 'Now, MH-Ten, the substation on Fifty-seven, is an area substation. The line coming in was high voltage. He could've rigged the cable anywhere on an area transmission line but that's real tricky, I guess, because the voltage is so high. So he was working on the *output* side of the area substation, where the voltage is only thirteen thousand eight hundred.'

'Phew,' Sellitto muttered. ''Only.''

'Then when it was rigged he set the circuit breakers higher and flooded the station with incoming juice.'

'And it blew,' Rhyme said.

She picked up an evidence bag containing teardrop-shaped bits of metal. 'And then it blew,' she repeated. 'These were all over the place. Like shrapnel.'

'What are they?' Sellitto asked.

'Molten droplets from the bus sign pole. Blew them everywhere. Nicked the concrete and went right through the sides of some cars. The vic was burned but that's not what killed him.' Her voice grew soft, Rhyme noticed. 'It was like a big shotgun blast. Cauterized the wounds.'

She grimaced. 'That kept him conscious for a while. Take a look.' A nod at Pulaski.

The officer plugged the flash cards into a nearby computer and created files for the case. A moment later these photos popped up on the high-def monitors nearby. After years and years in the crime scene business, Rhyme was largely inured to even the most horrific images; these, though, troubled him. The young victim's body had been riddled by the dots of metal. There was little blood, thanks to the searing heat of the projectiles. Had the perp known that's what his weapon would do, sealing the punctures? Keeping his victims conscious to feel the pain? Was this part of his MO? Rhyme could understand now why Sachs was so troubled.

'Christ,' the big detective muttered.

Rhyme shook aside the image and asked, 'Who was he?'

'Name was Luis Martin. Assistant manager in a music store. Twenty-eight. No record.'

'No connection to Algonquin, MTA . . . any reason anybody'd want him dead?'

'None,' Sachs said.

'Wrong time, wrong place,' Sellitto summarized.

Rhyme said, 'Ron. The coffee shop? What'd you find?'

'A man in dark blue overalls came into the place about ten forty-five. He had a laptop with him. He went online.'

'Blue overalls?' Sellitto asked. 'Any logo? ID?'

'Nobody saw. But the Algonquin workers there, their uniforms were the same dark blue.'

'Get a description?' the rumpled cop persisted.

'Probably white, probably forties, glasses, dark cap. Couple people said no glasses, and no cap. Blond hair, red hair, dark hair.'

'Witnesses,' Rhyme muttered disparagingly. You could have a shooter naked to the waist kill somebody in front of ten witnesses and each one would describe him as wearing ten different colored T-shirts. In the past few years his doubt about the value of eyewitnesses had tempered somewhat — because of Sachs's skill in interviewing and because of Kathryn Dance, who'd proved that analyzing body language was scientific enough in most cases to produce repeatable results. Still, he could never completely shake his skepticism.

'And what happened to this guy in the overalls?' Rhyme asked.

'Nobody's really sure. It was pretty chaotic. All they knew was that they heard this huge bang, the whole street went white with the flash and then everybody ran outside. Nobody could remember seeing him after that.'

'He took his coffee with him?' Rhyme asked. He loved beverage containers. They were like ID cards, with the DNA and fingerprint information they contained, along with trace that adhered because of the sticky nature of milk, sugar and other additives.

'Afraid he did,' Pulaski confirmed.

'Shit. What'd you find at the table?'

'This.' Pulaski pulled a plastic envelope out of a milk crate.

'It's empty.' Sellitto squinted and teased his imposing belly, maybe scratching an itch, maybe absently dismayed that his latest fad diet wasn't working.

But Rhyme looked at the plastic bag and smiled. 'Good job, Rookie.'

'Good job?' the lieutenant muttered. 'There's nothing there.'

'My favorite sort of evidence, Lon. The bits that're invisible. We'll get to that in a minute. I'm wondering about hackers,' Rhyme mused. 'Pulaski, what about wireless at the coffee shop? I was thinking about it and I'm betting they didn't have it.'

'You're right. How'd you know?'

'He couldn't take the chance that it'd be down. He's probably logging in through some cell phone connection. But we need to find out how he got into the Algonquin system. Lon, get

Computer Crimes on board. They need to contact somebody in Internet security at Algonquin. See if Rodney's available.'

The NYPD Computer Crimes Unit was an elite group of about thirty detectives and support staff. Rhyme worked with one of them occasionally, Detective Rodney Szarnek. Rhyme thought of him as a young man, but in fact he had no idea of his age since he had the boyish attitude, sloppy dress and tousled hair of a hacker — an image and avocation that tend to take years off people.

Sellitto placed the call and after a brief conversation hung up, reporting that Szarnek would call Algonquin's IT team immediately to see about hacking into the grid servers.

Cooper was looking reverently at the wire. 'So that's it?' Then lifting another of the bags that contained misshapen metal disks, the shrapnel, he added, 'Lucky nobody was walking by. If this'd happened on Fifth Avenue, there could be two dozen people dead.'

Ignoring the tech's unnecessary observation, Rhyme focused on Sachs. He saw that her eyes had gone still as she looked at the tiny disks.

In a voice perhaps harsher than necessary, to shake her attention away from the shrapnel, he called, 'Come on, people. Let's get to work.'

12

Easing into the booth, Fred Dellray found himself looking at a pale skinny man who could have been a wasted thirty or a preserved fifty.

The guy was wearing a sports jacket that was too big, its source either a very low-end thrift shop or a coat rack when nobody was looking.

'Jeep.'

'Uhm, that's not my name anymore.'

'Not your name? Like nacho cheese. Then whose cheese is it?'

'I don't get — '

'Whatcha name now?' Dellray asked, frowning deeply, playing a particular role, one he generally slipped into with people like this. Jeep, or Not Jeep, had been a sadistic junkie the FBI agent had collared in an undercover set that required Dellray to laugh his way through the man's graphic depiction of torturing a college kid who'd reneged on a drug payment. Then came the bust and, after some negotiation and time served, the man became one of Dellray's pets.

Which meant a tight leash that had to be jerked occasionally.

'It was Jeep. But I decided to change it. I'm Jim now, Fred.'

Changes. The magic word of the day.

'Oh, oh, speakin' of names: Fred . . . Fred? I'm your buddy, I'm your best friend? I didn't remember those introductions, signing your dance card, meetin' the parents.'

'Sorry, sir.'

'Tell ya what: Stick with 'Fred.' Don't believe you when you say 'sir.''

The man was a disgusting morsel of humanity but Dellray had learned you had to walk a fine line. Never contempt, yet never hesitate to dig in a knuckle or two, the pressure of fear.

Fear breeds respect. Just the way of the world.

'Now here's what we're doing. This's important. You got a date coming up, I'm recalling.'

A hearing, about leaving the jurisdiction. Dellray didn't care about losing him. Jeep's usefulness was pretty much gone. That was the nature of CIs; they have a shelf-life of fresh yogurt. Jeep-Jim was going to appeal to the New York State parole board about permission to move to Georgia. Of all places.

'If you'd put in a word, Fred, sir, that'd be great.' And he turned big soupy eyes the agent's way.

Wall Street should take a lesson from the confidential informant world. No derivatives, no default swaps, no insurance, no cooking the books. It was simple. You gave your snitch something of X value, and he gave you something equally important.

If he didn't produce, he was out. If you didn't pay, you got shit.

And all so very transparent.

'Okay,' Dellray said. 'Whatchu want's on the table. Now 'bout what I want. And what I have to say up front is it's time sensitive. You know what that means, Jim?'

'Somebody's gonna get fucked and pretty soon.'

'Rightie-ro. Now, listen close. I need to find Brent.'

A pause. 'William Brent? Why would I know where to find him?' Jeep-Jim, Slim-Jim, asked this with too much rise in his voice, telling Dellray that the snitch had at least *some* idea where to find the man.

Dellray sang, 'Georgia's on my mind.'

A full sixty seconds passed while Jeep did some negotiating with himself.

'I mean, maybe I could . . . the thing is, there's a possibility . . . '

'You gonna finish those sentences or can I eat 'em?'

'Lemme check something.'

Jeep-James-Jim rose and walked into the corner of the place and began texting, leaving Dellray amused at the paranoia about overhearing a text message. Jeepy boy would probably do well in Georgia.

Dellray sipped water the waiter had brought. He hoped the skinny guy's mission would be successful. One of the agent's biggest successes was running William Brent, a middle-aged white guy, unathletic and looking like a Wal-Mart checker. He'd been key in bringing down a very nasty conspiracy. A domestic terrorist group — racists and separatists — had a plan to blow up a number of synagogues on a Friday evening and blame Islamic fundamentalists for it. They had money but not the means, so they turned to a local organized crime family, who also had no love of either Jews or Muslims. Brent had been hired by the family to help and he'd fallen for Dellray's twitchy character — an arms dealer from Haiti selling rocket-propelled grenades.

Brent got collared and Dellray turned him. Surprising everyone, he took to confidential informing as if he'd studied all his life for the job. Brent infiltrated high up in both the racist group and the family and brought down the conspiracy. His debt to society paid, Brent nonetheless went on to work with Dellray in various personas — a mean-ass hired killer, a jewelry and bank heist mastermind, a radical anti-abortion activist. He proved to be one of the sharpest CIs the agent had ever run. And a chameleon in his own right. He was the flip side of Fred Dellray (some years ago it was even suspected, but never proven, that Brent had run a network of his own snitches — inside the NYPD itself).

Dellray ran him for a year until he got overexposed and Brent retired into the comfy quilt of witness protection. But word was that in one of his new personas he remained well connected, a player on the street.

Since none of Dellray's usual sources had come up with anything about Justice For or Rahman or the grid attack, the agent thought of William Brent.

Jimmy-Jeep returned and sat down on the squeaking bench. 'I think I can make it happen. But what's this about, man? I mean, I don't want him to clip me.'

Which was, Dellray reflected, one fairly

significant difference between Wall Street and the CI business.

He said, 'No, no, Jimmy boy, you're not hearing me. I'm not asking you t'turn inta a little fly on the wall. I'm asking you to play matchmaker is all. You get me a sit-down and you'll be eating peaches down in Georgia in no time.'

Dellray slid forward a card that contained only a phone number. 'This's what he should call. Go make it happen.'

'Now?'

'Now.'

Jeep nodded toward the kitchen. 'But my lunch. I didn't eat yet.'

'What kinda place is this?' Dellray barked suddenly, looking around, horrified.

'What do you mean, Fred?'

'You can't get food to go?'

13

Five hours had passed since the attack and the tension was climbing in Rhyme's townhouse. None of the leads was panning out.

'The wire,' he snapped urgently. 'Where'd it come from?'

Cooper shoved his thick glasses up on his nose again. He pulled on latex examining gloves but before touching the evidence he cleaned his hands with a pet hair roller and discarded the tape. Rhyme had been instructing his team to do this ever since he'd analyzed a case for the New Jersey State Police and found that some fiber evidence had come not from the suspect in custody but from the inside pocket of a detective's jacket. The investigator had stuffed a wad of loose rubber gloves there, after seeing some cop on a popular crime scene TV show do the same. The odds of contamination were slim but a forensic detective's job was only partly to find and analyze the evidence; they had to make sure it remained pristine enough to convict the bad guys in a courtroom filled with sharp defense lawyers.

After the infamous New Jersey fiber case, he insisted his people roll gloves after donning them if they hadn't been in contamination-free bags or boxes.

Using surgical scissors, Cooper cut the plastic wrapper off and exposed the wire. It was about fifteen feet long and most of it was covered with black insulation. The wire itself wasn't solid but comprised many silver-colored strands. At one end was bolted the thick, scorched brass plate. Attached to the other end were two large copper bolts with holes in the middle.

'They're called split bolts, the Algonquin guy told me,' Sachs said. 'Used for splicing wires. That's what he used to hook the cable to the main line.'

She then explained how he'd hung the plate — it was called a 'bus bar,' the worker had also explained — out the window. It was attached to the cable with two quarter-inch bolts. The arc had flashed from the plate into the nearest ground source, the pole.

Rhyme glanced at Sachs's thumb, ragged and dark with a bit of dried blood. She tended to chew her nails and worry her digits and scalp. Tension built up in her — like the voltage in the Algonquin substation. She dug into her thumb again and then — as if forcing herself to stop — pulled on latex gloves of her own.

Lon Sellitto was on the phone with the officers canvassing for witnesses up and down Fifty-seventh Street. Rhyme gave him a fast questioning glance but the detective's grimace — deeper than the one that usually graced his features — explained that the efforts so far were unfruitful. Rhyme turned his attention back to the wire.

'Move the camera over it, Mel,' Rhyme said. 'Slowly.'

Using a handheld video unit, the tech scanned

the wire from top to bottom, turned it over and went back the other way. What the camera saw was broadcast in high definition on the large screen in front of Rhyme. He stared intently.

He muttered, 'Bennington Electrical Manufacturing, South Chicago, Illinois. Model AM-MV-Sixty. Zero gauge, rated up to sixty thousand volts.'

Pulaski gave a laugh. 'You know that, Lincoln? Where'd you learn about wires?'

'It's printed on the side, Rookie.'

'Oh. I didn't notice.'

'Obviously. And our perp cut it to this length, Mel. What do you think? Not machine cut.'

'I'd agree.' Using a magnifying glass, Cooper was examining the end of the metal cable that had been bolted to the substation wire. He then focused the video on the cut ends. 'Amelia?'

Their resident mechanic looked it over. 'Hand hacksaw,' she offered.

The split bolts were unique to the power industry, it turned out, but they could have come from dozens of sources.

The bolts affixing the wire to the bus bar were similarly generic.

'Let's get our charts going,' Rhyme then said.

Pulaski wheeled several whiteboards forward from the corner of the lab. On the top of one Sachs wrote, *Crime Scene: Algonquin Substation Manhattan-10, West 57th Street.* On the other was *UNSUB Profile.* She filled in what they'd discovered so far.

'Did he get the wire at the substation?' Rhyme asked.

'No. There wasn't any stored there,' the young man said.

'Then find out where he *did* get it. Call Bennington.'

'Right.'

'Okay,' Rhyme continued. 'We've got metalwork and hardware. That means tool marks. The hacksaw. Let's look at the wire closely.'

Cooper switched to a large-object microscope, also plugged into the computer, and examined where the wire had been cut; he used low magnification. 'It's a new saw blade, sharp.'

Rhyme gave an envious glance toward the tech's deft hands, moving the focus and the geared stage of the 'scope. Then he returned to the screen. 'New, yes, but there's a broken tooth.'

'Near the handle.'

'Right.' Before people began to saw, they generally rested the blade on what they were about to cut, three or four times. Doing this, especially in soft aluminum like the wire, could reveal broken or bent saw teeth, or other unique patterns that could link tools found in the perp's possession to the one used in a crime.

'Now, the split bolts?'

Cooper found distinctive scratch marks on all the bolts, suggesting that the perp's wrench had probably left them.

'Love soft brass,' Rhyme muttered. 'Just love it. So he's got well-used tools. More and more, looking like he's an insider.'

Sellitto disconnected his call. 'Nothing. Maybe *somebody* saw *somebody* in a blue jumpsuit. But it might've been an hour after it happened. When

112

the whole friggin' block was crawling with Algonquin repair crews wearing friggin' blue jumpsuits.'

'What've you found out, Rookie?' Rhyme barked. 'I want sources for the wire.'

'I'm on hold.'

'Tell 'em you're a cop.'

'I did.'

'Tell 'em you're the chief cop. The big cheese.'

'I — '

But Rhyme's attention was already on something else: the iron bars forming the grate that barred entrance to the access tunnel.

'How'd he cut through them, Mel?'

A careful look revealed he hadn't used a hacksaw but a bolt cutter.

Cooper examined the ends of the bars through a microscope fitted with a digital camera and took pictures. He then transferred the shots to the central computer and assembled them onto one screen.

'Any distinctive marks?' Rhyme asked. As with the broken hacksaw tooth and scratches on the bolts and nuts, any unusual marking on the cutter would link its owner to the crime scene. 'How's that one?' Cooper asked, pointing at the screen.

There was a tiny crescent of scratch in roughly the same position on the cut surfaces of several of the bars. 'That'll do. Good.'

Then Pulaski cocked his head and readied his pen as somebody at Bennington Wire picked up the phone to speak to the young cop in his new capacity as the emperor of the New York City

Police Department.

After a brief conversation he hung up.

'What the hell's with the cable, Pulaski?'

'First of all, that model cable's real common. They — '

'*How* common?'

'They sell millions of feet of it every year. It's mostly for medium-voltage distribution.'

'Sixty thousand volts is medium?'

'I guess so. You can buy it from any electrical supply wholesaler. But he did say that Algonquin buys it in bulk.'

Sellitto asked, 'Who there would order it?'

'Technical Supplies Department.'

'I'll give 'em a call,' Sellitto said. He did so and had a brief conversation. He disconnected. 'They're going to check to see if anything's missing from inventory.'

Rhyme was gazing at the grating. 'So he climbed through the manhole earlier and into the Algonquin work space under the alley.'

Sachs said, 'He might've been down the steam pipe manhole to do some work and seen the grating that led to the tunnel.'

'Definitely suggests it's an employee.' Rhyme hoped this was the case. Inside jobs made cops' work a lot easier. 'Let's keep going. The boots.'

She said, 'Similar boot prints in both the access tunnel and near where the wire was rigged inside the substation.'

'And any prints from the coffee shop?'

'That one,' Pulaski responded, as he pointed to an electrostatic print. 'Under the table. Looks like the same brand to me.'

114

Mel Cooper examined it and concurred. The young officer continued, 'And Amelia had me check the boots of the Algonquin workers who were there. They were all different.'

Rhyme turned his attention to the boot. 'What's the brand, do you think, Mel?'

Cooper was browsing through the NYPD's footwear database, which contained samples of thousands of shoes and boots, the vast majority of which were men's shoes. Most serious felonies involving physical presence at the scene were committed by men.

Rhyme had been instrumental in creating the expanded shoe and boot database years ago. He worked out voluntary arrangements with all the major manufacturers to have scans of their lines sent into the NYPD regularly.

After returning to forensic work, following his accident, Rhyme had stayed involved in maintaining the department's product and materials databases, including this one. After working on a recent case involving data mining he'd come up with an idea that was now used in many police departments around the country: He'd recruited (well, bullied) the NYPD into hiring a programmer to create computer graphics images that depicted the sole of each shoe in the database in different stages of wear — new, after six months, one year and two years. And then to show images of the soles of shoes worn by people who had splayed feet or were pigeon-toed. He'd also gotten the computer guru to indicate wear patterns as a function of height and weight.

The project was expensive but took surprisingly little time to get online and resulted in nearly instantaneous answers to the questions of the brand and age of shoe, and the height, weight and stride characteristics of the wearer.

The database had already helped in the identification of three or four perps.

His fingers flying over the keys, Cooper said, 'Got a match. Albertson-Fenwick Boots and Gloves, Inc. Model E-20.' He perused the screen. 'Not surprising, they've got special insulation. They're for workers who have regular contact with live electrical sources. They meet ASTM Electrical Hazard Standard F2413-05. These're size eleven.'

Rhyme squinted as he looked them over. 'Deep treads. Good.' This meant they would retain significant quantities of trace material.

Cooper continued, 'They're fairly new so there're no distinctive wear marks that tell us much about his height, weight or other characteristic.'

'I'd say he walks straight, though. Agree?' Rhyme was looking at the prints on his screen, broadcast from a camera over the examining table.

'Yes.'

Sachs wrote this on the board.

'Good, Sachs. Now, Rookie, what's the invisible evidence you found?' Gazing at the plastic envelope labeled *Coffee Shop Opposite Blast* — Table Where Suspect Was Sitting.

Cooper was examining it. 'Blond hair. One inch long. Natural, not died.'

Rhyme loved hair as a forensic tool. It could often be used for DNA sampling — if the bulb was attached — and it could reveal a lot about the suspect's appearance, through color and texture and shape. Age and sex could also be reckoned with more or less accuracy. Hair testing was becoming more and more popular as a forensic and an employment tool since hair retained traces of drugs longer than urine or blood. An inch of hair held a two-month history of drug use. In England hair was frequently used to test for alcohol abuse.

'We're not sure it's his,' Sellitto pointed out.

'Of course not,' Rhyme muttered. 'We're not sure of anything at this point.'

But Pulaski said, 'It's pretty likely, though. I talked to the owner. He makes sure the bus boys wipe the table down after every customer. I checked. And nobody'd wiped it after the perp was there, because of the explosion.'

'Good, Rookie.'

Cooper continued, speaking of the hair, 'No natural or artificial curves. It's straight. No evidence of depigmentation, so I'd put him under fifty years old.'

'I want a tox-chem analysis. ASAP.'

'I'll send it to the lab.'

'A *commercial* lab,' Rhyme ordered. 'Wave a lot of money at them for fast results.'

Sellitto grumbled, 'We don't *have* a lot of money, and we've got our own perfectly good lab in Queens.'

'It's not perfectly good if they don't get me the results before our perp kills somebody else, Lon.'

'How's Uptown Testing?' Cooper asked.

'Good. Remember, wave money.'

'Jesus, the city doesn't revolve around *you*, Linc.'

'It doesn't?' Rhyme asked, with surprise in his eyes that was both feigned and genuine.

14

With the SEM-EDS — the scanning electron microscope and energy dispersive X-ray spectroscope, Mel Cooper analyzed the trace evidence Sachs had collected where the UNSUB had rigged the wire. 'I've got some kind of mineral, different from the substrata around the substation.'

'What's it made up of?'

'It's about seventy percent feldspar, then quartz, magnetite, mica, calcite and amphiboles. Some anhydrite too. Curious, large percentages of silicon.'

Rhyme knew the geology of the New York area well. When mobile, he'd strolled around the city, scooping up samples of dirt and rock and creating databases that could help him match perp and locale. But this combination of minerals was a mystery to him. It certainly wasn't from around here. 'We need a geologist.' Rhyme thought for a moment and made a call with speed dial.

'Hello?' a man's pleasant, soft voice answered.

'Arthur,' Rhyme said to his cousin, who lived not far away, in New Jersey.

'Hey. How are you?'

Rhyme reflected that it seemed *everybody* was asking about his health today, though Arthur was just making conversation.

'Good.'

'It was nice seeing you and Amelia last week.'

Rhyme had recently reconnected with Arthur Rhyme, who'd been like a brother to him and with whom he'd grown up outside Chicago. Though the criminalist was hardly one for weekends in the country, he'd astonished Sachs by suggesting that the two of them take up an invitation to visit Art Rhyme and his wife, Judy, at their small vacation house on the shore. Arthur revealed that he'd actually built a wheelchair ramp to make it accessible. They'd gone out to the place, along with Thom and Pammy and her dog, Jackson, for a couple of days.

Rhyme had enjoyed himself. While the women and canine hiked the beach, he and Arthur had talked science and academia and world events, their opinions growing inarticulate in direct proportion to the consumption of single malt scotch; Arthur, like Rhyme, had a pretty good collection.

'You're on speaker here, Art, with . . . well, a bunch of cops.'

'I've been watching the news. You're running this electricity incident, I'll bet. Terrible. The press is saying it's probably an accident but . . . ' He gave a skeptical laugh.

'No, not accidental at all. We don't know whether it's a disgruntled employee or a terrorist.'

'Anything I can do to help?'

Arthur was a scientist too and somewhat more broad-based than Rhyme.

'Actually, yes. I've got a fast question for you.

120

Well, I hope it's fast. We found some trace at the crime scene and it doesn't match any substrata nearby. In fact, it doesn't match any geologic formation in the New York area I'm familiar with.'

'I've got a pen. Give me what you found.'

Rhyme recited the results of their tests.

Arthur was silent. Rhyme pictured his cousin lost in thought as he gazed at the list he'd jotted, his mind running through possibilities. Finally he asked, 'How big are the particles?'

'Mel?'

'Hi, Art, it's Mel Cooper.'

'Hi, Mel. Been dancing lately?'

'We won the Long Island tango competition last week. We're going to regionals on Sunday. Unless I'm stuck here, of course.'

'Mel?' Rhyme urged.

'Particles? Yes, very small. About point two five millimeters.'

'Okay, I'm pretty sure it's tephra.'

'What?' Rhyme asked.

Arthur spelled it. 'Volcanic matter. The word's Greek for 'ash.' In the air, after it's blown out of the volcano, it's pyroclast — broken rock — but on the ground it's called tephra.'

'Indigenous?' Rhyme asked

In an amused voice, Arthur said, 'It's indigenous *somewhere*. But you mean around here? Not anymore. You could find a very minuscule trace amount in the Northeast given a major eruption on the West Coast and strong prevailing winds, but there haven't been any lately. In those proportions I'd say most likely the source was the Pacific Northwest. Maybe Hawaii.'

'So however this got to a crime scene it would have been carried there by the perp or somebody.'

'That'd be my call.'

'Well, thanks. We'll talk to you soon.'

'Oh, and Judy said she's going to email Amelia that recipe she wanted.'

Rhyme hadn't heard that part of the conversation during the weekend out of town. It must've occurred on one of the beach walks.

Sachs called, 'No hurry.'

After they disconnected, Rhyme couldn't help but look at her with a raised eyebrow. 'You're taking up cooking?'

'Pammy's going to teach me.' She shrugged. 'How hard can it be? I figure it's just like rebuilding a carburetor, only with perishable parts.'

Rhyme gazed at the chart. 'Tephra . . . So maybe our perp's been to Seattle or Portland recently or to Hawaii. I doubt that much trace would travel very well, though. I'm betting he was in or near a museum, school, geologic exhibit of some kind. Do they use volcanic ash in any kind of business? Maybe polishing stones. Like Carborundum.'

Cooper said, 'This's too varied and irregular to be milled commercially. Too soft too, I'd think.'

'Hm. How about jewelry? Do they make jewelry out of lava?'

None of them had ever heard of that, though,

and Rhyme concluded that the source had to be an exhibit or display that the perp had attended or that was near where he lived or where a future target was. 'Mel, have somebody in Queens start calling — check out any exhibits, traveling or permanent displays in the area that have anything to do with volcanoes or lava. Manhattan first.' He gazed at the access door, wrapped in plastic. 'Now, let's look at what Amelia went swimming with. Your turn at bat, Rookie. Make us proud.'

15

Cleaning his latex gloves with the pet-hair roller — and drawing an approving look from Rhyme — the young officer hefted the access door and surrounding frame, still connected. The door was about 18 inches square and the frame added another two or so inches. It was painted dark gray.

Sachs was right. It was a tight fit. The UNSUB very likely would have sloughed off something from his body as he entered the substation.

The door opened with four small turn latches on both sides. They would have been awkward to loosen with a gloved hand, so there was a chance he'd used bare fingers, especially since he'd planned on blowing up the door with the battery bomb and destroying evidence.

Fingerprints fall into one of three categories. Visible (the sort left by a bloody thumb on a white wall), impressible (left in pliable material, like plastic explosive), and latent (hidden to the unaided eye). There were dozens of good ways to raise latent prints but one of the best, on metal surfaces, was simply to use store-bought Super Glue, cyanoacrylate. The object would be put in an airtight enclosure with a container of the glue, which would then be heated until it turned gaseous. The vapors would bond with any number of substances left by the finger — amino and lactic acids, glucose, potassium and carbon trioxide — and the resulting reaction created a visible print.

The process could work miracles, raising prints that were completely invisible before.

Except not in this case.

'Nothing,' Pulaski said, discouraged, peering at the access door through a very Sherlock Holmesian magnifier. 'Only glove smudges.'

'Not surprising. He's been fairly careful so far. Well, collect trace from the inside of the frame, where he made contact.'

Pulaski did this, using a soft brush over the newsprint examination sheets and taking swabs. He placed whatever he found — to Rhyme it seemed like very little — into bags and organized them for Cooper to analyze.

Sellitto took a call and then said, 'Hold on. You're being speakered.'

'Hello?' came the voice.

Rhyme glanced at Sellitto. 'Who?' he whispered.

'Szarnek.'

The NYPD Computer Crimes expert.

'What do you have for us, Rodney?'

Rock music clattered around in the background. 'I can almost guarantee that whoever played with the Algonquin servers had the pass codes up front. In fact, I *will* guarantee that. First of all, we found no evidence of any attempted intrusion. No brute force attack. No shredded code of rootkits, suspicious drivers or kernel modules or — '

'Just the bottom line, you don't mind.'

'Okay, what I'm saying is we looked at every

port . . . ' He hesitated at Rhyme's sigh. 'Ah, bottom line. It was and wasn't an inside job.'

'Which means?' Rhyme grumbled.

'The attack was from outside Algonquin's physical building.'

'We know that.'

'But the perp had to get the codes from inside headquarters in Queens. Either him or an accomplice. They're kept in hard copies and on a random code generator that's isolated from networks.'

'So,' the criminalist summarized, just to make sure, 'no outside hackers, domestic or international.'

'Next to impossible. I'm serious, Lincoln. Not a single rootkit — '

'Got it, Rodney. Any trace on his line from the coffee shop?'

'Prepaid cell connecting through a USB port. Went through a proxy in Europe.'

Rhyme was tech enough to know that this meant the answer to his question was no.

'Thanks, Rodney. How do you get any work done with that music?'

The man chuckled. 'Call me anytime.'

The raucous hammering disappeared with the disconnecting click.

Cooper too was on the phone. He hung up and said, 'I've found somebody in Materials Analysis at HQ. She's got a geology background. She knows a lot of the schools that have regular exhibits for the public. She's checking on volcanic ash and lava.'

Pulaski, poring over the door, squinted. 'Got

something here, I think.'

He pointed to a portion of the door near the top latch. 'It looks like he wiped it off.' He grabbed the magnifying glass. 'And there's a burr of metal. Sharp. I think he cut himself and bled.'

'Really?' Rhyme was excited. There's nothing like DNA in forensic work.

Sellitto said, 'But if he cleaned it off, does it still do us any good?'

Before Rhyme could offer anything, Pulaski, still hunched over his find, mused, 'But what would he have to clean it off with? Maybe spit. That's as good as blood.'

This was going to have been Rhyme's conclusion. 'Use the ALS.'

Alternative light sources can reveal bodily fluids like traces of saliva, semen and sweat, all of which contain DNA.

All law enforcement agencies were now taking samples of DNA of suspects in certain types of offenses — sex crimes, for instance — and many were going further than that. If their UNSUB had committed a swabbable offense, he'd be in the Combined DNA Index System database, CODIS.

A moment later Pulaski, wearing goggles, paused the wand over a portion of the access door where he'd spotted the smear. There was a tiny yellowish glow. He called, 'Yessir, got something. Not much.'

'Rookie, you know how many cells are in the human body?'

'Well . . . No, I don't.'

'Over three trillion.'

'That's a lot of — '

'And do you know how many are needed for a successful DNA sample?'

He said, 'According to your book, Lincoln, about a hundred.'

Rhyme lifted an eyebrow. 'Impressive.' Then he added, 'You think you have a hundred cells there in that massive smear?'

'Probably, I would think.'

'You sure do. Sachs, looks like your swimming expedition wasn't in vain. If the battery had blown, it would have destroyed the sample. Okay, Mel, show him how to collect it.'

Pulaski ceded the tricky task to Cooper.

'STR?' Rhyme asked the tech. 'Or is the sample degraded?'

The polymerase chain reaction short tandem repeat method was the standard DNA test in criminal cases. It was fast and the most reliable system, with at least a billion to one accuracy. It could also determine the sex of the person from whom the sample came. But while the sample could be very small it had to be in good shape. If it had been damaged by the water or heat in the substation, a different test — mitochondrial DNA — would have to be used, a technique that took longer.

'I think it'll be fine.' The tech collected the DNA and called the lab for pickup. 'I know — ASAP,' he told Rhyme just as the criminalist had been about to crack the whip.

'And spare no expense.'

'That coming out of your fee, Linc?' Sellitto grumbled.

'I give you my best customer discount, Lon. And a good find, Pulaski.'

'Thanks, I — '

Having delivered enough compliments for the time being, Rhyme moved on, 'What about the trace from the *inside* of the door, Mel? You know, we're not moving very quickly here.'

Cooper took the samples and looked them over on the examining sheet or under the microscope. 'Nothing that doesn't match the samplars and substrata . . . except this.' It was a tiny pink dot.

'GC it,' Rhyme ordered.

A short time later Mel was reading results from the gas chromatograph, the mass spectrometer and several other analyses. 'We've got an acidic pH — about two — and citric acid and sucrose. Then . . . well, I'll put it up on the screen.'

The words appeared: *Quercetin 3-O-rutinoside-7-O-glucoside and chrysoeriol 6,8-di-C-glucoside (stellarin-2).*

'Fine,' Rhyme said impatiently. 'Fruit juice. With that pH, it's probably lemon.'

Pulaski couldn't help but laugh. 'How did you *know* that? I'm sorry, how did you know?'

'You only get out of a task what you bring to it, Rookie. Do your homework! Remember that.' He turned back to Cooper.

'Then vegetable oil of some sort, lots of salt and some compound that eludes me completely.'

'Made up of what?'

'It's protein rich. The amino acids are arginine, histidine, isoleucine, lysine and methionine. Also, plenty of lipids, mostly cholesterol and lecithin, then vitamin A, vitamins B2, B6, B12, niacin, pantothenic acid and folic acid. Large amounts of calcium, magnesium, phosphorus, potassium.'

'Tasty,' Rhyme said.

Cooper was nodding. 'It's food, sure. But what?'

Though his sensations of taste hadn't changed after the accident, food was to Lincoln Rhyme essentially fuel and he didn't get much pleasure out of it, unlike, of course, whisky.

'Thom?' There was no response so he took a deep breath. Before he could call again, the aide stuck his head in the door.

'Everything okay?'

'Why do you keep asking that?'

'What do you want?'

'Lemon juice, vegetable oil and egg.'

'You're hungry?'

'No, no, no. What would those ingredients be found in?'

'Mayonnaise.'

Rhyme lifted an eye to Cooper, who shook his head. 'Lumpy and kind of pinkish.'

The aide reconsidered. 'Then I'd go with taramasalata.'

'What? Is that a restaurant?'

Thom laughed. 'It's a Greek appetizer. A spread.'

'Caviar, right? You eat it with bread.'

Thom replied to Sachs, 'Well, it is fish eggs, but cod, not sturgeon. So it's not technically caviar.'

Rhyme was giving a nod. 'Ah, the elevated

saline. Fish. Sure. Is it common?'

'In Greek restaurants and grocery stores and delis.'

'Is there any place more common than others? A Greek area of the city?'

'Queens,' Pulaski said, who lived in the borough. 'Astoria. Lots of Greek restaurants there.'

'Can I get back now?' Thom asked.

'Yes, yes, yes . . . '

'Thanks,' Sachs called.

The aide waved a gloved hand, Playtex yellow, and disappeared.

Sellitto asked, 'Maybe he's been staking out someplace in Queens for the next attack.'

Rhyme shrugged, one of the few gestures he could still perform. He reflected: The perp would have to prepare the location, that was true. Still, he was leaning in a different direction.

Sachs caught his eye. 'You're thinking, Algonquin's headquarters're in Astoria, right?'

'Exactly. And everything's pointing to it being an inside job.' He asked, 'Who's in charge of the company?'

Ron Pulaski said he'd had a conversation with the workers outside the substation. 'They mentioned the president and CEO. The name's Jessen. Andy Jessen. Everybody seemed a little afraid of him.'

Rhyme kept his eyes on the charts for a moment and then said, 'Sachs, how'd you like to go for a drive in your fancy new wheels?'

'You bet.' She called, and arranged with the CEO's assistant for a meeting in a half hour.

It was then that Sellitto's cell rang. He pulled it out and took a look at caller-ID. 'Algonquin.' He hit a button. 'Detective Sellitto.' Rhyme noticed his face went still as he listened. Then he said, 'You're sure? . . . Okay. Who'd have access? . . . Thanks.' He disconnected. 'Son of a bitch.'

'What?'

'That was the supply division supervisor. He said one of the Algonquin warehouses in Harlem was burglarized last week. Hundred and eighteen Street. They thought it was an employee pilfering. Perp used a key. It wasn't broken into.'

Pulaski asked, 'And whoever it was stole the cable?'

Sellitto nodded. 'And those split bolts.'

But Rhyme could see another message in the detective's round face. 'How much?' he asked, his voice a whisper. 'How much wire did he steal?'

'You got it, Linc. Seventy-five feet of cable and a dozen bolts. What the hell was McDaniel talking about, a one-time thing? That's bullshit. This UNSUB's going to keep right on going.'

CRIME SCENE: ALGONQUIN SUBSTATION MANHATTAN-10, WEST 57TH STREET

- Victim (deceased): Luis Martin, assistant manager in music store.
- No friction ridge prints on any surface.
- Shrapnel from molten metal, as a result of the arc flash.
- o-gauge insulated aluminum strand cable.
  — Bennington Electrical Manufacturing, AM-MV-60, rated up to 60,000v.
  — Cut by hand with hacksaw, new blade, broken tooth.
- Two 'split bolts,' ¼ inch holes in them.
  — Untraceable.
- Distinctive tool marks on bolts.
- Brass 'bus' bar, fixed to cable with two ¼-inch bolts.
  — All untraceable.
- Boot prints.
  — Albertson-Fenwick Model E-20 for electrical work, size

Metal grating cut to allow access to substation, distinctive tool marks from bolt cutter.
- Access door and frame from basement.
  — DNA obtained. Sent out for testing.
  — Greek food, taramasalata.
- Blond hair, 1 inch long, natural, from someone 50 or under, discovered in coffee shop across the street from substation.
  — Sent out for tox-chem screening. Mineral trace: volcanic ash.
  — Not naturally found in New York area.
  — Exhibits, museums, geology schools?
- Algonquin Control Center software accessed by internal codes, not outside hackers.

UNSUB PROFILE

- Male.
- 40's.
- Probably white.
- Possibly glasses and cap.
- Possibly with short, blond hair.
- Dark blue overalls, similar to those worn by Algonquin workers.
- Knows electrical systems very well.
- Boot print suggests no physical condition affecting posture or gait.
- Possibly same person who stole 75 feet of similar Bennington cable and 12 split bolts. More attacks in mind? Access to Algonquin warehouse where theft occurred with key.
- Likely he is Algonquin employee or has contact with one.
- Terrorist connection? Relation to Justice For [unknown]? Terror group? Individual named Rahman involved? Coded references to monetary disbursements, personnel movements and something 'big.'

16

Looming.

That was the word that came to mind as Amelia Sachs climbed out of her Torino Cobra in the parking lot of Algonquin Consolidated Power and Light in Astoria, Queens. The facility covered a number of blocks but it was anchored by a complicated, soaring building made of grim red and gray panels that rose two hundred feet into the air. The massive edifice dwarfed the employees now leaving at the end of the day, walking through dollhouse doorways in the panoramic sheets of the walls.

Pipes evacuated the building in dozens of places and, as she'd expected, there were wires everywhere, only 'wires' didn't quite suit. These were thick and inflexible cables, some insulated, some silver gray bare metal glistening under security lights. They must have carried hundreds of thousands of volts from the guts of the building through a series of metallic and, she supposed, ceramic or other insulated fittings, into even more complicated scaffoldings and supports and towers. They divided and ran in different courses, like bones extending from the arm to the hand to the fingers.

Tilting her head back, she saw high above her the four towers of the smokestacks, also grimy red and sooty gray, blinking with warning lights bright in the hazy dusk. She'd been aware of the stacks for years, of course; no one who'd been to New York even once missed them, the dominant feature of the bland industrial shore of the East River. But she'd never been this close and they now captivated her, piercing the dull sky. She remembered, in winter, seeing exhaust of smoke or steam, but now there was nothing escaping except heat or invisible gas, distorting with ripples the smooth plain of the heavens above.

Sachs heard some voices and looked over the parking lot to see a crowd of maybe fifty protesters standing in a large cluster. Posters were held aloft and there was a little amiable chanting, probably complaining about the big bad wolf of the oil-guzzling power company. They didn't notice that she'd arrived here in a car that used five times as much black gold as one of their Priuses.

Underneath her feet she believed she could feel a rumbling like massive nineteenth-century engines groaning away. She heard a low hum.

She closed the car door and approached the main entrance. Two guards were watching her. They were clearly curious about the tall redhead, curious about her arrival in an old ruddy muscle car, but they also seemed amused at her reaction to the building. Their faces said, Yeah, it's really something, isn't it? After all these years here you never get over it.

Then, with her ID and shield flashed, their expressions became alert and — apparently expecting a cop, though not in this package — they ushered her immediately through the halls of what was the executive headquarters portion of Algonquin Consolidated.

Unlike the slick office building in Midtown of a massive data mining company involved in a case she'd recently worked, Algonquin seemed like a museum diorama of life in the 1950s: blond wood furniture, framed gaudy photographs of the facility and transmission towers, brown carpet. The clothing of the employees — nearly all of them men — was ultra conservative: white shirts and dark suits. The hair was trimmed short, nearly military style.

They continued down the boring halls, decorated with pictures of magazines that featured articles about Algonquin. *Power Age. Electricity Transmission Monthly. The Grid.*

The time was nearly six-thirty and yet there were dozens of employees here, ties loosened, sleeves rolled up, faces troubled.

At the end of the corridor the guard delivered her to the office of A. R. Jessen. Although the drive here had been eventful — involving speeds of close to 70 on one stretch of highway — Sachs had managed to do a bit of research. Jessen was not an Andy but an *Andi*, for Andrea. Sachs always made it a point to do homework like this, learn what she could about the principals. It was important in maintaining control of interviews and interrogations. Ron had assumed that the CEO was a man. She imagined how her credibility would have fallen had she arrived and asked for *Mr.* Jessen.

Inside, Sachs paused just inside the doorway of the ante-office. A secretary, or personal assistant, in a tight black tank top and wearing

137

bold high heels, rose on precarious toes to dig into a filing cabinet. The short blonde, in her early forties or late thirties, Sachs reckoned, was frowning, frustrated at being unable to find something her boss wanted.

In the doorway to the main office stood an imposing woman with salt and pepper hair and wearing a severe brown suit and high neck blouse. She too frowned as she watched the file cabinet excavation and crossed her arms.

'I'm Detective Sachs, I called earlier,' she said when the dour woman turned her way.

It was then that the younger woman plucked a folder from the cabinet and handed it to the older, then said, 'I found it, Rachel. My mistake, I filed it when you were at lunch. If you could make five copies, I'd appreciate it.'

'Yes, Ms. Jessen,' she said. And stepped to a copier.

The CEO strode forward on the dangerous heels, looked up into Sachs's eyes and shook her hand firmly. 'Come on inside, Detective,' she said. 'Looks like we have a lot to talk about.'

Sachs glanced over at the brown-suited personal assistant and followed the real Andi Jessen into her office.

So much for homework, she reflected ruefully.

17

Andrea Jessen seemed to catch on to the near faux pas. 'I'm the second youngest and the *only* woman head of a major power company in the country. Even with me having the final say on hiring, Algonquin has a tenth the women as in most other big companies in the US. It's the nature of the industry.'

Sachs was about to ask why Jessen had gone into the field when the CEO said, anticipating her, 'My father was in the business.'

The detective nearly told her that she was a cop exclusively because of her own father, a 'portable,' or foot patrolman, with the NYPD for many years. But she refrained.

Jessen's face was angular, with the slightest dusting of makeup. Wrinkles were present but subdued, radiating timidly from the corners of her green eyes and bland lips. Otherwise the skin was smooth. This was not a woman who got outside much.

She in turn examined Sachs closely, then nodded toward her large coffee table, surrounded by office chairs. The detective sat while Jessen grabbed the phone. 'Excuse me for a moment.' Her manicured but unpolished nails clacked against the number pad.

She called three different people — all about the attack. One, to a lawyer, the detective could tell, one to the public relations department or an outside PR firm. She spent most of the time on the third call, apparently making sure extra security personnel were on site at all the company's substations and other facilities. Jotting tiny notes with a gold-plated pencil, Jessen spoke in clipped tones, using staccato words with not a single filler like 'I mean,' or 'you know.' As Jessen rattled off instructions, Sachs took in the office, noting on the broad teak desk a picture of a teenage Andi Jessen and her family. She deduced from the series of photos of the children that Jessen had one brother, a few years younger. They resembled each other, though he was brown-haired and she blonde. Recent pictures showed him to be a handsome, fit man in an army uniform. There were other pictures of him on travels, occasionally with his arm around a pretty woman, different in every shot.

There were no pictures of Jessen with any romantic partners.

The walls were covered with bookcases and pictures of old-time prints and maps that might have come out of a museum display about the history of power. One map was labeled *The First Grid*, and showed a portion of lower Manhattan around Pearl Street. She saw in legible script *Thomas A. Edison*, and she guessed that was the inventor's actual signature.

Jessen hung up and sat forward, elbows on her desk, her eyes bleary but jaw and narrow lips firm. 'It's been over seven hours since the . . . incident. I was hoping you'd have somebody in custody. I guess if you'd caught them,' she muttered, 'I would've had a phone call. Not a visit in person.'

'No, I'm here to ask you some questions about things that have come up in the investigation.'

Again a careful appraisal. 'I've been talking with the mayor and the governor and the head of the FBI's New York office. Oh, Homeland Security too. I was expecting to see one of them, not a police officer.'

This wasn't a put-down, not intentionally, and Sachs took no offense. 'NYPD is running the crime scene portion of the case. My questions have to do with that.'

'That explains it.' Her face softened slightly. 'Woman to woman, I get a bit defensive. I was thinking the big boys weren't taking me seriously.' A faintly conspiratorial smile. 'It happens. More than you'd think.'

'I understand that.'

'I imagine you do. A detective, hm?'

'That's right.' Then Sachs, feeling the urgency of the case, asked, 'We get to those questions?'

'Of course.'

The phone kept ringing, but according to Jessen's instructions to her PA, who'd returned to the ante-office a moment ago, the unit chirped only once and fell silent as the woman fielded the calls.

'First of all, just a preliminary matter. Have you changed the access codes to the grid software?'

A frown. 'Of course. That's the first thing we did. Didn't the mayor or Homeland security tell you?'

No, they hadn't, Sachs reflected.

Jessen continued, 'And we've put in an extra set of firewalls. The hackers can't get in any longer.'

'It's probably not hackers.'

Jessen cocked her head. 'But this morning Tucker McDaniel was saying that it was probably terrorists. The FBI agent?'

'We have more recent information.'

'How else could it have happened? Somebody from the outside was rerouting the supply and altering the circuit breakers at MH-Ten — the substation on Fifty-Seventh Street.'

'But we're pretty sure he got the codes from the inside.'

'That's impossible. It has to be terrorists.'

'That's definitely a possibility and I want to ask you about that. But even if so they were using an insider. An officer in our Computer Crimes division had a conversation with your IT people. He said there was no evidence of independent hacking.'

Jessen fell silent and examined her desk. She didn't seem happy — because of this news about the insider? Or because somebody in her company was talking to the police without her knowing? She jotted a note and Sachs wondered if it was to remind her to reprimand the technology security man.

Sachs continued, 'The suspect was seen in an Algonquin uniform. Or at least blue coveralls that were very similar to what your employees wear.'

'Suspect?'

'A man was spotted in a coffee shop around the time of the attack, across from the substation. He was seen with a laptop.'

'Did you get any details about him?'

'White male, forties probably. Nothing else.'

'Well, about the uniform, you could buy one or make one.'

'Yes. But there's more. The cable he used to rig the arc flash? It was Bennington brand. That's what your company regularly uses.'

'Yes, I know. Most power companies do too.'

'Last week, seventy-five feet of Bennington cable, the same gauge was stolen from one of your warehouses in Harlem, along with a dozen split bolts. They're used for splicing — '

'I know what they're used for.' The wrinkles in Jessen's face grew severe.

'Whoever broke into the warehouse, he used a key to get in. He also got into the access tunnel under the substation through an Algonquin steam pipe manhole.'

Jessen said quickly, 'Meaning he *didn't* use the electronic keypad to get into the substation?'

'No.'

'So, there's some evidence that it's *not* an employee.'

'It's a possibility, like I said. But there's something else.' Sachs added that they'd found traces of Greek food, suggesting a nearby connection.

Seemingly bewildered at the extent of their knowledge, the CEO repeated, exasperated, '*Taramasalata?*'

'There are five Greek restaurants within

walking distance of your headquarters here. And twenty-eight within a ten-minute cab ride. And since the trace was fairly recent, it makes sense that he's a current employee or at least got the codes from a current employee. Maybe they met at a restaurant nearby.'

'Oh, please, there are plenty of Greek restaurants around the city.'

'Let's just assume the computer codes came from inside. Who'd have access to them?' Sachs asked. 'That's really the threshold issue.'

'Very limited and very tightly controlled,' she said fast, as if she were on trial for negligence. The line seemed rehearsed.

'Who?'

'I do. A half dozen senior staff. That's all. But, Detective, these're people who've been with the company for years. They wouldn't possibly do this. Inconceivable.'

'You keep the codes separate from the computers, I understand.'

A blink at this knowledge too. 'Yes. They're set randomly by our senior control center supervisor. And kept in a safe file room next door.'

'I'd like names and to find out if there's been any unauthorized access to that room.'

Jessen was clearly resistant to the idea that the perp was an employee, but she said, 'I'll call our security director. He should have that information.'

'And I'll need the names of any workers in the past few months who were assigned to repair steam lines in that manhole across from the substation. It's in an alleyway about thirty feet north of the station.'

The CEO picked up the phone and asked her PA to summon two employees to her office. The request was polite. While some people in this position would have barked the order, Jessen remained in control and reasonable. Which, to Sachs, made her seem all the harder. It was the weak and insecure who blustered. Happened in the policing business all the time.

Just a moment after she hung up, one of the men she'd asked to join them arrived. His office might've been next door to hers. He was a stocky, middle-aged businessman in gray slacks and a white shirt.

'Andi. Anything new?'

'A few things. Sit down.' Then she turned to Sachs.

'This is Bob Cavanaugh, senior VP of Operations. Detective Sachs.'

They shook hands.

He asked Sachs, 'Any headway? Any suspects?'

Before the detective could answer, Andi Jessen said stoically, 'They think it's somebody inside, Bob.'

'Inside?'

'That's what it's looking like,' Sachs said, and explained what they'd learned so far. Cavanaugh too seemed dismayed that their company might possibly be harboring a traitor.

Jessen asked, 'Could you find out from Steam Maintenance who's been assigned to inspect the pipes down the manhole near MH-Ten?'

'For how long back?'

'Two, three months,' Sachs said.

145

'I don't know if we'll have the assignment sheets, but I'll see.' He made the call and requested the information then he turned back to the women.

Sachs said, 'Now, let's talk a little more about the terrorist connection.'

'I thought you were accusing an employee.'

'It's not unusual for a terror cell to recruit an insider.'

'Should we look at Muslim employees?' Cavanaugh asked.

'I was thinking of the protesters outside,' Sachs said. 'What about ecoterrorism?'

Cavanaugh shrugged. 'Algonquin's been criticized in the press for not being green enough.' He said this delicately, not looking Jessen's way. This was apparently a familiar and tedious issue.

Jessen said to Sachs, 'We *have* a program for renewable energy. We're pursuing it. But we're being realistic about the subject, not wasting our time. It's politically correct to wave the renewables flag. But most people don't know the first thing about it.' She waved her hand dismissively.

Thinking of the severity of some ecoterror incidents in the recent past, Sachs asked her to elaborate.

It was as if she'd pushed an On button.

'Hydrogen fuel cells, biofuels, wind farms, solar farms, geothermal, methane generation, ocean wave generators . . . you know how much they produce? Less than three percent of all the energy consumed in the country. Half the electrical service supply in the US comes from

146

coal. Algonquin uses natural gas; that's twenty percent. Nuclear's about nineteen. Hydro's seven percent.

'Sure, the renewable will be growing but very, very slowly. For the next hundred years, they'll be a drop in the bucket of juice, if I can quote myself.' The president was growing even angrier. 'The start-up costs are obscene, the gadgets to create the juice are ridiculously expensive and unreliable, and since the generators're usually located away from major load centers, transportation is another huge cost. Take solar farms. The wave of the future, right? Do you know they're one of the biggest users of water in the power business? And where are they located? Where there's the most sun and therefore the least water.

'But say that out loud and you get jumped by the media. And by Washington and Albany too. You hear about those senators coming to town for Earth Day?'

'No.'

Jessen continued, 'They're on the Joint Energy Resources Subcommittee, working with the President on environmental issues. They'll be at that big rally in Central Park Thursday night. And what'll they be doing? Beating us up. Oh, they won't mention Algonquin by name, but I guarantee one of them'll point our way. You can see the smokestacks from the park. I'm convinced that's why the organizers put the stage where it is . . . All right, those're my views. But is that enough to make Algonquin a target? I just don't see it. Some political or religious fundamentalists going after the American infra-structure, sure. But not eco.'

Cavanaugh agreed. 'Ecoterror? Never had any problems that I can remember. And I've been here for thirty years — I worked with Andi's father when he ran the place. We burned coal back then. We were always expecting Greenpeace or some liberals to sabotage us. But nothing.'

Jessen confirmed, 'No, we tend to get boycotts and protesters.'

Cavanaugh gave a sour smile. 'And they don't see the irony that half of them took a subway over here from the New Energy Expo at the convention center, courtesy of Algonquin-generated current. Or made their little posters last night by the light provided by us. Forget irony. How's hypocrisy?'

Sachs said, 'Until we get some communication from somebody, though, or learn more, I'd still like to consider ecoterrorists. Have you heard anything about a group that starts with the words "Justice For"?'

'For what?' Cavanaugh asked.

'We don't know.'

'Well, I never have,' Jessen said. Cavanaugh hadn't either. But he said he'd check with the regional offices of Algonquin to see if they had heard anything.

He took a call. He lifted his eyes to Andi Jessen. He listened then disconnected and said to Sachs, 'No service in the steam access manhole for over a year. Those lines're shut down.'

'Okay.' Sachs was discouraged at the news.

Cavanaugh said, 'If you don't need me, I'll go check with the regional offices now.'

After he left, a tall African American appeared in the doorway — the second of the men she'd summoned — and Jessen motioned him to sit. She introduced them. Security Director Bernard Wahl was, Sachs realized, the only nonwhite she'd seen in the company not in worker's overalls. The strongly built man was draped in a dark suit and white shirt, heavily starched. His tie was red. His head was shaved and glistened in the overhead lights. Glancing up, Sachs saw that every other lightbulb was missing from the ceiling fixtures. An economy move? Or, given her anti-green stance, had Jessen decided that reducing energy use would be advantageous from a public relations standpoint?

Wahl shook Sachs's hand and snuck a glimpse at the bulge on her hip where her Glock resided. Somebody who'd come out of law enforcement would not have any interest in her piece, which was just a tool of the trade like cell phones or ball-point pens. It was the amateur cops who were fascinated with armament.

Andi Jessen briefed him and asked about access to the codes for the computers.

'The codes? That's just a few people. I mean, they're very senior. You ask me, it'd be too obvious. You sure we weren't hacked? Those kids're real smart nowadays.'

'Ninety-nine percent sure,' Sachs said.

'Bernie, have somebody check on access to the safe file room beside the control center.'

Wahl pulled out his mobile phone and placed

a call, told an assistant to handle the request. He disconnected and then added, 'I've been waiting for a terrorist announcement. But you're thinking it's from the inside?'

'We think it was either inside or with the *help* of somebody inside. But we did want to ask about ecoterror threats.'

'Not in my four years here. Just protesters.' A nod out the window.

'Have you ever heard of a group called Justice For something? Having to do with environmental issues?'

'No, ma'am.' Wahl was placid, exuded no emotion whatsoever.

Sachs continued, 'Any problems with employees who've been fired recently, who've had complaints with the company?'

'With the *company*?' Wahl asked. 'They tried to take out a city bus. It wasn't the company they were after.'

Jessen said, 'Our stock's down eight percent, Bernie.'

'Oh, sure. I didn't think about that. There're a few. I'll get the names.'

Sachs continued, 'I'd also like any information you have about employees with mental issues, anger management problems, or who've shown some instability.'

Wahl said, 'Security doesn't generally get their names unless it's serious. Some risk of violence to themselves or others. I can't think of anybody off the top of my head. But I'll check with HR and our medical department. Some details'll be confidential but I'll get you

150

the names. You can go from there.'

'Thanks. Now, we think he might've stolen the cable and hardware from an Algonquin warehouse, the one on a Hundred and Eighteenth Street.'

'I remember that,' Wahl said, a grimace on his face. 'We looked into it but the loss was only a few hundred dollars. And there were no leads.'

'Who'd have the keys?'

'They're standard. All our field workers have a set. In the region? Eight hundred people. Plus the supervisors.'

'Any employees fired or under suspicion of pilfering or stealing recently?'

He glanced at Jessen to make sure he should be answering the questions. He got the subtle message that he should.

'No. Not that my department's been aware of.' His cell phone chirped and he looked at the screen. 'Excuse me. Wahl here.' Sachs watched his face as he took in some troubling news. He looked from one to the other then disconnected. He cleared his throat in a baritone rumble. 'It's possible — I'm not sure — but it's possible we had a security breach.'

'What?' Jessen snapped, face reddening.

'The log-in records of Nine East.' He looked at Sachs. 'The wing where the control center and the safe file room are.'

'And?' Jessen and Sachs asked this simultaneously.

'There's a security door between the control room and the safe files. It should close on its own, but the smart lock records show it was open for about two hours a couple of days ago. A malfunction or it got jammed somehow.'

'Two hours? Unsupervised?' Andi Jessen was furious.

'That's right, ma'am,' he said, lips taut. He rubbed his glistening scalp. 'But it wasn't like anybody from the outside could get in. There was no breach in the lobby.'

Sachs asked, 'Security tapes?'

'We don't have them there, no.'

'Anybody sitting near the room?'

'No, it opens on an empty corridor. It's not even marked, for security.'

'How many people could've gotten into the room?'

'As many as had clearance to Nine through Eleven East.'

'Which is?'

'A lot,' he admitted, eyes downcast.

Discouraging news, though Sachs hadn't expected more. 'Can you get me the list of anybody who had access that day?'

He made another call while Jessen herself picked up the phone and raised hell about the breach. A few minutes later a young woman in a lavish gold blouse and teased hair stepped shyly into the doorway. She glanced once at Andi Jessen and then offered sheets of paper to Wahl. 'Bernie, I've got those lists you wanted. The one from HR too.'

She turned and was happy to flee the lioness's den.

Sachs looked at Wahl's face as he reviewed the list. Apparently the task of compiling it hadn't taken long but the results weren't good. Forty-six people, he explained, would have had access to the room.

'Forty-six? Oh, Christ.' Jessen slumped, staring out the window.

'All right. What we need to find out is who among them — ' Gesturing at the access list. ' — had alibis and who had the skill to reroute the computer and rig the wire at the bus stop.'

Jessen stared at her immaculate desk top. 'I'm not a technical expert. I got my father's talent for the business side of the power industry — generation, transportation, brokering.' She thought for a moment. 'But I know somebody who could help.'

She made another phone call, then looked up. 'He should be here in a few minutes. His office is on the other side of the Burn.'

'The . . . ?'

'The turbine room.' A gesture outside the window at the portion of the building from which the smokestacks blossomed. 'Where we produce the steam for the generators.'

Wahl was looking over the shorter list: 'Employees we've had to discipline or let go for various problems over the past six months — some mental problems, a few drug test failures, drinking on the job.'

'Only eight,' Jessen said.

Was there pride in her voice?

Sachs compared the two lists. None of those on the shorter one — the problem employees — had access to the computer codes. She was disappointed; she'd hoped it would pay off.

Jessen thanked Wahl.

'Anything else I can do, Detective, just call me.'

She too thanked the security chief, who left. Then she said to Jessen, 'I'd like copies of their résumés. Everybody on the list. Or if you have employee profiles, CVs. Anything.'

'Yes, I can arrange for that.' She asked her assistant to make a copy of the list and pull together personnel information for everybody on it.

Another man, slightly out of breath, arrived in Jessen's office. Midforties, Sachs estimated. He was a little doughy and had unruly brown hair, mixed with gray. 'Cute' seemed to fit. There was a boyish quality about him, Sachs decided. Sparkling eyes and raised eyebrows and a fidgety nature. The sleeves of his wrinkled striped shirt were rolled up. Food crumbs, it seemed, dusted his slacks.

'Detective Sachs,' Jessen said. 'This is Charlie Sommers, Special Projects manager.'

He shook the detective's hand.

The president looked at her watch, stood and donned a suit jacket she'd selected from a large closet of clothes. Sachs wondered if she pulled all-nighters. Jessen brushed at skin flakes or dust on the shoulders. 'I have to meet with our PR firm and then hold a press conference. Charles, could you take Detective Sachs back to your office? She's got some questions for you. Help her however you can.'

'Sure. Be happy to.'

Jessen was looking out the window, at her

dynasty — the massive building, the superstructure of towers and cables and scaffolding. With the fast-flowing East River glistening in the background, she seemed like the captain of a huge ship. The woman was obsessively rubbing her right thumb and forefinger together, a gesture of stress that Sachs recognized immediately, since she often did the same. 'Detective Sachs, how much wire did he use for that attack?'

Sachs told her.

The CEO nodded and kept looking out the window. 'So he's got enough left for six or seven more. If we can't stop him.'

Andi Jessen didn't seem to want a response. She didn't even seem to be speaking to the other people in the room.

18

After work, a different social tone emerged in Tompkins Square Park in the East Village. Young couples, some in Brooks Brothers, some pierced and sporting tats, strolling with their toddlers. Musicians, lovers, clusters of twenty-somethings headed home from despised day jobs and filled with expanding joy at what the night might hold. The smells here were hot dog water, pot, curry and incense.

Fred Dellray was on a bench near a large, spreading elm tree. He'd glanced at the plaque when he'd arrived and learned this was where the founder of the Hari Krishna movement had chanted the group's mantra in 1966 for the first time outside India.

He'd never known that. Dellray preferred secular philosophy to theology but had studied all major religions and he knew that the Hari Krishna sect included four basic rules in order to follow dharma, the righteous path: mercy, self-control, honesty and cleanliness of body and spirit.

He was reflecting on those qualities and how they figured in today's New York City versus South Asia, when feet scuffled behind him.

His hand hadn't even made it halfway to his weapon when he heard the voice, 'Fred.'

It troubled Dellray deeply that he'd been caught off guard. William Brent wasn't a threat but he easily could have been.

Another sign of losing his touch?

He nodded to the man to sit. Wearing a black suit that had seen better days, Brent was nondescript, a little jowly with direct eyes under swept back hair, sprayed into place. He wore steel-rimmed glasses that had been out of style when Dellray had been running him. But they were practical. Typical of William Brent.

The CI crossed his legs and glanced at the tree. He wore argyle socks and scuffed penny loafers.

'Been well, Fred?'

'Okay. Busy.'

'You always were.'

Dellray didn't bother to ask what Brent had been up to. Or what his present name was, for that matter. Or career. It would have been a waste of energy and time.

'Jeep. Strange creature, isn't he?'

'Is,' Dellray agreed.

'How long you think he'll live?'

Dellray paused but then answered honestly, 'Three years.'

'Here. But if Atlanta works out, he'd probably last for a while. If he doesn't get stupid.' Dellray was encouraged by the extent of his knowledge. Even Dellray hadn't known exactly where Jeep was going.

'So, Fred, you know I'm a working man now. Legitimate. What'm I doing here?'

'Because you listen.'

'Listen?'

'Why I liked running you. You always listened.

You heard things. Got this feeling you hear things still.'

'This about that explosion at the bus stop?'

'Uh-huh.'

'Some electrical malfunction.' Brent smiled. 'The news said that. I've always wondered about this obsession we have with the media. Why should I believe anything? They tell us that untalented actors and twenty-nine-year-old pop stars with excessive tits and cocaine problems behave badly. Why does that merit more than a millisecond of our consciousness? . . . That bus stop, Fred. Something else happened there.'

'Something else happened.' Dellray had been assuming one role with Jeep. That was a made-for-TV movie, melodramatic. But here, with William Brent, he was a Method actor. Subtle and real. The lines had been written over the years but the performance came from his heart. 'I really need to know what.'

'I liked working with you, Fred. You were . . . difficult but you were always honest.'

So, I'm one quarter of the way to dharmic enlightenment. The agent said, 'Are we going to keep going here?'

'I'm retired. Being a snitch can be detrimental to your health.'

'People come outa retirement all the time. Economy's fucked. Their social security checks don't go as far as they thought.' Dellray repeated, 'We going to keep going here?'

Brent stared at the elm tree for a long, long fifteen seconds. 'We'll keep going. Give me some deets and I'll see if it's worth my time and the risk. To both of us.'

To both of us? Dellray wondered. Then continued, 'We don't *have* many details. But there's maybe a terror group called Justice For we don't know what. The leader might be somebody named Rahman.'

'They were behind it, the bus stop?'

'Possibly. And somebody who might be connected with the company. No ID yet. Man, woman, we don't know.'

'What exactly happened that they aren't saying? A bomb?'

'No. The perp manipulated the grid.'

Brent's eyebrow rose behind the archaic glasses. 'The grid. Electricity . . . think about it. That's worse than an IED. With the grid, the explosive's already there, in everybody's house, in everybody's office. All he has to do is pull a few switches. I'm dead, you're dead. And not a pretty way to go.'

'Why I'm here.'

'Justice For something . . . Any idea what's on their to-do list?'

'No. Islamic, Aryan, political, domestic, foreign, eco. We don't know.'

'Where'd the name come from? Translated?'

'No. Was intercepted that way. 'Justice.' And 'For.' In English. Other words too. But they didn't get 'em.'

''They.'' Brent gave a furrow of a smile, and Dellray wondered if he knew exactly what Dellray was doing here, that he'd been tweaked aside by the brave new world of electronics.

SIGINT. 'Anybody take credit?' the man asked in his soft voice.

'Not yet.'

Brent was thinking, hard. 'And it would take a whole lot of planning to put something like this together. Lot of strands to get woven.'

'Would, sure.'

And a flutter of muscles in Brent's face told Dellray that some pieces were falling together. He was thrilled to see this. But of course revealed nothing.

Brent confirmed in a whisper, 'I have heard something, yes. About somebody doing some mischief.'

'Tell me.' Trying not to sound too eager.

'There's not enough to tell. It's smoke.' He added, 'And the people who can tell me? I can't let you contact them directly.'

'Could it be terror related?'

'I don't know.'

'Which means you can't say it isn't.'

'True.'

Dellray felt an uneasy clicking in his chest. He'd run snitches for years and he knew he was close to something important. 'If this group or whoever it is keeps going . . . a lot of people could be hurt. Hurt really bad.'

William Brent made a faint, candle-extinguishing noise. Which meant that he didn't care one bit, and that appeals to patriotism and what was right were a waste of breath.

Wall Street should take a lesson . . .

Dellray nodded. Meaning the negotiation was under way.

Brent continued, 'I'll give you names and locations. Whatever I find, you get it. But *I* do the work.'

Unlike Jeep, Brent had himself displayed several qualities of dharmic enlightenment when Dellray had been running him. Self-control. Cleanliness of spirit — well, body at least.

And the all-important honesty.

Dellray believed he could trust him. He snared him in a tight gaze. 'Here it is. I can live with you doing the work. I can live with being cut out. What I can't live with is slow.'

Brent said, 'That's one of the things you'd be paying for. Fast answers.'

'Which brings us to . . . ' Dellray had no problem paying his snitches. He preferred to bargain favors — reducing sentences, cutting deals with parole board case officers, dropping charges. But money worked too.

Paying value, getting value.

William Brent said, 'The world's changing, Fred.'

Oh, we're back to that? Dellray mused to himself.

'And I've got some new prospects I need to pursue. But what's the problem? What's always the problem?'

Money, of course.

Dellray asked, 'How much?'

'One hundred thousand. Up front. And you have a guarantee. I *will* get you something.'

Dellray coughed a laugh. He'd never paid more than five large to a snitch in all his years running them. And that princely sum had bought them indictments in a major dockside corruption case.

One hundred *thousand* dollars?

'It's just not there, William,' he said, not thinking about the name, which Brent probably hadn't used in years. 'That's more than our entire snitch bag put together. That's more than *everybody*'s snitch bag put together.'

'Hm.' Brent said nothing. Which is exactly what Fred Dellray himself would have done, had he been on the other side of the negotiation.

The agent sat forward, his bony hands clasped. 'Give me a minute.' Like Jeep in the stinky diner earlier, Dellray rose and walked past a skateboarder, two giggling Asian girls, and a man handing out fliers, looking surprisingly rational and cheerful, considering his cause was the 2012 end of days. Near the dharma tree he pulled out his phone and made a call.

'Tucker McDaniel,' was the clipped greeting.

'It's Fred.'

'You got something?' The ASAC sounded surprised.

'Maybe. A CI of mine, from The day. Nothing concrete. But he's been solid in the past. Only he wants some money.'

'How much?'

'How much we got?'

McDaniel paused. 'Not a lot. What's he got that's gold?'

'Nothing yet.'

'Names, places, acts, numbers? Scraps? . . . *Anything*?'

Like a computer rattling off data in a list.

'No, Tucker. Nothing yet. It's like an investment.'

Finally the ASAC said, 'I could do six, eight thousand probably.'

'That's all?'

'How the hell much does he want?'

'We're negotiating.'

'Fact is, we've had to adjust bottom lines for this one, Fred. Took us by surprise. You know.'

McDaniel's reluctance to spend was suddenly clear. He'd moved all the money in the Bureau operating accounts to the SIGINT and T and C teams. Naturally one of the first places he'd raided was the snitch fund.

'Start with six. See the merchandise. If it's meat, maybe I could go nine or ten. Even that's pushing it.'

'I think he could be on to something, Tucker.'

'Well, let's see some proof . . . Hold on . . . Okay, Fred, it's T and C on the other line. I better go.'

Click.

Dellray snapped the phone shut and stood for a moment, staring at the tree. He heard around him a swirl of voices. 'She was hot, you know, but there was this one thing didn't seem right . . . no, it's the Mayan calendar, I mean, maybe Nostradamus . . . that's totally fucked up . . . yo, where you been, dog?'

But what he was really hearing was his partner in the FBI some years ago saying, 'No problem, Fred. I'll take it.' And going on a trip that Dellray had been scheduled to handle.

And then hearing the voice of his special agent

163

in charge of the New York office two days later, that voice choking, telling Dellray that the partner had been one of the people killed in a terrorist bombing in the Oklahoma City federal building. The man had been in the conference room that Dellray should have been occupying.

At that moment, Fred Dellray, in a comfortable air-conditioned conference room of his own many miles from the smoking crater, had decided that a priority in his law enforcement career from then on would be to pursue terrorists and anyone else who killed men, women and children, en masse in the name of ideas, whether political or religious or social.

Yes, he was being marginalized by the ASAC He wasn't even being taken seriously. But what Dellray was about to do had very little to do with vindicating himself, or striking a blow for the old ways.

It was about stopping what he thought was the worst of evils: killing innocents.

He returned to William Brent, sat down. He said, 'Okay. One hundred thousand.'

They exchanged numbers — both cold phones, prepaid mobiles that would be discarded after a day or so. Dellray looked at his watch. He said, 'Tonight. Washington Square. Near the law school, by the chess boards.'

'Nine?' Brent asked.

'Make it nine-thirty.' Dellray rose and, according to the tradecraft of the CI world, left the park alone, with William Brent remaining behind to pretend to read the paper or contemplate the Krishna elm.

Or figure out how to spend his money.

But the CI was soon lost to thought, and Fred Dellray was considering how best to plan the set, what part the chameleon should now play, how to cast his eyes, how to convince and wheedle and call in favors. He was pretty sure he could pull it off; these were skills he'd honed for years.

He'd just never thought he'd ever be using his talents to rob his employer — the American government and the American people — of $100,000.

19

As Amelia Sachs followed Charlie Sommers to his office on the other side of the Burn in Algonquin Consolidated, she was aware that the heat was rising along the complicated route he was taking. And the rumble filling the halls was getting louder with every step.

She was totally lost. Up stairways, down stairways. As she followed him she sent and received several text messages on her BlackBerry but as they moved lower and lower she had to concentrate on where she was walking; the hallways became increasingly visitor-hostile. Cell reception finally turned to dust and she put her phone away.

The temperature rose higher.

Sommers stopped at a thick door, beside which were a rack of hard hats.

'You worried about your hair?' he asked, his voice rising, since the rumbling from the other side of the door was very loud now.

'I don't want to lose it,' she called back. 'But otherwise, no.'

'Just getting mussed a bit. This is the shortest way to my office.'

'Shorter's better. I'm in a hurry.' She grabbed a hat and squashed it onto her head.

'Ready?'

'I guess. What's through there exactly?'

Sommers thought for a moment and said,

'Hell.' And nodded her forward.

She recalled the seared polka-dot wounds that covered Luis Martin. Her breath was coming fast and she realized that her hand, moving toward the door handle, had slowed. She gripped and pulled the heavy steel portal open.

Yep, hell. Fire, sulfur, the whole scene.

The temperature in the room was overwhelming. Well over a hundred degrees and Sachs felt not only a painful prickle on her skin but a curious lessening of the pain in her joints as the heat deadened her arthritis.

The hour was late — it was close to eight p.m. — but there was a full staff at work in the Burn. The hunger for electricity might ebb and flow throughout the day but never ceased completely, of course.

The dim space, easily two hundred feet high, was filled with scaffolding and hundreds of pieces of equipment. The centerpiece was a series of massive light-green machines. The largest of them was long with a rounded top, like a huge Quonset hut, from which many pipes and ducts and wires sprouted.

'That's MOM,' Sommers called, pointing to it. '*M-O-M*. Midwest Operating Machinery, Gary, Indiana. They built her in the 1960s.' This was all shouted with some reverence. Sommers added that she was the biggest of the five electrical generators here in the Queens complex. He continued, explaining that when first installed, Mom was the biggest electrical generator in the country. In addition to the other electrical generators — they were only numbered, without names — were four units that provided superheated steam to the New York City area.

Amelia Sachs was indeed captivated by the massive machinery. She found her step slowing as she gazed at the huge components and tried to figure out the parts. Fascinating what the human mind could put together, what human hands could build.

'Those're the boilers.' He pointed to what seemed to Sachs to be a separate building within a building. They must've been ten or twelve stories tall. 'They produce steam, over three thousand pounds per square inch.' He drew a breath. 'It goes into two turbines, a high-pressure and a low-pressure one.' He pointed to part of Mom. 'Then into the generator. She's got a continuous output — thirty-four thousand amps, eighteen thousand volts, but it's stepped up once it gets outside for transport to over three hundred thousand.'

Despite the squashing heat, she felt a shiver, hearing those figures and flashing on the memory of Luis Martin, his skin punctured by hot metal raindrops.

Sommers added with some pride, it seemed to Sachs, that the output of the entire Queens facility — Mom plus several other turbines — was close to 2,500 megawatts. About 25 percent of the city's entire usage.

He pointed to a series of other tanks. 'That's where the steam is condensed to water and pumped back to the boilers. Starts all over again.' Proudly he continued, shouting, 'She's got three hundred and sixty miles of tubes and pipes, a million feet of cable.'

But then, despite her fascination and the massive scale, Sachs found herself gigged in the belly by her claustrophobia. The noise was relentless, the heat.

Sommers seemed to understand. 'Come on.' He gestured her to follow and in five minutes they were out the other door and hanging up their hats. Sachs was breathing deeply. The corridor, while still warm, was blessedly cool after her minutes in hell.

'It gets to you, doesn't it?'

'Does.'

'You all right?'

She diverted a tickling stream of sweat and nodded. He offered her a paper towel from a roll kept there for mopping faces and necks, it seemed, and she dried off.

'Come on this way.'

He led her down more corridors and into another building. More stairs and finally they arrived at his office. She stifled a laugh at the clutter. The place was filled with computers and instruments she couldn't recognize, hundreds of bits of equipment and tools, wires, electronic components, keyboards, metal and plastic and wood items in every shape and color.

And junk food. Tons of junk food. Chips and pretzels and soda, Ding Dongs and Twinkies. And hostess powdered sugar donuts, which explained the dandruff on his clothes.

'Sorry. It's the way we work in Special

Projects,' he said, shoveling aside computer printouts from an office chair for her to sit in. 'Well, the way I work, at least.'

'What exactly do you do?'

He explained, somewhat abashedly, that he was an inventor. 'I know, sounds either very nineteenth century or very infomercial. But that's what I do. And I'm the luckiest guy in the world. I do for a living exactly what I wanted to when I was a kid and building dynamos, motors, lightbulbs — '

'You made your own lightbulbs?'

'Only set fire to my bedroom twice. Well, three times, but we only had to call the fire department twice.'

She looked at a picture of Edison on the wall.

'My hero,' Sommers said. 'Fascinating man.'

'Andi Jessen had something about him on her wall too. A photo of the grid.'

'It's Thomas Alva's original signature. But Jessen's more Samuel Insull, I'd say.'

'Who?'

'Edison was the scientist. Insull was a businessman. He headed Consolidated Edison and created the first big monopolistic power utility. Electrified the Chicago trolley system, practically gave away the first electrical appliances — like irons — to get people addicted to electricity. He was a genius. But he ended up disgraced. This sound familiar? He was way overleveraged and when the Depression came, the company went under and hundreds of thousands of shareholders lost everything. Little like Enron. You want to know some trivia: The accounting firm Arthur Andersen was involved with both Insull and Enron.

'But me? I leave the business to other people. I just create things. Ninety-nine per cent amounts to nothing. But . . . well, I've got twenty-eight patents in my name and I've created nearly ninety processes or products in Algonquin's. Some people sit in front of the TV or play video games for fun. I . . . well, invent things.' He pointed to a large cardboard box, brimming with squares and rectangles of paper. 'That's the Napkin File.'

'The what?'

'I'm out at Starbucks or a deli and I get an idea. I jot it down on a napkin and come back here to draw it up properly. But I save the original, toss it in there.'

'So if there's ever a museum about you there'll be a Napkin Room.'

'It has occurred to me.' Sommers was blushing, from forehead to ample chin.

'What exactly do you invent?'

'I guess my expertise is the opposite of what Edison did. He wanted people to use electricity. I want people not to.'

'Does your boss know that's your goal?'

He laughed. 'Maybe I should say I want people to use it more efficiently. I'm Algonquin's negawatt maven. That's 'nega' with an n.'

'Never heard about that.'

'A lot of people haven't, which is too bad. It came from a brilliant scientist and environmentalist, Amory Lovins. The theory is to create incentives to *reduce* demand and use electricity more efficiently, rather than trying to build new power plants to increase supply. Your typical power generation station wastes nearly half of the heat generated — right up the smoke stack. Half! Think about that. But we've got a series of thermal collectors on the stacks and cooling towers here. At Algonquin we lose only twenty-seven percent.

'I've been coming up with ideas for portable nuclear generators — on barges, so they can be moved around from region to region.' He leaned forward, eyes sparkling again. 'And the big new challenge: storing electricity. It's not like food. You can't make it and put it on the shelf for a month. You use it or lose it — instantly. I'm creating new ways to store it. Flywheels, air pressure systems, new battery technology . . .

'Oh, and lately I've been spending half my time traveling around the country linking up small alternative and renewable companies, so they can get onto the major grids like the Northeastern Interconnection — that's ours — and sell juice to *us*, rather than us selling to small communities.'

'I thought Andi Jessen wasn't very supportive of renewables and alternative energy.'

'No, but she's not crazy either. It's the wave of the future. I think we just disagree about when that future's going to arrive. I think sooner.' A whimsical smile. 'Of course, you did notice that her office is the size of my entire department, and it's on the ninth floor with a view of Manhattan . . . I'm in the basement.' His face grew solemn. 'Now, what can I do to help?'

172

Sachs said, 'I have a list of people at Algonquin who might've been behind the attack this morning.'

'Somebody here?' He appeared dismayed.

'It's looking that way. Or at least they were working with the perp. Now, he's probably a man, though he could be working with a woman. He or she had access to the computer codes that let them get into grid control software. He kept shutting down substations so that the electricity was rerouted into the substation on Fifty-Seventh Street. And he reset the circuit breakers higher than they should have been.'

'So that's how it happened.' His face was troubled. 'The computers. I wondered. I didn't know the details.'

'Some of them will have alibis — *we'll* take care of checking that out. But I need you to give me some idea of who'd have the ability to reroute the electricity and rig the arc flash.'

Sommers seemed amused. 'I'm flattered. I didn't know Andi even knew much about what happens down here.' Then the cherubic look was gone, replaced by a wry smile. 'Am I a suspect?'

She'd spotted his name when Jessen had first mentioned him. She held his eye. 'You're on the list.'

'Hm. You're sure you want to trust me?'

'You were on conference call from ten-thirty until nearly noon today, when the attack happened, and you were out of town during the window when the perp could have gotten the computer codes. The key data shows you didn't log into the safe file room at any other time.'

173

Sommers was lifting an eyebrow.

She tapped her BlackBerry. 'That's what I was texting about on the way here. I had somebody in the NYPD check you out. So you're clean.'

She supposed she sounded apologetic for not trusting him. But Sommers said, his eyes sparkling, 'Thomas Edison would have approved.'

'What do you mean?'

'He said a genius is just a talented person who does his homework.'

20

Amelia Sachs didn't want to show Sommers the list itself; he might know some of the employees and be inclined to dismiss the possibility of their being suspects, or, on the other hand, he might call her attention to somebody simply because he thought they were otherwise suspicious.

She didn't explain her reluctance but said simply she just wanted a profile of somebody who could have arranged the attack and used the computer.

He opened a bag of Doritos, offered Sachs some. She declined and he chomped down a handful. Sommers didn't look like an inventor. He was more of a middle-aged advertising copywriter, with his tousled hair and slightly untucked blue-and-white-striped shirt. Bit of a belly. His glasses were stylish, though Sachs suspected that on the frames were the words 'Made in' preceding some Asian rim country. Only up close could you see the wrinkles near his eyes and mouth.

He washed the food down with soda and said, 'First, rerouting the juice to get it to the substation on Fifty-seventh Street? That'll narrow things down. Not everybody who works here could do it. Not many people could at all, in fact. They'd need to know SCADA. That's our Supervisory Control and Data Acquisition program. It runs on Unix computers. He'd also probably have to know EMP — energy management programs. Ours is Enertrol. It's Unix-based too. Unix is a pretty complicated operating system. It's used in the big internet routers. It's not like Windows or Apple. You couldn't just look up online how to do it. You'd need somebody who'd studied SCADA and EMP, taken courses in it or, at the very least, apprenticed in a control room for six months, a year.'

Sachs jotted notes, then asked, 'And about the arc flash. Who'd know about rigging that?'

'Tell me how he did it exactly.'

Sachs explained about the cable and the bus bar.

He asked, 'It was aimed out the window? Like a gun?'

She nodded.

Sommers went silent for a moment. He focused elsewhere. 'That could've killed dozens of people . . . And the burns. Terrible.'

'Who could do it?' Sachs persisted.

Sommers was looking off again, which he did a lot, she'd noticed. After a moment: 'I know you're asking about Algonquin employees. But you ought to know that arc flashes are the first thing that all electricians learn about. Whether they're working as licensed tradesmen, in construction, for manufacturing companies, the army or navy . . . any field at all, as long as they're around electrical service lines with enough juice for arcs to be a problem, they'll learn the rules.'

'So you mean that anybody who knows how to

176

avoid arcs or prevent them knows how to create them.'

'Exactly.'

Another note in her quick handwriting. Then she looked up. 'But let's just talk for the moment about employees.'

'Okay, who here could rig something like that? There'd be live wire work involved, so it'd have to be somebody who is or has been a licensed master electrician in private contracting or been a lineman or a troubleman for a utility.'

'A what? Troubleman?'

Sommers laughed. 'Great job title, hm? Those're supervisors who arrange for the repairs when a line goes down or there's a short circuit or other problem. And remember that a lot of the senior people here have risen through the ranks. Just because they do energy brokerage now and sit behind a desk doesn't mean they can't rewire a three-phase service panel in their sleep.'

'And make an arc flash gun.'

'Exactly. So you should be looking for somebody with computer training in Unix control and energy management programs. And somebody with a career as a lineman or troubleman or in the contracting trades. Military too. Army, navy and air force produce a lot of electricians.'

'Appreciate this.'

A knocking on the door frame intruded. A young woman stood there with a large Redweld expanding envelope in her arms. 'Ms. Jessen said you wanted these? From Human Resources?'

177

Sachs took the résumés and employee files and thanked the woman.

Sommers had dessert, a Hostess cupcake. Then its twin. He sipped more soda. 'Want to say something.'

She lifted an eyebrow.

'Can I give you a lecture?'

'Lecture?'

'Safety lecture.'

'I don't have much time.'

'It'll be quick. But it's important. I was just thinking, you're at a big disadvantage, going after this . . . what'd you call him?'

'We say 'perp.' For 'perpetrator.''

''Perp' sounds sexier. Say you're going after your usual perp. Bank robbers, hitmen . . . You know that they might have a gun or knife. You're used to that. You know how to protect yourself. You've got procedures on how to handle them. But electricity as a weapon or a booby trap . . . that's a whole different ball game. The thing about juice? It's invisible. And it's all over the place. I mean, everywhere.'

She was recalling the bits of hot metal. The horrid round holes in Luis Martin's tan skin.

Sachs had a scent memory of the scorch at the crime scene. She shivered in disgust.

Sommers gestured toward a sign on his wall.

REMEMBER NATIONAL FIRE PROTECTION ASSOCIATION GUIDELINE 70. READ IT, LEARN IT. NFPA 70 CAN SAVE YOUR LIFE!

She felt an urgency to get on with the case but she also wanted to hear what he had to say. 'I don't have much time, but please, go ahead.'

'First, you have to know how dangerous electricity is. And that means knowing about amperage, or current. You know what that is?'

'I . . . ' Sachs had thought she did, until she realized she couldn't define it. 'No.'

'Let's compare an electric circuit to a plumbing system: water pumped through pipes. Water pressure is created by the pump, which moves a certain amount of water through the pipes at a certain speed. It moves more or less easily depending on the width and condition of the pipes.

'Now, in an *electrical* system, it's the same thing. Except you have electrons instead of water, wires or some conductive material instead of pipes and a generator or battery instead of the pump. The pressure pushing the electrons is the voltage. The amount of electrons moving through the wire is the amps, or current. The resistance — called ohms — is determined by the width and nature of the wires or whatever the electrons're flowing through.'

So far, so good. 'That makes sense. Never heard it put that way before.'

'Now we're talking about *amps*. Remember: That's the amount of moving electrons.'

'Good.'

'How much amperage does it take to kill you? At fifteen milliamps, you're in excruciating pain and you're experiencing respiratory arrest. At a hundred milliamps of AC current, your heart will fibrillate and you'll die. That's one *tenth* of one amp. Your typical Rite Aid hair dryer pulls ten amps.'

'Ten?' Sachs whispered.

'Yes, ma'am. A hair dryer. Ten amps, which, by the way, is all you need for an electric chair.'

As if she weren't uneasy enough.

He continued, 'Electricity is like Frankenstein's monster — who was animated with lightning, by the way. It's stupid and it's brilliant. Stupid because once it's created it wants to do only one thing: Get back to the ground. Brilliant because it instinctively knows the best way to do that. It always takes the path of least resistance. You can grab on to a hundred-thousand-volt line but if it's easier for the electricity to get back through the wire, you're perfectly safe. If *you're* the best conductor to the ground . . . ' His pointed nod explained the consequences.

'Now, for your lesson. My three rules for dealing with juice: First, avoid it if at all possible. This guy is going to know you're after him and he might be rigging traps with live lines. Stay away from metal — handrails, doors and doorknobs, uncarpeted flooring, appliances, machinery. Wet basements, standing water. Have you ever seen transformers and switchgear on the street?'

'No.'

'Yes, you have. But you're not aware of them because our city fathers hide and disguise them. The working parts of transformers're scary and ugly. In the city, they're underground or in

180

innocuous buildings or neutral-painted enclo-sures. You could be standing right next to a transformer taking in thirteen thousand volts and not know it. So keep an eye out for anything that says Algonquin on it. And stay away if you can.

'Now, you have to remember that even if you *think* you're avoiding it, you could still be in danger. There's something called 'islanding.''

'Islanding?'

'Say the grid is down in some part of town, like happened today. You think all the circuits're dead, right? Of *course* you're safe. Well, maybe and maybe not. Andi Jessen would like Algonquin to be the only game in town, but we're not. Power nowadays is supplied through what's called distributed generation, where smaller energy producers pump juice into our grid. Islanding would happen when the Algon-quin supply is offline but some smaller source is still supplying juice to the grid — an island of electricity in the void.

'Then there's backfeed. You cut the breakers and go to work, so the supply isn't feeding into the line. But the *low*-voltage lines downstream may start feeding juice *back* into the trans-former — '

Sachs understood. 'And the transformer steps it back *up*.'

'Exactly. And the line you thought was dead is alive. Really alive.'

'With enough juice to hurt you.'

'Oh, yeah. And then there's induction. Even if you're sure you shut off the circuits — it's

181

completely dead, and there's no islanding or backfeed possible — the wire you're working on can *still* become charged again with deadly voltage if there's another live wire nearby. That's because of induction. The current in one wire can energize another, even a dead one, if it's close enough.

'So, rule one: avoid the juice. What's rule two? If you can't avoid it, protect yourself against it. Wear PPE, personal protective equipment. Rubber boots and gloves and not those sissy little ones they wear on that *CSI* TV show. Thick, industrial, rubber work gloves. Use insulated tools or, even better, a hot stick. They're fiberglass, like hockey sticks, with tools attached to the end. We use them for working live lines.

'Protect yourself,' he repeated. 'Remember the path of least resistance rule. Human skin is a pretty poor conductor if it's dry. If it's wet, especially with sweat, because of the salt, resistance drops dramatically. And if you've got a wound or a burn, skin becomes a *great* conductor. Dry leather soles of your shoes are fairly good insulators. Wet leather's like skin — especially if you're standing on a conductive surface like damp ground or a basement floor. Puddles of water? Uh-oh.

'So, if you have to touch something that could be live — say, opening a metal door, make sure you're dry and wearing insulated shoes or boots. Use a hot stick or an insulated tool if you can and use only one hand — your right since it's slightly farther from the heart — and keep your other hand in your pocket so you don't touch anything accidentally and complete a circuit. Watch where you put your feet.

'You've seen birds sitting on uninsulated high-tension wires? They don't wear PPE. How can they roost on a piece of metal carrying a hundred thousand volts? Why don't we have roast pigeons falling from the skies?'

'They don't touch the other wire.'

'Exactly. As long as they don't touch a return or the tower, they're fine. They have the same charge as the wire, but there's no current — no amps — going through them . . . You've got to be like that bird on the wire.'

Which, to Sachs, made her sound pretty damn fragile.

'Take off all metal before you work with juice. Jewelry especially. Pure silver is the best conductor on earth. Copper and aluminum are at the top too. Gold isn't far behind. At the other end are the dielectrics — insulators. Glass and Teflon, then ceramic, plastics, rubber, wood. Bad conductors. Standing on something like that, even a thin piece, could mean the difference between life and death.

'That's rule number two, protection.' Sommers continued, 'Finally, rule three: If you can't avoid juice and can't protect yourself against it, cut its head off. All circuits, big or small, have a way to shut them down. They all have switches, they all have breakers or fuses. You can stop the juice instantly by flipping the switch or the breaker off, or removing a fuse. And you don't even need to know where the breaker is to pop it.

183

What happens if you stick two pieces of wire into the holes in a household outlet and touch the ends?'

'The circuit breaker pops.'

'Exactly. You can do the same thing with any circuit. But remember rule number two. Protect yourself when you do that. Because at bigger voltages touching the two wires will produce one hell of a spark and it could be an arc flash.'

Sommers was on to another junk food course, pretzels. He washed down the noisy bite with more soda. 'I could go on for an hour but those're the basics. You get the message?'

'I do. This's really helpful, Charlie. I appreciate it.'

His advice sounded so simple but, though Sachs had carefully listened to everything Sommers had told her, she couldn't escape the fact that this particular weapon was still very alien to her.

How could Luis Martin have avoided it, protected himself against it, or cut the beast's head off? The answer was, he couldn't.

'If you need me for anything else technical, just give me a call.' He gave her two cell phone numbers. 'And, oh, hold on . . . here.' He handed her a black plastic box with a button on the side and an LCD screen at the top. It looked like an elongated cell phone. 'One of my inventions. A noncontact current detector. Most of them only register up to a thousand volts and you have to be pretty close to the wire or terminal for it to read. But this goes to ten thousand. And it's very sensitive. It'll sense voltage from about four or five feet away and give you the level.'

'Thanks. That'll be helpful.' She gave a laugh, examining the instrument. 'Too bad they don't make these to tell you if a guy on the street's carrying a gun.'

Sachs had been joking. But Charlie Sommers was nodding, a glaze of concentration on his face; he seemed to be considering her words very seriously. As he said good-bye to her, he shoved some corn chips into his mouth and frantically began drawing a diagram on a slip of paper. She noticed that a napkin was the first thing he'd grabbed.

21

'Lincoln, this is Dr. Kopeski.'

Thom was standing in the doorway of the lab with a visitor.

Lincoln Rhyme looked up absently. The time was now about 8:30 p.m. and, though the urgency of the Algonquin case was pulsing through the room, there was little he could do until Sachs returned from meeting the power company executive. So he'd reluctantly agreed to see the representative from the disability rights group giving Rhyme his award.

Kopeski's not going to come here and cool his heels like some courtier waiting for an audience with the king . . .

'Call me Arlen, please.'

The soft-spoken man, in a conservative suit and white shirt, a tie like an orange and black candy cane, walked up to the criminalist and nodded. No vestigial offer of a handshake. And he didn't even glance down at Rhyme's legs or at the wheelchair. Since Kopeski worked for a disability rights organization Rhyme's condition was nothing to him. An attitude that Rhyme approved of. He believed that we were all disabled in one way or another, ranging from emotional scar tissue to arthritis to Lou Gehrig's Disease. Life was one big disability; the question was simple: What did we do about it? Rhyme rarely dwelt on the subject.

He'd never been an advocate for disabled rights; that struck him as a diversion from his job. He was a criminalist who happened to be able to move with less facility than most. He compensated as best he could and got on with his work.

Rhyme glanced at Mel Cooper and nodded toward the den, across the foyer from the lab. Thom ushered Kopeski inside, with Rhyme following in his chair, and eased the pocket doors partially together. He disappeared.

'Sit down, if you like,' Rhyme said, the last clause offered to temper the first, hoping that the man would remain standing, get to business and get out. He was carrying a briefcase. Maybe the paperweight was in there. The doc could present it, get a photo and leave. The whole matter would be put to rest.

The doctor sat. 'I've followed your career for some time.'

'Have you?'

'Are you familiar with the Disability Resources Council?'

Thom had briefed him. Rhyme remembered little of the monologue. 'You do some very good work.'

'Good work, yes.'

Silence.

If we could move this along. Rhyme glanced out the window intently as if a new assignment were winging its way toward the townhouse like the falcon earlier. Sorry, have to go, duty calls . . .

'I've worked with many disabled people over

the years. Spinal cord injuries, spina bifida, ALS, a lot of other problems. Cancer too.'

Curious idea. Rhyme had never thought about that disease being a disability, but he supposed some types could fit the definition. A glance at the wall clock, ticking away slowly. And then Thom brought in a tray of coffee and, oh, for Christ's sake, cookies. The glance at the aide — meaning this was not a fucking tea party — rolled past like vapor.

'Thank you,' Kopeski said, taking a cup. Rhyme was disappointed that he added no milk, which would have cooled the beverage so he could drink it, and leave, more quickly.

'For you, Lincoln?'

'I'm fine, thank you,' he added with a chill that Thom ignored as effectively as he had the searing glance a moment ago. He left the tray and scooted back to the kitchen.

The doctor eased down into the sighing leather chair. 'Good coffee.'

I'm so very pleased. A cock of the head.

'You're a busy man, so I'll get to the point.'

'I'd appreciate that.'

'Detective Rhyme ... Lincoln. Are you a religious man?'

The disability group must have a church affiliation; they might not want to honor a heathen.

'No, I'm not.'

'No belief in the afterlife?'

'I haven't seen any objective evidence that one exists.'

'Many, many people feel that way. So, for you,

188

death would be equal to, say, peace.'

'Depending on how I go.'

A smile in the kind face. 'I misrepresented myself somewhat to your aide. And to you. But for a good reason.'

Rhyme wasn't concerned. If the man had pretended to be somebody else to get in and kill me, I'd be dead now. A raised eyebrow meant: Fine. Confess and let's move forward.

'I'm not with DRC.'

'No?'

'No. But I sometimes say I'm with one group or another because my real organization sometimes gets me kicked out of people's homes.'

'Jehovah's Witnesses?'

A chuckle. 'I'm with Die with Dignity. It's a euthanasia advocacy organization based in Florida.'

Rhyme had heard of them.

'Have you ever considered assisted suicide?'

'Yes, some years ago. I decided not to kill myself.'

'But you kept it as an option.'

'Doesn't everybody, disabled or not?'

A nod. 'True.'

Rhyme said, 'It's pretty clear that I'm not getting an award for picking the most efficient way of ending my life. So what can I do for you?'

'We need advocates. People like yourself, with some public recognition factor. Who might consider making the transition.'

Transition. Now, there's a euphemism for you.

'You could make a video for YouTube. Give

189

some interviews. We were thinking that someday you might decide to take advantage of our services.' He withdrew from his briefcase a brochure. It was subdued and printed on nice card stock and had flowers on the front. Not lilies or daisies, Rhyme noticed. Roses. The title above the flora was 'Choices.'

He set it on the table near Rhyme. 'If you'd be interested in letting us use you as a celebrity sponsor we could not only provide you with our services for free, but there'd be some compensation, as well. Believe it or not, we do okay, for a small group.'

And presumably they pay up front, Rhyme thought. 'I really don't think I'm the man for you.'

'All you'd have to do is talk a bit about how you've always considered the possibility of assisted suicide. We'd do some videos too. And —'

A voice from the doorway startled Rhyme. 'Get the fuck out of here!' He noticed Kopeski jump at the sound.

Thom stormed into the room, as the doctor sat back, spilling coffee as he dropped the cup, which hit the floor and shattered. 'Wait, I —'

The aide, usually the picture of control, was red-faced. His hands were shaking. 'I said out.'

Kopeski rose. He remained calm. 'Look, I'm having a conversation with Detective Rhyme here,' he said evenly. 'There's no reason to get upset.'

'Out! Now!'

'I won't be long.'

'You'll leave now.'

'Thom — ' Rhyme began.

'Quiet,' the aide muttered.

The look from the doctor said, You let your assistant talk to you like that?

'I'm not going to tell you again.'

'I'll leave when I've finished.' Kopeski eased closer to the aide. The doctor, like many medical people, was in good shape.

But Thom was a caregiver, which involved getting Rhyme's ass into and out of beds and chairs and exercise equipment all day long. A physical therapist too. He stepped right into Kopeski's face, ready to go at it, if he needed to.

But the confrontation only lasted a few seconds. The doctor backed down. 'All right, all right, all right.' He held his hands up. 'Jesus. No need to — '

Thom picked up the man's briefcase and shoved it into his chest and led him out the door. A moment later the criminalist heard the door slam. Pictures on the wall shook.

The aide appeared a moment later, evidently mortified. He cleaned up the broken china, mopped the coffee. 'I'm sorry, Lincoln. I checked. It was a real organization . . . I thought.' His voice cracked. He shook his head, the handsome face dark, hands shaking.

As Rhyme wheeled back toward the lab he said, 'It's fine, Thom. Don't worry . . . And there's a bonus.'

The man turned his troubled eyes toward Rhyme, to find his boss smiling.

'I don't have to waste time writing an acceptance speech for any goddamn award. I can get back to work.'

22

Electricity keeps us alive; the impulse from the brain to the heart and lungs is a current, like any other.

And electricity kills too.

You can't separate it from death.

At 9 p.m., just nine and a half hours after the attack at Algonquin substation MH-10, the man in the dark-blue Algonquin Consolidated overalls surveyed the scene in front of him: his killing zone.

Electricity and death . . .

He was standing in a construction site, out in the open, but no one paid him any attention . . . because he was a worker among fellow workers. Different uniforms, different hard hats, different companies. But one thing tied them all together: those who made a living with their hands were looked down on by 'real people,' the ones who relied on their services, the rich, the comfortable, the ungrateful.

Safe in this invisibility, he was in the process of installing a much more powerful version of the device he'd tested earlier at the health club. In the nomenclature of electrical service, 'high voltage' didn't begin until you hit 70,000v. For what he had planned, he needed to be sure all the systems could handle at least two or three times that much juice.

He looked over the site of tomorrow's attack

one more time. As he did he couldn't help but think about voltage and amperage . . . and death.

There'd been a lot of misreporting about Ben Franklin and that insane key-in-the-thunderstorm thing. Actually Franklin had stayed completely off damp ground, in a barn, and was connected to the wet kite string with a dry silk ribbon. The kite itself was never actually struck by lightning; it simply picked up static discharge from a gathering storm. The result wasn't a real bolt but rather elegant blue sparks that danced from the back of Franklin's hand like fish feeding at the surface of a lake.

One European scientist duplicated the experiment not long afterward. He didn't survive.

From the earliest days of power generation, workers were constantly being burned to death or having their hearts switched off. The early grid took down a number of horses, thanks to metal shoes on wet cobble-stones.

Thomas Alva Edison and his famous assistant Nikola Tesla battled constantly over the superiority of DC, direct current (Edison), versus AC, alternating current (Tesla), trying to sway the public by horror stories of danger. The conflict became known as the Battle of the Currents and it made front-page news regularly. Edison constantly played the electrocution card, warning that anyone using AC was in danger of dying and in a very unpleasant way. It was true that it took less AC current to cause injury, though any type of current powerful enough to be useful could also kill you.

194

The first electric chair was built by an employee of Edison's, rather tactically using Tesla's alternating current. The first execution via the device was in 1890, under the direction not of an executioner but a 'state electrician.' The prisoner did die, though the process took eight minutes. At least he was probably unconscious by the time he caught fire.

And then there were always stun guns. Depending on who was getting shot and what part of the body, they could be counted on for the occasional death. And the fear of everyone in the industry: arc flashes, of course, like the attack he'd engineered this morning.

Juice and death . . .

He wandered through the construction site, feigning end of day weariness. The site was now staffed by a skeleton crew of night-shift workers. He moved closer, and still no one noticed him. He was wearing thick-framed safety glasses, the yellow Algonquin hard hat. He was as invisible as electricity in a wire.

The first attack had made the news in a big way, of course, though the stories were limited to an 'incident' in a Midtown substation. The reporters were abuzz with talk of short circuits, sparks and temporary power outages. There was a lot of speculation about terrorists but no one had found any connection.

Yet.

At some point, somebody would have to consider the possibility of an Algonquin Power worker running around rigging traps that resulted in very, very unpleasant and painful deaths, but that hadn't happened.

He now left the construction site and made his way underground, still unchallenged. The uniform and the ID badge were like magic keys. He slipped into another grimy, hot access tunnel and, after donning personal protective gear, continued to rig the wiring.

Juice and death.

How elegant it was to take a life this way, compared, say, with shooting your victim at five hundred yards.

It was so pure and so simple and so natural.

You could stop electricity, you could direct it. But you couldn't trick it. Once juice was created it would instinctively do whatever it could to return to the earth, and if the most direct way was to take a human life in the process, it would do so in, literally, a flash.

Juice had no conscience, felt no guilt.

This was one of the things he'd come to admire about his weapon. Unlike human beings, electricity was forever true to its nature.

23

The city came alive at this time of night.

9 p.m. was like a green flag for a car race.

The dead time in New York wasn't night; it was when the city was spiritually numb, ironically when it was at its busiest: rush hour, mid-morning and — afternoon. Only now were people shedding the workaday numbness, refocusing, coming alive.

Making all-important decisions: which bar, which friends, which shirt? Bra, no bra?

Condoms? . . .

And then out onto the street.

Fred Dellray now loped through the cool spring air, sensing the energy rise like what was humming through the electrical cables beneath his feet. He didn't drive much, didn't own a car, but what he was feeling now was akin to punching the accelerator and burning gas in a frenzy, as the power flung you toward your fate.

Two blocks from the subway, three, four.

And something else burned. The $100,000 in his pocket.

As he moved along the sidewalk Fred Dellray couldn't help but thinking, Have I ruined it all? Yes, I'm doing the morally right thing. I'd risk my career, I'd risk jail, if this thin thread of a lead ultimately revealed the perp, whether it was Justice For or anyone else. Anything to save the lives of citizens. Of course, the $100,000 was nothing to the entity he'd taken it from. And the cash might, thanks to bureaucratic myopia, never be missed. But even if it wasn't, and even if William Brent's lead blossomed and they were successful in stopping more attacks, would Dellray's malfeasance gnaw at him, the guilt growing larger and larger like a spiky tumor?

Would he fall into such guilt that his life would be altered forever, turned gray, turned worthless?

Change . . .

He was close to turning around and returning to the federal building, putting the money back.

But, no. He was doing the right thing. And he'd live with the consequences, whatever they were.

But, goddamn, William, you better come through for me.

Dellray now crossed the street in the Village and wandered right up to William Brent, who blinked in faint surprise, as if he'd believed Dellray wouldn't come. They stood together. This wasn't a set — an undercover operation — and it wasn't a recruiting session. It was just two guys meeting on the street to conduct business.

Behind them an unclean teenage boy, strumming a guitar and bleeding from a recent lip piercing, moaned out a song. Dellray motioned Brent along the sidewalk. The smell and the sound faded.

The agent asked, 'You found anything more?'

'Have, yes.'

'What?' Once again, trying not to sound desperate.

'It wouldn't do any good to say at this point. It's a lead to a lead. I'll guarantee you something by tomorrow.'

Guarantee? Not a word you heard often in the snitch business.

But William Brent was your Armani of CIs.

Besides, Dellray had no choice.

'Say,' Brent said casually, 'you through with the paper?'

'Sure. Keep it.' And handed the folded-up *New York Post* to Brent.

They'd done this all before, of course, a hundred times. The CI slipped the newspaper into his attaché case without even feeling for the envelope inside, much less opening it up and counting the money.

Dellray watched the money disappear as if he were watching a coffin submerge into a grave.

Brent didn't ask the source of the cash. Why should he? It wasn't relevant to him.

The C.I. now summarized, half musing, 'White male, a lot of mediums. Employee or inside connection. Justice For something. Rahman. Terrorism, possibly. But it could be something else. And he knows electricity. And significant planning.'

'That's all we have for now.'

'I don't think I need anything else,' Brent said without a hint of ego. Dellray took the words and this attitude as encouragement. Normally, even parting with a typical snitch gratuity — $500 or so — he felt like he was getting robbed. Now, he had a gut sense that Brent would deliver.

Dellray said, 'Meet me tomorrow. Carmella's.

The Village. Know it?'

'I do. When?'

'Noon.'

Brent further wrinkled his wrinkled face. 'Five.'

'Three?'

'Okay.'

Dellray was about to whisper, 'Please,' which he didn't think he'd ever said to a CI. He canned the desperation but had a tough time keeping his eyes off the attaché case, whose contents might just be the ashes of his career. And, for that matter, his entire life. An image of his son's ebullient face rose. He forced it away.

'Pleasure doing business with you, Fred.' Brent smiled and nodded a farewell. The streetlight glinted off his oversized glasses and then he was gone.

24

'That's Sachs.'

The deep bubble of a car engine sounded outside the window and fell to silence.

Rhyme was speaking to Tucker McDaniel and Lon Sellitto, both of whom had arrived not long before, around the time the Death Doctor had exited so abruptly.

Sachs would be throwing the *NYPD Official Business* placard on the dash and heading toward the house. And, yes, a moment later the door opened and her footsteps, spaced far apart because of her long legs, and because of the urgency she wore like her weapon, resounded on the floor.

She nodded to those present and spent a second longer examining Rhyme. He noted the expression: tenderness blended with the clinical eye typical of those in relationships with the severely disabled. She'd studied quadriplegia more than he had, she could handle all the tasks involved in his intimate, day-to-day routine, and did occasionally. Rhyme was, at first, embarrassed by this but when she pointed out, with humor and maybe a little flirtation, 'How's it different from any other old married couple, Rhyme?' he'd been brought up short. 'Good point' was his only response.

Which didn't mean her doting, like anyone else's, didn't rankle occasionally and he glanced at her once and then turned to the evidence charts.

Sachs looked around. 'Where's the award?'

'There was an element of misrepresentation involved.'

'What do you mean?'

He explained to her about Dr. Kopeski's bait and switch.

'No!'

Rhyme nodded. 'No paperweight.'

'You threw him out?'

'That was Thom. And a very fine job he did of it. But I don't want to talk about that now. We have work to do.' He glanced at her shoulder bag. 'So what do we have?'

Pulling several large files out, she said, 'Got the list of people who had access to the Algonquin computer pass codes. And their résumés and employee files.'

'What about disgruntled workers? Mental problems?'

'None that're relevant.'

She gave more details of her meeting with Andi Jessen: There was no record of employees in the steam tunnel work area near the substation on Fifty-seventh Street. There had been no obvious terrorist threats but an associate was looking into the possibility. 'Now, I spoke to somebody who works in the Special Projects Division — that's alternative energy, basically. Charlie Sommers. Good guy. He gave me the profile of the sort of person who could rig an arc flash. A master electrician, military electrician, a power company lineman or troubleman — '

'Now that's a job description for you,' Sellitto remarked.

'It's really trouble*shooter*, a foreman basically. You need on-the-job experience to make one of these arc flashes happen. You can't just look it up on the Internet.'

Rhyme nodded at the whiteboard and Sachs wrote her summary. She added, 'As for the computer, you'd need to have classroom training or a fair amount of training on the job. That's pretty tricky too.' She explained about the SCADA and EMP programs that the UNSUB would have to be competent in.

She added these details to the chart too.

Sellitto asked, 'How many're on the list?'

'Over forty.'

'Ouch,' McDaniel muttered.

Rhyme supposed that one of the names on the list could be the perp, and maybe Sachs or Sellitto could narrow it down to a more reasonable number. But what he wanted at the moment was evidence. Of which there was very little, at least little that was productive.

Nearly twelve hours had elapsed since the attack and they were no closer to finding the man who'd been in the coffee shop, or any other suspect.

The lack of leads was frustrating but more troubling was a simple entry in the UNSUB's profile chart: *Possibly same person who stole 75 feet of similar Bennington cable and 12 split bolts. More attacks in mind?*

Was he rigging something right now? There'd been no warning about the bus attack. Maybe that was the MO for his crimes. Any moment the networks could report a story that perhaps dozens of people had been killed in a second arc flash explosion.

Mel Cooper made a copy of the list and they divided up the names. Sachs, Pulaski and Sellitto took half, McDaniel the rest, for his federal agents to follow up on. Sachs then looked through the personnel files she'd gotten at Algonquin and kept the ones that corresponded to the names they'd selected, gave the others to McDaniel.

'This Sommers, you trust him?' Rhyme asked.

'Yes. He checked out. And he gave me this.' She whipped out a small black electronic device and pointed it toward a wire near Rhyme. She pressed a button and read a screen. 'Hm. Two hundred forty volts.'

'And how about me, Sachs? Am I fully charged?'

She laughed, playfully aimed it at him. Then lifted what he thought was a seductive eyebrow his way. Her phone buzzed and she glanced at the screen, answered. She had a brief conversation and hung up. 'That was Bob Cavanaugh, the Operations vice president. He was the one checking out terrorists connections at the company branches around the region. No evidence of ecoterror groups threatening Algonquin or attacking their power plants. But there was a report of infiltration in one of the company's main Philadelphia substations. White male in his forties got inside. Nobody knows who he was or what he was doing there. No security tape and he got away before the police arrived. This was last week.'

Race, sex and age . . . 'That's our boy. But what did he want?'

'No other intrusions in the company's facilities.'

Was the perp's mission to get information about the grid, the security in substations? Rhyme could only speculate and, accordingly, filed the incident away for the time being.

McDaniel got a phone call. He stared absently at the evidence chart whiteboards, then disconnected. 'T and C's had more chatter about the Justice For terrorist group.'

'What?' Rhyme asked urgently.

'Nothing big. But one thing interesting: they're using code words that've been used in the past for large-scale weapons. 'Paper and supplies' were the ones our algorithms isolated.'

He explained that underground cells often did this. An attack in France was averted recently when chatter among known negatives included the words '*gâteau*,' '*farine*' and '*beurre*.' French for 'cake,' 'flour' and 'butter.' They really referred to a bomb and it's ingredients: explosives and detonator.

'The Mossad's reported that Hezbollah cells sometimes use 'office supplies' or 'party supplies' for missiles or high explosives. Now, we also think that two people in addition to Rahman have been involved. Man and a woman, the computer's telling us.'

Rhyme asked, 'Have you told Fred?'

'Good idea.' McDaniel pulled out his BlackBerry and made a speakerphone call.

'Fred, it's Tucker. You're on speaker at Rhyme's. You had any luck?'

'My CI's on it. Following up on some leads.'

'Following up? Nothing more concrete than that?'

A pause. Dellray said, 'I don't have anything more. Not yet.'

'Well, T and C's found a few things.' He updated the agent on the code words and the fact that a man and woman were likely involved.

Dellray said he'd report that to his contact.

McDaniel asked, 'So he was willing to work within the budget?'

'That's right.'

'I knew he would. These people'll take advantage of you if you let them, Fred. That's the way CIs work.'

'Happens,' Dellray said somberly.

'Stay in touch.' McDaniel disconnected, stretched. 'This damn cloud zone. We're not hoovering up nearly as much as we'd like.'

Hoovering?

Sellitto tapped the stack of personnel files from Algonquin. 'I'll go downtown. Get people started on them. Brother, it's going to be a long night.' The time was now 11:10.

It *was*, Rhyme reflected. For him too. Particularly because there wasn't much for him to do at this point but wait.

Oh, how he hated waiting.

Eyes straying to the skimpy evidence boards, he thought: We're moving too damn slow.

And here we are, trying to find a perp who attacks with the speed of light.

UNSUB PROFILE

- Male.
- 40's.
- Probably white.
- Possibly glasses and cap.
- Possibly with short, blond hair.
- Dark blue overalls, similar to those worn by Algonquin workers.
- Knows electrical systems very well.
- Boot print suggests no physical condition affecting posture or gait.
- Possibly same person who stole 75 feet of similar Bennington cable and 12 split bolts. More attacks in mind? Access to Algonquin warehouse where theft occurred with key.
- Likely he is Algonquin employee or has contact with one.
- Terrorist connection? Relation to Justice For [unknown]? Terror group? Individual named Rahman involved?

Coded references to monetary disbursements, personnel movements and something 'big.'
— Algonquin security breach in Philadelphia might be related.
— SIGINT hits: code word reference to weapons, 'paper and supplies' (guns, explosives?).
— Personnel include man and woman.

- Would have studied SCADA —Supervisory Control and Data Acquisition program. And EMP — energy management programs. Algonquin's is Enertrol. Both Unix-based.
- To create arc flash would probably have been or currently is lineman, troubleman, licensed tradesman, generator construction, master electrician, military.

II

THE PATH OF LEAST RESISTANCE

SIXTEEN HOURS UNTIL EARTH DAY

'Someday, man will harness the rise and fall of the tides, imprison the power of the sun, and release atomic power.'

— THOMAS ALVA EDISON, on the future of producing electricity

209

25

8 a.m.

Low morning light poured into the town-house. Lincoln Rhyme blinked and maneuvered out of the blinding stream as he steered his Storm Arrow wheelchair out of the small elevator that connected his bedroom with the lab below.

Sachs, Mel Cooper and Lon Sellitto had assembled an hour earlier.

Sellitto was on the phone and said, 'Okay, got it.' He crossed through another name. He hung up. Rhyme couldn't tell if he'd changed clothes. Maybe he'd slept in the den or downstairs bedroom. Cooper had been home, at least for a time. And Sachs had slept beside Rhyme — for a portion of the night. She was up at 5:30 a.m. to keep reviewing employee files and narrowing the list of suspects.

'Where are we?' Rhyme now asked.

Sellitto muttered, 'Just talked to McDaniel. They've got six and we've got six.'

'You mean we're down to twelve suspects? Let's — '

'Uhm, no, Linc. We've *eliminated* twelve.'

Sachs said, 'The problem is that a lot of the employees on the list are senior. They didn't put their early careers on their résumés or all of the continuing education computer courses. We have to do a lot of digging to find out if they had the

211

skill to manipulate the grid and rig the device.'

'Where the hell's the DNA?' Rhyme snapped.

'Shouldn't be long,' Cooper said. 'They're expediting it.'

'Expediting,' was Rhyme's sour response. The new tests generally could be done in a day or two, unlike the old RFPL tests, which could take a week. He didn't understand why the results weren't back already.

'And nothing more about Justice For . . . ?'

Sellitto said, 'Our people've been through all their files. McDaniel's too. And Homeland Security and ATF and Interpol. Nothing on them or Rahman. Zip. Fucking creepy, that cloud zone thing. Sounds like something out of a Stephen King novel.'

Rhyme started to call the lab running the DNA analysis but just as he flicked a finger to the touchpad to make a call, the phone buzzed. He lifted an eyebrow and instantly hit ANSWER CALL.

'Kathryn. Morning. You're up early.' It was 5 a.m. in California.

'A bit.'

'Anything more?'

'Logan was spotted again — near where he'd been seen before. Now, I just talked to Arturo Diaz.'

The law enforcer was up early too. A good sign.

'His boss is on the case now. The one I mentioned. Rodolfo Luna.'

Luna was, it turned out, very senior indeed: the second in command of the Mexican

Ministerial Federal Police, the equivalent of the FBI. Though burdened with the overwhelming task of running drug enforcement operations — and rooting out corruption in government agencies themselves — Luna had eagerly taken over the chance to apprehend the Watchmaker, Dance explained. A threat of another killing in Mexico wasn't much news, and hardly required someone as high up as Luna, but he was ambitious and he'd be thinking that his cooperation with the NYPD would pay dividends with their Mexico's tenuous allies to the north.

'He's larger than life. Drives around in his own Lexus SUV, carries two guns . . . a real cowboy sort.'

'But is he honest?'

'Arturo was telling me that he plays the system but, yes, he's honest enough. And he's good. He's a twenty-year veteran and sometimes goes into the field himself to work a case. He even collects evidence on his own.'

Rhyme was impressed. He'd done the same when he was an active captain on the force and working as head of Investigation Resources. He remembered many times when a young technician was startled to turn around at the sound of a voice and see his boss's boss's boss holding a pair of tweezers in gloved hands as he examined a fiber or hair.

'He's made a name for himself cracking down on economic crimes and human trafficking and terrorism. Put some big people behind bars.'

'And he's still alive,' Rhyme said. He wasn't

being flippant. The head of the Mexico City police force had been assassinated not long ago.

'He does have a huge security detail,' Dance explained. Then added, 'He'd like to talk to you.'

'Give me the number.'

Dance did. Slowly. She'd met Rhyme and knew about his disability. He moved his right index finger over the special touchpad and typed the numbers. They appeared on the flat screen in front of him.

She then said that the DEA was continuing its interview with the man who'd delivered a package to Logan. 'He's lying when he says he doesn't know what was inside. I watched the video and gave the agents some advice on how to handle the interrogation. The worker would've thought drugs or cash and taken a fast look. The fact he didn't steal it means that it wasn't those two things. They're about to start with him again.'

Rhyme thanked her.

'Oh, one thing?'

'Yes?'

Dance gave him a URL of a website. This too Rhyme slowly typed, into his browser.

'Go to that site. I thought you'd like to see Rodolfo. I think it's easier to understand someone when you can picture them.'

Rhyme didn't know if that was the case or not. In his line of work, he tended not to see many people at all. The victims were usually dead and the ones who'd killed them were long gone by the time he got involved. Given his druthers he'd rather not see anyone.

After disconnecting, though, he called the site up. It was a Mexican newspaper story in Spanish about a huge drug bust, Rhyme deduced. The officer in charge was Rodolfo Luna. The photo accompanying the story showed a large man surrounded by fellow federal policemen. Some wore black ski masks to hide their identities, others had the grim, vigilant look of people whose jobs turned them into marked men.

Luna was a broad-faced, dark-complexioned man. He wore a military cap but it seemed that he had a shaved head underneath. His olive drab uniform was more military than police and he was decked out with plenty of shiny gingerbread on the chest. He had a bushy black mustache, surrounded by jowl lines. Frowning with an intimidating visage, he was holding a cigarette and pointing toward something to the left of the scene.

Rhyme placed the call to Mexico City, again using the touchpad. He could have used the voice recognition system, but since he'd regained some motion in his right hand he tended to prefer to use the mechanical means.

Placing the call took only a country code's extra effort and soon he was talking to Luna, who had a surprisingly delicate voice with only a slight and completely unrecognizable accent. He would be Mexican, of course, but his vowels seemed tinged with French.

'Ah, ah, Lincoln Rhyme. This is very much a pleasure. I've read about you. And, of course, I have your books. I made sure they were in the course curriculum for my investigators.' A moment's pause. He asked, 'Forgive me. But are you going to update the DNA section — ?'

Rhyme had to laugh. He'd been considering doing exactly that just a few days ago. 'I'm going to. As soon as this case is finished. Inspector . . . are you an inspector?'

'Inspector? I'm sorry,' said the good-natured voice, 'but why does everybody think that officers in other countries than the US are inspectors?'

'The definitive source for law enforcement training and procedures,' Rhyme said. 'Movies and TV.'

A chuckle. 'What would we poor police do without cable? But no. I'm a commander. In my country the army and the police, we're often interchangeable. And you are a captain RET, I see from your book. Does that mean resident expert technician? I was wondering.'

Rhyme laughed aloud. 'No, it means I'm retired.'

'Really? And yet here you are working.'

'Indeed. I appreciate your help with this case. This is a very dangerous man.'

'I'm pleased to be of assistance. Your colleague, Mrs. Dance, she's been very helpful in getting some of our felons extradited back to our own country, when there was considerable pressure not to.'

'Yes, she's good.' He got to the meat of his question: 'I understand you've seen Logan.'

'My assistant, Arturo Diaz, and his team have spotted him twice. Once yesterday in a hotel. And then not long ago nearby — among office buildings on Avenue Bosque de Reforma in the business district. He was taking pictures of the buildings. That aroused suspicion — they are hardly architectural marvels — and a traffic officer recognized Logan's picture. Arturo's men got there quickly. But your Mr. Watchmaker vanished before backup arrived. He's very elusive.'

'That describes him pretty well. Who are the tenants in the offices he was taking pictures of?'

'Dozens of companies. And some small government ministries. Satellite offices. Transport and commerce operations. A bank on the ground floor of one. Would that be significant?'

'He's not in Mexico for a robbery. Our intelligence is that this is a murder he's planning.'

'We're looking into the personnel and the purposes of all the offices right now to see if there might be a likely victim.'

Rhyme knew the delicate game of politics but he had no time for finesse, and he had a feeling Luna didn't either. 'You have to keep your teams out of sight, Commander. You must be much more careful than usual.'

'Yes, of course. This man has the eye, does he?'

'The eye?'

'Like second sight. Kathryn Dance was telling me he's like a cat. He knows when he's in danger.'

No, Rhyme thought; he's just very smart and can anticipate exactly what his opponents are likely to do. Like a master chess player. But he said, 'That's it exactly, Commander.'

Rhyme stared at the picture of Luna on his computer. Dance was right: Conversations seemed to have more to them when you could visualize the person you were speaking with.

'We have a few of those down here too.' Another chuckle. 'In fact, I'm one of them. It's why I'm still alive when so many of my colleagues are not. We will continue the surveillance — subtly. When we capture him, Captain, perhaps you would like to come for the extradition.'

'I don't get out much.'

Another pause. Then a somber, 'Ah, forgive me. I forgot about your injury.'

The one thing, Rhyme reflected, with equal sobriety, that he himself never could. He said, 'No apologies are necessary.'

Luna added, 'Well, we are very — what do you say? — *accessible* here in Mexico City. You would be welcome to come, and very comfortable. You could stay at my house and my wife will cook for you. I have no stairs to trouble you.'

'Perhaps.'

'We have very good food, and I am a collector of mescal and tequilas.'

'In that case a celebration dinner might be in order,' Rhyme said to placate him.

'I will earn your presence by capturing this man . . . and perhaps you could lecture to my officers.'

Now Rhyme laughed to himself. He hadn't realized they'd been negotiating. Rhyme's appearance in Mexico would be a feather in this man's cap; it was one of the reasons he'd been so cooperative. This was probably the way all business — whether it was law enforcement or commerce — worked in Latin America.

'It would be a pleasure.' Rhyme glanced up and saw Thom gesturing to him and pointing to the hallway.

'Commander, I have to go now.'

'I'm grateful you contacted me, Captain. I will be in touch as soon as I learn anything. Even if it seems insignificant, I will absolutely call you.'

26

Thom led trim, energetic Assistant Special Agent in Charge Tucker McDaniel into the lab again. He was accompanied by an associate, spiffy and young and compensating, whose name Rhyme immediately forgot. He was easier to think of as the Kid, capital K, anyway. He blinked once at the quadriplegic and looked away.

The ASAC announced, 'We've eliminated a few more names from the list. But there's something else. We've got a demand letter.'

'Who from?' Lon Sellitto asked from an examination table, where he sat wrinkled as a deflated ball. 'Terrorists?'

'Anonymous and unspecified,' McDaniel said, pronouncing every syllable primly. Rhyme wondered if he disliked the man as much as he thought he did. Partly it was how he'd treated Fred Dellray. Partly it was just his style. And sometimes, of course, you just didn't need a reason.

Cloud zone . . .

The agent continued, 'Sounds mostly like a crank, eco issues, but who knows what it's a front for.'

Unspiffy Sellitto continued, 'We sure it's him?'

After an apparently motiveless attack, it wasn't unusual for a number of people to take credit for it. And threaten to repeat the incident if some demands weren't met, even though they themselves had nothing to do with it.

McDaniel said in a stiff voice, 'He confirmed details of the bus attack. Of *course* we checked that.'

The condescension explained some of Rhyme's distaste.

'Who received it and how?' Rhyme asked.

'Andi Jessen. I'll let her give you the details. I wanted to get it to you as fast as possible.'

At least the fed wasn't fighting a turf war. The dislike eased a bit.

'I've told the mayor, Washington and Homeland Security. We conferenced about it on the way over.'

Though without our presence, Rhyme noted.

The fed opened his briefcase and took out a sheet of paper in a clear plastic envelope. Rhyme nodded to Mel Cooper, who, in gloved hands, removed the sheet and placed it on an examining table. First, he photographed it and an instant later the handwritten text appeared on the computer screens around the room:

To Andi Jessen, CEO, and Algonquin Consolidated Power:

At around 11:30 a.m. yesterday morning there was an arc flash incident at the MH-10 substation on W 57 Street in Manhattan, this happened by securing a Bennington cable and bus bar to a post-breaker line with two split bolts. By shutting down four substations and raising the breaker limit at MH-10 an overload of close to two hundred thousand volts caused the flash.

This incident was entirely your fault and due to your greed and selfishness. This is typical of the industry and it is reprehensable. Enron destroyed the financial lives of people, your company destroys our physical lives and the life of the earth. By exploiting electricity without regard for it's consequences you are destroying our world, you insideously work your way into our lives like a virus, until we are dependent on what is killing us.

People must learn they do not need as much electricity as you tell them they do. You have to show them the way. You are to execute a rolling brownout across the New York City service grid today — reduce levels to fifty per cent of offpeak load for a half hour, starting at 12:30. If you don't do this, at 1 p.m. more people will die.

Rhyme nodded toward the phone and said to Sachs, 'Call Andi Jessen.'

She did and a moment later the woman's voice came through the speaker. 'Detective Sachs? Have you heard?'

'Yes, I'm here with Lincoln Rhyme and some people from the FBI and the NYPD. They've brought the letter.'

Rhyme heard exasperation and anger as the woman said, 'Who's behind it?'

'We don't know,' Sachs said.

'You have to have some idea.'

McDaniel identified himself and said, 'The

investigation's moving along, but we don't have a suspect yet.'

'The man in the uniform at the coffee shop yesterday morning, by the bus stop?'

'We don't have his identity. We're going through the list you gave us. But nobody's a clear suspect yet.'

'Ms. Jessen, this is Detective Sellitto, NYPD. Can you do it?'

'Do what?'

'What he's asking for. You know, reduce the power.'

Rhyme didn't see any problem playing games with the bad guys, if a little negotiation gave extra time to analyze the evidence or run surveillance on a terrorist. But it wasn't his call.

'This is Tucker again, Ms. Jessen. We strongly recommend against negotiating. In the long run, that just encourages them to up their demands.' His eyes were on the large detective who stared right back.

Sellitto persisted, 'It could buy us some breathing room.'

The ASAC was hesitating, perhaps debating the wisdom of not presenting a united front. Still he said, 'I would firmly recommend against it.'

Andi Jessen said, 'It's not even an issue. A citywide fifty percent decrease below offpeak load? It's not like turning a dimmer switch. It would throw off the load patterns throughout the Northeast Interconnection. We'd have dropouts and blackouts in dozens of places. And we've got millions of customers with on-off systems that'd shut down cold with that drop in power. There'd

223

be data dumps and resets'd go to default. You can't just turn them back on again; it would take days of reprogramming, and a lot of data would be lost altogether.

'But worse, *some* of the life-critical infrastructure has battery or generator backup, but not all of it. Hospitals have only so much and some of those systems never work right. People will die as a result of it.'

Well, thought Rhyme, the writer of the letter had one point right: Electricity, and Algonquin and the power companies, have indeed worked their way into our lives. We're dependent on juice.

'There you have it,' said McDaniel. 'It can't be done.'

Sellitto grimaced. Rhyme looked toward Sachs. 'Parker?'

She nodded and scrolled through her Black-Berry to find the number and email of Parker Kincaid in Washington, D.C. He was a former FBI agent and now a private consultant, the best document examiner in the country, in Rhyme's opinion.

'I'll send it now.' She dropped into a chair in front of one of the work-stations, wrote an email, scanned the letter then sent them on their way.

Sellitto snapped open his phone and contacted NYPD Anti-Terror, along with the Emergency Service Unit — the city's version of SWAT — and told them that another attack was planned for around one p.m.

Rhyme turned to the phone. 'Ms. Jessen, Lincoln again. That list you gave Detective Sachs yesterday? The employees?'

'Yes?'

'Can you get us samples of their handwriting?'

'Everybody?'

'As many as you can. As soon as you can.'

'I suppose. We have signed confidentiality statements from just about everybody. Probably health forms, requests, expense accounts.'

Rhyme was somewhat skeptical of signatures as representative of handwriting. Though he was no document examiner, you can't be the head of a forensics unit without developing some knowledge of the subject. He knew that people tended to scrawl their names carelessly (very bad practice, he'd also learned, since a sloppy signature was easier to forge than a precise one). But people wrote memos and took notes in a more legible way, which was more indicative of how they wrote in general. He told this to Jessen, and she responded that she'd put several assistants on the job of finding as many nonsignature examples of handwriting as she could. She wasn't happy but seemed to be softening her position that an Algonquin employee couldn't be involved.

Rhyme turned away from the phone and called, 'Sachs! Is he there? Is Parker there? What's going on?'

She nodded. 'He's at some function or something. I'm getting patched through.'

Kincaid was a single father of two children, Robby and Stephanie, and he carefully balanced his personal and professional lives — his commitment to his kids was why he'd quit the

FBI to become, like Rhyme, a consultant. But Rhyme knew too that for a case like this, Kincaid would get on board instantly and do what he could to help.

The criminalist turned back to the phone. 'Ms. Jessen, could you scan them and send them to . . . ?' An eyebrow raised toward Sachs, who called out Parker Kincaid's email address.

'I've got it,' Jessen said.

'Those are terms in the business, I assume?' Rhyme asked. ''Rolling brownout,' 'shedding load,' 'service grid,' 'offpeak load.''

'That's right.'

'Does that give us any details about him?'

'Not really. They're technical aspects of the business but if he could adjust the computer and rig a flash arc device, then he'd know those too. Anybody in the power industry would know them.'

'How did you get the letter?'

'It was delivered to my townhouse.'

'Is your address public?'

'I'm not listed in the phone book but I suppose it wouldn't be impossible to find me.'

Rhyme persisted, 'How exactly did you receive it?'

'I live in a doorman building, Upper East Side. Somebody rang the back delivery bell in the lobby. The doorman went to go see. When he got back, the letter was at his station. It was marked, *Emergency. Delivery immediately to Andi Jessen.*'

'Is there video security?' Rhyme asked.

'No.'

'Who handled it?'

'The doorman. Just the envelope, though. I had a messenger from the office pick it up. He would have touched it too. And I did, of course.'

McDaniel was about to say something but Rhyme beat him to it. 'The letter was time sensitive, so whoever left it knew you had a doorman. So that it would get to you immediately.'

McDaniel was nodding. Apparently that would have been his comment. The bright-eyed Kid nodded as well, like a bobble-head dog in the back window of a car.

After a moment: 'I guess that's right.' The concern was obvious in her voice. 'So that means he knows about me. Maybe knows a *lot* about me.'

'Do you have a bodyguard?' Sellitto asked.

'Our security director, at work. Bernie Wahl. You met him, Detective Sachs. He's got four armed guards on staff, each shift. But not at home. I never thought . . . '

'We'll get somebody from Patrol stationed outside your apartment,' Sellitto said. As he made the call, McDaniel asked, 'What about family in the area? We should have somebody look out for them.'

Momentary silence from the speaker. Then: 'Why?'

'He might try to use them as leverage.'

'Oh.' Jessen's otherwise rugged voice sounded small at the implication of those close to her being hurt. But she explained, 'My parents are in Florida.'

Sachs asked, 'You have a brother, don't you? Didn't I see his picture on your desk?'

'My brother? We don't stay in touch much. And he doesn't live here either.' Another voice interrupted her. Jessen came back on the line. 'Look, I'm sorry, the governor's calling. He's just heard the news.'

With a click she disconnected.

'So.' Sellitto lifted his palms. His eyes grazed McDaniel but then settled on Rhyme. 'This makes it all pretty fucking easy.'

'Easy?' asked the Kid.

'Yeah.' Sellitto nodded at the digital clock on a nearby flat-screen monitor. 'If we can't negotiate, all we gotta do is find him. In under three hours. Piece of cake.'

27

Mel Cooper and Rhyme were working on the analysis of the letter. Ron Pulaski had arrived too, a few minutes earlier. Lon Sellitto was speeding downtown to coordinate with ESU, in the event they could either ID a suspect or find his possible target.

Tucker McDaniel looked over the demand letter as if it were some type of food he'd never encountered. Rhyme supposed this was because handwriting on a piece of paper didn't fall into cloud zone law enforcement. It was the antithesis of high-tech communications. His computers and sophisticated tracing systems were useless against paper and ink.

Rhyme glanced at the script. He knew from his own training, as well as from working with Parker Kincaid, that handwriting doesn't reveal anything about the personality of the writer, whatever the grocery store check-out stand books and news pundits suggested. Analysis could be illuminating, of course, if you had another, identified sample to compare it with, so you could determine if the writer of the second document was the same as the one who wrote the first. Parker Kincaid would be doing this now, running a preliminary comparison with handwriting samples of known terror suspects — and comparing them with the writing of those Algonquin employees who were on the company list.

Handwriting and content could also suggest right- or left-handedness, level of education, national and regional upbringing, mental and physical illnesses and intoxication or drug-impaired states.

But Rhyme's interest in the note was more basic: the source of the paper, source of the ink, fingerprints and trace embedded in the fibers.

All of which, after Cooper's diligent analysis, added up to a big fat nothing.

The sources for both paper stock and ink were generic — they could have come from one of thousands of stores. Andi Jessen's prints were the only ones on the letter and those on the envelope were from the messenger and the doorman; McDaniel's agents had taken samples of their prints and forwarded them to Rhyme.

Useless, Rhyme reflected bitterly. The only deduction was that the perp was smart. And had a great sense of survival.

But ten minutes later, they had a break-through, of sorts.

Parker Kincaid was on the line from his document examination office in his house in Fairfax, Virginia.

'Lincoln.'

'Parker, what've we got?'

Kincaid said, 'First, the handwriting comparison. The control samples from Algonquin itself were pretty sparse, so I couldn't do the complete analysis I would have liked.'

'I understand that.'

'But I've narrowed it down to twelve employees.'

'Twelve. Excellent.'

'Here are the names. Ready?'

Rhyme glanced at Cooper, who nodded. The tech jotted them down as Kincaid dictated.

'Now, I can give you a few other things about him. First, he's right-handed. Then I picked some characteristics from the language and word choice.'

'Go ahead.'

At Rhyme's nod, Cooper walked to the profile board.

'He's a product of high school and probably some college. And it was an American education. There are a few spelling, grammatical and punctuation mistakes but mostly with more difficult words or constructions. I put those down to the stress of what he's doing. He was probably born here. I can't say for sure that he *isn't* of foreign extraction, but English is his first and, I'm almost positive, only language.'

Cooper wrote this down.

Kincaid continued, 'He's also pretty clever. He doesn't write in the first person and avoids the active voice.'

Rhyme understood. 'He never says anything about himself.'

'Exactly.'

'Suggesting there could be others working with him.'

'It's a possibility. Also, there's some variation on ascenders and descenders. You get that when a subject is upset, emotional. They're writing in anger or distress, and broader strokes tend to be emphasized.'

'Good.' Rhyme nodded at Cooper, who jotted this too onto the profile board.

'Thanks, Parker. We'll get to work.'

They disconnected. 'Twelve.' Rhyme sighed. He looked over the evidence and profile chart, then the names of the suspects. 'Don't we have any way to narrow it down faster?' he asked bitterly, watching his clock advance one more minute toward the approaching deadline.

CRIME SCENE: ALGONQUIN SUBSTATION MANHATTAN- 10, WEST 57TH STREET

- Victim: Luis Martin, assistant manager in music store.
- No friction ridge prints on any surface.
- Shrapnel from molten metal, as a result of the arc flash.
- o-gauge insulated aluminum strand cable.
  — Bennington Electrical Manufacturing, AM-MV-60, rated up to 60,000v.
  — Cut by hand with hacksaw, new blade, broken tooth.
- Two 'split bolts,' ¼

inch holes in them.
  — Untraceable.
- Distinctive tool marks on bolts.
- Brass 'bus' bar, fixed to cable with two ¼-inch bolts.
  — All untraceable.
- Boot prints. —
  — Albertson-Fenwick Model e-20 for electrical work, size 11.
- Metal grating cut to allow access to substation, distinctive tool marks from bolt cutter.
- Access door and frame from basement.
  — DNA obtained.

Sent out for testing.
— Greek food, taramasalata.

- Blond hair, 1 inch long, natural, from someone 50 or under, discovered in coffee shop across the street from substation.
  — Sent out for tox-chem screening.
- Mineral trace: volcanic ash.
  — Not naturally found in New York area.
  — Exhibits, museums, geology schools?
- Algonquin Control Center software accessed by internal codes, not outside hackers.

DEMAND NOTE

- Delivered to Andi Jessen at home.
  — No witnesses.
- Handwritten.
  — Sent to Parker Kincaid for analysis.
- Generic paper and ink.

— Untraceable.
- No friction ridge prints, other than A. Jessen, doorman, messenger.
- No discernible trace discovered in paper.

UNSUB PROFILE

- Male.
- 40's.
- Probably white.
- Possibly glasses and cap.
- Possibly with short, blond hair.
- Dark blue overalls, similar to those worn by Algonquin workers.
- Knows electrical systems very well.
- Boot print suggests no physical condition affecting posture or gait.
- Possibly person who stole 75 feet of similar Bennington cable and 12 split bolts. More attacks in mind? Access to the warehouse where theft occurred with key.

- Likely he is Algonquin employee or has contact with one.
- Terrorist connection? Relation to Justice For [unknown]? Terror group?
- Individual named Rahman involved? Coded references to monetary disbursements, personnel movements and something 'big.'
  — Algonquin security breach in Philadelphia might be related.
  — SIGINT hits: code word reference to weapons, 'paper and supplies' (guns, explosives?).
  — Personnel include man and woman.
- Would have studied SCADA — Supervisory Control and Data Acquisition program. And EMP — energy management programs. Algonquin's is Energy control. Both Unix-based.
- To create arc flash would probably have been or currently is lineman, troubleman, licensed tradesman, generator construction, master electrician, military.
- Profile from Parker Kincaid, re: handwriting:
  — Right handed.
  — High school education at least, probably college.
  — American educated.
  — English first and probably only language.
  — Writes with passive voice, to keep from giving away accomplices.
  — Could match one of 12 Algonquin employees.
  — Emotional, angry, distressed writing the letter.

28

Mel Cooper, in front of his computer, sat up quickly. 'I think I've got one.'

'One *what*?' Rhyme asked acerbically.

'A way to narrow down the list.' Cooper sat up straighter yet and shoved his glasses higher onto the bridge of his nose as he read an email. 'The hair. That we got from the coffee shop across from the substation?'

'No bulb so there's no DNA,' Rhyme pointed out abruptly. He was still irritated that the analysis wasn't ready yet.

'I don't mean that, Lincoln. I've just got the tox-chem screening from the hair itself. Vinblastine and prednisone in significant quantities, and traces of etoposide.'

'Cancer patient,' Rhyme said, leaning his head forward — his version of Cooper's own posture adjustment. 'He's on a chemotherapy regimen.'

'Has to be.'

The young FBI protégé of McDaniel's barked a laugh. 'How do you know that?' Then to his boss: 'That's pretty good.'

'You'd be surprised,' Ron Pulaski said.

Rhyme ignored them both. 'Call Algonquin and see if any of the twelve on the list made health claims for cancer treatment in the past five or six months.'

Sachs called Algonquin. Andi Jessen was on the phone — probably with the governor or mayor — and Sachs was transferred to the company's security chief, Bernard Wahl. Through speakerphone, the deep, African-American-inflected voice reassured them that he'd look into it immediately.

It wasn't quite immediate but it was good enough for Rhyme. Three minutes later Wahl came back on the line.

'There're six cancer patients on the original list — of the forty-two. But only two on the list of the twelve, the one whose handwriting could match the demand letter. One of those is a manager in the energy brokerage department. He was supposedly flying into town from a business trip at the time of the attack.' Wahl gave the relevant information. Mel Cooper took it down and, at a nod from Rhyme, called the airline to check. Transportation Security had become an unwitting partner in general law enforcement because identification requirements were now so stringent that the whereabouts of people flying could be verified easily.

'He checks out.'

'What about the other one?'

'Yessir, well, he's a possibility. Raymond Galt, forty. He's made health claims for leukemia treatment over the past year.'

Rhyme shot a glance to Sachs, who knew instinctively what the look meant. They communicated this way often. She dropped into a chair and began keyboarding.

'His history?' Rhyme said.

Wahl answered, 'Started with a competitor in the Midwest and then joined Algonquin.'

'Competitor?'

He paused. 'Well, not really competitor, like carmakers are. That's just how we refer to other power companies.'

'What does Galt do for you now?'

'He's a troubleman,' Wahl said.

Rhyme was staring at the profile on his computer screen. A troubleman would have enough experience to put together an arc flash weapon like the sort at the substation, according to Charlie Sommers. He asked, 'Mel, take a look at Galt's file. Would he know SCADA and the energy management program?'

Cooper opened the man's personnel file. 'Doesn't say specifically. Just that he's taken a lot of continuing education courses.'

'Mr. Wahl, is Galt married, single?' Rhyme asked the security chief.

'Single. Lives in Manhattan. You want his address, sir?'

'Yes.'

Wahl gave it to them.

'This is Tucker McDaniel. What about whereabouts, Mr. Wahl?' McDaniel asked urgently.

'That's the thing. He called in sick two days ago. Nobody knows where he is.'

'Any chance he's done some traveling lately? Maybe to Hawaii or Oregon? Someplace where there's a volcano?'

'Volcano? Why?'

Struggling to be patient, Rhyme asked, 'Just, has he traveled?'

'According to his time sheets, no. He's taken a

few days' medical — I guess for the cancer treatment — but he hasn't been on a vacation since last year.'

'Could you check with his fellow employees and see if they know about places he goes, friends outside of the company, any groups he's in?'

'Yessir.'

Thinking of the Greek food connection, Rhyme asked, 'And anybody he goes to lunch with regularly.'

'Yessir.'

'Mr. Wahl, what about Galt's next of kin?' McDaniel asked.

Wahl reported that Galt's father was dead but his mother and a sister lived in Missouri. He recited the names, addresses and phone numbers.

Rhyme — and McDaniel too — could think of nothing else to ask the security chief. The criminalist thanked him and they disconnected.

McDaniel instructed his underling to contact the FBI's resident agency in Cape Girardeau, Missouri, and have them start surveillance.

'Probable cause to get a tap?' the Kid asked.

'Doubt it. But push for one. Get a pen register, at least.'

'I'm on it.'

'Rhyme,' Sachs called.

He looked up at the screen, which revealed the fruits of Sachs's frantic keyboarding. The DMV picture showed a pale man, gazing unsmiling at the camera. He was blond, hair trimmed short. About an inch long.

'So,' McDaniel said, 'we've got a suspect. Good job, Lincoln.'

'We'll congratulate ourselves when he's in custody.'

He then squinted at the DMV information, which confirmed the address. 'His place is on the Lower East Side? . . . Not many colleges or museums there. I think the volcanic ash must've come from the place he's going to attack. Maybe the next target. And he'd want a public location, lots of people.'

Lots of victims . . .

A glance at the clock. It was ten-thirty.

'Mel, check again with your geology person at HQ. We need to move!'

'I'm on it.'

McDaniel said, 'I'll call a magistrate for a warrant and get a tac team ready to hit Galt's place.'

Rhyme nodded and called Sellitto, still en route to city hall.

The detective's voice rattled from the speaker, 'I've just blown through about five hundred traffic lights, Linc. I'm thinking if this asshole shuts down the grid and the lights go, we're fucked. No way to — '

Rhyme cut him off. 'Lon, listen, we've got a name. Raymond Galt. He's a troubleman at Algonquin. Not absolute but it looks likely. Mel's going to email you the particulars.'

Cooper, juggling the phone call about the lava search, began typing the relevant information about the suspect into a text.

'I'll get ESU down there now,' Sellitto called.

'We're sending our tac team,' McDaniel said quickly.

Like school kids, Rhyme thought. 'Whoever it is, I don't think matters. But the point is *now*.'

Via speaker conference, the detective and the agent agreed to taskforce the raid and each arranged to assemble and deploy teams.

Rhyme then warned, 'We're getting close to the deadline, so he probably won't be there. If not, then I want only my person running the scene at Galt's apartment.

'No problem,' McDaniel said.

'Me?' Sachs lifted an eyebrow.

'No. If we get any leads to the next attack, I want you there.' He glanced at Pulaski.

'Me?' Same pronoun, different tone.

'Get going, Rookie. And remember — '

'I know,' Pulaski said. 'Those arc things're five thousand degrees Fahrenheit. I'll be careful.'

Rhyme grunted a laugh. 'What I was *going* to say was: Don't fuck up . . . Now, move!'

29

Plenty of metal. Metal everywhere.

Ron Pulaski glanced at his watch. 11 a.m. Two hours until another attack.

Metal . . . wonderfully conductive, and possibly connected to wires that ran to one of the invisible sources of juice in the bowels of the lousy apartment building he was standing in.

Armed with a warrant, the FBI and ESU teams had found — to everyone's disappointment but no one's surprise — that Galt wasn't there. Pulaski then shooed the officers out. And was now surveying the dim apartment, the basement unit in an old decrepit brownstone on the Lower East Side. He and three tactical officers had cleared the place — only the four of them, as Rhyme had ordered, to minimize contamination of the scene.

The team was now outside and Pulaski was examining the small place by himself. And seeing a lot of metal that could be rigged, the way the battery was rigged in the substation — that trap that had nearly killed Amelia.

Also picturing the metal disks on the sidewalk, seeing the scars in the concrete and in the body of poor young Luis Martin. And he recalled something else too, something even more troubling: Amelia Sachs's eyes looking spooked. Which they never did. If this electricity crap could scare her . . .

Last night, after his wife, Jenny, had gone to bed, Ron Pulaski went online to learn what he could about electricity. If you understand something, Lincoln Rhyme had told him, you fear it less. Knowledge is control. Except with electricity, with power, with juice, that wasn't quite the case. The more he learned, the more uneasy he grew. He could grasp the basic concept but he kept coming back to the fact it was so damn invisible. You never knew exactly where it was. Like a poisonous snake in a dark room.

He then shook himself out of these thoughts. Lincoln Rhyme had entrusted the scene to him. So get to work. On the drive here, he'd called in and asked if Rhyme wanted him to hook up via radio and video and walk him through the scene like he sometimes did with Amelia.

Rhyme had said, 'I'm busy, Rookie. If you can't run a scene by now there's no damn hope for you.'

Click.

Which to most people would've been an insult, but it put a big grin on Pulaski's face and he wanted to call his twin brother, a uniform down in the Sixth Precinct, and tell him what had happened. He didn't, of course; he'd save that for when they went out for beers this weekend.

And so, solo, he started the search, pulling on the latex gloves.

Galt's apartment was a cheesy, depressing place, clearly the home of a bachelor who cared zero about his environment. Dark, small, musty.

Food half fresh and half old, some of it *way* old. Clothes piled up. The immediate search, as Rhyme had impressed on him, was not to gather evidence for trial — though he 'better not fuck up the chain of custody cards' — but to find out where Galt might be going to attack again and what, if any, connection he had with Rahman and Justice For . . .

Presently he was searching fast through the unsteady, scabby desk and the battered filing cabinets and boxes for references to motels or hotels, other apartments, friends, vacation houses. A map with a big red X and a note: *Attack here!*

But of course there wasn't anything that obvious. In fact, there was very little helpful at all. No address books, notes, letters. The call log, in and out, on the phone had been wiped and, hitting REDIAL, he heard the electronic voice ask what city and state he needed a number for. Galt had taken his laptop with him and there was no other computer here.

Pulaski found sheets of paper and envelopes similar to what had been used for the demand note. A dozen pens too. He collected these and bagged them.

When he found nothing else helpful he began walking the grid, laying the numbers, photographing. And collecting samples of trace.

He moved as quickly as he could, though, as often, wrestling with the fear, which was always with him. Afraid that he'd get hurt again, which made him timid and want to pull back.

But that in turn led to another fear: that if he

didn't do 100 hundred percent, he wouldn't live up to expectations. He'd disappoint his wife, his brother, Amelia Sachs.

Disappoint Lincoln Rhyme.

But it was so hard to shake the fear.

His hands started to quiver, breath came fast, and he jumped at the sound of a creak.

Calming, remembering his wife's comforting voice, whispering, 'You're okay, you're okay, you're okay . . . '

He started again. He located a back closet and was about to open it. But he noted the metal handle. He was on linoleum but he didn't know if that was safe enough. He was too spooked to open the door even with the CS latex gloves. He picked up a rubber dish mat and used that to grip the knob. He opened the door.

And inside was proof positive that Ray Galt was the perp: a hacksaw with a broken blade. The bolt cutter too. He knew his job here was only to walk the grid and collect evidence but he couldn't help pulling a small magnifier from his pocket and looking over the tool, noting that it had a notch on the blade that could have left the distinctive mark on the grating bar he'd collected at the substation scene near the bus stop. He bagged and tagged them. In another small cabinet he discovered a pair of Albertson-Fenwick boots, size eleven.

His phone trilled, startling him. It was Lincoln Rhyme on caller-ID. Pulaski answered at once. 'Lincoln, I — '

'You find anything about hidey-holes, Rookie? Vehicles he might've rented? Friends he might be staying with? Anything at all about target locations?'

'No, he's kind of sanitized the place. I found the tools and boots, though. It's definitely him.'

'I want *locations. Addresses.*'

'Yessir, I — '

Click.

Pulaski snapped the phone shut and carefully bagged the evidence he'd collected so far. Then he went through the entire apartment twice, including the refrigerator, the freezer, all the closets. Even food cartons large enough to hide something.

Nothing . . .

Now the fear was replaced by frustration. He'd found evidence that Galt was the attacker but nothing else about him. Where he might be, what his target was. Then his eyes settled on the desk again. He was looking at a cheap computer printer. On the top a yellow light was blinking. He approached it. The message was: *Clear jam.*

What had Galt been printing?

The cop carefully opened the lid and peered into the guts of the machine. He could see the tangle of paper.

He could also see a sign that warned, *Danger! Electric Shock Risk! Unplug before clearing jam or servicing!*

Presumably there might be other pages in the queue, something that could be helpful. Maybe even key. But if he unplugged the unit, the memory would dump the remaining pages of the job.

He started to reach in carefully. Then he

pictured the molten bits of metal again.

Five thousand degrees . . .

A glance at his watch.

Shit. Amelia had told him not to go near electricity with anything metallic on. He'd forgotten about it. Goddamn head injury! Why couldn't he think straighter? He pulled the watch off. Put it in his pocket. Jesus our Lord, what good is that going to do? He put the Seiko on the desk, far away from the printer.

One more attempt, but the fear got to him again. He was furious with himself for hesitating.

'Shit,' he muttered, and returned to the kitchen. He found some bulky pink Playtex gloves. He pulled them on and, looking around to make sure no FBI agents or ESU cops were peering in at the ridiculous sight, walked back to the printer.

He opened the evidence collection kit and selected the best tool to clear the jam and get the printer working again: tweezers. They were, of course, metal ones, just the ticket to make a nice, solid connection to any exposed electric wires Galt had rigged inside the printer.

He glanced at his watch, six feet away. Less than an hour and a half until the next attack.

Ron Pulaski leaned forward and eased the tweezers between two very thick wires.

30

News stations were broadcasting Galt's picture, former girlfriends were being interviewed, as was his bowling team and his oncologist. But there were no leads. He'd gone underground.

Mel Cooper's geology expert at Queens CS had found twenty-one exhibits in the New York metropolitan area that might involve volcanic ash, including an artist in Queens who was using lava rock to make sculpture.

Cooper muttered, 'Twenty thousand dollars for something the size of a watermelon. Which is what it looks like, by the way.'

Rhyme nodded absently and listened to McDaniel, now back at Federal Plaza, explain on speakerphone that Galt's mother hadn't heard from him for a few days. But that wasn't unusual. He'd been upset lately because he'd been sick. Rhyme asked, 'You get a Title Three on them?'

The agent explained testily that the magistrate hadn't been persuaded to issue a wiretap on Galt's family members.

'But we've got a pen.' A pen register phone tap wouldn't allow agents to listen to the conversation but would reveal the numbers of anyone who called them and of anybody they'd phoned. Those could then be traced.

Impatient, Rhyme had contacted Pulaski again, who'd responded immediately and with a shaking voice, saying the buzzing phone had scared the 'you know what out of me.'

The young officer told Rhyme he was extracting information from Raymond Galt's computer printer.

'Jesus, Rookie, don't do that yourself.'

'It's okay, I'm standing on a rubber mat.'

'I don't mean that. Only let experts go through a computer. There could be data-wipe programs — '

'No, no, there's no computer. Just the printer. It's jammed and I'm — '

'Nothing about addresses, locations of the next attack?'

'No.'

'Call the minute, call the *second* you find something.'

'I — '

Click.

The joint task force had had little luck in canvassing people on Fifty-seventh Street and in Ray Galt's neighborhood. The perp — no longer an UNSUB — had gone underground. Galt's mobile was 'dead': The battery had been removed so it couldn't be traced, his service provider reported.

Sachs was on her own phone, head down, listening. She thanked the caller and disconnected. 'That was Bernie Wahl again. He said he'd talked to people in Galt's department — New York Emergency Maintenance — and everybody said he was a loner. He didn't socialize. Nobody regularly had lunch with him. He liked the solitude of working on the lines.'

Rhyme nodded at this information. He then told the FBI agent about the sources for the lava. 'We've found twenty-one locations. We're — '

'Twenty-two,' Cooper called, on the phone with the CS woman in Queens. 'Brooklyn art gallery. On Henry Street.'

McDaniel sighed. 'That many?'

'Afraid so.' Then Rhyme said, 'We should let Fred know.'

McDaniel didn't respond.

'Fred Dellray.' *Your* employee, Rhyme added silently. 'He should tell his CI about Galt.'

'Right. Hold on. I'll conference him in.'

There were some clicks and a few heartbeats of silence. Then they heard, ''Lo? This's Dellray.'

'Fred, Tucker here. With Lincoln. On conference. We've got a suspect.'

'Who?'

McDaniel glanced at Rhyme, who explained about Ray Galt. 'We don't have a motive, but it's pointing to him.'

'You found him?'

'No. He's MIA. We've got a team at his apartment.'

'The deadline's still a go?'

McDaniel said, 'We have no reason to think otherwise. You found *anything*, Fred?'

'My CI's got some good leads. I'm waiting to hear.'

'Anything you can share?' the ASAC asked pointedly.

'Not at this point. I'm meeting him at three. He tells me he's got something. I'll call him and give him Galt's name. Maybe that'll speed things up.'

They disconnected. Only a moment later Rhyme's phone rang again. 'Is this Detective Rhyme?' a woman asked.

'Yes. That's me.'

'It's Andi Jessen. Algonquin Consolidated.'

McDaniel identified himself, then: 'Have you heard anything more from him?'

'No, but there's a situation I have to tell you about.' Her husky, urgent voice got Rhyme's full attention.

'Go ahead.'

'Like I told you, we changed the computer codes. So he couldn't repeat what happened yesterday.'

'I remember.'

'And I ordered security around all the substations. Twenty-four/seven. But about fifteen minutes ago a fire started in one of our Uptown substations. One in Harlem.'

'Arson?' Rhyme asked.

'That's right. The guards were in front. It looks like somebody threw a firebomb through the back window. Or something. The fire's been extinguished but it caused a problem. Destroyed the switchgear. That means we can't manually take that substation offline. It's a runaway. There's no way to stop the electricity flowing through the transmission lines without shutting down the entire grid.'

Rhyme sensed she was concerned but he didn't grasp the implications. He asked her to clarify.

She said, 'I think he's done something that's pretty crazy — he cut directly into an area transmission line running from the substation that burned. That's nearly a hundred and fifty thousand volts.'

'How could he do it?' Rhyme asked. 'I thought he used the substation yesterday because it was too dangerous to splice into a main line.'

'True, but, I don't know, maybe he's developed some kind of remote switchgear to let him rig a splice, then activate it later.'

McDaniel asked, 'Any idea where?'

'The line I'm thinking of is about three-quarters of a mile long. It runs under Central and West Harlem to the river.'

'And you absolutely can't shut it down?'

'Not until the switchgear's repaired in the burned substation. That'll take a few hours.'

'And this arc flash could be as bad as yesterday's?' Rhyme asked.

'At least. Yes.'

'Okay, we'll check it out.'

'Detective Rhyme? Tucker?' Her voice was less brittle than earlier.

It was the FBI agent who said, 'Yes?'

'I'm sorry. I think I was being difficult yesterday. But I honestly didn't believe that one of my employees would do this.'

'I understand,' McDaniel said. 'At least we've got the name now. If we're lucky we'll stop him before more people get hurt.'

As they disconnected, Rhyme was shouting, 'Mel, you get that? Uptown? Morningside Heights, Harlem. Museum, sculptor, whatever.

Now, find me a possible target!' Rhyme then called the temporary head of the Crime Scene Unit in Queens — the man with his former job — and asked him to send a team to the substation closed because of the arson. 'And have them bring back whatever they find, stat.'

'Got a possibility!' Cooper called, tilting his head away from the phone. 'Columbia University. One of the biggest lava and igneous rock collections in the country.'

Rhyme turned to Sachs. She nodded. 'I can be there in ten minutes.'

They were both glancing at the digital clock on Rhyme's computer screen.

The time was 11:29.

31

Amelia Sachs was on the Columbia University campus, Morningside Heights, in northern Manhattan.

She had just left the Earth and Environmental Science Department office, where a helpful receptionist had said, 'We don't have a volcano exhibit, as such, but we have hundreds of samples of volcanic ash, lava and other igneous rock. Whenever some undergrads come back from a field project, there's dust all over the place.'

'I'm here, Rhyme,' she said into the mike and told him what she'd learned about the volcanic ash.

He was saying, 'I've been talking to Andi Jessen again. The transmission line goes underground basically all the way from Fifth Avenue to the Hudson. It roughly follows a Hundred and Sixteen Street. But the lava dust means the arc is rigged somewhere near the campus. What's around there, Sachs?'

'Just classrooms, mostly. Administration.'

'The target could be any of them.'

Sachs was looking from right to left. A clear, cool spring day, students meandering or jogging. Sitting on the grass, the library steps. 'I don't see a lot of likely targets, though, Rhyme. The school's old, mostly stone and wood, it looks like. No steel or wires or anything like that. I don't know how he could rig a large trap here to hurt a significant number of people.'

Then Rhyme asked, 'Which way is the wind blowing?'

Sachs considered this. 'To the east and northeast, it looks like.'

'Logically, what would you think? Dust wouldn't blow that far. Maybe a few blocks.'

'I'd think. That'd put him in Morningside Park.'

Rhyme told her, 'I'll call Andi Jessen or somebody at Algonquin and find out where the transmission lines are under the park. And, Sachs?'

'What?'

He hesitated. She guessed — no, *knew* — that he was going to tell her to be careful. But that was an unnecessary comment.

'Nothing,' he said.

And disconnected abruptly.

Amelia Sachs walked out one of the main gates in the direction the wind was blowing. She crossed Amsterdam and headed down a street in Morningside Heights east of the campus, toward beige apartments and dark row houses, solidly built of granite and brick.

When her phone trilled she glanced at caller ID. 'Rhyme. What do you have?'

'I just talked to Andi. She said the transmission line jogs north around a Hundred Seventeenth then runs west under the park.'

'I'm just about there, Rhyme. I don't see . . . oh, no.'

'What, Sachs?'

Ahead of her was Morningside Park, filled with people as the hour approached lunchtime. Children, nannies, businesspeople, Columbia students, musicians . . . hundreds of them, just hanging out, enjoying the beautiful day. People on the sidewalks too. But the number of targets was only part of what dismayed Sachs.

'Rhyme, the whole west side of the park, Morningside Drive?'

'What?'

'They're doing construction. Replacing water mains. They've big iron pipes. God, if he's rigged the line to them . . . '

Rhyme said, 'Then the flash could hit anywhere on the street. Hell, it could even get inside any building, office, dorm, a store nearby . . . or maybe miles away.'

'I've got to find where he connected it, Rhyme.' She slipped her phone into its holster and jogged to the construction site.

32

Sam Vetter had mixed feelings about being in New York.

The sixty-eight-year-old had never been here before. He'd always wanted to make the trip from Scottsdale, where he'd lived for 100 percent of those years, and Ruth had always wanted to see the place, but their vacations found them in California or Hawaii or on cruises to Alaska.

Now, ironically, his first business trip after her death had brought him to New York, all expenses paid.

Happy to be here.

Sad Ruth couldn't be.

He was having lunch, sitting in the elegant, muted Battery Park Hotel dining room, chatting with a few of the other men who were here for the construction finance meeting, sipping a beer.

Businessman talk. Wall Street, team sports. Some individual sports talk too, but only golf. Nobody ever talked about tennis, which was Vetter's game. Sure, Federer, Nadal . . . but tennis wasn't a war story sport. The topic of women didn't much enter into the discussion; these men were all of an age.

Vetter looked around him, through the panoramic windows, and worked on his impression of New York because his secretary and associates back home would want to know what he thought. So far: really busy, really rich, really loud, really gray — even though the sky was cloudless. Like the sun knew that New Yorkers didn't have much use for light.

Mixed feelings . . .

Part of which was a little guilt about enjoying himself. He was going to see *Wicked*, to see if it stacked up to the Phoenix version, and probably *Billy Elliot*, to see if it stacked up to the trailers of the movie. He was going to have dinner in Chinatown with two of the bankers he'd met that morning, one based here and one from Santa Fe.

Maybe there was a hint of infidelity about the whole enjoyment thing.

Of course, Ruth wouldn't've minded.

But still.

Vetter also had to admit he was feeling a little out of his element here. His company did general construction, specializing in the basics: foundations, driveways, platforms, walkways, nothing sexy, but necessary and oh-so profitable. His outfit was good, prompt and ethical . . . in a business where those qualities were not always fully unfurled. But it was small; the other companies that were part of the joint venture were bigger players. They were more savvy about business and regulatory and legislative matters than he was.

The conversation at the lunch table kept slipping from the Diamondbacks and the Mets to collateral, interest rates and high-tech systems that left Vetter confused. He found himself looking out the windows again at a large construction site next to the hotel, some big office building or apartment going up.

As he watched, one worker in particular caught his eye. The man was in a different outfit — dark blue overalls and yellow hard hat — and was carrying a roll of wire or cable over his shoulder. He emerged from a manhole near the back of the job site and stood, looking around, blinking. He pulled out a mobile phone and placed a call. Then he snapped it closed and wandered through the site and, instead of leaving, walked toward the building next door to the construction. He looked at ease, walking with a bounce in his step. Obviously he was enjoying whatever he was doing.

It was all so normal. That guy in the blue could have been Vetter thirty years ago. He could have been any one of Vetter's employees now.

The businessman began to relax. The scene made him feel a lot more at home — watching the guy in the blue uniform and the others in their Carhartt jackets and overalls, carrying tools and supplies, joking with one another. He thought of his own company and the people he worked with, who were like family. The older white guys, quiet and skinny and sunburned all of them, looking like they'd been born mixing concrete, and the newer workers, Latino, who chatted up a storm and worked with more precision and pride.

It told Vetter that maybe New York and the people he was doing this deal with *were* in many ways similar to his world and those who inhabited it.

258

Relax.

Then his eyes followed the man in the blue overalls and yellow hardhat as he disappeared into a building across from the construction site. It was a school. Sam Vetter noted some signs in the window.

POGO STICK MARATHON FUNDRAISER.
MAY 1.
JUMP FOR THE CURE!

CROSS-GENDERED STUDENTS DINNER
MAY 3.
SIGN UP NOW!

THE EARTH SCIENCES DEPARTMENT
PRESENTS
'VOLCANOES: UP CLOSE AND PERSONAL'
APRIL 20 — MAY 15. IT'S FREE
AND IT'S FIERY!
OPEN TO THE PUBLIC.

Okay, he admitted, with a laugh, maybe New York *is* a little different from Scottsdale, after all.

33

Rhyme continued to look over the evidence, trying desperately to find, in the seemingly unrelated bits of metal and plastic and dust that had been collected at the scenes, some connection to spark his imagination and help Sachs figure out where exactly Galt had rigged the deadly cable to the water line running through Morningside Heights and Harlem.

If that's in fact what he'd done.

Spark his imagination . . . Bad choice of word, he decided.

Sachs continued to search Morningside Park, looking for the spliced wire running from the transmission cable to the pipes. He knew she'd be uneasy — there was no way to find the wire except to get close to it, to find where it had been attached to the water pipes. He recalled the tone of her voice, her hollow eyes as she'd described the shrapnel from the arc flash yesterday, peppering Luis Martin's body.

There were dozens of uniformed officers from the closest precinct, clearing Morningside Park and the buildings in the vicinity of the water pipe project. But couldn't the electricity follow a cast-iron pipe anywhere? Couldn't it produce an arc flash in a kitchen a mile away?

In his own kitchen, where Thom was now standing at the sink?

Rhyme glanced at the clock on his computer

screen. If they didn't find the line in sixty minutes they'd have their answer.

Sachs called back. 'Nothing, Rhyme. Maybe I'm wrong. And I was thinking at some point the line has to cross the subway. What if he's rigged it to hit a car? I'll have to search there too.'

'We're still on the horn with Algonquin, trying to narrow it down, Sachs. I'll call you back.' He shouted to Mel Cooper, 'Anything?'

The tech was speaking with a supervisor in the Algonquin control center. Following Andi Jessen's orders, he and his staff were trying to find if there had been any voltage fluctuation in specific parts of the line. This might be possible to detect, since sensors were spaced every few hundred feet to alert them if there were problems with insulation or degradation in the electric transmission line itself. There was a chance they could pinpoint where Galt had tapped into the line to run his deadly cable to the surface.

But from Cooper: 'Nothing. Sorry.'

Rhyme closed his eyes briefly. The headache he'd denied earlier had grown in intensity. He wondered if pain was throbbing elsewhere. There was always that concern with quadriplegia. Without pain, you never know what the rebellious body's up to. A tree falls in the forest, of course it makes a sound, even if nobody's there. But does pain exist if you don't perceive it?

These thoughts left a morbid flavor, Rhyme realized. And he understood too that he'd been having similar ones lately. He wasn't sure why.

261

But he couldn't shake them.

And, even stranger, unlike his jousting with Thom yesterday at this same time of day, he didn't want any scotch. Was nearly repulsed by the idea.

This bothered him more than the headache.

His eyes scanned the evidence charts but they skipped over the words as if they were in a foreign language he'd studied in school and hadn't used for years. Then they settled on the chart again, tracing the flow of juice from power generation to household. In decreasing voltages.

One hundred and thirty-eight thousand volts . . .

Rhyme asked Mel Cooper to call Sommers at Algonquin.

'Special Projects.'

'Charlie Sommers?'

'That's right.'

'This is Lincoln Rhyme. I work with Amelia Sachs.'

'Oh, sure. She mentioned you.' In a soft voice he said, 'I heard it was Ray Galt, one of our people. Is that true?'

'Looks that way. Mr. Sommers — '

'Hey, call me Charlie. I feel like I'm an honorary cop.'

'Okay, Charlie. Are you following what's happening right now?'

'I've got the grid on my laptop screen right here. Andi Jessen — our president — asked me to monitor what's going on.'

'How close are they to fixing the, what's it

called? Switchgear in the substation where they had that fire?'

'Two, three hours. That line's still a runaway. Nothing we can do to shut it down, except turn off the switch to most of New York City. Is there anything I can do to help?'

'Yes. I need to know more about arc flashes. It looks like Galt's spliced into a major line, a transmission level line and hooked his wire to the water main, then — '

'No, no. He wouldn't do that.'

'Why not?'

'It's a ground. It'd short out the instant it touched.'

Rhyme thought for a minute. Then another idea occurred to him. 'What if he was just hinting at tapping into the transmission line? Maybe he actually rigged a smaller trap, someplace else. How much voltage would you need for an arc?'

'A hundred and thirty thousand is your arc flash of mass destruction but, sure, you can have one with a lot less juice. The key is that the voltage exceeds the capacity of the line or terminal that's carrying it. The arc jumps from that to another wire — that's phase to phase. Or to the ground. Phase to ground. With house current, you'll get a spark but not an arc flash. That's at most about two hundred volts. When you're closer to four hundred, yes, a small arc is possible. Over six hundred, it's a strong possibility. But you're not going to see any serious length until you get into medium to high voltages.'

'So a thousand volts could do it?'

'If the conditions were right, sure.'

Rhyme was staring at the map of Manhattan, focusing on where Sachs was at the moment. This news exponentially increased the number of places where Galt might have planned his attack.

'But why're you asking about arcs?' Sommers wondered.

'Because,' Rhyme said absently, 'Galt's going to kill somebody with one in less than an hour.'

'Oh, did Galt's note say something about an arc?'

Rhyme realized that it didn't. 'No.'

'So you're just assuming that's what he'd do.'

Rhyme hated the word 'assumption' and all its derivatives. He was furious with himself, wondering if they'd missed something important. 'Go on, Charlie.'

'An arc is spectacular but it's also one of the least efficient ways to use electricity as a weapon. You can't control it very well, you're never sure where it's going to end up. Look at yesterday morning. I mean, Galt had a whole bus for a target and he missed. You want to know how *I'd* kill somebody with electricity?'

Lincoln Rhyme said quickly, 'Yes, I very much would,' and tilted his head to the phone to listen with complete concentration.

34

Thomas Edison introduced overhead transmission, those ugly towers, in New Jersey in 1883, but the first grid ran beneath the streets of lower Manhattan, starting from his generating station on Pearl Street. He had a grand total of fifty-nine customers.

Some linemen hated the underground grid — the dark grid, as it was sometimes called — but Joey Barzan loved it down here. He'd been with Algonquin Power for only a couple of years but had been in the electrical trades for ten years, since he'd started working at eighteen. He'd worked private construction before joining the company, moving his way up from apprentice to journeyman. He was thinking of going on and becoming a master electrician, and he would someday, but for now he liked working for a big company.

And what bigger outfit could he find than Algonquin Consolidated, one of the top premier energy companies in the country?

A half hour earlier he and his partner had gotten a call from his troubleman that there'd been a curious fluctuation in power in the supply to a subway system near Wall Street. Some of the MTA lines had their own power plants, miniature versions of Algonquin's MOM. But this line, the one rumbling nearby right now, was powered purely by Algonquin juice. The company transmitted 27,500 volts from Queens to substations along the line, which stepped it down and converted it to 625 volts, DC, for the third rails.

A gauge in a nearby MTA substation reported that for a fraction of a second there'd been a dropout. Not enough to cause any disruption of subway service but enough to be concerned — considering the incident at the bus station early yesterday.

And, damn, an Algonquin employee was the one behind it. Ray Galt, a senior troubleman in Queens.

Barzan had seen arc flashes — everyone in the business had at one time or another — and the spectacle of the burning lightning, the explosion, the eerie hum was enough to make him promise himself he'd never take a chance with juice. PPE gloves and boots, insulated hot sticks, no metal on the job. A lot of people thought they could outthink juice.

Well, you can't. And you can't outrun it either.

Now — his partner up top briefly — Barzan was looking for anything that might've caused the current to dip. It was cool here and deserted, but not quiet. Motors hummed and subways shook the ground like earthquakes. Yep, he liked it here, among the cables and the smell of hot insulation, rubber, oil. New York city is a ship, with as much structure under the surface as above. And he knew all the decks as well as he knew his neighborhood in the Bronx.

He couldn't figure out what had caused the

fluctuation. The Algonquin lines all seemed fine. Maybe —

He paused, seeing something that made him curious.

What *is* that? he wondered. Like all linemen, whether up top or in the dark grid, he knew his territory and at the dim end of the tunnel was something that wasn't right: A cable was spliced to one of the breaker panels feeding the subway system for no logical reason. And, instead of running down into the ground, to reach the subway, this went up and ran across the ceiling of the tunnel. It was well spliced — you judged a lineman's skill by how well he joined lines — so it'd been done by a pro. But who? And why?

He stood and started to follow it.

Then gasped in fright. Another Algonquin worker was standing in the tunnel. The man seemed even more surprised to run into somebody. In the dimness Barzan didn't recognize him.

'Hi, there.' Barzan nodded. Neither shook hands. They were wearing PPE gloves, bulky — thick enough for live-wire work provided the rest of the dielectric was adequate.

The other guy blinked and wiped sweat. 'Didn't expect anybody down here.'

'Me either. You hear about the fluctuation?'

'Yeah.' The man said something else but Barzan wasn't really listening. He was wondering what the guy was doing exactly, looking at his laptop — all linemen used these, of course, everything on the grid being computerized. But he wasn't checking voltage levels or switchgear integrity. On the screen was a video image. It looked like the construction site that was pretty much overhead. Like what you'd see from a security camera with good resolution.

And then Barzan glanced at the guy's Algonquin ID badge.

Oh, shit.

Raymond Galt, Senior Technical Service Operator.

Barzan felt his breath hiss from his lungs, recalling the supervisor that morning calling in all the linemen and explaining about Galt and what he'd done.

He now realized that the spliced cable was rigged to create another arc flash!

Be cool, he told himself. It was pretty dark down here and Galt couldn't see his face very well; he might've missed Barzan's reaction. And the company and the police had made the announcement only a little while ago. Maybe Galt had been down here for the past couple of hours and didn't know the cops were looking for him.

'Well, lunchtime. I'm starving.' Barzan started to pat his stomach and then decided that was overacting. 'Better get back upstairs. My partner'll be wondering what I'm doing down here.'

'Hey, take care,' Galt said and turned back to the computer.

Barzan too turned to head toward the closest exit, stifling the urge to flee.

He should have given into it, he quickly realized.

The instant Barzan turned, he was aware of Galt reaching down fast and lifting something from beside him.

Barzan started to run but Galt was even faster and, glancing back, Barzan had only a brief image of a lineman's heavy fiberglass hot stick, swinging in an arc into his hard hat. The blow stunned him and sent him tumbling to the filthy floor.

He was focused on a line carrying 138,000v, six inches from his face, when the stick slammed into him once more.

35

Amelia Sachs was doing what she did best.

Perhaps not best.

But doing what she loved most. What made her feel the most alive.

Driving.

Pushing metal and flesh to its limits, speeding fast along city streets, seemingly impossible routes, considering the dense traffic, human and vehicular. Weaving, skidding. When you drove fast, you didn't ease the vehicle along the course, you didn't dance; you pounded the car through its moves, you slammed and jerked and slugged.

These were called muscle cars for a reason.

The 1970 model year 428 Ford Torino Cobra, heir to the Fairlane, pushed out 405 horsepower with a nifty 447 foot pounds of torque. Sachs had the optional four-speed transmission, of course, which she needed for her heavy foot. The shifter was tough and sticky and if you didn't get it right you'd have adjustments aplenty, which might include flushing gear teeth out of the reservoir. It wasn't like today's forgiving six-speed syncromeshes made for mid-life crisis businessmen with Bluetooths stuck into their ear and dinner reservations on their mind.

The Cobra wheezed, growled, whined; it had many voices.

Sachs tensed. She gave a touch of horn but before the sound waves made it to the lazy driver about to change lanes without looking, she was past him.

Sachs admitted that she missed her most recent car, a Chevy Camaro SS, the one she and her father had worked on together. It had been a victim of the perp in a recent case. But her father had reminded her it wasn't wise to put too much person into your car. It was part of you, but it wasn't you. And it wasn't your child or your best friend. The rods, wheels, the cylinders, the drums, the tricky electronics could turn indifferent or lazy and strand you. They could also betray and kill you, and if you thought the conglomeration of steel and plastic and copper and aluminum cared, you were wrong.

'Amie, a car has only the soul you put into it. No more and no less. And never forget that.'

So, yes, she regretted the loss of her Camaro and always would. But she now drove a fine vehicle that suited her. And that, incongruously, sported as a steering wheel ornament the Camaro's insignia, a present from Pammy, who'd removed it reverently from the Chevy's corpse for Sachs to mount on the Ford.

Pound on the brake for the intersection, heel-toe downshift to rev match, check left, check right, clutch out and rip up through the gears. The speedometer hit fifty. Then kissed sixty, seventy. The blue light on the dashboard, which she hardly even saw, flashed as fast as a pounding heart.

Sachs was presently on the West Side Highway, venerable Route 9A, having made the transition from the Henry Hudson several miles

271

behind her. Heading south, she streaked past familiar sights, the helipad, Hudson River Park, the yacht docks, and the tangled entrance to the Holland Tunnel. Then with the financial center buildings on her right, she hurried on past the massive construction site where the towers had been, aware even at this frantic time that if ever a void could cast a shadow it was here.

A controlled skid angled the Cobra onto Battery Place and Sachs flew east into the warren of lower Manhattan.

She had the tip of the ear bud inserted and a crackling sound interrupted her concentration as she deftly skidded around two cabs, noting the shocked expression below the Sikh's turban.

'Sachs!'

'What, Rhyme?'

'Where are you?'

'Almost there.'

She lost rubber on all four tires as she made a ninety-degree turn and inserted the Ford between curb and car, one needle never below 45, the other never below 5,000.

She was making for Whitehall Street. Near Stone. Rhyme had had a conversation with Charlie Sommers, and it had yielded unexpected results. The Special Projects man had speculated that Galt might try something other than an arc flash; Sommers was betting the man would simply try to electrify a public area with enough voltage to kill passersby. He'd turn them into part of the circuit and run juice through them somehow. It was easier and more efficient, the man had explained, and you didn't need nearly as much voltage.

Rhyme had concluded that the fire in the uptown substation was really a distraction to keep them focused away from Galt's attack on the real location: probably downtown. He'd looked over the list of lava and volcano exhibits, and found the one that was the farthest away from Harlem, where everybody was looking: Amsterdam College. It was a community college specializing in office skills and associate degrees in the business professions. But their liberal arts division was having a show on geologic formations, including an exhibit about volcanoes.

'I'm here, Rhyme.' Sachs skidded the Torino to stop in front of the school, leaving twin tails of black on the gray asphalt. She was out of the car before the tire smoke from the wheel wells had dissipated. The smell ominously reminded her of Algonquin substation MH-10 . . . and though she tried to avoid it, a repeat image of the black-and-red dots in the body of Luis Martin. As she jogged toward the school's entrance, she was, for once, thankful that a jolt of arthritic pain shot through her knees, partially taking her attention off the harsh memories.

'I'm looking the place over, Rhyme. It's big. Bigger than I expected.' Sachs wasn't searching a scene so she'd foregone the video uplink.

'You've got eighteen minutes until the deadline.'

She scanned the six-story community college, from which students, professors and staff were

273

leaving, quickly, uneasiness on their faces. Tucker McDaniel and Lon Sellitto had decided to evacuate the place. They hurried outside, clutching purses and computers and books, and moved away from the building. Almost everyone looked up at one point in their exodus.

Always, in a post 9/11 world, looking up.

Another car arrived, and a woman in a dark suit climbed out. It was a fellow detective, Nancy Simpson. She jogged up to Sachs.

'What do we have, Amelia?'

'Galt's rigged something in the school, we think. We don't know what yet. I'm going inside and looking around. Could you interview them — ' a nod at the evacuees, ' — and see if anybody spotted Galt? You have his picture?'

'On my PDA.'

Sachs nodded and turned to the front of the school once more, uncertain how to proceed, recalling what Sommers had said. She knew where a bomb might be set, where a sniper would position himself. But the threat from electricity could come from anywhere.

She asked Rhyme, 'What exactly did Charlie say Galt might rig?'

'The most efficient way would be to use the victim like a switch. He'd wire door handles or stair railings with the hot source and then the floor with the return. Or the floor might just be a natural ground if it was wet. The circuit's open until the vic touches the handle or railing. Then the current flows through them. It wouldn't take much voltage at all to kill somebody. The other way is to just have somebody touch a live source

274

with two hands. That could send enough voltage through your chest to kill you. But it's not as efficient.'

Efficient . . . sick word to use under the circumstances.

Sirens chirped and barked behind her. Fire, NYPD Emergency Service Unit and medical personnel had begun to arrive.

She waved a greeting to Bo Haumann, the head of ESU, a lean, grizzled former drill sergeant. He nodded back and began deploying his officers to help get the evacuees to safety and to form into tactical response teams, searching for Raymond Galt and any accomplices.

Hesitating, then pushing on the glass portion of the door rather than the metal handle, she walked into the lobby of the school, against the crowd. She wanted to call out to everyone not to touch any metal but was afraid if she did that, she'd start a panic and people would be injured or killed in a crush. Besides, they still had fifteen minutes until the deadline.

Inside there were plenty of metal railings, knobs, stairs and panels on the floor. But no visual clues about whether or not they were connected to a wire somewhere.

'I don't know, Rhyme,' she said uncertainly. 'There's metal, sure. But most of the floor's carpeted or covered with linoleum. That's gotta be a bad conductor.'

Was he just going to start a fire and burn the place down?

Thirteen minutes.

'Keep looking, Sachs.'

She tried Charlie Sommers's noncontact current detector and it gave occasional indications of voltage but nothing higher than house current. And the source wasn't in the places that would be the most likely to kill or injure anyone.

Through the window, a flashing yellow light caught her eye. It was an Algonquin Consolidated truck with a sign on the side, reading *Emergency Maintenance*. She recognized two of the four occupants, Bernie Wahl, the security chief, and Bob Cavanaugh, the Operations VP. They ran up to a cluster of officers, including Nancy Simpson.

It was as she was looking through the plate glass at the three of them that Sachs noticed for the first time what was next door to the school. A construction site for a large high-rise. The crews were doing the iron-work, bolting and welding the girders into place.

Metal. The entire structure was pure metal.

'Rhyme,' she said softly, 'I don't think it's the school at all.'

'What do you mean?'

She explained.

'Steel . . . Sure, Sachs, it makes sense. Try to get the workers down. I'll call Lon and have him coordinate with ESU.'

She pushed out the door and ran toward the trailer that was the general contractor's office for the high-rise construction. She glanced up at the twenty, twenty-five stories of metal that were about to become a live wire, on which easily two hundred workers were perched. And counted only two small elevators to carry them down to safety.

The time was ten minutes until one p.m.

36

'What's going on?' Sam Vetter asked the waiter in the hotel dining room. He and his fellow lunchers were staring out the window at what seemed to be an evacuation of both the school and the construction site between the college and the hotel. Police cars and fire trucks were pulling up.

'It's safe, isn't it?' a patron asked. 'Here, I mean?'

'Oh, yessir, very safe,' the waiter assured.

Vetter knew the man didn't have a clue what was safe and what wasn't. And being in the construction business, Vetter immediately checked out the ratio of emergency exits to occupancy.

One of the businessmen at his table, the man from Santa Fe, asked, 'You hear about that thing yesterday? The explosion at the power station? Maybe it's related to that. They were talking terrorists.'

Vetter had heard a news story or two, but only in passing. 'What happened?'

'Some guy doing something to the grid. You know, the electric company.' The man nodded out the window. 'Maybe he did the same thing at the school. Or the construction site.'

'But not us,' another patron worried. 'Not at the hotel.'

'No, no, not us.' The waiter smiled and vanished. Vetter wondered which exit route he was presently sprinting down.

People were rising and walking to the windows. From here the restaurant offered a good view of the excitement.

Vetter heard: 'Naw, it's not terrorists. It's some disgruntled worker. Like a lineman for the company. They showed his picture on TV.'

Then Sam Vetter had a thought. He asked one of his fellow businessmen, 'You know what he looks like?'

'Just he's in his forties. And is maybe wearing company overalls and a yellow hard hat. The overalls're blue.'

'Oh, my God. I think I saw him. Just a little while ago.'

'*What?*'

'I saw a worker in blue overalls and a yellow hard hat. He had a roll of electrical cable over his shoulder.'

'You better tell the cops.'

Vetter rose. He started away, then paused, reaching into his pocket. He was worried that his new friends might think he was trying to stiff them for the bill. He'd heard that New Yorkers were very suspicious of people and he didn't want his first step into the world of big-city business to be marred by something like that. He peeled off a ten for his sandwich and beer, then remembered where he was and left twenty.

'Sam, don't worry about it! Hurry.'

He tried to remember exactly where the man had climbed from the manhole and where he'd stood to make his phone call before walking into the school. If he could recall the time of the call, more or less, maybe the police could trace it. The cell company could tell them who he'd been talking to.

Vetter hurried down the escalator, two steps at a time, and then ran into the lobby. He spotted a police officer, who was standing near the front desk.

'Officer, excuse me. But I just heard . . . you're looking for somebody who works for the electric company? That man who was behind that explosion yesterday?'

'That's right, sir. Do you know anything about it?'

'I think I might've seen him. I don't know for sure. Maybe it's not him. But I thought I should say something.'

'Hold on.' The man lifted his bulky radio and spoke into it. 'This is Portable Seven Eight Seven Three to Command Post. I think I've got a witness. Might've seen the suspect, K.'

'Roger.' Clattering from the speaker. 'Hold on, K . . . All right, Seven Eight, send him outside. Stone Street. Detective Simpson wants to talk to him, K.'

'Roger. Seven Eight, out.' Turning to Vetter, the cop said, 'Go out the front doors and turn left. There's a detective there, a woman. Nancy Simpson. You can ask for her.'

Hurrying through the lobby, Vetter thought: Maybe if the man is still around they'll capture him before he hurts anybody else.

My first trip to New York, and I might just make the newspapers. A hero.

What would Ruth have said?

37

'Amelia!' Nancy Simpson shouted from the sidewalk. 'I've got a witness. Somebody in the hotel next door.' Sachs hurried up to Simpson, who said, 'He's coming out to see us.'

Sachs, via the microphone, relayed this information to Rhyme.

'Where was Galt seen?' the criminalist asked urgently.

'I don't know yet. We're going to talk to the wit in a second.'

Together, she and Simpson hurried to the entrance of the hotel to meet the wit. Sachs looked skyward at the steel superstructure of the building under construction. Workers were leaving fast. Only a few minutes remained until the deadline.

Then she heard: 'Officer!' A man's voice called from behind her. 'Detective!'

She turned and saw Algonquin vice president Bob Cavanaugh running toward her. The large man was breathing heavily and sweating as he pulled up. His expression said, Sorry, I forgot your name.

'Amelia Sachs.'

'Bob Cavanaugh.'

She nodded.

'I heard that you're clearing the construction site?'

'That's right. We couldn't find anywhere he'd

attack in the school. It's mostly carpet and — '

'But a job site makes no sense,' Cavanaugh said, gesturing frantically toward it.

'Well, I was thinking . . . the girders, the metal.'

'Who's there, Sachs?' Rhyme broke in.

'The operations director of Algonquin. He doesn't think the attack's going to be at the job site.' She asked Cavanaugh, 'Why not?'

'Look!' he said desperately, pointing to a cluster of workers standing nearby.

'What do you mean?'

'Their boots!'

She whispered, 'Personal protective equipment. They'd be insulated.'

If you can't avoid it, protect yourself against it . . .

Some were wearing gloves too and thick jackets.

'Galt would know they're in PPE,' the operations man said. 'He'd have to pump so much juice into the superstructure to hurt anybody that the grid'd shut down in this part of town.'

Rhyme said, 'Well, if it's not the school and it's not the job site, then what's his target? Or did we get it wrong in the first place? Maybe it's not there at all. There was *another* volcano exhibit.'

Then Cavanaugh gripped her arm and gestured behind them. 'The hotel!'

'Jesus,' Sachs muttered, staring at the place. It was one of those minimalist, chic places filled with stark stone, marble, fountains . . . and metal. Lots of metal. Copper doors and steel stairs and flooring.

Nancy Simpson too turned to gaze at the building.

'What?' Rhyme asked urgently into her ear.

'It's the *hotel*, Rhyme. That's what he's attacking.' She grabbed her radio to call ESU's chief. She lifted it to her mouth, as she and Simpson sprinted forward. 'Bo, it's Amelia. He's going after the *hotel*, I'm sure of it. It's not the construction site. Get your people there now! Evacuate it!'

'Roger that, Amelia, I'll — '

But Sachs didn't hear the rest of his transmission. Or rather, whatever he said was lost completely to her as she stared through the hotel's massive windows.

Though it was before the deadline, one o'clock, a half dozen people inside the Battery Park Hotel stopped in their tracks. Their animated faces instantly went blank. They became doll faces, they were caricatures, grotesques. Spittle appeared in the corners of lips taut as ropes. Fingers, feet, chins began quivering.

Onlookers gasped and then screamed in panic at the otherworldly sight — humans turned to creatures out of a sick horror film, zombies. Two or three were caught with their hands on the push panels of revolving doors, jerking and kicking in the confined spaces. One man's rigid leg kicked through the door glass, which severed his femoral artery. Blood sprayed and smoked. Another man, young, student age, was gripping a large brass door to a function room, and bent forward, urinating and shivering. There were two others, their hands on the rails of the low steps to the lobby bar. Frozen, shaking, as the life evaporated from their bodies.

And even outside, Sachs could hear an unearthly moan from deep in the smoldering throat of a woman, caught in midstep.

A heavy-set man plunged forward to save a guest — to push him away from the elevator panel the smoking victim's hand was frozen to. The good Samaritan may have believed he could body-slam the poor guy away from the panel. But he hadn't reckoned on the speed and the power of juice. The instant he contacted the victim he too became part of the circuit. His face twisted into a mass of wrinkles from the pain. Then the expression melted into that of an eerie doll and he began the terrible quivering too.

Blood ran from mouths as teeth cut into tongues and lips. Eyes rolled back into sockets.

A woman with her fingers around a door handle must have made particularly good contact; her back arched at an impossible angle, her unseeing eyes gazing at the ceiling. Her silver hair burst into flames.

Sachs whispered, 'Rhyme . . . Oh, it's bad, real bad. I'll have to call back.' She disconnected without waiting for a response.

Sachs and Simpson turned and began beckoning the ambulances forward. Sachs was horrified by the spectacle of arms and legs convulsing, muscles frozen, muscles quivering, veins rising, spittle and blood evaporating on

284

faces from the blisteringly hot skin.

Cavanaugh called, 'We've got to stop them from trying to get out. They can't touch anything!'

Sachs and Simpson ran to the windows and gestured people back from the doors, but everyone was panicked and continued to stream for the exits, stopping only when they saw the terrible scene.

Cut its head off . . .

She spun to Cavanaugh, crying, 'How can we shut the current off here?'

The Operations VP looked around. 'We don't know what he's rigged it to. Around here we've got subway lines, transmission lines, feeders . . . I'll call Queens. I'll cut everything off in the area. It'll shut down the Stock Exchange but we don't have any choice.' He pulled out his phone. 'But it'll take a few minutes. Tell people in the hotel to stay put. Not to touch anything!'

Sachs ran close to a large sheet of plate glass and gestured people back frantically. Some understood and nodded. But others were panicking. Sachs watched a young woman break free from her friends and race for the emergency exit door, in front of which lay the smoking body of a man who'd tried to exit a moment before. Sachs pounded on the window. 'No!' she cried. The woman looked at Sachs but kept going, arms outstretched.

'No, don't touch it!'

The woman, sobbing, sped onward.

Ten feet from the door . . . Five feet . . .

No other way, the detective decided.

'Nancy, the windows! Take 'em out!' Sachs drew her Glock. Checked the backdrop. And firing high, used six bullets to take out three of the massive windows in the lobby.

At the sound of the gunshots the woman screamed and dove to the ground just before she grabbed the deadly handle.

Nancy Simpson blew out the windows on the other side of the doors.

Both detectives leapt inside. They ordered people not to touch anything metal and began organizing the exodus through the jagged window frames, as smoke, unbelievably vile, filled the lobby.

38

Bob Cavanaugh called, 'Power's off!'

Sachs nodded and directed emergency workers to the victims, then scanned the crowds outside, looking for Galt.

'Detective!'

Amelia Sachs turned. A man in an Algonquin Consolidated uniform was running in her direction. Seeing the dark blue outfit worn by a white male, she thought immediately that it might be Galt. The witness in the hotel had apparently reported that the suspect was nearby and the police had only a bad DMV picture of the attacker to identify him.

But as the man approached it was clear that he was much younger than Galt.

'Detective,' he said breathlessly, 'that officer there said I should talk to you. There's something I thought you should know.' His face screwed up as he caught a whiff of the smoke from inside the hotel.

'Go on.'

'I'm with the power company. Algonquin. Look, my partner, he's in one of our tunnels, underneath us?' Nodding toward Amsterdam College. 'I've been trying to reach him, but he's not responding. Only, the radios're working fine.'

Underground. Where the electric service was.

'I was thinking this Raymond Galt guy, maybe he was down there and Joey ran into him. You know. I'm worried about him.'

Sachs called two patrolmen to join her. They and the Algonquin worker hurried to the school. 'We have an easement through the basement. It's the best way to get down to the tunnel.'

So that's how Galt had picked up the volcanic ash trace, slipping through the exhibit hall of the college. Sachs called Rhyme and explained what had happened. Then added, 'I'm going tactical, Rhyme. He might be in the tunnel. I'll call you when I know something. You found anything else in the evidence that might help?'

'Nothing more, Sachs.'

'I'm going in now.'

She disconnected before he responded and she and the officers followed the worker to the door that led to the basement. The electricity was off in the building, but emergency lights glowed like red and white eyes. The worker started for the door.

'No,' Sachs said. 'You wait here.'

'Okay. You go down two flights and you'll see a red door. It'll say 'Algonquin Consolidated' on it. That'll lead to stairs going down to the service tunnel. Here's the key.' He handed it to her.

'What's your partner's name?'

'Joey. Joey Barzan.'

'And where was he supposed to be?'

'At the bottom of the access stairs, turn left. He was working about a hundred feet, hundred and fifty, away. It'd sort of be under where the hotel is.'

'What's visibility down there?'

'Even with the juice off, there'll be some work

lights on battery power.'

Battery. Great.

'But it's really dark. We always use flashlights.'

'Are there live lines there?'

'Yeah, it's a transmission tunnel. The feeders here are off now, but others're live.'

'Are they exposed?'

He gave a surprised blink. 'They've got a hundred and thirty thousand volts. No, they're not exposed.'

Unless Galt had exposed them.

Sachs hesitated then swept the voltage detector over the door handle, drawing a glance of curiosity from the Algonquin worker. She didn't explain about the invention, but merely gestured everybody back and flung the door open, hand on her weapon's grip. Empty.

Sachs and the two officers started down the murky stairwell — her claustrophobia kicked in immediately but at least here the disgusting smell of burned rubber and skin and hair was less revolting.

Sachs was in the lead, the two patrolmen behind. She was gripping the key firmly but when they got to the red door, giving access to the tunnel, she found it was partially open. They all exchanged glances. She drew her weapon. They did the same and she gestured the patrolmen to move forward slowly behind her, then eased the door open silently with her shoulder.

In the doorway she paused, looked down.

Shit. The stairs leading to the tunnel — about two stories, it seemed — were metal. Unpainted.

Her heart tripping again.

If you can, avoid it.

If you can't do that, protect yourself against it.

If you can't do that, cut its head off.

But none of Charlie Sommers's magic rules applied here.

She was now sweating furiously. She remembered that wet skin was a far better conductor than dry. And hadn't Sommers said something about salty sweat making it even worse?

'You see something, Detective?' A whisper.

'You want me to go?' the second officer asked.

She didn't respond to the questions but whispered back, 'Don't touch anything metal.'

'Sure. Why not?'

'A hundred thousand volts. That's why.'

'Oh. Sure.'

She plunged down the stairs, half expecting to hear a horrific crack and see her vision fill with a blinding burst of spark. Down the first flight of stairs, then down the second one.

The estimate was wrong. The journey was down *three* very steep flights.

As they approached the bottom, they heard rumbling and hums. Loud. It was also twenty degrees hotter down here than outside and the temperature was rising with every step of the descent.

Another level of hell.

The tunnel was bigger than she expected, about six feet across and seven high, but much dimmer. Many of the emergency lighting bulbs here were missing. To the right, she could just make out the end of the tunnel, about fifty feet away. There were no doors Galt could have escaped through, no places to hide. To the left, though, where Joey Barzan was supposed to be, the corridor disappeared in what seemed to be a series of bends.

Sachs motioned the other two to stay behind her as they moved to the first jog in the tunnel. There they stopped. She didn't believe Galt was still here — he would get as far away as he could — but she was worried about traps.

Still, it was a *belief*, not a certainty, that he'd fled. So when she looked around the bend she was crouching and had her Glock ready, though not preceding her, where Galt might knock it aside or grab it.

Nothing.

She looked down at the water covering the concrete floor. Water. Naturally. Plenty of conductive water.

She glanced at the wall of the tunnel, on which were mounted thick black cables.

DANGER !!! HIGH VOLTAGE
CALL ALGONQUIN CONSOLIDATED POWER
BEFORE WORKING

She remembered the Algonquin worker's comment a moment ago about the voltage.

'Clear,' she whispered.

And motioned the officers along behind her, hurrying. She certainly was concerned about the Algonquin worker, Joey Barzan, but more important she hoped to find some clues as to where Galt might've gone.

But could they? These tunnels would go on for miles, she guessed. They would have been a perfect route by which to escape. The floors were dirt and concrete, but no footprints were obvious. The walls were sooty. She could collect trace evidence for days and not come up with a single thing that might yield a clue as to where he'd gone. Maybe —

A scraping sound.

She froze. Where had it come from? Were there side passages where he might be hiding?

One of the officers held up a hand. He pointed at his own eyes and then forward. She nodded, though she thought the military signal wasn't really necessary here.

But whatever makes you comfortable in situations like this.

Though not much was making Sachs comfortable at the moment. Again, the bullets of molten metal zinged, hissing, through her mind's eye.

Still, she couldn't pull back.

Another deep breath.

Another look . . . Again, the stretch of tunnel ahead of them was empty. It was also dimmer than the other. And she saw why: most of the lightbulbs were missing here too, but these had been broken out.

A trap, she sensed.

They had to be directly beneath the hotel, she figured, when they came to a ninety-degree turn to the right.

Again she took a fast look, but this time it was hard to see anything at all because of the greater darkness here.

Then she heard noises again.

One patrolman eased close. 'A voice?'

She nodded.

'Keep low,' she whispered.

They eased around the corner and made their way up the tunnel, crouching.

Then she shivered. It wasn't a voice. It was a moan. A desperate moan. Human.

'Flashlight!' she whispered. As a detective, she wore no utility belt, just weapons and cuffs, and she felt the painful blow as the officer behind her shoved the light into her side.

'Sorry,' he muttered.

'Get down,' she told the patrolmen softly. 'Prone. Be prepared to fire. But only on my command . . . unless he takes me out first.'

They eased to the filthy floor, guns pointed down the tunnel.

She aimed in that direction too. Holding the flashlight out to her side at arm's length so she wouldn't present a vital-zone target, she clicked it on, the blinding beam filling the grim corridor.

No gunshots, no arc flashes.

But Galt had claimed another victim.

About thirty feet away an Algonquin worker lay on his side, duct tape over his mouth, hands tied behind him. He was bleeding from the temple and behind his ear.

'Let's go!'

The other officers rose and the three of them hurried down the tunnel to the man she supposed was Joey Barzan. In the beam she could see it wasn't Galt. The worker was badly injured and bleeding heavily. As one of the

293

patrolmen hurried toward him to stop the hemorrhaging, Barzan began to shake his head frantically and wail beneath the tape.

At first Sachs assumed he was dying and that death tremors were shaking his body. But as she got closer to him she looked at his wide eyes and glanced down, following their path. He was lying not on the bare floor but on a thick piece of what looked like Teflon or plastic.

'Stop!' she shouted to the officer reaching forward to help the man. 'It's a trap!'

The patrolman froze.

She remembered what Sommers had told her about wounds and blood making the body much less resistant to electricity.

Then, without touching the worker, she walked around behind him.

His hands were bound, yes. But not with tape or rope — with bare copper wire. Which had been spliced into one of the lines on the wall. She grabbed Sommers's voltage detector and aimed it at the wire wrapped around Barzan's flesh.

The meter jumped off the scale at 10,000v. Had the patrolman touched him, the juice would have streaked through him, through the officer and into the ground, killing them instantly.

Sachs stepped back and turned up the volume on her radio to call Nancy Simpson and have her find Bob Cavanaugh and tell the operations director he needed to cut the head off another snake.

39

Ron Pulaski had managed to nurse Ray Galt's damaged computer printer back to life. And he was grabbing the hot sheets of paper as they eased into the output tray.

The young officer pored over them desperately, searching for clues as to the man's whereabouts, accomplices, the location of Justice For . . . anything that might move them closer to stopping the attacks.

Detective Cooper sent him a text, explaining that they hadn't successfully stopped Galt at a hotel downtown. They were still searching for the killer in the Wall Street area. Did Pulaski have anything that could help?

'Not yet. Soon, I hope.' He sent the message, turned back to the printouts.

Of the eight remaining pages in the print queue, nothing was immediately relevant to finding and stopping the killer. But Pulaski did learn something that might become helpful: Raymond Galt's motive.

Some of the pages were printouts of postings that Galt had made on blogs and online newsletters. Others were downloads of medical research, some very detailed and written by doctors with good credentials. Some were written by quacks in the language and tone of conspiracy theorists.

One had been written by Galt himself and

posted on a blog about environmental causes of serious disease.

My story is typical of many. I was a lineman and later a troubleman (like a supervisor) for many years working for several power companies in direct contact with lines carrying over one hundred thousand volts. It was the electromagnetic fields created by the transmission lines, that are uninsulated, that led to my leukemia, I am convinced. In addition it has been proven that power lines attract aerosol particles that lead to lung cancer among others, but this is something that the media doesn't talk about.

We need to make all the power companies but more important the public aware of these dangers. Because the companies won't do anything voluntarily, why should they? if the people stopped using electricity by even half we could save thousands of lives a year and make them (the companies) more responsible. In turn they would create safer ways to deliver electricity. And stop destroying the earth too.

People, you need to take matters into your own hands!

— Raymond Galt.

So that was it. He was ill, he felt, because of companies like Algonquin. And he was fighting back in the time he had left. Pulaski knew the man was a killer, yet he couldn't help but feel a bit of sympathy for him. The officer had found liquor bottles, most of them at least half empty, in one of the cupboards. Sleeping pills too. And antidepressants. It was no excuse to kill anybody, suffering from such a terrible disease and the people responsible for your death not caring? Well, Pulaski could understand where the anger came from.

He continued through the printouts, but found only more of the same: rants and medical research. Not even emails whose addresses they might trace to see if they could find Galt's friends and clues to his whereabouts.

He looked through them once more, thinking about Assistant Special Agent in Charge Tucker McDaniel's weird theory about cloud zone communications, looking for code words and secret messages that might be embedded in the text. Then he decided he'd wasted enough time on that and bundled up the printouts. He then spent a few minutes bagging the rest of the evidence, collecting the trace and attaching chain-of-custody cards. Then he laid the numbers and photographed the entire site.

When he was finished, Pulaski looked up the dim hallway to the front door and felt the uneasiness return. He started toward the door, noting again that both the knob and the door itself were metal. What's the problem, he asked himself angrily. You opened it to get inside an hour ago! Leaving on the latex exam gloves, he tentatively reached out and pulled the door open, then, with relief, he stepped outside.

Two NYPD cops and an FBI agent were

nearby. Pulaski nodded a greeting.

'You hear?' the agent asked.

Pulaski paused in the doorway of the apartment, then stepped farther away from the steel door. 'About the attack? Yeah. I heard he got away. I don't know any details.'

'He killed five people. Would've been more but your partner saved a lot of them.'

'Partner?'

'That woman detective. Amelia Sachs. Bunch were injured. Badly burned.'

Pulaski shook his head. 'That's tough. That same way, the arc flash?'

'I don't know. He electrocuted them, though. That's all I heard.'

'Jesus.' Pulaski looked around the street. He'd never noticed how much metal there was on a typical residential block. A creepy feeling was flooding over him, the paranoia. There were metal posts and bars and rods everywhere, it seemed. Fire escapes, vents, pipes going into the ground, those metal sheets covering under-sidewalk elevators. Any one of them could be energized enough to send a charge right through you or to explode in a shower of metal shrapnel.

Killed five people . . .

Third-degree burns.

'You okay there, Officer?'

Pulaski gave a reflexive laugh. 'Yeah.' He wanted to explain his fear, but of course he didn't. 'Any leads to Galt?'

'No. He's gone.'

'Well, I gotta get this back to Lincoln Rhyme.'

'Find anything?'

'Yeah. Galt's definitely the one. But I couldn't find anything about where he is now. Or what he's got planned next.'

The FBI agent asked, 'Who's going to do surveillance?' He nodded at the apartment. 'You want to leave some of your people here?'

The implication being that the feds were perfectly happy to come along for the bust but since Galt wasn't here and probably wouldn't return — he must've heard on the news that they'd identified him — they didn't want to bother leaving their people on guard detail.

'That's not my call,' the young officer said. He radioed Lon Sellitto and told him what he'd found. The lieutenant would arrange for two NYPD officers to remain on site, though hidden, until an official undercover surveillance team could be put together, just in case Galt tried to sneak back.

Pulaski then walked around the corner and into the deserted alleyway behind the building. He popped the trunk and loaded the evidence inside.

He slammed it, and looked around uneasily.

At all the metal, surrounded by metal.

Goddamn it, stop thinking about that! He got into the driver's seat and started to insert the key into the steering column. Then he hesitated. The car had been parked here, up the alley, out of sight of the apartment in case Galt *did* come back. If the perp was still free, was there a chance he'd returned and rigged some kind of trap on Pulaski's car?

No, too far-fetched.

Pulaski grimaced. He started the car and put it in reverse.

His phone buzzed. He glanced at the screen. It was his wife, Jenny. He debated. No, he'd call her later. He slipped the phone away.

Glancing out the window he saw an electrical service panel on the side of a building, three large wires running from it. Shivering at the sight, Pulaski gripped the key and turned it. The starter gave that huge grinding sound when the engine's already running. In panic, believing that he was being electrocuted, the young cop grabbed the door handle and yanked it open. His foot slipped off the brake and landed on the accelerator. The Crown Victoria screeched backward, tires skidding. He slammed on the brake.

But not before there was a sickening thud and a scream and he caught a glimpse of a middle-aged man who'd been crossing the alley, carting a load of groceries. The pedestrian flew into the wall and collapsed on the cobblestones, blood streaming from his head.

40

Amelia Sachs was taking stock of Joey Barzan.

'How you doing?'

'Yeah. I guess.'

She wasn't sure what that meant and didn't think he knew either. She glanced at the EMS medic who was bent over Barzan. They were still in the tunnel beneath the Battery Park Hotel.

'Concussion, lost some blood.' He turned to his patient, who was sitting unsteadily against the wall. 'You'll be all right.'

Bob Cavanaugh had managed to find the source of the juice and shut down the line that Galt had used for the trap. Sachs had confirmed that the electrical supply was dead, using Sommers's current detector, and quickly — really quickly — undone the wire attached to the feeder line.

'What happened?' she asked Barzan.

'It was Ray Galt. I found him down here. He hit me with a hot stick, knocked me out. When I woke up he'd wired me to the line. Jesus. That was sixty-thousand volts, a subway feeder. If you'd touched me, if I'd rolled a few inches to the side . . . Jesus.' Then he blinked. 'I heard the sirens on the street. The smell. What happened?'

'Galt ran some wires into the hotel next door.'

'God, no. Is anybody hurt?'

'There are casualties. I don't know the details yet. Where'd Galt go?'

'I don't know. I was out. If he didn't leave through the college, he had to go that way, through the tunnel.' He cast his eyes to the left. 'There's plenty of access to the subway tunnels and platforms.'

Sachs asked, 'Did he say anything?'

'Not really.'

'Where was he when you saw him?'

'Right there.' He pointed about ten feet away. 'You can see where he rigged the line. There's some kind of box on it. I've never seen that before. And he was watching the construction site and the hotel on his computer. Like it was hooked into a security camera.'

Sachs rose and looked over the cable, the same Bennington brand as at the bus stop yesterday. No sign of the computer or hot stick, which she recalled Sommers telling her about — a fiberglass pole for live-wire work.

Then Barzan said in a soft voice, 'The only reason I'm alive now is that he wanted to use me to kill people, isn't that right? He wanted to stop you from chasing him.'

'That's right.'

'That son of a bitch. And he's one of us. Linemen and troublemen stick together. It's like a brotherhood, you know. We have to be. Juice is so dangerous.' He was furious at the betrayal.

Sachs rolled the man's hands, arms and legs for trace and then nodded to the medics. 'He can go now.' She told Barzan if he thought of anything else to give her a call and handed him a card. A medic radioed his colleague and said that the scene was clear and that they could bring the stretcher down the tunnel to evacuate the worker. Barzan sat back against the tunnel wall and closed his eyes.

Sachs then contacted Nancy Simpson and told her what had happened. 'Get ESU into the Algonquin tunnels for a half mile around. And the subways too.'

'Sure. Amelia. Hold on.' Simpson came back on a moment later. 'They're on their way.'

'What about our witness from the hotel?'

'I'm still checking.'

Sachs's eyes were growing more accustomed to the dark. She squinted. 'I'll get back to you, Nancy. I see something.' She moved through the tunnel in the direction that Barzan indicated Galt probably had fled.

About thirty feet away, sandwiched behind a grating in a small recess, she found a set of Algonquin dark blue overalls, hard hat and gear bag. She'd seen a flash of yellow from the safety hat. Of course, Galt would now know that everybody was looking for him, so he'd stripped off the outfit and hidden it here with the tool bag.

She called back Simpson and asked her to contact Bo Haumann and ESU and let them know that Galt would be in different clothes. Then she donned latex gloves and reached forward to pull the evidence out from behind the metal.

But then she stopped fast.

Now, you have to remember that even if you think you're avoiding it, you could still be in danger.

303

Sommers's words resounded in her head. She took the current detector and swept it over the tools.

The needle jumped: 603 volts.

Gasping, Sachs closed her eyes and felt the strength drain from her legs. She looked more carefully and saw a wire. It ran from the grating underground to the conduit behind which the evidence was stashed. She'd have to touch the pipe to pull the items out. The power was technically off in the tunnel but maybe this was a case of islanding or backfeed, if she remembered what Sommers had told her.

How much amperage did it take to kill you?

Less than one tenth of one amp.

She returned to Barzan, who gazed at her blearily, his bandaged head still resting against the tunnel wall.

'I need some help. I need to collect some evidence, but there's still power in one of the lines.'

'What line?'

'Up there. Six hundred volts. He's wired it to some conduit.'

'Six hundred? It's DC, backfeed from the third rail supply on the subway. Look, you can use my hot stick. See it there?' He pointed. 'And my gloves. The best thing is to run another wire to a ground from the conduit. You know how to do that?'

'No.'

'I'm in no shape to help you. Sorry.'

'That's okay. Tell me how to use the stick.' She pulled on Barzan's gloves over the latex ones and took the tool, which ended with a clawlike attachment on the end, covered in rubber. It gave her some, but not a lot of, confidence.

'Stand on the rubber mat and pull whatever you saw out one by one. You'll be fine . . . To be safe do it one-handed. Your right hand.'

Farthest from the heart . . .

Which thudded furiously as she walked up to the recess, lay the Teflon sheets down and began slowly to collect the evidence.

Pictured yet again young Luis Martin's torn body, the shivering creatures dying in the hotel lobby.

Hated being distracted.

Hated being up against an enemy she couldn't see.

Holding her breath — though she didn't know why — she pulled out the overalls and hard hat. Then the gear bag. *R. Galt* was written in sloppy marker on the red canvas.

Exhaling long.

Finally she assembled and bagged the evidence.

A crime scene technician from Queens had arrived with CS equipment suitcases in hand. Even though the scene was now vastly contaminated, Sachs dressed in the blue Tyvek jumpsuit and continued to run the scene like any other. She laid out the numbers, took pictures and walked the grid. Using Sommers's detector, she double-checked the lines and then quickly unbolted the Bennington cable and a square black plastic box that connected it to the main feeder line. Galt's wire ran to the steel girder of

305

the hotel, which would carry the juice to energize the metal fixtures of the door handles, revolving doors and stair rails. She bagged everything she'd found, then took samples from where Galt had stood to mount the cable and where he'd attacked Joey Barzan.

She looked again for the hot stick Galt had hit his fellow worker with but couldn't find it. Nor was there any sign of where he'd cut into any video feeds to use the school's or construction site's security cameras to look over the site of the attack, as Barzan had told her.

After she'd finished bagging the evidence, she called Rhyme and gave him an update.

'Get back here as soon as you can, Sachs. We need that evidence.'

'What'd Ron find?'

'According to Lon, nothing spectacular. Hm. Wonder what's going on. He should be here by now.' His impatience was obvious.

'It'll just be a few minutes. I want to find that witness. Somebody having lunch apparently got a good look at Galt. I'm hoping he can tell us something specific.'

They disconnected and Sachs returned to the surface, and found Nancy Simpson. The detective was in the hotel lobby, which was now largely empty. Sachs started for one of the revolving doors not sealed off with police tape but stopped. She turned and climbed through the shattered window.

Simpson's hollow face revealed that she was still shaken. 'Just talked to Bo. No idea where Galt got out of the system. With the power off he might've just walked down the subway tracks to Canal Street, got lost in Chinatown. Nobody knows.'

Sachs looked at where blood and scorch marks stained the marble floors, outlining where the victims had been.

'Final count?'

'Five dead, looks like eleven injured, all seriously. Burns are mostly third degree.'

'You canvass?'

'Yep. But nobody saw anything. Most of the guests who were here just vanished. They weren't even checking out.' Simpson added that they had just fled, with spouses, children, associates and suitcases in tow. The hotel staff had done nothing to stop them. Half the employees had left too, it seemed.

'What about our witness?'

'I'm trying to track him down. I found some people he was having lunch with. They said he saw Galt. That's why I'd really love to find him.'

'Who is he?'

'His name's Sam Vetter. Was here from Scottsdale on business. His first trip to the city.'

A patrolman walked past. 'Excuse me, I heard you mention the name Vetter?'

'Right. Sam Vetter.'

'He came up to me in the lobby. Said he had some information about Galt.'

'Where is he?'

'Oh, you didn't know?' the officer said. 'He was one of the victims. Was in the revolving door. He's dead.'

41

Amelia Sachs returned with the evidence.

Rhyme's eyes narrowed as she walked quickly into the townhouse. In her wake was a repulsive odor. Burned hair, burned rubber, burned flesh. Some crips believed they'd have an increased sense of smell because of their disability; Rhyme wasn't sure if this was true but in any case he had no problem detecting the stench.

He looked over the evidence Sachs and a Crime Scene tech from Queens had carted in. The hungry itch to tackle the mysteries the clues might reveal filled him. As Sachs and Cooper laid it out, Rhyme asked, 'ESU find where Galt got out of the tunnel?'

'No sign of him. None at all.' She looked around. 'Where's Ron?'

Rhyme said that the rookie still wasn't back. 'I called, left a message. I haven't heard from him. The last he said he'd found Galt's motive, but didn't go into it. What, Sachs?'

He'd caught her gazing out the window, her face still.

'I got it wrong, Rhyme. I wasted time evacuating the construction site and missed the real target completely.'

She explained that it had been Bob Cavanaugh who figured out that the target was the hotel. She was sighing. 'If I'd thought it out better, I might've saved them.' She walked to a whiteboard and with a firm hand wrote, 'Battery Park Hotel,' at the top and just below that the names of the deceased victims, apparently a husband and wife and a businessman from Scottsdale, Arizona, a waiter and an advertising executive from Germany.

'It could've been a lot more. I heard you took out the windows and got people out that way.'

Her response was a shrug.

Rhyme felt that 'what if' had no part in the policing business. You did the best you could, you play the odds.

Though he too was feeling what Sachs was, angry that, despite their race against the clock and their correct deduction about the general locale where the attack would be, not only had they failed to save victims but they'd missed their chance to collar Galt.

But he wasn't as upset as she was. However many people were at fault and whatever their degree of blame, Sachs was always hardest on herself. He could have told her that undoubtedly more people would have died if she hadn't been there, and that Galt now knew that he'd been identified and nearly outthought. He might very well stop the attacks altogether and give up. But saying this to her would smack of condescension and, had it been directed at Rhyme himself, he wouldn't even have listened.

Besides, the stark truth was, yes, the perp got away because they'd got it wrong.

Sachs returned to assembling the evidence on the examining table.

Her face was paler than normal; she was a

minimalist when it came to makeup. And Rhyme could see that this crime scene too had affected her. The bus incident had spooked her — and some of that was still in her eyes, a patina of ill ease. But this was a different horror, the residue of the image of the people in the hotel dying in such terrible ways. 'They were . . . it was like they were dancing while they died, Rhyme,' she'd described it to him.

She'd collected Galt's Algonquin overalls and hardhat, the gear bag containing tools and supplies, another of the heavy-duty cables, identical to the one Galt had used for the arc flash yesterday morning. There were also several bags of trace. Another item, too, in a thick plastic bag: connecting the cable to the main line involved something different from what Galt had used at the Algonquin substation on Fifty-seventh Street, she explained. He'd used split bolts but between the two wires was a plastic box, about the size of a hard-cover book.

Cooper scanned it for explosives and then opened it up. 'Looks home-made but I have no idea what it is.'

Sachs said, 'Let's talk to Charlie Sommers.'

In five minutes they were on a conference call with the inventor from Algonquin. Sachs described the attack at the hotel.

'I didn't know it was that bad,' he said in a soft voice.

Rhyme said, 'Appreciate your advice earlier — how he'd be rigging the current like he did, instead of the arc.'

'Didn't help much, though,' the man muttered.

'Can you look over this box we recovered?' Sachs asked. 'It was connecting the Algonquin line to the one he ran to the hotel.'

'Of course.'

Cooper gave Sommers a URL for a secure streaming video and then turned the high-def camera over the guts of the box.

'Got it. Let me take a look . . . Go back to the other side . . . Interesting. Not commercial. Made by hand.'

'That's what it looks like to us,' Rhyme said.

'I've never seen anything like it. Not this compact. It's switchgear. That's our term for the switches in substations and on transmission systems.'

'Just shuts a circuit on and off?'

'Yep. Like a wall switch, except I'd say it could handle a hundred thousand volts easy. A built-in fan, a solenoid and a receiver. Remote control.'

'So he hooked the wires together without transferring any current, then when he was safely away he hit the switch. Andi Jessen said he might try something like that.'

'Did she? Hm. Interesting.' Then Sommers added, 'But I don't think the issue is safety. Any troubleman knows how to splice wires safely. He did this for another reason.'

Rhyme understood. 'To time the attack — he'd turn on the juice the moment when most victims were exposed.'

'I think that's it, yes.'

Sachs added, 'One of the workers who saw

311

him said he was watching the scene on his laptop — it was probably hooked into a nearby security camera. I couldn't find where he cut in, though.'

'Maybe that's why he hit the switch a few minutes early,' Rhyme said. 'He had the chance to target more people. And he knew Algonquin wasn't going to give in to his demand at that point anyway.'

Sommers sounded impressed when he said, 'He's talented. That's a clever piece of work. The switch seems simple but it was a lot harder to make than you'd think. There's a lot of electromagnetic power in voltage lines that big and he'd have to shield the electronics. He's smart. Which, I guess, is bad news.'

'Where could he get the parts, the solenoid, the receiver, the fan?'

'In any one of a hundred electrical supply stores in the area, two hundred . . . Any serial numbers?'

Cooper examined them carefully. 'No. Model numbers, that's all.'

'Then, you're out of luck.'

Rhyme and Sachs thanked Sommers and they hung up.

Sachs and Cooper examined Galt's gear kit and the Algonquin overalls and hard hat. No notes or maps, nothing to indicate where he might be hiding out or what his next target might be. That didn't surprise them, since Galt had intentionally ditched the items and would know they'd been discovered.

Detective Gretchen Sahloff, from Crime Scene HQ, had collected samplars of Galt's fingerprints from his office and a thumbprint on file from Algonquin Human Resources. Cooper now examined all of the items collected and compared them against these prints. He found only Galt's on the collected evidence. Rhyme was frustrated at this. Had they found others, that could have led them to a friend of Galt's or an accomplice or someone in the Justice For cell, if it was involved in the attacks.

Also Rhyme noted that the hacksaw and bolt cutter weren't in the bag, but this didn't surprise him. The kit was for smaller hand tools.

The wrench, however, *was*, and it had tool marks that were identical to those on the bolts at the substation on Fifty-seventh Street.

The crime scene team from the arson incident at the substation in Harlem arrived. They had very little. Galt had used a simple Molotov cocktail — a glass bottle filled with gasoline and a cloth rag stuck into the top. It had been thrown against the barred but open window and the burning gas had flowed inside, igniting rubber and plastic insulation. The bottle was for wine — there were no threads for a screw-top cap — and was manufactured by a glassworks that sold to dozens of wineries, which in turn sold to thousands of retail outlets. The label had been soaked off. Untraceable.

The gasoline was BP, regular grade, and the cloth was from a T-shirt. None of these items could be traced to a specific location, though a rat-tail file was found in Galt's gear bag with glass dust that could be associated with the bottle — from scoring it, so that it would be certain to break.

There was no security camera outside or in the substation.

A knock on the door sounded.

Thom went to open it and a moment later Ron Pulaski entered, with the evidence he'd gathered at Galt's apartment, several milk crates full of items, the bolt cutter and the hacksaw, along with a pair of boots.

Well, at last, Rhyme thought, irritated at the delay, though pleased at the arrival of the evidence.

Unsmiling, Pulaski looked at no one as he stacked up the evidence on the table. Then Rhyme noticed that his hand was shaking.

'Rookie, you all right?'

The young man, his back to them all, paused, looking down, hands flat on the table in front of him. Then he turned. Took a breath. 'There was an accident at the scene. I hit somebody with my car. Somebody innocent, just happened to be there. He's in a coma. They think he might die.'

42

The young officer told them what had happened.

'I just wasn't thinking. Or maybe I was thinking too much. I got spooked. I was worried Galt might've gotten to my car and rigged a trap or something.'

'How could he have done that?' Rhyme asked.

'I don't *know*,' Pulaski said emotionally. 'I didn't remember I'd already started the engine. I turned the key again and the noise . . . well, it scared me. I guess my foot slipped off the brake.'

'Who was he?'

'Just some guy, Palmer's his name. Works nights at a trucking company. He was taking a shortcut back from a grocery store . . . I hit him pretty hard.'

Rhyme thought about the head injury that Pulaski himself had suffered. He'd be troubled by the fact that his carelessness had now seriously injured someone else.

'Internal Affairs's going to talk to me. They said the city'll probably be sued. They told me to contact the PBA about a lawyer. I . . . ' Words failed him. Finally he repeated manically, 'My foot slipped off the brake. I didn't even remember putting the car in gear or starting it.'

'Well, Rookie, blame yourself or not, but the point is this Palmer's not a player in the Galt case, is he?'

'No.'

'So deal with it after hours,' Rhyme said firmly.

'Yessir, sure. I will. I'm sorry.'

'So, what'd you find?'

He explained about the sheets he'd managed to tease out of Galt's printer. Rhyme complimented him on that — it was a good save — but the officer didn't even seem to hear. Pulaski continued, explaining about Galt's cancer and the high-tension wires.

'Revenge,' Rhyme mused. 'The old standby. An okay motive. Not one of my favorites. Yours?' He glanced at Sachs.

'No,' she replied seriously. 'Greed and lust're mine. Revenge's usually an antisocial personality disorder thing. But this could be more than revenge, Rhyme. From the demand note he's on a crusade. Saving the people from the evil energy company. A fanatic. And I still think we may find a terrorist connection.'

Apart from the motive, though, and the evidence tying Galt to the crime scenes, Pulaski had found nothing that suggested his present whereabouts or where he might be going to attack next. This was disappointing but didn't surprise Rhyme; the attacks were obviously well planned and Galt was smart. He'd have known from the start that his identity might be learned, and he would have made arrangements for a hideout.

Rhyme scrolled through numbers and placed a call.

'Andi Jessen's office,' came the weary voice

through the speaker-phone.

Rhyme identified himself and a moment later was talking to the CEO of the power company. She said, 'I just talked to Gary Noble and Agent McDaniel. There're five people dead, I heard. And more in the hospital.'

'That's right.'

'I'm so sorry. How awful. I've been looking at Ray Galt's employee file. His picture's up in front of me right now. He doesn't look like the kind of person who'd do something like this.'

They never do.

Rhyme explained, 'He's convinced he got cancer from working on the electric lines.'

'Is *that* why he's doing this?'

'It seems. He's crusading. He thinks working on high-power lines is a big risk.'

She sighed. 'We've got a half dozen suits pending on the issue. High-voltage cables give off EMFs — electromagnetic fields. Insulation and walls shield the electrical field, but not the magnetic. There're arguments that that can cause leukemia.'

Reading over the pages from Galt's printer, now scanned and up on the monitor in front of him, Rhyme said, 'He also talks about the lines attracting airborne particles that can cause lung cancer.'

'None of that's ever been proven. I dispute it. I dispute the leukemia thing too.'

'Well, Galt doesn't.'

'What does he want us to do?'

'I guess we won't know that until we get

another demand note or he contacts you some other way.'

'I'll make a statement — ask him to give himself up.'

'It couldn't hurt.' Though Rhyme was thinking that Galt had come too far simply to make a point and surrender. He had more retribution in mind, they had to assume.

Seventy-five feet of cable and a dozen split bolts. So far he'd used about thirty feet of the stolen wire.

As he disconnected, Rhyme noticed that Pulaski was on the phone, head down. The officer looked up and met his boss's eyes. He ended his call quickly — and guiltily — and walked over to the evidence table. He started to reach for one of the tools he'd collected and then froze, realizing he didn't have latex gloves on. He pulled on a pair, cleaned the rubber fingers and palm with the dog hair roller. Then he picked up the bolt cutter.

A comparison of the tool marks showed that both it and the hacksaw were the same tools used to create the trap at the bus stop, and the boots were the same brand and size too.

But that just confirmed what they already knew: that Raymond Galt was the perp.

They took a look at the paper and the pens the young officer had collected from Galt's apartment. They could determine no source, but the paper and the ink in the Bics were virtually the same as had been used in the demand note.

Cooper was reading the results from the gas

chromatograph/mass spectrometer. He said, 'Got some trace here. Found it in two separate locations: the lace of the boots and the handle of the bolt cutter in Galt's apartment. And then the sleeve of the worker who'd been attacked by Galt in the tunnel downtown, Joey Barzan.'

'And?' Rhyme asked.

'It's a kerosene derivative, with minute amounts of phenol and dinonylnaphthylsulfonic acid added.'

Rhyme said, 'Jet fuel. The phenol is an antigumming substance and the acid is an antistatic agent.'

'But there's more,' Cooper continued. 'Something odd, a form of natural gas. Liquefied, but stable across a wide range of temperatures. And . . . get this, traces of biodiesel.'

'Check the fuel database, Mel.'

A moment later the tech said, 'Got it. It's an alternative aviation fuel that's being tested now. Mostly in military fighters. It's cleaner and it cuts down on fossil-fuel use. They say it'll be the wave of the future.'

'Alternative energy,' Rhyme mused, wondering how this piece of the puzzle fit. But one thing he knew. 'Sachs, call Homeland Security and the Department of Defense. FAA too. Tell them our boy may have been checking out fuel depots or air bases.'

An arc flash was bad enough. Combined with jet propellant, Rhyme couldn't even imagine the devastation.

CRIME SCENE:
BATTERY PARK HOTEL AND SURROUNDINGS

- Victims (deceased):
  — Linda Kepler, Oklahoma City, tourist.
  — Morris Kepler, Oklahoma City, tourist.
  — Samuel Vetter, Scottsdale, businessman.
  — Ali Mamoud, New York City, waiter.
  — Gerhart Schiller, Frankfurt, Germany, advertising executive.
- Remote control switch for turning on current.
  — Components not traceable.
- Bennington cable and split bolts, identical to first attack.
- Galt's Algonquin uniform, hard hat and gear bag with his friction ridge prints, no others.
  — Wrench with tool marks that can be associated with tool marks on bolts at first crime scene.
  — Rat-tail file with glass dust that can be associated with glass from bottle found at substation scene in Harlem.
  — Probably working alone.
- Trace from Algonquin worker Joey Barzan, assault victim of Galt.
  — Jet fuel and alternative jet fuel.
  — Attack at military base?

CRIME SCENE:
GALT'S APARTMENT, 227 SUFFOLK ST., LOWER EAST SIDE

- Bic SoftFeel fine-point pens, blue ink, associated with ink used in demand letter.
- Generic 8½ × 11" white computer paper, associated with demand letter.
- Generic No. 10 size envelope, associated with envelope containing demand letter.
- Bolt cutter, hacksaw with tool marks matching those at initial scene.
- Computer printouts:
  — Articles about medical research on cancer linked to high-power electric lines.
  — Blog postings by Galt re: same.
- Albertson-Fenwick Model E-20 boots for electrical work, size 11, with treads the same as prints at initial scene.
- Additional traces of jet fuel and alternative jet fuel.
  — Attack at military base?
- No obvious leads as to where he might be hiding, or location of future attacks.

CRIME SCENE:
ALGONQUIN SUBSTATION MH-7, E.
119TH STREET, HARLEM

- Molotov cocktail: 750-ml wine bottle, no source.
- BP gas used as accelerant.
- Cotton cloth strips, probably white T-shirt, used as fuse, no source determined.

PROFILE

- Identified as Raymond Galt, 40, single, living in Manhattan, 227 Suffolk St.
- Terrorist connection? Relation to Justice For [unknown]? Terror group? Individual named Rahman involved?

References to monetary disbursements, personnel movements and something 'big.'
— Algonquin security breach in Philadelphia might be related.
— SIGINT hits: code word reference to weapons, 'paper and supplies' (guns, explosives?).
— Personnel include man and woman.
— Galt's involvement unknown.

- Cancer patient; presence of vinblastine and prednisone in significant quantities, traces of etoposide. Leukemia.

43

Lincoln Rhyme's main phone trilled.

The caller ID registered a number he'd been hoping to see, though not at this particular moment. Still he immediately clicked ANSWER.

'Kathryn, what do you have?'

No time for pleasantries at the moment. But Dance would understand. She was the same way when it came to a case.

'The DEA guys in Mexico City got the worker to talk — the man who gave the package to Logan just after he slipped into the country. He did take a look at what was inside, like we thought. I'm not sure it's helpful but here it is: a dark blue booklet with lettering on it. He didn't remember the words. Two letter C's, he thought. A logo of a company maybe. Then a sheet of paper that had a capital letter I followed by six lines. Like blanks to be filled in.'

'He have any idea what they were?'

'No . . . Then a slip of paper containing some numbers. All he remembers is five hundred seventy and three hundred seventy-nine.'

'*The Da Vinci Code*,' Rhyme said, discouraged.

'Exactly. I like puzzles but not on the job.'

'True.'

I – – – – – –

Fill in the blanks.

And: *Five hundred seventy and three hundred seventy-nine* . . .

Dance added, 'Then he found something else. A circuit board. A small one.'

'For a computer?'

'He didn't know. He was disappointed. He said he would have stolen it if it'd been something he could sell more easily.'

'And he'd be dead now if he did.'

'I think he's relieved to be in jail. For that very reason . . . I've had a talk with Rodolfo. He'd like you to call.'

'Of course.'

Rhyme thanked Dance and disconnected. He then called the Commander Rodolfo Luna, in Mexico City.

'Ah, Captain RET Rhyme, yes. I just spoke to Agent Dance. The mystery . . . the numbers.'

'An address?'

'Perhaps it is. But . . . ' His fading voice meant, of course, that in a city of 8 million people one would need more than a few numbers to find a specific location.

'And maybe related, maybe not.'

'Two separate meanings.'

'Yes,' Rhyme said. 'Do they have any significance at all regarding the places he's been spotted?'

'No.'

'And those buildings? The tenants?'

'Arturo Diaz and his officers are speaking with them now, explaining the situation. The ones there who are legitimate businesspeople are mystified because they cannot believe they are in danger. The ones who are themselves criminals are mystified because they are better armed than my troops and believe no one would dare attack them.'

Five hundred seventy and three hundred seventy-nine . . .

Phone numbers? Coordinates? Parts of an address?

Luna continued, 'We've reconstructed the route the truck took from the airport to the capital. They were pulled over once. But you may have heard about our traffic police? A 'fine' was paid immediately and no questions were asked. Arturo tells me those officers — who are, by the way, now looking for new jobs — identified your Mr. Watchmaker. There was no one else in the truck other than the driver, and, of course, they didn't bother to look over his license. And there was, in the back, no equipment or contraband that would lead us in one direction or another. So we are left to focus on the buildings *he* seems to be focusing on. And hope — '

' — that he isn't sneaking up behind his real victim, five miles away.'

'Very much what I was going to say.'

'Do you have any thoughts about the circuit board that Logan was given?'

'I'm a soldier, Captain Rhyme, not a hacker. Or a sixteen-year-old boy. And so naturally I thought it was not a piece of computer hardware but a remote detonator for explosives. The booklet was perhaps an instruction manual.'

'Yes, I was thinking that too.'

'He would not want to travel with such a device. It would make sense to acquire it here. And I understand, from our news, that you have your hands full there. Some terrorist group?'

'We don't know.'

'I wish I could help *you*.'

'Appreciated. But keep your attention focused on the Watchmaker, Commander.'

'Good advice.' Luna gave a sound between a growl and a laugh. 'Cases are so much easier to run when you start with a corpse or two. I hate it when the bodies are still alive and being elusive.'

Rhyme smiled at that. And couldn't disagree.

44

At 2:40 p.m. Algonquin security chief Bernard Wahl was walking along the sidewalk in Queens, coming back from his investigation. That's how he liked to think of it. *His* investigation about *his* company, the number-one energy provider in the East, maybe in the entire North American grid.

He wanted to help. Especially now, since the horrific attack this afternoon at the Battery Park Hotel.

Ever since he'd heard that woman, Detective Sachs, mention to Ms. Jessen about the Greek food, he'd been devising a strategy.

'Microinvestigation' was how he thought of what he was doing. Wahl had read about it somewhere, or maybe seen it on the Discovery Channel. It was all about looking at the small clues, the small connections. Forget geopolitics and terrorists. Get a single fingerprint or hair and run with it. Until you collared the perp. Or it turned out to be a dead end and you went in a different direction.

So he'd been on a mission of his own — checking out the nearby Greek restaurants in Astoria, Queens. He'd learned that apparently Galt enjoyed that cuisine.

And just a half hour ago he'd hit pay dirt.

A waitress, Sonja, more than cute, earned a twenty-dollar tip by reporting that twice in the past week, a man wearing dark slacks and a knit

Algonquin Consolidated shirt — the sort worn by middle managers — had been in for lunch. The restaurant was Leni's, known for its moussaka and grilled octopus ... and, more significant, home-made taramasalata, bowls of which were brought to everyone who sat down, lunch and dinner, along with wedges of pita bread and lemon.

Sonja 'couldn't swear to it,' but when shown a picture of Raymond Galt, she said, 'Yeah, yeah, that looks like him.'

And the man had been online the entire time — on a Sony VAIO computer. While he'd only picked at most of his food he'd eaten all his taramasalata, she'd noted.

Online the whole time ...

Which meant to Wahl that there might be some way to trace what Galt had searched for or who he'd emailed. Wahl watched all those crime shows on TV, and did some continuing education in security on his own dime. Maybe the police could get the identification number of Galt's computer and find out where he was hiding.

Sonja had reported the killer had also made a lot of cell phone calls.

That was interesting. Galt was a loner. He was attacking people because he was pissed off about getting cancer from high-tension wires. So who was he calling? A partner? Why would he have one? That was something they could find out too.

Hurrying back to the office now, Wahl considered how best to handle this. Of course he'd have to get word back to the police as fast as he could. His heart was slamming at the thought of being instrumental in catching the killer. Maybe Detective Sachs would be impressed enough to get him a job interview with the NYPD.

But, hold on, don't be cagey here, he cautioned himself. Just do what's best and deal with the future in the future. Call everybody — Detective Sachs, Lincoln Rhyme and the others: FBI agent McDaniel and that police lieutenant, Lon Sellitto.

And, of course, tell Ms. Jessen.

He walked quickly, tense and exhilarated, seeing ahead of him the red and gray smoke stacks of Algonquin Consolidated. And in front of the building, those damn protesters. He enjoyed a brief image of turning a water cannon on them. Or, even more fun, a Taser. The company that made them also had a sort of a shotgun Taser, which would fire a number of barbs into a crowd for riot control.

He was smiling at the thought of them dancing around on the ground, when the man got him from behind.

Wahl gasped and barked a cry.

A muzzle of a gun appeared against his right cheek. 'Don't turn around,' was the whisper. The gun now pressed against his back. The voice told him to walk into an alley between a closed car repair shop and a darkened warehouse.

A harsh whisper: 'Just do what I say, Bernie, and you won't get hurt.'

'You know me?'

329

'It's Ray,' came the whisper.

'Ray Galt?' Wahl's heart thudded hard. He wondered if he'd be sick. 'Oh, man, look. What're you — '

'Shhh. Keep going.'

They continued into the alley for another fifty feet or so, and turned a corner into a dim recess.

'Lie down, facefirst. Arms out at your sides.'

Wahl hesitated, thinking for some ridiculous reason about the suit he'd proudly put on that morning, an expensive one. 'Always look better than your job title,' his father had told him.

The .45 nudged his back. He dropped like a stone into the greasy dirt.

'I don't go to Leni's anymore, Bernie. You think I'm stupid?'

Which told him that Galt had been tailing him for a while.

And I hadn't even noticed. Oh, some fucking cop I'd be. Jesus.

'And I don't use their broadband. I use a prepaid cell connection.'

'You killed those people, Ray. You — '

'They're not dead because of me. They're dead because Algonquin and Andi Jessen killed them! Why didn't she listen to me? Why didn't she do what I asked?'

'They wanted to, man. There just wasn't enough time to shut the grid down.'

'Bullshit.'

'Ray, listen. Turn yourself in. This is crazy, what you're doing.'

A bitter laugh. 'Crazy? You think I'm crazy?'

'I didn't mean that.'

330

'I'll tell you what's crazy, Bernie: companies that burn gas and oil and fuck up the planet. And that pump juice through wires that kills our children. Just because we like fucking blenders and hair dryers and TVs and microwaves . . . don't you think *that*'s what's crazy?'

'No, you're right, Ray. You're right. I'm sorry. I didn't know all the shit you'd been through. I feel bad for you.'

'Do you mean it, Bernie? Do you really mean it or are you just trying to save your ass?'

A pause. 'Little bit of both, Ray.'

To Bernard Wahl's surprise, the killer gave a laugh. 'That's an honest answer. Maybe one of the only honest answers that's ever come out of somebody who works for Algonquin.'

'Look, Ray, I'm just doing my job.'

Which was a cowardly thing to say and he hated himself for saying it. But he was thinking of his wife and three children and his mother, who lived in their home on Long Island.

'I don't have anything against you personally, Bernie.'

And with that, Wahl suspected that he was a dead man. He struggled not to cry. In a shaky voice he asked, 'What do you want?'

'I need you to tell me something.'

The security code for Andi Jessen's town-house? What garage she parked her car in. Wahl didn't know either of those.

But the killer's request was something very different. 'I need to know who's looking for me.'

Wahl's voice cracked. 'Who's . . . ? Well, the police're, the FBI. Homeland Security . . . I mean, *everybody*. There's hundreds of them.'

'Tell me something I don't know, Bernie. I'm talking about *names*. And at Algonquin too. I know employees're helping them.'

Wahl was going to cry. 'I don't know, Ray.'

'Of course you know. I need names. Give me names.'

'I can't do that, Ray.'

'They almost figured out about the attack at the hotel. How did they know that? They almost got me there. Who's behind this?'

'I don't know. They don't talk to me, Ray. I'm a security guard.'

'You're chief of security, Bernie. Of course they talk to you.'

'No, I really — '

He felt his wallet coming out of his pocket.

Oh, not that . . .

A moment later Galt recited Wahl's home address, tucked the wallet back.

'What's the service in your house, Bernie? Two hundred amps?'

'Oh, come on, Ray. My family never did anything to you.'

'I never did anything to anybody and *I* got sick. You're part of the system that made me sick, and your family benefited from that system . . . Two hundred amps? Not enough for an arc. But the shower, the bathtub, the kitchen . . . I could just play with the ground fault interrupts and your whole house'd become one big electric chair, Bernie. Now, talk to me.'

45

Fred Dellray was walking down a street in the East Village, past a row of gardenias, past a gourmet coffee shop, past a clothing store.

My, my . . . Was that $325 for a *shirt*? Without a suit, tie and pair of shoes attached?

He continued past storefronts in which sat complicated espresso machines and overpriced art and the sorts of glittery shoes that a girl would lose at 4 a.m. en route from one hazy downtown club to another.

Thinking how the Village had changed in the years since he'd started being an agent.

Change . . .

Used to be a carnival, used to be crazy, used to be gaudy and loud, laughter and madness, lovers entwined or shrieking or floating sullenly down the busy sidewalks . . . all the time, all the time. Twenty-four hours. Now this portion of the East Village had the formula and sound track of a homogenized sitcom.

Man, had this place changed. And it wasn't just the money, not just the preoccupied eyes of the professionals who lived here now, cardboard coffee cups replacing chipped porcelain . . .

No, that wasn't what Dellray kept seeing.

What he saw was everybody on fucking cell phones. Talking, texting . . . and, Jesus our Savior in heaven, here were two tourists right in front of him using *GPS* to find a restaurant!

In the East fucking Village.

Cloud zone . . .

Everywhere, more evidence that the world, even this world — Dellray's world — was now Tucker McDaniel's. Back in the day, Dellray would play dress-up here, looking homeless, pimp, dealer. He was good at pimp, loved the colored shirts, purple and green. Not because he worked vice, which wasn't a federal crime, but because he knew how to fit.

The chameleon.

He fit in places like this. And that meant people talked to him.

But now, hell, there were more people on phones than there weren't. And every one of those phones — depending on the inclination of the federal magistrate — could be tapped into and give up information that it would have taken Dellray days to get. And even if they weren't tapped, there apparently were still ways to get that information, or some of it.

Out of the air, out of clouds.

But maybe he was just overly sensitive, he told himself, using a word that had rarely figured in the psyche of Fred Dellray. Ahead of him he saw Carmella's — the old establishment that may very well have been a whorehouse a long time ago and was presently an island of tradition here. He walked inside and sat down at a rickety table. He ordered a regular coffee, noting that, yes, espresso and cappuccino and latte were on the menu, but of course, they always had been. Long before Starbucks.

God bless Carmella.

And around him, of the ten people here — he counted — only two were on cell phones.

This was the world of Mama behind the cash register, her pretty boy sons waiting tables and even now, midafternoon, customers twirling pasta, glistening orange not supermarket red. And sipping from small hemispheres of wineglasses. The whole place filled with animated talk, punctuating gestures.

This filled him with comfort. He believed that he was doing this the right way. He believed in William Brent's reassurance. He was about to receive some value, *something* for the dubious one hundred thousand dollars. Only a tenuous lead but it would be enough. That was something else about Street Dellray. He'd been able to weave cloth from the tiny threads his CIs delivered, usually they themselves oblivious to the value of what they'd found.

A single hard fact that would lead to Galt. Or to the site of the next attack. Or to the elusive Justice For.

And he was well aware that fact, that find, that save . . . they'd vindicate him too, Dellray, the old-school street agent, far from the cloud zone.

Dellray sipped the coffee and snuck a glance at his watch. Exactly 3 p.m. He'd never known William Brent to be late, even by sixty seconds. ('Not efficient,' the CI had said, of being either early or tardy. 'And possibly fucking dangerous.')

Forty-five minutes later, without as much as a phone call from Brent, a grim-faced Fred Dellray checked his messages once more on the cold phone. Nothing. He tried Brent's for the sixth time. Still straight to the robotic voice telling him to leave a message.

Dellray gave it ten minutes longer, tried once more, then called in a big favor from a buddy of his at one of the mobile providers and learned that the battery had been removed from Brent's phone. The only reason to do that was to prevent tracing, of course.

A young couple approached and the girl asked if Dellray was using the other chair at his table. The responsive glance must have been pretty intimidating because they retreated instantly and the boyfriend didn't even try for a moment of chivalric bravado.

Brent's gone.

I've been robbed and he's gone.

Replaying the man's confidence, his reassurance.

Guarantee, my ass . . .

One hundred thousand dollars . . . He should have known that something was going on when Brent had insisted on that huge sum, considering the shabby suit and threadbare argyle socks.

Dellray wondered whether the man had decided to settle in the Caribbean or South America on his windfall.

46

'We've had another demand.'

Grim Andi Jessen was staring out of Rhyme's flat-screen monitor, on a video conference call. Her blond hair stiff, oversprayed. Or perhaps she'd spent the night in the office and hadn't showered that morning.

'*Another* one?' Rhyme glanced at Lon Sellitto, Cooper and Sachs, all frozen in various places and attitudes around the lab.

The big detective tossed down half the muffin that he'd snagged from a plate Thom had brought in. 'We just *had* an attack, and he's hitting us again?'

'He wasn't happy we ignored him, I suppose,' Jessen said brittlely.

'What does he want?' Sachs asked, at the same time as Rhyme said, 'I'd like the note here. ASAP.'

Jessen answered Rhyme first. 'I gave it to Agent McDaniel. It's on its way to you now.'

'What's the deadline?'

'Six p.m.'

'*Today*?'

'Yes.'

'Jesus,' Sellitto muttered. 'Two hours.'

'And the demand?' Sachs repeated.

'He wants us to stop all the DC — the direct current — transmission to the other North American grids for an hour, starting at six. If we

337

don't he'll kill more people.'

Rhyme asked, 'What does that mean?'

'Our grid is the Northeastern Interconnection, and Algonquin's the big energy producer in it. If a power company in another grid needs supply, we sell it to them. If they're more than five hundred miles away, we use DC transmission, not AC. It's more cost effective. Usually it goes to smaller companies in rural areas.'

'What's the, you know, significance of the demand?' Sellitto asked.

'I don't know why he's asking. It doesn't make any sense to me. Maybe his point is reducing cancer risk to people near the transmission lines. But I'd guess fewer than a thousand people in North America live near DC lines.'

Rhyme said, 'Galt isn't necessarily behaving rationally.'

'True.'

'Can you do it? Meet his demand?'

'No, we can't. It's impossible. It's just like before, with the grid in New York City, except worse. It would cut out service to thousands of small towns around the country. And there are direct feeds into military bases and research facilities. Homeland Security's saying to shut it down would be a national security risk. The Defense Department concurs.'

Rhyme added, 'And presumably you'd be losing millions of dollars.'

A pause. 'Yes. We would. We'd be in breach of hundreds of contracts. It would be a disaster for the company. But, anyway, the argument about complying is moot. We physically couldn't do this in the time he's given us. You don't just flip a wall switch with seven hundred thousand volts.'

'All right,' Rhyme said. 'How did you get the note?'

'Galt gave it to one of our employees.'

Rhyme and Sachs exchanged glances.

Jessen continued, explaining that Galt accosted security chief Bernard Wahl as the man was returning from lunch.

'Is Wahl there with you?' Sachs asked.

'Hold on a minute,' Jessen said. 'He was being debriefed by the FBI . . . Let me see.'

Sellitto whispered, 'They didn't fucking bother to even tell us they were talking to him, the feebies? It had to come from *her*?'

A moment later solid-shouldered Bernard Wahl appeared on the screen and sat down next to Andi Jessen. His round, black scalp glistened.

'Hello,' Sachs said.

The handsome face nodded.

'Are you all right?'

'Yes, Detective.'

He wasn't all right, though, Rhyme could see. His eyes were hollow. They were avoiding the webcam.

'Tell us what happened.'

'I was coming back from lunch. And Galt came up behind me with a gun and took me to an alleyway. Then he shoved the letter into my pocket and said get it to Ms. Jessen right away. Then he was gone.'

'That's all?'

339

A hesitation. 'Pretty much. Yes, ma'am.'

'Did he say anything that might lead us to where he's hiding out or where the next target might be?'

'No. Mostly he just rambled about electricity causing cancer and being dangerous and how nobody cares.'

Rhyme was curious about something. 'Mr. Wahl? Did you see the weapon? Or was he bluffing?'

Another hesitation. Then the security man said, 'I caught a look. A forty-five. Nineteen-eleven. The old army model.'

'Did he grab you? We could get some trace evidence off your clothes.'

'No. Only his gun.'

'Where'd this happen?'

'Somewhere in an alley near B and R Auto Repair. I don't really remember, sir. I was pretty shaken up.'

Sachs asked, 'And that was it? He didn't ask anything about the investigation?'

'No, ma'am, he didn't. I think all he cared about was getting the letter to Ms. Jessen right away. He couldn't think of another way to do it except to stop an employee.'

Rhyme had no more questions for him. He glanced to Sellitto, who shook his head.

They thanked him, and Wahl moved off camera. Jessen looked up, nodding at somebody who'd come into the doorway. Then back to the camera for the video conference. 'Gary Noble and I are meeting with the mayor. Then I'm doing a press conference. I'll make that personal appeal to Galt. Do you think that'll work?'

No, Rhyme didn't think it would work. But he said, 'Anything you can do — even if it just buys us some time.'

After they disconnected the call, Sellitto asked, 'What wasn't Wahl telling us?'

'He got scared. Galt threatened him. He probably gave up some information. I'm not too worried. He was out of the loop pretty much. But whatever he spilled, frankly, we can't worry about that now.'

At that moment the doorbell rang. It was Tucker McDaniel and the Kid.

Rhyme was surprised. The FBI agent would have known there was a pending press conference and yet here he was, not leveraging his way onto the podium. He'd yielded to Homeland Security so he could bring evidence to Rhyme in person.

The ASAC's stock rose slightly once more.

After being briefed about Galt and his motive, the agent asked Pulaski, 'And in his apartment you found no reference to Justice For or Rahman? Terrorist cells?'

'No, nothing.'

The agent looked disappointed but said, 'Still, that doesn't contradict a symbiosis construct.'

'Which is?' Rhyme asked.

'A traditional terror operation using a front man, with mutually aligned goals. They may not even like each other but they want the same thing in the end. An important aspect is that the professional terror cell keeps themselves completely isolated from the primary negative actor. And all communications is — '

'Cloud?' Rhyme asked, the agent's index dipping a bit now.

'Exactly. They have to minimize any contact. Two different agendas. They want societal destruction. He wants revenge.' McDaniel nodded at the profile on the whiteboard. 'What Parker Kincaid was saying. Galt didn't use pronouns — didn't want to give away any clue that he was working with somebody else.'

'Eco or political/religious?'

'Could be either.'

It was hard to picture al-Qaida or the Taliban in league with an unstable employee bent on revenge because his company had given him cancer. But an eco-terror group made some sense. They'd need somebody to help them get into the system. Rhyme would find it more credible, though, if there was some *evidence* to support that supposition.

McDaniel added that he'd heard from the warrants people, who'd gotten the okay for the T & C teams to go through Galt's email and social networking accounts. Galt had emailed and posted comments in a number of places about his cancer and its relationship to high-power lines. But nothing in the hundreds of pages he'd written had given them any clues to where he was or what he might have in store.

Rhyme was growing impatient at the speculation. 'I'd like to see the note, Tucker.'

'Sure.' The ASAC gestured at the Kid.

342

Please, be chock full of trace. Something helpful.

In sixty seconds they were looking at the second demand letter.

To Andi Jessen, CEO and Algonquin Consolidated Power and Light:

You've made the decision to ignore my earlier request and that's not acceptable. You could have responded to that reasonable request for a brownout but you didn't, YOU have raised the stakes, no one else has. Your callusness and greed lead to the deaths this afternoon. You MUST show the people they do not need the drug that you've addicted them to. They can return to a PURER way of life. They don't think they can but they can be shown the way. You will cease all high voltage DC transmission to the other North American Interconnections for one hour starting at 6 p.m. this evening. This is non-negotiable.

Cooper began his analysis of the letter. Ten minutes later he said, 'There's nothing new, Lincoln. Same paper, same pen. Unsourceable. As far as trace goes, more jet fuel. That's about it.'

'Shit.' Like opening a beautifully wrapped box on Christmas morning and finding it empty.

Rhyme noticed Pulaski in the corner. His head, with the blond spiky hair, was cast forward as he spoke softly into his mobile. The conversation seemed furtive and Rhyme knew it didn't have anything to do with the Galt case. He'd be calling the hospital about the man he'd run into. Or maybe he'd gotten the name of the next of kin and was offering condolences.

'You with us, Pulaski?' Rhyme called harshly.

Pulaski snapped his phone shut. 'Sure, I — '

'Because I really need you with us.'

'I'm with you, Lincoln.'

'Good. Call FAA and TSA and tell them we've had another demand and that we've found more jet fuel on the second note. They should step up security at all the airports. And call the Department of Defense too. It could be an attack on a military airfield, especially if Tucker's terrorist connection pans out. You up for that? Talking to the Pentagon? Impressing the risk on them?'

'Yes, I'll do it.'

Turning back to the evidence charts, Rhyme sighed. Symbiotic terrorist cells, cumulonimbus communications and an invisible suspect with an invisible weapon.

And as for the other case, the attempt to trap the Watchmaker in Mexico City? Nothing but the mysterious circuit board, its owner's manual and two meaningless numbers:

Five hundred seventy and three hundred seventy-nine . . .

Which put him in mind of other digits. Those on the clock nearby, the clock counting down to the next deadline.

SECOND DEMAND NOTE

- Delivered to Bernard Wahl, Algonquin security chief.
  — Assaulted by Galt.
  — No physical contact; no trace.
  — No indication of whereabouts or site of next attack.
- Paper and ink associated with those found in Galt's apartment.
- Additional traces of jet fuel and alternative jet fuel embedded in paper.
  — Attack on military base?

PROFILE

- Identified as Raymond Galt, 40, single, living In Manhattan, 227 Suffolk St.
- Terrorist connection? Relation to Justice For [unknown]? Terror group? Individual named Rahman involved? References to monetary disbursements, personnel movements and something 'big.'
  — Algonquin security breach in Philadelphia might be related.
  — SIGINT hits: code word reference to weapons, 'paper and supplies' (guns, explosives?).
  — Personnel include man and woman.
  — Galt's relationship unknown.
- Cancer patient; presence of vinblastine and prednisone in significant quantities, traces of etoposide. Leukemia.
- Galt is armed with military 1911 Colt .45.

47

The TV was on in Rhyme's lab.

As a prelude to Andi Jessen's press conference, which would start in a few minutes, a story about Algonquin Consolidated and Jessen herself was airing. Rhyme was curious about the woman and paid attention to the anchorman as he traced Jessen's career in the business. How her father had been president and CEO of the company before her. There was no nepotism involved, though; the woman had degrees in engineering and business and had worked her way up, actually starting as a lineman in upstate New York.

A life-long employee of Algonquin, she was quoted as saying how devoted she was to her career and to her goal of building the power company into the number-one player in both the generation of electricity and the brokering of it. Rhyme had not known that because of deregulation a few years ago power companies had increasingly taken to brokerage: buying electricity and natural gas from other companies and selling it. Some had even sold off their interest in the generation and transmission of power and were, in effect, commodity dealers, with no assets other than offices, computers and telephones.

And very large banks behind them.

This was, the reporter explained, the thrust of Enron's business.

Andi Jessen, though, had never slipped over to the dark side, extravagance, arrogance, greed. The compact, intense woman ran Algonquin with an old-fashioned austerity and shunned the splashy life. She was divorced and had no children. Jessen seemed to have no life other than Algonquin. Her only family was a brother, Randall Jessen, who lived in Philadelphia. He was a decorated soldier in Afghanistan and had been discharged after an injury by a roadside bomb.

Andi was one of the country's most outspoken advocates for the megagrid — one unified power grid that connected all of North America. This was, she felt, a far more efficient way to produce and deliver electricity to consumers. (With Algonquin as the major player, Rhyme supposed.)

Her nickname — though apparently one never used to her face or in her presence — was 'the All-Powerful.' Apparently this was a reference to both her take-no-prisoners management style, and to her ambitions for Algonquin.

Her controversial reservations about green power were on blunt display in one interview.

'First of all, I wanted to say that we at Algonquin Consolidated are committed to renewable energy sources. But at the same time I think we all need to be realistic. The earth was here billions of years before we lost our gills and tails and started burning coal and driving internal combustion cars and it'll be here, doing just fine, long, long after we're history.

'When people say they want to save the earth, what they really mean is that they want to save their *lifestyle*. We have to admit we want energy and a lot of it. And that we *need* it — for civilization to progress, to be fed and educated, to use fancy equipment to keep an eye on the dictators of the world, to help Third World countries join the First. Oil and coal and natural gas and nuclear power are the best ways to create that power.'

The pieces ended and pundits leapt in to criticize or say hurrah. It was more politically correct, and produced better ratings, to eviscerate her, however.

Finally the camera went live to City Hall, four people on the dais; Jessen, the mayor, the police chief and Gary Noble, from Homeland Security.

The mayor made a brief announcement and then turned over the microphone. Andi Jessen, looking both harsh and reassuring, told everyone that Algonquin was doing all it could to control the situation. A number of safeguards had been put into place, though she didn't say what those might be.

Surprising Rhyme, and everyone else in the room, the group had made the decision to go public about the second demand letter. He supposed that the reasoning was if they were unsuccessful in stopping Galt and somebody else died in another attack, the public relations, and perhaps legal, consequences to Algonquin would have been disastrous.

The reporters leapt on this instantly and

pelted her with questions. Jessen coolly silenced them and explained that it was impossible to meet the extortionist's requirements. A reduction in the amount of power he wanted would result in hundreds of millions of dollars in damages. And very likely *many* more deaths.

She added that it would be a national security risk because the demands would hamper military and other governmental operations. 'Algonquin is a major player in our nation's defense and we will not do anything to jeopardize that.'

Slick, thought Rhyme. She's turning the whole thing around.

Finally, she ended with a personal statement to Galt to turn himself in. He'd be treated fairly. 'Don't let your family or anyone else suffer because of the tragedy that's happened to you. We'll do whatever we can to ease your suffering. But please, do the right thing, and turn yourself in.'

She took no questions and was off the dais seconds after she finished speaking, her very high heels clattering loudly.

Rhyme noticed that while her sympathy was heartfelt she never once admitted that the company had done anything wrong or that high-voltage lines might in fact have led to Galt's or anyone else's cancer.

Then the police chief took over and tried his best to offer concrete reassurance. Police and federal agents were out in force looking for Galt, and National Guard troops were ready to assist if there were more attacks or the grid was compromised.

He ended with a plea to citizens to report anything unusual.

Now *that's* helpful, Rhyme thought. If there's one thing that's the order of the day in New York City, it's the unusual.

And he turned back to the paltry evidence.

48

Susan Stringer left her office on the eighth floor of an ancient building in Midtown Manhattan at 5:45 p.m.

She said hello to two other men also making their way to the elevator. One of them she knew casually because they'd run into each other occasionally in the building. Larry left at about this same time every day. The difference was that he'd be returning to his office, to work through the night.

Susan, on the other hand, was heading home.

The attractive thirty-five-year-old was an editor for a magazine that had a specialized field: art and antiques restoration, primarily eighteenth and nineteenth century. She also wrote poetry occasionally, and was published. These passions gave her only a modest income but if she ever had any doubts about the wisdom of sticking to her career, all she had to do was listen to a conversation like the one Larry and his friend were having at the moment, and she knew she could never go into that side of business — law, finance, banking, accounting.

The two men wore very expensive suits and nice watches and elegant shoes. But there was a harried quality about them. Edgy. It didn't seem they liked their jobs much. The friend was complaining about his boss breathing down his neck. Larry was complaining about an audit that

351

was in the 'fucking tank.'

Stress, unhappiness.

And that *language* too.

Susan was pleased she didn't have to deal with that. Her life was the Rococo and neoclassical designs of craftsmen, from Chippendale to George Hepplewhite to Sheraton.

Practical beauty, she phrased their creations.

'You look wasted,' the friend said to Larry.

He did, Susan agreed.

'I am. Bear of a trip.'

'When'd you get back?'

'Tuesday.'

'You were senior auditor?'

Larry nodded. 'The books were a nightmare. Twelve-hour days. The only time I could get out on the golf course was Sunday and the temperature hit a hundred and sixteen.'

'Ouch.'

'I've got to go back. Monday. I mean, I just don't know where the hell the money's going. Something's fishy.'

'Weather that hot, maybe it's evaporating.'

'Funny,' Larry muttered in an unfunny way.

The men continued their banter about financial statements and disappearing money but Susan tuned them out. She saw another man approach, wearing a workman's brown overalls and a hat, as well as glasses. Eyes down, he carried a tool kit and a large watering can, though he must've been working in a different office since there were no decorative plants in the hallway here, and none in her office. Her publisher wouldn't pay for any flora and he sure

352

wouldn't pay for a person to water them.

The elevator car came and the two business-men let her precede them inside, and she reflected that at least some semblance of chivalry remained in the twenty-first century. The workman entered too and hit the button for the floor two down. But, unlike the others, he rudely pushed past her to get to the back of the car.

They started to descend. A moment later Larry glanced down and said, 'Hey, mister, watch it. You're leaking there.'

Susan looked back. The workman had accidentally tilted the can and a stream of water was pouring onto the stainless-steel floor of the car.

'Oh, sorry,' the man mumbled unapologeti-cally. The whole floor was soaked, Susan noted.

The door opened and the worker got out. Another man entered.

Larry's friend said in a loud voice, 'Careful, that guy just spilled some water in here. Didn't even bother to clean it up.'

But whether the culprit had heard or not, Susan couldn't say. Even if he had she doubted he cared.

The door closed and they continued their journey downward.

49

Rhyme was staring at the clock. Ten minutes until the next deadline.

The last hour or so had involved coordinated searches throughout the city by the police and FBI, and, in the townhouse here, a frantic analysis of the evidence once more. Frantic ... and futile. They were no closer to finding Galt or his next target location than they'd been just after the first attack. Rhyme's eyes swung to the evidence charts, which remained an elusive jumble of puzzle pieces.

He was aware of McDaniel's taking a call. The agent listened, nodding broadly. He shot a look to his protégé. He then thanked the caller and hung up.

'One of my T and C teams had another hit about the terror group. A small one but it's gold. Another word in the name is 'Earth.''

'Justice For the Earth,' Sachs said.

'Could be more to it but we know those words for certain. 'Justice.' 'For.' And 'Earth.''

'At least we know it's ecoterror,' Sellitto muttered.

'No hits on any database?' Rhyme wondered aloud.

'No, but remember, this is all cloud-zone. And there was another hit. Rahman's second in command seems to be somebody named Johnston.'

'Anglo.'

But how does this help? Rhyme wondered angrily to himself. How does any of this help us find the site of the attack, which's going to happen in just a few minutes?

And what the hell kind of weapon has he devised this time? Another arc flash? Another deadly circuit in a public place?

Rhyme's eyes were riveted on the evidence whiteboards.

McDaniel said to the Kid, 'Get me Dellray.'

A moment later the agent's voice came through the speaker. 'Yes, who's this? Who's there?'

'Fred. It's Tucker. I'm here with Lincoln Rhyme and some other people from the NYPD.'

'At Rhyme's?'

'Yes.'

'How you doing, Lincoln?'

'Been better.'

'Yeah. True about all of us.'

McDaniel said, 'Fred, you heard about the new demand and deadline.'

'Your assistant called me. She told me about the motive too. Galt's cancer.'

'We've got a confirmation that it's probably a terror group. Ecoterror.'

'How does that play with Galt?'

'Symbiosis.'

'What?'

'A symbiotic construct. It was in my memo . . . They're working together. The group's called Justice For the Earth. And Rahman's second in command is named Johnston.'

355

Dellray asked, 'Sounds like they have different agendas. How'd they hook up? Galt and Rahman?'

'I don't know, Fred. That's not the point. Maybe they contacted him, read his postings about the cancer. It was all over the internet.'

'Oh.'

'Now, the deadline's coming up at any minute. Has your CI found *anything*?'

A pause. 'No, Tucker. Nothing.'

'The debriefing. You said it was at three.'

Another hesitation. 'That's right. But he doesn't have anything concrete yet. He's going a little farther underground.'

'The whole fucking world's underground,' the FBI agent snapped, surprising Rhyme; he couldn't imagine an expletive issuing from the man's smooth lips. 'So, call your guy up and get him the information about Justice For the Earth. And the new player, Johnston.'

'I'll do it.'

'Fred?'

'Yes?'

'He's the only one has any leads, this CI of yours?'

'That's right.'

'And he didn't hear anything, not a name, nothing?'

'Afraid not.'

McDaniel said distractedly, 'Well, thanks, Fred. You did what you could.' As if he hadn't expected to learn anything helpful anyway.

A pause. 'Sure.'

They disconnected. And Rhyme and Sellitto

both were aware of McDaniel's sour expression.

'Fred's a good man,' the detective said.

'He is a good man,' the ASAC replied quickly. Too quickly.

But the subject of Fred Dellray and McDaniel's opinion of him vanished as everyone in the townhouse, except Thom, got a cell call, all within five seconds of each other.

Different sources, but the news was the same.

Although the deadline was still seven minutes away, Ray Galt had struck again, once more killing innocents in Manhattan.

It was Sellitto's caller who gave them the details. Through speaker-phone the NYPD patrolman, sounding young and distracted, started to give an account of the attack — a Midtown office building elevator car in which four passengers were riding. 'It was . . . it was pretty bad.' Then the officer choked, his voice dissolved in coughing — maybe from smoke created by the attack. Or maybe it was simply to cover up his emotion.

The officer excused himself and said he'd call back in a few minutes.

He never did.

50

That smell again.

Could Amelia Sachs ever escape it?

And even if she scrubbed and scrubbed and threw her clothes out, could she ever *forget* it? Apparently the sleeve and hair of one of the victims had caught fire in the elevator car. The flames hadn't been bad but the smoke was thick and the smell was repulsive.

Sachs and Ron Pulaski were suiting up in their overalls. She asked one of the Emergency Service officers, 'DCDS?' Gesturing toward the hazy air of the car.

Deceased, confirmed dead at scene.

'That's right.'

'Where're the bodies?'

'Up the hall. I know we fucked up the scene in the elevator, Detective, but there was so much smoke, we didn't know what was going on. We had to clear it.'

She told him that was all right. Checking on the conditions of victims is the first priority. Besides, nothing contaminates a crime scene like fire. A few emergency worker footprints would make little difference.

'How'd it work?' she asked the ESU officer.

'We aren't sure. The building supervisor said the car stopped just above the ground floor. Then smoke started. And the screams. By the time they got the car down to the main floor and

358

the door opened, it was all over.'

Sachs shivered at the thought. The molten metal disks were bad enough, but, being claustrophobic, she was even more troubled by the thought of those four people in a confined space filled with electricity . . . and one of them burning.

The ESU officer looked over his notes. 'The vics were an editor of an arts magazine, a lawyer and an accountant on the eighth floor. A computer parts salesman from the sixth. If you're interested.'

Sachs was *always* interested in anything that made the victims real. Partly this was to keep her heart about her, to make certain she didn't become callous because of what she encountered on the job. But partly it was because of what Rhyme had instilled in her. For a man who was pure scientist, a rationalist, Rhyme's talent as a forensic expert was also due to his uncanny ability to step into the mind of the perp.

Years ago, at the very first scene they'd worked, a terrible crime also involving death by a utility system — steam, in that case — Rhyme had whispered to her something that seated itself in her mind every time she walked the grid: 'I want you to be him,' he'd told her, speaking of the perp. 'Just get into his head. You've been thinking the way we think. I want you to think the way he does.'

Rhyme had told her that while he believed forensic science could be taught, this empathy was an innate talent. And *Sachs* believed the best way to maintain this connection — this *wire*, she thought now, between your heart and your skill — was never to forget the victims.

'Ready?' she asked Pulaski.

'I guess.'

'We're going to do the grid, Rhyme,' she said into the microphone.

'Okay, but do it without me, Sachs.'

She was alarmed. Despite his protests to the contrary, Rhyme hadn't been well. She could tell easily. But it turned out that there was another reason he was signing off. 'I want you to walk the grid with that guy from Algonquin.'

'Sommers?'

'Right.'

'Why?'

'For one thing, I like his mind. He thinks broadly. Maybe it's his inventor's side. I don't know. But beyond that, something's not right, Sachs. I can't explain it. I feel we're missing something. Galt had to have planned this out for a month, at least. But now it looks like he's accelerating the attacks — two in one day. I can't figure that out.'

'Maybe,' she suggested, 'it's because we've gotten on to him faster than he hoped.'

'Could be. I don't know. But if that's the case it also means he'd love to take us out too.'

'True.'

'So I want a fresh perspective. I've already called Charlie, and he's willing to help . . . Does he always eat when he talks on the phone?'

'He likes junk food.'

'Well, when you're on the grid, make sure he's

got something that doesn't crunch. Communications will patch you in, whenever you're ready. Just get back here ASAP with whatever you find. For all we know Galt's rigging another attack right now.'

They disconnected. She glanced at Ron Pulaski, who was still clearly troubled.

I need you with us, Rookie . . .

She called him over. 'Ron, the major scene's downstairs, where he probably rigged the wires and that device of his.' She tapped her radio. 'I'll be online with Charlie Sommers. I need you to run the elevator.' Another pause. 'And process the bodies too. There probably won't be much trace. His MO is he doesn't have any direct contact with the vics. But it needs to be done. Are you okay with that?'

The young officer nodded. 'Anything you need, Amelia.' Sounding painfully sincere. He was making amends for the accident at Galt's apartment, she guessed.

'Let's get to it. And Vicks.'

'What?'

'In the kit. Vick's VapoRub. Put some underneath your nose. For the smell.'

In five minutes she was online with Charlie Sommers, grateful that he was helping her in running the scene — to give 'technical support,' which he defined, in his irreverent way, as helping to 'save her ass.'

Sachs clicked on her helmet light and started down the stairs into the basement of the building, describing to Charlie Sommers exactly what she saw in the dank, filthy area at the base of the elevator shaft. She was linked to him only through audio, not video, as she usually was with Rhyme.

The building had been cleared by ESU, but she was very aware of what Rhyme had told her earlier — that Galt could easily have decided to start targeting his pursuers. She looked around for a moment, taking only a few detours to shine the light on shadows that had a vaguely human form.

They turned out to be only shadows that had a vaguely human form.

He asked, 'You see anything bolted to the railings the elevator rides on?'

She focused again on her search. 'No, nothing on the rails. But . . . there's a piece of that Bennington cable bolted to the wall. I'm . . . '

'Test the voltage first!'

'Was just going to say that.'

'Ah, a born electrician.'

'No way. After this, I'm not even going to change my car batteries.' She swept with the detector. 'It's zero.'

'Good. Where does the line go?'

'On one end, to a bus bar that's dangling in the shaft. It's resting against the bottom of the elevator car. It's scorched where it's made contact. The other end goes to a thick cable that runs into a beige panel on the wall, like a big medicine cabinet. The Bennington wire is connected to a main line with one of those remote switches like at the last scene.'

'That's the incoming service line.' He added that an office building like this didn't receive electricity the way a residence did. It took in a much larger amount, like a street transformer: 13,800 volts, which was then stepped down for distribution to the offices. It was a spot network. 'So the car would descend and hit the hot bus bar . . . But there has to be another switch somewhere, one that controls the power to the elevator. He needed to stop the car just before it got to the lobby. So the victims inside would hit the call button. Then the passenger's hand on the panel and his feet on the floor completed the circuit and electrocuted him and anybody who touched him or he was brushing up against.'

Sachs looked around and found the other device. She told Sommers this.

He explained exactly how to dismantle the cables and what to look for. Before she removed any evidence, though, Sachs laid the numbers and photographed the scene. Then she thanked Sommers and told him that was all she needed for now. They disconnected and she walked the grid, including the entrance and exit routes — which turned out to be in all likelihood a door nearby that led to the alley. It had a flimsy lock and had recently been jimmied open. She took pictures of this too.

She was about to go upstairs and join Pulaski when she paused.

Four victims here in the elevator.

Sam Vetter and two others dead at the hotel, a number in the hospital, Luis Martin.

And fear throughout the city, fear of this invisible killer.

In her imagination she heard Rhyme say, 'You

have to become him.'

Sachs rested the evidence by the stairs and returned to the base of the elevator shaft.

I'm him, I'm Raymond Galt . . .

Sachs had trouble summoning the fanatic, the crusader, since that emotion didn't jibe, in her mind, with the extreme calculation that the man had shown so far. Anybody else would just have taken a shot at Andi Jessen or firebombed the Queens plant. But Galt was going to these precise, elaborate lengths to use a very complicated weapon to kill.

What did it mean?

I'm him . . .

I'm Galt.

Then her mind went still, and up bubbled the answer: I don't care about motive. I don't care why I'm doing this. None of that matters. All that's important is to focus on technique, like focusing on making the most perfect splice or switch or connection I can to cause the most harm.

That's the center of my universe.

I've become addicted to the process, addicted to the juice . . .

And with that thought came another: It's all about angles. He had to get . . . *I* have to get the bus bar in just the right position to kiss the floor of the elevator car when it's *near* the lobby but not yet there.

Which means I have to watch the elevator in operation from all different perspectives down here to make sure the counterweight, the gears, the motor, the cables of the elevator don't knock

364

aside the bus bar or otherwise interfere with the wire.

I have to study the shaft from all angles. I *have* to.

On her hands and knees Sachs made a circuit of the filthy basement all around the base of the shaft — anywhere that Galt could have seen the cable and bar and contacts. She found no footprints, no fingerprints. But she did find places where the ground had been recently disturbed, and it was not unreasonable to think that he'd crouched there to examine his deadly handiwork.

She took samples from ten locations and deposited them into separate evidence bags, marking them according to positions of the compass: '10° away, northwest.' '7° away, south.' She then gathered all the other evidence and climbed painfully on her arthritic legs to the lobby. Joining Pulaski, Sachs looked into the interior of the elevator. It wasn't badly damaged. There were some smoke marks — accompanied by that terrible smell. She simply couldn't imagine what it would have been like to be riding in that car and suddenly have thirteen thousand volts race through your body. At least, she supposed, the vics would have felt nothing after the first few seconds.

She saw that he'd laid the numbers and taken pictures. 'You find anything?'

'No. I searched the car too. But the panel hadn't been opened recently.'

'He rigged everything from downstairs. And the bodies?'

His face was troubled and she could tell that it had been a difficult chore. Still, he said evenly, 'No trace. But there was something interesting. All three of them had wet soles. All their shoes.'

'The fire department?'

'No, the fire was out by the time they got here.'

Water. That was interesting. To improve the connection. But how did he get their shoes wet? Sachs then asked, 'You said *three* bodies?'

'That's right.'

'But that ESU guy said there were four vics.'

'There were, but only three of them died. Here.' He handed her a piece of paper.

'What's this?' On the slip was a name and phone number.

'The survivor. I figured you'd want to talk to her. Her name's Susan Stringer. She's at St. Vincent's. Smoke inhalation, some burns. But she'll be okay. They'll be releasing her in an hour or so.'

Sachs was shaking her head. 'I don't see how anybody could've survived. There were thirteen thousand volts in here.'

Ron Pulaski replied, 'Oh, she's disabled. In a wheelchair. Rubber tires, you know. Guess that insulated her.'

51

'How'd he do?' Rhyme asked Sachs, who'd just returned to the lab.

'Ron? Little distracted. But he did a good job. Processed the bodies. That was tough. But he found something interesting. Somehow the vics all had wet shoes.'

'How'd Galt manage that?'

'I don't know.'

'You don't think Ron's too shaken up?'

'Not *too*. But *some*. But he's young. Happens.'

'That's no excuse.'

'No, it's not. It's an explanation.'

'They're both the same to me,' Rhyme muttered. 'Where is he?'

The hour was after 8 p.m. 'He went back to Galt's, thought he might've missed something.'

Rhyme thought this wasn't a bad idea, though he was confident that the young officer had searched the scene well the first time. He added, 'Just keep an eye on him. I won't risk anybody's life because he's distracted.'

'Agreed.'

The two of them and Cooper were here alone in the lab. McDaniel and the Kid were back at the federal building, meeting with Homeland Security, and Sellitto was down at the Big Building — One Police Plaza. Rhyme wasn't sure whom he was meeting with but there'd undoubtedly be a long list of people who wanted explanations about why there was no suspect in custody.

Cooper and Sachs were laying out the evidence that Sachs had collected at the office building. The tech then examined the cable and other items from the base of the elevator shaft.

'There's one other thing.' Sachs probably thought her voice was casual; in fact it was tripping with meaning to Rhyme. Tough to be in love with somebody; you can read them so well when they're up to something.

'What?' He gave her his inquisitor's gaze.

'There was a witness. She was in the elevator when the other people died.'

'She hurt bad?'

'Apparently not. Smoke inhalation mostly.'

'That would've been unpleasant. Burning hair.' His nostrils flared slightly.

Sachs sniffed at her red strands. Her nose wrinkled too. 'I'm taking a really long shower tonight.'

'What'd she have to say?'

'I didn't get a chance to interview her. She's coming over here as soon as she's released.'

'Here?' Rhyme asked with surprise. Not only was he skeptical of witnesses in the first place, but there was a security question about letting a stranger into the lab. If a terrorist cell was behind the attacks, they might want to sneak one of their members into the inner sanctum of the investigators.

But Sachs laughed, deducing his thoughts. 'I checked her out, Rhyme. She's clean. No record, no warrants. Longtime editor of some furniture magazine. Besides, I thought it wasn't a bad idea — I wouldn't have to spend the time getting to and from the hospital. I can stay here and work the evidence.'

'What else?'

She hesitated. Another smile. 'I was explaining too much?'

'Uh-huh.'

'Okay. She's disabled.'

'Is she now? That's still not answering my question.'

'She wants to meet you, Rhyme. You're a celebrity.'

Rhyme sighed. 'Fine.'

Sachs turned to him, eyes narrowed. 'You're not arguing.'

Now *he* laughed. 'Not in the mood. Let her come over. I'll interview her myself. Show you how it's done. Short and sweet.'

Sachs gave a cautious look.

Rhyme then asked, 'What do you have, Mel?'

Peering through the eyepiece of a microscope, the tech said, 'Nothing helpful for sourcing him.'

' "Sourcing." Missed that word when I was in verb school,' Rhyme said sourly.

'But I've got one thing,' Cooper said, ignoring Rhyme's remark and reading the results from the chromatograph. 'Traces of substances that the database is saying are ginseng and wolfberry.'

'Chinese herbs, maybe tea,' Rhyme announced. A case several years ago had involved a snake-head, a smuggler of illegal aliens, and much of the investigation had centered around China-town. A police officer from mainland China, helping in the case, had taught Rhyme about herbalism, thinking it might help his condition. The substances had no effect, of course, but Rhyme had found the subject potentially helpful in investigations. At the moment he noted the find, but agreed with Cooper that it wasn't much of a lead. There was a time when those sub-stances would have been found only in Asian specialty shops and what Rhyme called 'woo-woo stores.' Now products like that were in every Rite Aid pharmacy and Food Emporium throughout the city.

'On the board, if you please, Sachs.'

As she wrote, he looked over a series of small evidence bags lined up in a row, with her handwriting on the chain-of-custody cards. They were labeled with directions from the compass.

'Ten little Indians,' Rhyme said, intrigued. 'What do we have there?'

'I got mad, Rhyme. No, I got fucking furious.'

'Good. I find anger liberating. Why?'

'Because we can't find him. So I took samples of substrate from where he might've been. I crawled around in some pretty lousy places, Rhyme.'

'Hence the smudge.' He looked at her forehead.

She caught his eye. 'I'll wash it off later.' A smile. Seductive, he believed.

He lifted an eyebrow. 'Well, get searching. Tell me what you find.'

She pulled on gloves and poured the samples

into ten examining dishes. Donning magnifying goggles, she began sifting through them, using a sterile probe to search the contents of each bag. Dirt, cigarette butts, the scraps of paper, the nuts and bolts, the bits of what seemed to be rodent shit, hairs, scraps of cloth, candy and fast food wrappers, grains of concrete, metal and stone. The epidermis of underground New York.

Rhyme had learned long ago that in searching for evidence at crime scenes, the key was finding patterns. What repeated itself frequently? Objects in that category could be presumptively eliminated. It was the unique items, those out of place, that might be relevant. Outliers, statisticians and sociologists called them.

Nearly everything that Sachs had found was repeated in every dish of the samples. But there was only one thing that was in a category of its own: a very tiny band of curved metal, nearly in a circle, about twice the width of a pencil lead. Though there were many other bits of metal — parts of screws and bolts and shavings — nothing resembled this.

It was also clean, suggesting it had been left recently.

'Where was this, Sachs?'

Rising from her hunched-over pose and stretching, she looked at the label on the bag in front of the dish.

'Twenty feet from the shaft, southwest. It's where he would've had a view of all the wiring connections he'd made. It was under a beam.'

So Galt would have been crouching. The metal bit could have fallen from his cuff or

371

clothing. He asked Sachs to hold it up for him to examine closely. She put magnifying goggles on him, adjusted them. Then she took tweezers and picked up the bit, holding it close.

'Ah, bluing,' he said. 'Used on iron. Like on guns. Treated with sodium hydroxide and nitrite. For corrosion resistance. And good tensile properties. It's a spring of some kind. Mel, what's your mechanical parts database like?'

'Not as updated as when you were chief, but it's something.'

Rhyme went online, laboriously typing the pass code. He could use voice recognition, but characters like @% $* — which the department had adopted to improve security — were troublesome to interpret vocally.

The NYPD forensic database main screen popped up and Rhyme started in the *Miscellaneous Metals — Springs* category.

After ten minutes of scrolling through hundreds of samples he announced, 'It's a hairspring, I think.'

'What's that?' Cooper asked.

Rhyme was grimacing. 'I'm afraid it's bad news. If it's his, it means he might be changing his approach to the attacks.'

'How?' Sachs wondered aloud.

'They're used in timers. I'd bet he's worried we're getting close to him. And he's going to start using a timed device instead of a remote control. When the next attack happens, he could be in a different borough.'

Rhyme had Sachs bag the spring and mark a chain-of-custody card.

'He's smart,' Cooper observed. 'But he'll slip up. They always do.'

They *often* do, Rhyme corrected silently.

The tech then said, 'Got a pretty good print from one of the remote switches.'

Rhyme hoped it was from somebody else, but, no, it was just one of Galt's — he didn't need to be diligent about obscuring his identity now that they'd learned his name.

The phone buzzed and Rhyme blinked to see the country code. He answered at once.

'Commander Luna.'

'Captain Rhyme, we have, perhaps, a development.'

'Go ahead, please.'

'An hour ago there was a false fire alarm in a wing of the building Mr. Watchmaker was observing. On that floor is an office of a company that brokers real estate loans in Latin America. The owner's a colorful fellow. Been under investigation a few times. It made me suspicious. I looked into the background of this man and he's had death threats made before.'

'By whom?'

'Clients whose deals turned out to be less lucrative than they would have wanted. He performs some other functions too, which I cannot find out about too easily. And if I cannot find out about them the answer is simple: He's a crook. Which means he has a very large and efficient security staff.'

'So he's the sort of target that would require a killer like the Watchmaker.'

'Exactly.'

'But,' Rhyme continued, 'I'd also keep that in mind the target could be at the exact opposite end of the complex from that office.'

'You think the fire alarm was a feint.'

'Possibly.'

'I'll have Arturo's men consider that too. He's put his best — and most invisible — surveillance people on the case.'

'Have you found anything more about the contents of the package that Logan received? The letter I with the blanks? The circuit board, the booklet, the numbers?'

'Nothing but speculation. And, as I think you would too, Captain, I feel speculation is a waste of time.'

'True, Commander.'

Rhyme thanked the man again and they disconnected. He glanced at the clock. The time was 10 p.m. Thirty-five hours since the attack at the substation. Rhyme was in turmoil. On the one hand, he was aware of the terrible pressure to move forward with a case in which the progress was frustratingly slow. On the other, he was exhausted. More tired than he remembered being in a long time. He needed sleep. But he didn't want to admit it to anyone, even Sachs. He was staring at the silent box of the phone, considering what the Mexican police commander had just told him, when he was aware of sweat dotting his forehead. This infuriated him. He wanted to wipe it before anyone noticed, but of course that was a luxury not available to him. He jerked his head from side to side. Finally the motion dislodged the drop.

But it also caught Sachs's attention. He sensed she was about to ask if he was feeling all right. He didn't want to tell her that he wasn't, nor did he want to lie to her. He wheeled abruptly to an evidence whiteboard and studied the script intently. Without seeing the words at all.

Sachs was starting toward him when the doorbell rang. A moment later there was some motion from the doorway and Thom entered the room with a visitor. Rhyme easily deduced the person's identity; she was in a wheelchair made by the same company that had produced his.

52

Susan Stringer had a pretty, heart-shaped face and a sing-songy voice. Two adjectives stood out: pleasant and sweet.

Her eyes were quick, though, and lips taut, even when smiling, as befit somebody who had to maneuver her way through the streets of New York using only the power of her arms.

'An accessible townhouse on the Upper West Side. That's a rarity.'

Rhyme gave her a smile in return — he was reserved. He had work to do, and very little of it involved witnesses; his comments to Sachs earlier about his interviewing Susan Stringer were, of course, facetious.

Still, she'd nearly been killed by Ray Galt — in a particularly horrible way — and might have some helpful information. And if, as Sachs had reported, she wanted to meet him in the process, he could live with that.

She nodded at Thom Reston with a knowing look about the importance of — and burdens upon — caregivers. He asked if there was anything she wanted and she said no. 'I can't stay long. It's late and I'm not feeling too well.' Her face had a hollow look; she'd undoubtedly be thinking of the terrible moments in the elevator. She wheeled closer to Rhyme. Susan's arms clearly worked fine; she was a paraplegic and would probably have suffered a thoracic injury, in her mid or upper back.

'No burns?' Rhyme asked.

'No. I didn't get a shock. The only problem was smoke — from the . . . from the men in the elevator with me. One caught fire.' The last sentence was a whisper.

'What happened?' Sachs asked.

A stoic look. 'We were near the ground floor when the elevator stopped suddenly. The lights went out, except for the emergency light. One of the businessmen behind me reached for the panel to hit the Help button. As soon as he touched it he just started moaning and dancing around.'

She coughed. Cleared her throat. 'It was terrible. He couldn't let go of the panel. His friend grabbed him or he brushed against him. It was like a chain reaction. They just kept jerking around. And one of them caught fire. His hair . . . the smoke, the smell.' Susan was whispering now. 'Horrible. Just horrible. They were dying, right around me, they were dying. I was screaming. I realized it was some electrical problem and I didn't want to touch the metal hand rim of the chair or the metal door frame. I just sat there.'

Susan shuddered. Then repeated, 'I just sat there. Then the car moved down the last few feet and the door opened. There were dozens of people in the lobby, they pulled me out . . . I tried to warn them not to touch anything but the electricity was off by then.' She coughed softly for a moment. 'Who is this man, Ray Galt?' Susan asked.

Rhyme told her, 'He thinks he got sick from power lines. Cancer. He's out for revenge. But there may be an ecoterror connection. He might've been recruited by a group that's opposed to traditional power companies. We don't know yet. Not for sure.'

Susan blurted, 'And he wants to kill innocent people to make his point? What a hypocrite.'

Sachs said, 'He's a fanatic so he doesn't even register hypocrisy. Whatever *he* wants to do is good. Whatever stops him from doing what he wants is bad. Very simple universe.'

Rhyme glanced at Sachs, who caught the cue and asked Susan, 'You said there was something that might help us?'

'Yes, I think I saw him.'

Despite his distrust of witnesses, Rhyme said encouragingly, 'Go ahead. Please.'

'He got onto the elevator at my floor.'

'You think it was him? Why?'

'Because he spilled some water. Accidentally, it seemed, but now I know he did it on purpose. To improve the connection.'

Sachs said, 'The water that Ron found on the soles of their shoes. Sure. We wondered where that came from.'

'He was dressed like a maintenance man with a watering can for the plants. He was wearing brown overalls. Kind of dirty. It seemed odd. And the building doesn't have plants in the hall and we don't in our office.'

'There's still a team there?' Rhyme asked Sachs.

She said that there would be. 'Fire, maybe. Not PD.'

'Have them call the building manager, wake him up if they have to. See if they have a plant maintenance service. And check video security.'

A few minutes later they had their answer: no plant waterers for the building or any of the companies on the eighth floor. And security cameras were only in the lobby, with wide-angle lenses uselessly showing 'a bunch of people coming, a bunch of people going,' one of the fire marshals reported. 'Can't make out a single face.'

Rhyme called up the DMV picture of Galt on the screen. 'Is that him?' he asked Susan.

'Could be. He didn't look at us and I didn't look at him really.' A knowing glance toward Rhyme. 'His face wasn't exactly at eye level.'

'Anything else you remember about him?'

'When he was walking toward the car and then when he first got in, he kept looking at his watch.'

'The deadline,' Sachs pointed out. Then added, 'He set it off early, though.'

'Only a few minutes,' Rhyme said. 'Maybe he was worried that somebody'd recognized him in the building. He wanted to finish up and get out. And he was probably monitoring Algonquin's electrical transmissions and knew the company wasn't going to shut down the juice by the deadline.'

Susan continued, 'He was wearing gloves. Tan gloves. They were leather . . . Those *were* at eye level. And I remember them because I was thinking his hands must be sweating. It was hot in the car.'

'Did the uniform have any writing on it?'

'No.'

'Anything else?'

She shrugged. 'Not that it's helpful, but he was rude.'

'Rude?'

'When he got on the elevator he pushed past me. Didn't apologize or anything.'

'He actually touched you?'

'Not me.' She nodded down. 'The chair. It was kind of a tight squeeze.'

'Mel!'

The tech's head swiveled toward them.

'Susan,' Rhyme asked. 'Do you mind if we examine that spot on your chair?'

'No, not at all.'

Cooper carefully looked over the side of the chair she indicated, using a magnifying glass. Rhyme couldn't see exactly what he found but the tech lifted away two items from bolts at joints in the upright pieces.

'What?'

'Fibers. One dark green and one brown.' Cooper was examining them through the microscope, then turned to a computer database of similar fiber. 'Cotton, heavy duty. Could be military, army surplus.'

'Enough to test?'

'Plenty.' The tech and Sachs ran a portion of each of the samples through the gas chromatograph/mass spectrometer.

Finally, as Rhyme waited impatiently, she called, 'Got the results.' A printout eased from the machine and Cooper looked it over.

'More aviation fuel on the green fiber. But

something else. On the brown fiber there's diesel fuel. And more of those Chinese herbs.'

'Diesel.' Rhyme was considering this. 'Maybe it's not an airport. Maybe it's a refinery he's after.'

Cooper said, 'That'd be one hell of a target, Lincoln.'

It sure would. 'Sachs, call Gary Nobel. Tell him to step up security in the ports. Refineries and tankers especially.'

She grabbed the phone.

'Mel, add everything we've got so far to the chart.'

CRIME SCENE:
OFFICE BUILDING AT 235 W. 54TH STREET

- Victims (deceased):
  — Larry Fishbein, New York City, accountant.
  — Robert Bodine, New York City, attorney.
  — Franklin Tucker, Paramus, New Jersey, salesman.
- One friction ridge of Raymond Galt.
- Bennington cable and split bolts, same as at other scenes.
- Two hand-made remote relay switches:
  — One to shut off power to elevator.
  — One to complete circuit and electrify elevator car.
- Bolts and smaller wires connecting panel to elevator, not traceable.
- Victims had water on shoes.
- Trace:
  — Chinese herbs, ginseng and wolf-berry.
  — Hairspring (plan-ning on using timer,

rather than remote for future attacks?).
— Dark green cotton heavy-duty clothing fiber.
— containing trace of jet fuel and alternative jet fuel.
— Attack on military base?
• Dark brown cotton heavy-duty clothing fiber.
— Containing trace of diesel fuel.
— Containing additional Chinese herbs.

PROFILE

• Identified as Raymond Galt, 40, single, living in Manhattan, 227 Suffolk St.
• Terrorist connection? Relation to Justice For the Earth? Suspected ecoterror group. No profile in any U.S. or international database. New? Underground? Individual named Rahman involved. Also Johnston.
• References to monetary disbursements, personnel movements and something 'big.'
— Algonquin security breach in Philadelphia might be related.
— SIGINT hits: code word reference to weapons, 'paper and supplies' (guns, explosives?).
— Personnel include man and woman.
— Galt's relationship unknown.
• Cancer patient; presence of vinblastine and prednisone in significant quantities, traces of etoposide. Leukemia.
• Galt is armed with military 1911 Colt .45.
• Masquerading as maintenance man in dark brown overalls. Dark green, as well?
• Wearing tan leather gloves.

Cooper organized the evidence, and marked chain of custody cards, while Sachs was on the phone with Homeland Security about the risk to the ports in New York and New Jersey.

Rhyme and Susan Stringer found themselves alone. As he stared at the chart he was aware that the woman was looking him over closely. Uneasy, he turned toward her, trying to figure out how to get her to leave. She'd come, she'd helped, she'd met the celebrity crip. Time to get on with things.

She asked, 'You're C4, right?'

This meant his injury was at the fourth cervical vertebra, four bones down in his spine from the base of the skull.

'Yes, though I've got a little motion in my hands. No sensation.'

Technically his was a 'complete' injury, meaning that he'd lost all sensory function below the site of the injury ('incomplete' patients can have considerable movement). But the human body is quirky, and a few electric impulses escaped over the barricade. The wiring was faulty but not wholly severed.

'You're in good shape,' she said. 'Muscle-wise.'

Eyes back on the whiteboards, he said absently, 'I do range-of-motion exercises every day and functional electric stimulation to keep the tone up.'

Rhyme had to admit that he enjoyed the exercise. He explained that he worked out on a treadmill and stationary bike. The equipment moved *him*, not the other way around, but it still built up muscles and seemed to have been

383

responsible for the recent movement he'd regained in his right hand, whereas after the accident only his left ring finger worked.

He was in better shape now than before the injury.

He told her this and he could see from her face that she understood; she flexed. 'I'd ask you to arm wrestle, but . . . '

A genuine laugh from Rhyme's throat.

Then her face grew solemn and she glanced around to see if anyone else could hear. When it was clear that nobody could she turned back, held his eyes and said, 'Lincoln, do you believe in fate?'

53

There is a certain camaraderie in the world of the disabled.

Some patients have the band of brothers attitude — it's us against them. Don't mess with us. Others take a more huggy approach. Hey, you ever need to cry on somebody's shoulder, I'm there for you. We're all in this together, friend.

But Lincoln Rhyme didn't have time for either. He was a criminalist who happened to have a body that didn't operate the way he would have liked. Like Amelia Sachs was a cop with arthritis and a love of fast cars and guns.

Rhyme didn't define himself by his disability. It was an afterthought. There were pleasant crips and witty ones and those who were insufferable pricks. Rhyme judged them one by one, as he did everybody else.

He thought Susan Stringer was a perfectly pleasant woman and respected her courage in coming here when she could have stayed home and nursed her wounds and exploited her trauma. But they had nothing in common other than a spinal cord injury, and Rhyme's mind was already back to the Galt case; he suspected Susan was soon to be disappointed that the famous gimp criminalist she'd come to see had little time for her.

And he sure as hell wasn't anybody to talk to about fate.

'No,' he answered her, 'probably not in the sense you mean.'

'I'm referring to what seems to be coincidence actually could be events that were meant to happen.'

He confirmed, 'Then, no.'

'I didn't think so.' She was smiling. 'But the good news for people like you is that there are people like me who *do* believe in fate. I think there's a reason I was in that elevator and I'm here now.' The smile turned into a laugh. 'Don't worry. I'm not a stalker.' A whisper. 'I'm not after a donation . . . or after your body. I'm happily married and I can see that you and Detective Sachs are together. It's not about that. It's solely about you.'

He was about to . . . well, he wasn't sure *what* he was about to do. He simply wanted her to leave but didn't quite know how to engineer it. So he lifted a curious, and cautious, eyebrow.

She asked, 'Have you heard about the Pembroke Spinal Cord Center, over on Lexington?'

'I think so. I'm not sure.' He was forever getting information about spinal cord injury rehab and products and medical updates. He'd stopped paying much attention to the flood of material; his obsession with the cases he was running for the Bureau and the NYPD greatly limited his time for extracurricular reading, much less chasing around the country in search of new treatments.

Susan said, 'I've been in several programs there. Some people in my SCI support group have too.'

SCI support group. His heart sank. He saw what was coming.

But again, she was a step ahead. 'I'm not asking you to join us, don't worry. You don't look like you'd be a good member.' The eyes sparkled humorously in her heart-shaped face. 'Of anything.'

'No.'

'All I'm asking tonight is that you hear me out.'

'I can do that.'

'Now, Pembroke is the D-day of spinal cord treatment. They do everything.'

There were many promising techniques to help people with severe disabilities. But the problem was funding. Even though the injuries were severe, and the consequences lifelong, the reality was that when compared with other maladies, serious spinal cord problems were relatively rare. Which meant that government and corporate research money went elsewhere, to procedures and medicines that would help more people. So most of the procedures that promised significant improvements in patients' conditions remained experimental and unapproved in America.

And some of the results *were* remarkable. In research labs, rats with severed spinal cords had actually learned to walk again.

'They have a critical response unit, but that won't do us any good, of course.'

The key to minimizing spinal cord damage is to treat the affected area immediately after the accident with medications that prevent swelling and future killing of the nerves at the site of the injury. But there's a very small window of opportunity to do that, usually hours or at the most days after the injury.

As veteran patients, Rhyme and Susan Stringer could take advantage only of techniques to *repair* the damage. But that always ran up against the intractable problem: central nervous system cells — those in the brain and spinal cord — don't regenerate the way the skin on your finger does after a cut.

This was the battle that SCI doctors and researchers fought daily, and Pembroke was in the vanguard. Susan described an impressive array of techniques that the center offered. They were working with stem cells, doing nerve rerouting — using peripheral nerves (any nerve *outside* the spinal cord, which *can* regenerate) — and treating the injured areas with drugs and other substances to promote regeneration. They were even building noncellular 'bridges' around the location of the injury to carry nerve impulses between the brain and the muscles.

The Center also had an extensive prosthetics department.

'It was amazing,' she told him. 'I saw a video of this paraplegic who'd been implanted with a computer controller and a number of wires. She could walk almost normally.'

Rhyme was staring at the length of the

Bennington cable that Galt had used in the first attack.

Wires . . .

She described something called the Freehand system, and others like it, that involved implanting stimulators and electrodes in the arms. By shrugging your shoulders or moving your neck in a certain way, you could trigger coordinated movements of the arm and hands. Some quads, she explained, could even feed themselves.

'None of that bullshit quackery you see, doctors preying on the desperate.' Susan angrily mentioned a doctor in China who'd pocket $20,000 to drill holes in patients' heads and spines to implant tissue from embryos. With, of course, no discernible effect — other than exposing the patient to risk of death, further injury and bankruptcy.

The people on the staff at Pembroke, she explained, were all from the top medical schools from around the world.

And the claims were realistic — that is, modest. A quad like Rhyme wouldn't be able to walk, but he could improve his lung functioning, perhaps get other digits to work and, most important, get back control of bowel and bladder. This would greatly help in reducing the risk of dysreflexia attacks — that skyrocketing of the blood pressure that could lead to stroke that could render him even more disabled than he was. Or kill him.

'It's helped me a lot. I think in a few years I'll be able to walk again.'

Rhyme was nodding. He could think of nothing to say.

'I don't work for them. I'm not a disability rights advocate. I'm an editor who happens to be a paraplegic.' This echo made Rhyme offer a faint smile. She continued, 'But when Detective Sachs said she was working with you, I thought, Fate. I was meant to come tell you about Pembroke. They can help you.'

'I . . . appreciate it.'

'I've read about you, of course. You've done a lot of good for the city. Maybe it's time you did some good for yourself.'

'Well, it's complicated.' He had no idea what that meant, much less why he'd said it.

'I know, you're worried about the risk. And you should be.'

True, surgery would be riskier for him, as a C4, than for her. He was prone to blood pressure, respiratory and infection complications. The question was balance. Was the surgery worth it? He'd nearly undergone an operation a few years ago but a case had derailed the plans for the procedure. So he'd postponed any medical treatment of that sort.

But now? He considered: Was his life the way he wished it to be? Of course not. But he was content. He loved Sachs, and she him. He lived for his job. He wasn't eager to throw all that away chasing an unrealistic dream.

Normally buttoned tight about his personal feelings, he nonetheless told Susan Stringer this, and she understood.

Then he surprised himself further by adding

390

something he hadn't told many people at all. 'I feel that I'm mostly my mind. That's where I live. And I sometimes think that's one of the reasons I'm the criminalist that I am. No distractions. My power comes from my disability. If I were to change, if I were to become, quote, 'normal,' would that affect me as a forensic scientist? I don't know. But I don't want to take that chance.'

Susan was considering this. 'It's an interesting thought. But I wonder if that's a crutch, an excuse *not* to take the risk.'

Rhyme appreciated that. He liked blunt talk. He nodded at his chair. 'A crutch is a step up in my case.'

She laughed.

'Thanks for your thoughts,' he added, because he felt he ought to, and she fixed him with another of those knowing looks. The expression was less irritating now, though it remained disconcerting.

She backed away in the chair and said, 'Mission accomplished.'

His brow furrowed.

Susan said, 'I found you two fibers you might not otherwise have.' She smiled. 'Wish it were more.' Eyes back on Rhyme. 'But sometimes it's the little things that make all the difference. Now, I should go.'

Sachs thanked her and Thom saw her out.

After she'd left, Rhyme said, 'This was a setup, right?'

Sachs replied, 'It was *sort of* a setup, Rhyme. We needed to interview her anyway. When I called about arranging it, we got to talking. When she heard I worked with you she wanted to make her sales pitch. I told her I'd get her in to see the chairman.'

Rhyme gave a brief smile.

Then it faded as Sachs crouched and said in a voice that Mel Cooper couldn't hear, 'I don't want you any different than you are, Rhyme. But I want to make sure you're healthy. For me, that's all I care about. Whatever you choose is fine.'

For a moment Rhyme recalled the title of the pamphlet left by Dr. Kopeski, with Die With Dignity.

Choices.

And she leaned forward and kissed him. He felt her hand touching the side of his head with a bit more palm than made sense for a gesture of affection.

'I have a temperature?' he asked, smiling at catching her.

She laughed. 'We *all* have temperatures, Rhyme. Whether or not you have a fever, I can't tell.' She kissed him again. 'Now get some sleep. Mel and I'll keep going here for a while. I'll be up to bed soon.' She returned to the evidence she'd found.

Rhyme hesitated but then decided that he was tired, too tired to be much help at the moment. He wheeled toward the elevator, where Thom joined him and they began their journey upward in the tiny car. Sweat continued to dot his forehead and it seemed to him that his cheeks were flushed. These were symptoms of dysreflexia. But he didn't have a headache and he didn't feel the onset of the sensation that preceded an attack. Thom got him ready for bed and handled the evening detail. The blood pressure cuff and thermometer were handy. 'Little high,' he said of the former. As to the latter, Rhyme didn't, in fact, have a fever.

Thom executed a smooth transfer to get him into bed, and Rhyme heard in his memory Sachs's comment from a few minutes earlier.

We all have a temperature, Rhyme . . .

He couldn't help reflecting that clinically this was true. We all did. Even the dead.

54

He awoke fast, from a dream.

He tried to recall it. He couldn't remember enough to know whether it had been bad or simply odd. It was certainly intense, though. The likelihood, however, was that it was bad, since he was sweating furiously, as if he were walking through the turbine room at Algonquin Consolidated.

The time was just before midnight, the faint light of the alarm clock reported. He'd been asleep for a short time and he was groggy; it took a moment to orient himself.

He'd ditched the uniform and hard hat and gear bag after the attack at the hotel, but he'd kept one of his accoutrements, which was now dangling from a chair nearby: the ID badge. In the dim, reflected light he stared at it now: His sullen picture, the impersonal typeface of 'R. Galt' and, above that, in somewhat more friendly lettering:

ALGONQUIN CONSOLIDATED POWER
ENERGIZING YOUR LIFE™

Considering what he'd been up to for the past several days, he appreciated the irony of that slogan.

He lay back and stared at the shabby ceiling in the East Village weekly rental, which he'd taken a month ago under a pseudonym, knowing the police would find the apartment sooner or later.

Sooner, as it turned out.

He kicked the sheets off. His flesh was damp with sweat.

Thinking about the conductivity of the human body. The resistance of our slippery internal organs can be as low as 85 ohms, making them extremely susceptible to current. Wet skin, 1,000 or less. But dry skin has a resistance of 100,000 ohms or more. That's so high that significant amounts of voltage are needed to push that current through the body, usually 2,000 volts.

Sweat makes the job a lot easier.

His skin cooled as it dried, and his resistance climbed.

His mind leapt from thought to thought: the plans for tomorrow, what voltages to use, how to rig the lines. He thought about the people he was working with. And he thought about the people pursuing him. That woman detective, Sachs. The younger one, Pulaski. And, of course, Lincoln Rhyme.

Then he was meditating on something else entirely: two men in the 1950s, the chemists Stanley Miller and Harold Urey, at the University of Chicago. They devised a very interesting experiment. In their lab they created their version of the primordial soup and atmosphere that had covered the earth billions of years ago. Into this mix of hydrogen, ammonia and methane, they fired sparks mimicking the lightning that blanketed the earth back then.

And what happened?

A few days later they found something thrilling: In the test tubes were traces of amino acids, the so-called building blocks of life.

They had discovered evidence suggesting that life had begun on earth all because of a spark of electricity.

As the clock approached midnight, he composed his next demand letter to Algonquin and the City of New York. Then with sleep enfolding him he thought again about juice. And the irony that what had, in a millisecond burst of lightning, created life so many, many years ago would, tomorrow, take it away, just as fast.

III

JUICE

EARTH DAY

'I haven't failed. I've just found ten thousand ways that won't work.'

— THOMAS ALVA EDISON

55

'Please leave a message at the tone.'

Sitting in his Brooklyn townhouse at 7:30 a.m., Fred Dellray stared at his phone, flipped it closed. He didn't bother to leave another message, though, not after leaving twelve earlier ones on William Brent's cold phone.

I'm screwed, he thought.

There was the chance the man was dead. Even though McDaniel's phrasing was fucked-up (*symbiosis construct?*), his theory might not be. It made sense that Ray Galt was the inside man seduced into helping Rahman and Johnston and their Justice For the Earth group target Algonquin and the grid. If Brent had stumbled into their cell, they'd have killed him in an instant.

Ah, Dellray thought angrily: blind, simple-minded politics — the empty calories of terrorism.

But Dellray'd been in this business a long time and his gut told him that William Brent was very much alive. New York City is smaller than people think, particularly the underside of the Big Apple. Dellray had called up other contacts, a lot of them: other CIs and some of the undercover agents he ran. No word about Brent. Even Jimmy Jeep knew nothing — and he definitely had a motive to track down the man again, to make sure Dellray still backed the upcoming march through Georgia. Yet nobody'd heard about anybody ordering a clip or a cleaner. And no surprised garbage men had wheeled a Dumpster to their truck and found nestled inside the pungent sarcophagus an unidentified body.

No, Dellray concluded. There was only the obvious answer, and he could ignore it no more: Brent had fucked him over.

He'd checked Homeland Security to see if the snitch, either as Brent or as one of his half-dozen undercover identities, had booked a flight anywhere. He hadn't, though any professional CI knows where to buy airtight identity papers.

'Honey?'

Dellray jumped at the sound and he looked up and saw Serena in the doorway, holding Preston.

'You're looking thoughtful,' she said. Dellray continued to be struck by the fact she looked like Jada Pinkett Smith, the actress and producer.

'You were brooding before you went to bed, you started brooding when you woke up. I suspect you were brooding in your sleep.'

He opened his mouth to spin a tale, but then said, 'I think I got my ass fired yesterday.'

'What?' Her face was shocked. 'McDaniel fired you?'

'Not in so many words — he thanked me.'

'But — '

'Some thank-you's mean thank you. Others mean pack up your stuff . . . Let's just say I'm being eased out. Same thing.'

'I think you're reading too much into it.'

'He keeps forgetting to call me with updates on the case.'

'The grid case?'

'Right. Lincoln calls me, Lon Sellitto calls me. Tucker's *assistant* calls me.'

Dellray didn't go into the part about another source of the brooding: the possible indictment for the stolen and missing $100,000.

But more troubling was the fact that he really did believe William Brent had had a solid lead, something that might let them stop these terrible attacks. A lead that had vanished with him.

Serena walked over and sat beside him, handed over Preston, who, grabbing Dellray's lengthy thumb in enthusiastic fingers, took away some of the brooding. She said to him, 'I'm sorry, honey.'

He looked out the window of the townhouse into the complex geometry of buildings and beyond, where he could just see a bit of stonework from the Brooklyn Bridge. A portion of Walt Whitman's poem 'Crossing Brooklyn Ferry' came to mind.

The best I had done seem'd to me blank
and suspicious;
My great thoughts, as I supposed them,
were they not in reality meagre?

These words were true of him as well. The façade of Fred Dellray: hip, ornery, tough, man of the street. Occasionally thinking, *more* than occasionally thinking, What if I'm getting it wrong?

401

The beginning lines of the next stanza of Whitman's poem, though, were the kicker:

It is not you alone who know what it is to be evil;
I am he who knew what it was to be evil . . .

'What'm I going to do?' he mused.

Justice For the Earth . . .

He ruefully recalled turning down the chance to go to a high-level conference on satellite and data intelligence gathering and analysis. The memo had read, 'The Shape of the Future.'

Slipping into Street, Dellray had said, 'Here's the shape of the fewture.' And rolled the memo into a ball, launching it into a trash bin for a three-pointer.

'So, you're just . . . home?' Serena asked, wiping Preston's mouth. The baby giggled and wanted more. She obliged and tickled him too.

'I had one angle on the case. And it vanished. Well, I lost it. I trusted somebody I shouldn't've. I'm outta the loop.'

'A snitch? Walked out on *you*?'

An inch away from mentioning the one hundred thousand. But he didn't go there.

'Gone and vanished,' Dellray muttered.

'Gone *and* vanished? Both?' Serena's face grew theatrically grave. 'Don't tell me he absconded and disappeared too?'

The agent could resist the smile no longer. 'I only use snitches with extra-ordinary talents.' Then the smile faded. 'In two years he never missed a debriefing or call.'

Of course, in those two years I never paid him till *after* he'd delivered.

Serena asked, 'So what're you going to do?'

He answered honestly, 'I don't know.'

'Then you can do me a favor.'

'I suppose. What?'

'You know all that stuff in the basement, that you've been meaning to organize?'

Fred Dellray's first reaction was to say, You've got to be kidding. But then he considered the leads he had in the Galt case, which were none, and, hefting the baby on his hip, rose and followed her downstairs.

56

Ron Pulaski could still hear the sound. The thud and then the crack.

Oh, the crack. He hated that.

Thinking back to his first time working for Lincoln and Amelia: how he'd gotten careless and had been smacked in the head with a bat or club. He *knew* about the incident though he couldn't remember a single thing about it. Careless. He'd turned the corner without checking on the whereabouts of the suspect and the man had clocked him good.

The injury had made him scared, made him confused, made him disoriented. He did the best he could — oh, he tried hard — though the trauma kept coming back. And even worse: It was one thing to get lazy and walk around a corner when he should've been careful, but it was something very different to make a mistake and hurt somebody else.

Pulaski now parked his squad car in front of the hospital — a different vehicle. The other one had been impounded for evidence. If he was asked, he was going to say he was here to take a statement from somebody who'd been in the neighborhood of the man committing the terrorist attacks on the grid.

I'm trying to ascertain the perpetrator's whereabouts . . .

That was the sort of thing he and his twin

brother, also a cop, would say to each other and they'd laugh their asses off. Only it wasn't funny now. Because he knew the guy he'd run over, whose body had thudded and whose head had cracked, was just some poor passerby.

As he walked inside the chaotic hospital, a wave of panic hit him.

What if he had *killed* the guy?

Vehicular manslaughter, he supposed the charge could be. Or criminally negligent homicide.

This could be the end of his career.

And even if he didn't get indicted, even if the attorney general didn't go anywhere with the case, he could still be sued by the guy's family. What if the man ended up like Lincoln Rhyme, paralyzed? Did the police department have insurance for this sort of thing? His own coverage sure wouldn't pay for anything like lifelong care. Could the vic sue Pulaski and take away everything? He and Jenny'd be working for the rest of their lives just to pay off the judgment. The kids might never go to college; the tiny fund they'd already started would disappear like smoke.

'I'm here to see Stanley Palmer,' he told the attendant sitting behind a desk. 'Auto accident yesterday.'

'Sure, officer. He's in four oh two.'

Being in uniform, he walked freely through several doors until he found the room.

He paused outside to gather his courage. What if Palmer's entire family was there? Wife and children? He tried to think of something to say.

But all he heard was *thud*. Then *crack*.

Ron Pulaski took a deep breath and stepped into the room. Palmer was alone. He lay unconscious, hooked to all sorts of intimidating wires and tubes, electronic equipment as complicated as the things in Lincoln Rhyme's lab.

Rhyme . . .

How he'd let down his boss! The man who'd inspired him to remain a cop because Rhyme had done the same after his own injury. And the man who kept giving him more and more responsibility. Lincoln Rhyme believed in him.

And look what I've done now.

Pulaski stared at Palmer, lying absolutely still — even stiller than Rhyme, because *nothing* on the patient's body was moving, except his lungs, though even the lines on the monitor weren't doing much. A nurse passed by and Pulaski called her in. 'How is he?'

'I don't know,' she replied in a thick accent he couldn't identify. 'You have to talk to, you know, the doctor.'

After staring at Palmer's still form for some time, Pulaski looked up to see a middle-aged man of indeterminate race in blue scrubs. *M.D.* was embroidered after his name. Again because of Pulaski's own uniform, it seemed, the medico gave him information he might not otherwise have doled out to a stranger. Palmer had undergone surgery for severe internal injuries. He was in a coma and they weren't able to give a prognosis at this point.

He didn't have any family in the area, it

seemed. He was single. He had a brother and parents in Oregon and they'd been contacted.

'Brother,' Pulaski whispered, thinking of his own twin.

'That's right.' Then the doctor lowered the chart and cast a look at the cop. After a moment he said, with a knowing gaze, 'You're not here to take his statement. This has nothing to do with the investigation. Come on.'

'What?' Alarmed, Pulaski could only stare.

Then a kind smile blossomed in the doctor's face. 'It happens. Don't worry about it.'

'Happens?'

'I've been an ER doctor in the city for a long time. You never see veteran cops come in person to pay respects to victims, only the young ones.'

'No, really. I was just checking to see if I could take a statement.'

'Sure . . . But you could've called to see if he was conscious. Don't play all hard ass, Officer. You've got a good heart.'

Which was pounding all the harder now.

The doctor's eyes went to Palmer's motionless form. 'Was it a hit-and-run?'

'No. We know the driver.'

'Good. You nailed the prick. I hope the jury throws the book at him.' Then the man, in his stained outfit, was walking away.

Pulaski stopped at the nurses' station and, once more under the aura of his uniform, got Palmer's address and social security number. He'd find out what he could about him, his family, dependents. Even though he was single, Palmer was middle-aged so he might have kids.

He'd call them, see if he could help in some way. Pulaski didn't have much money, but he'd give whatever moral support he could.

Mostly the young officer just wanted to unburden his soul for the pain he'd caused.

The nurse excused herself and turned away, answering an incoming call.

Pulaski turned too, even more quickly, and before he left the nurses' station, he pulled on sunglasses so nobody could see the tears.

57

At a little after 9 a.m. Rhyme asked Mel Cooper to turn on the TV in the lab, though to keep the sound down.

Since the feds had seemed slow to share up-to-the-minute information with the NYPD, at least with Rhyme, he wanted to make certain he learned the latest developments.

What better source than CNN?

The case was front and center, of course. Galt's picture was flashed about a million times and there were nearly as many references to the mysterious Justice for the Earth ecoterror group. And sound bites from anti-green Andi Jessen.

But most of the coverage of the Galt attacks involved windstorms of speculation. And many anchors, of course, wondered if there was a connection to Earth Day.

Which was also the subject of much reportage. There were a number of celebrations in the city: a parade, schoolchildren planting trees, protests, the New Energy Expo at the convention center and the big rally in Central Park, at which two of the President's key allies on the environment would be speaking, up-and-coming senators from out west. Following that would be a concert by a half dozen famous rock groups. Attendance would be close to a half million people. Several stories dealt with the increased security at all the events because of the recent attacks.

Gary Noble and Tucker McDaniel had told Rhyme that not only were two hundred extra agents and NYPD officers assigned to security, the FBI's technical support people had been working with Algonquin to make sure that all the electrical lines in and around the park were protected from sabotage.

Rhyme now looked up as Ron Pulaski walked into the room.

'Where've you been, Rookie?'

'Uhm . . . ' He held up a white envelope. 'The DNA.'

He'd been someplace else — Rhyme believed he knew where. The criminalist didn't press it but he said, 'That wasn't a priority. We know who the perp is. We'll need it for the trial. But we've got to catch him first.'

'Sure.'

'You find anything else yesterday at Galt's?'

'Went over it again top to bottom, Lincoln. But nothing, sorry.'

Sellitto too arrived, looking more disheveled than usual. The outfit seemed the same — light blue shirt and navy suit. Rhyme wondered if he'd slept in his own office last night. The detective gave them a synopsis of how things were unfolding downtown — the case had bled over into the public relations world. Political careers could be at stake and while local, state and federal officials were putting bodies on the street and bringing 'resources to bear,' each was also carefully suggesting that it was doing more than the others.

Settling into a noisy wicker chair, he loudly slurped coffee and muttered, 'But the bottom line's nobody knows how to run this thing. We've got portables and feebies and National Guard at the airports, subways, train stations. All the refineries and docks. Special harbor patrols around the tankers — though I don't know how the fuck he'd attack a ship with an arc flash or whatever. And they've got people on all the Algonquin substations — '

'He's not going after the substations anymore,' Rhyme complained.

'I know that. And so does everybody, but nobody knows where exactly to expect him. It's everywhere.'

'What is?'

'This fucking juice. Electricity.' He waved his hand, apparently indicating the entire city. 'Everybody's goddamn house.' He eyed outlets in Rhyme's wall. Then said, 'At least we haven't got any more demands. Christ, two yesterday, within a few hours. I was thinking he just got pissed off and decided to kill those guys in an elevator, no matter what.' The big man sighed. 'I'll be taking the stairs for a while, I'll tell you. Good for the weight, at least.'

Eyes sweeping across the evidence boards, Rhyme was in agreement about the rudderless nature of the case. Galt was smart but he wasn't brilliant, and he was leaving ample trace behind. It just wasn't leading them anywhere, other than offering general ideas of his targets.

An airport?

An oil depot?

Though Lincoln Rhyme was also thinking something else: Are the paths there and am I just missing them?

And felt again the tickle of sweat, the faint recurring headache that had plagued him recently. He'd successfully ignored it for a time but the throbbing had returned. Yes, he was feeling worse, there was no doubt about it. Was that affecting his mental skills? He would admit to no one, not even Sachs, that this was perhaps the most terrifying thing in the world to him. As he'd told Susan Stringer last night, his mind was all he had.

He found his eyes drawn to the den across the hall. The table where Dr. Arlen Kopeski's Die with Dignity brochure rested.

Choices . . .

He then tipped the thought away.

Just then Sellitto took a call, sitting up as he listened and setting down his coffee quickly. 'Yeah? . . . Where?' He jotted in his limp notebook.

Everyone in the room was watching him intently. Rhyme was thinking: a new demand?

The phone clicked closed. He looked up from his notes. 'Okay, may have something. A portable downtown, near Chinatown, calls in. Woman'd come up to him and says she thinks she saw our boy.'

'Galt?' Pulaski asked.

Sourly: 'What other boy we interested in, Officer?'

412

'Sorry.'

'She thinks she recognized the picture.'

'Where?' Rhyme snapped.

'There's an abandoned school, near China-town.' Sellitto gave them the address. Sachs was writing.

'The portable checked it out. Nobody there now.'

'But if he *was* there, he'd've left something behind,' Rhyme said.

At his nod, Sachs stood. 'Okay, Ron, let's go.'

'You better take a team.' Sellitto added wryly, 'We've probably got a *few* cops left who aren't guarding fuse boxes or wires around town.'

'Let's get ESU in the area,' she said. 'Stage nearby but keep 'em out of sight. Ron and I'll go in first. If he's there after all and we need a takedown, I'll call. But we don't want a team running through the place, screwing up the evidence, if it's empty.'

The two of them headed out the door.

Sellitto called Bo Haumann of Emergency Service and briefed him. The ESU head would get officers into the area and coordinate with Sachs. The detective disconnected and looked around the room, presumably for something to accompany the coffee. He found a plate of pastry, courtesy of Thom, and grabbed a bear claw. Dunked it and ate. Then he frowned.

Rhyme asked, 'What?'

'Just realized I forgot to call McDaniel and the feds and tell 'em about the operation in Chinatown — at the school.' Then he grimaced and held up his phone theatrically. 'Aw, shit. I

413

can't. I didn't pay for a cloud zone SIM chip. Guess I'll have to tell him later.'

Rhyme laughed and ignored the searing ache that spiked momentarily in his head.

Just then his phone rang and both humor and headaches vanished.

Kathryn Dance was calling.

His finger struggled to hit the keypad. 'Yes, Kathryn? What's going on?'

She said, 'I'm on the phone with Rodolfo. They've found the Watchmaker's target.'

Excellent, he reflected, though part of him was also thinking: Why now? But then he decided: the Watchmaker's the priority, at least for the moment. You've got Sachs and Pulaski and a dozen ESU troops after Galt. And the last time you had a chance at the Watchmaker, you turned away from the search to focus on something else, and he killed his victim and got away.

Not this time. Richard Logan isn't escaping this time.

'Go ahead,' he told the CBI agent, forcing himself to turn away from the evidence boards.

There was a click.

'Rodolfo,' Dance said. 'Lincoln's on the line. I'll leave you two to talk. I've got to see TJ.'

They said good-bye to her.

'Hello, Captain.'

'Commander. What do you have?'

'Arturo Diaz has four undercover officers in the office complex I was telling you about. About ten minutes ago Mr. Watchmaker, dressed as a businessman, entered the building. From the lobby he used a pay phone to call a company on

414

the sixth floor — on the opposite side of where the fire alarm was yesterday. Just like you thought. He spent about ten minutes inside and then left.'

'He vanished?' Rhyme asked, alarmed.

'No. He's now outside in a small park between the two main buildings in the complex.'

'Just sitting there?'

'So it seems. He's made several mobile calls. But the frequency is unusual or they're scrambled, Arturo tells me. So we can't intercept.'

Rhyme supposed rules about eavesdropping in Mexico might be somewhat less strict than in the U.S.

'They're sure it's the Watchmaker?'

'Yes. Arturo's men said they had a clear view. He has a satchel with him. He still is carrying it.'

'He is?'

'Yes. We still can't be sure what it is. A bomb, perhaps. With the circuit board detonator. Our teams are surrounding the facility. All plain-clothed but we have a full complement of soldiers nearby. And the bomb squad.'

'Where are you, Commander?'

A laugh. 'It was very considerate of your Watchmaker to pick this place. The Jamaican consulate is here. They have bomb barriers up and we're behind those. Logan can't see us.'

Rhyme hoped that was true.

'When will you move in?'

'As soon as Arturo's men say it's clear. The park is crowded with innocents. A number of children. But he won't get away. We have most of the roads sealed off.'

A trickle of sweat slipped down Rhyme's temple. He grimaced and twisted his head to the side to wipe it on the headrest.

The Watchmaker . . .

So close.

Please. Let this work out. Please . . .

And again squelched the frustration that he felt from working on such an important case at a distance.

'We'll let you know soon, Captain.'

They disconnected the call and Rhyme forced himself to focus on Raymond Galt once again. Was the lead to his whereabouts solid? He looked like an everyman, approaching middle age, not too heavy, not too slim. Average height. And in the paranoid climate he'd created, people were undoubtedly primed to see things that weren't there. Electrical traps, arc flash risks . . . and the killer himself.

Then he started, as Sachs's voice snapped through the radio. 'Rhyme, you there, K?'

She'd ended her transmission with the traditional conclusion of a comment or question in the police radio parlance, *K*, to let the recipient know it was okay to transmit. He and she usually disposed of this formality, and for some reason Rhyme found it troubling that she'd used the shorthand.

'Sachs, go ahead. What do you have?'

'We just got here. We're about to go in. I'll let you know.'

58

A maroon Torino Cobra made for a bad undercover car, so Sachs had glided it to a stop about two blocks away from the school where Galt had been sighted.

The school had closed years ago and, according to the signage, was soon to be demolished and condominiums built on the grounds.

'Good hidey-hole,' she said to Pulaski as they jogged close, noting the seven-foot-high wooden fence around the grounds. Covered with graffiti and posters of alternative theater, performance pieces and music groups plummeting to obscurity. *The Seventh Seal. The Right Hands. Bolo.*

Pulaski, who seemed to be forcing himself to concentrate, nodded. She'd have to keep an eye on him. He'd done well at the elevator crime scene in Midtown but it seemed that the accident at Galt's apartment — hitting that man — was bothering him again.

They paused in front of the fence. The demolition hadn't started yet; the gate — two hinged pieces of plywood chained together and padlocked — had enough play so they could have squeezed through, which is probably how Galt had gotten in, if in fact he had. Sachs stood to the side of the gap and peered in. The school was largely intact, though it seemed that a portion of the roof had fallen in. Most of the glass had been stoned out of the windows but you could see virtually nothing inside.

Yep, it was a good hidey-hole. And a nightmare to assault. There'd be a hundred good defensive positions.

Call in the troops? Not yet, Sachs thought. Every minute they delayed was a minute Galt could be finishing the last touches on his new weapon. And every ESU officer's footfall might destroy trace evidence.

'He could have it booby-trapped,' Pulaski whispered in an unsteady voice, looking at the metal chain. 'Maybe it's wired.'

'No. He wouldn't risk somebody just touching it casually and getting a shock; they'd call the police right away.' But, she continued, he could easily have something rigged to tell him of intruders' presence. So, sighing and with a grimace on her face, she looked up the street. 'Can you climb that?'

'What?'

'The fence?'

'I guess I could. If I were chasing or being chased.'

'Well, I can't, unless you give me a boost. Then you come after.'

'All right.'

They walked to where she could make out, through a crack in the fence, some thick bushes on the other side, which would both break their fall and give them some cover. She recalled that Galt was armed — and with a particularly powerful gun, the .45. She made sure her Glock holster was solidly clipped into her waistband

and then nodded. Pulaski crouched down and laced his fingers together.

Mostly to put him at ease, she whispered gravely, 'One thing to remember. It's important.'

'What's that?' He looked into her eyes uneasily.

'I've gained a few pounds,' said the tall policewoman. 'Be careful of your back.'

A smile. It didn't last long. But it was a smile nonetheless.

She winced from the pain in her leg as she stepped onto his hands, and twisted to face the wall.

Just because Galt hadn't electrified the chain didn't mean he hadn't rigged something on the other side. She saw in her mind's eye once more the holes in Luis Martin's flesh. Saw too the sooty floor of the elevator car yesterday, the quivering bodies of the hotel guests.

'No backup?' he whispered. 'You're sure?'

'I'm sure. On three. One . . . Two . . . Three.'

And up she went, Pulaski much stronger than she'd expected, launching her nearly six-foot frame straight up. Her palms caught the top and she lodged there, sitting momentarily. A glance at the school. No sign of anyone. Then a look downward, and she saw beneath her only the bushes, nothing to burn her flesh with five-thousand-degree arc flashes, no metal wires or panels.

Sachs turned her back to the school, gripped the top of the fence and lowered herself as far as she could. Then, when she knew she'd have to let go, she let go.

She hit rolling, and the pain rattled through her knees and thighs. But she knew her malady of arthritis as intimately as Rhyme knew his bodily limitations and she understood this was merely a temporary protest. By the time she'd taken cover behind the thickest stand of shrub, gun drawn and looking for any presenting targets, the pain had diminished.

'Clear,' she whispered through the fence.

There was a thump and a faint grunt and, like some kung-fu movie actor, Pulaski landed deftly and silently beside her. His weapon too appeared in his hand.

There was no way they could approach the front without being seen if Galt happened to look out. They'd go around to the back but Sachs needed to do one thing first. She scanned the grounds and, gesturing Pulaski to follow her, stayed behind the bushes and Dumpsters awaiting filling, heading to the right side of the school.

With Pulaski covering her, she moved fast to where two large rusting metal boxes were fitted to the brick. Both had peeling decals with the name Algonquin Consolidated on the side and a number to call in an emergency. She took from her pocket Sommers's current detector, turned it on and swept the unit over the boxes. The display showed zero.

Not surprising, since the place had been deserted for years, it seemed. But she was happy to see the confirmation.

'Look,' Pulaski whispered, touching her arm.

Sachs gazed at where he was pointing, through

a greasy window. It was dim and hard to make out anything inside clearly, but after a moment she could see the faint movement of a flashlight, she believed, slowly scanning. Possibly — the shadows were deceptive — she was looking at a man poring over a document. A map? A diagram of an electrical system he was going to turn into a deadly trap?

'He *is* here,' Pulaski whispered excitedly.

She pulled the headset on and called Bo Haumann, the ESU head.

'What do you have, Detective? K.'

'There's somebody here. I can't tell if it's Galt or not. He's in the middle part of the main building. Ron and I are going to flank him. What's your ETA? K.'

'Eight, nine minutes. Silent roll-up, K.'

'Good. We'll be in the back. Call me when you're ready for the take-down. We'll come in from behind.'

'Roger, out.'

She then called Rhyme and told him that they might have the perp. They'd go in as soon as ESU was on site.

'Look out for traps,' Rhyme urged.

'There's no power. It's safe.'

She disconnected the transmission and glanced at Pulaski. 'Ready?'

He nodded.

Crouching, she moved quickly toward the back of the school, gripping her weapon tightly and thinking: Okay, Galt. Haven't got your juice to protect you here. You've got a gun, I've got a gun. Now, we're on *my* turf.

421

59

As he disconnected from Sachs, Rhyme felt another tickle of sweat. He finally had to resort to calling Thom and asking him to wipe it off. This was perhaps the hardest for Rhyme. Relying on somebody for the big tasks wasn't so bad: the range-of-motion exercises, bowel and bladder, the sitting transfer maneuver to get him into the wheelchair or bed. The feeding.

It was the tiny needs that were the most infuriating . . . and embarrassing. Flicking away an insect, picking fuzz off your slacks.

Wiping away a rivulet of sweat.

The aide appeared and easily took care of the problem without a thought.

'Thank you,' the criminalist said. Thom hesitated at the unexpected show of gratitude.

Rhyme turned back to the evidence boards, but in fact he wasn't thinking much of Galt. It was possible that Sachs and the ESU team were about to collar the crazed employee at the school in Chinatown.

No, what was occupying his overheated mind exclusively was the Watchmaker in Mexico City. Goddamn it, why wasn't Luna or Kathryn Dance or *somebody* calling to give him a blow-by-blow description of the takedown?

Maybe the Watchmaker had already planted

the bomb in the office building and was using his own presence as a diversion. The satchel he carried might be filled with bricks. Why exactly was he hanging out in the office park like some goddamn tourist trying to figure out where to get a margarita? And could it be a different office altogether he was targeting?

Then Rhyme said, 'Mel, I want to see where the takedown's happening. Google Earth . . . or whatever it's called. Pull it up for me. Mexico City.'

'Sure.'

'Avenue Bosque de Reforma . . . How often do they update the images?'

'I don't know. Probably every few months. It's not real time, though, I don't imagine.'

'I don't care about that.'

A few minutes later they were looking at a satellite image of the area: a wide road, Avenue Bosque de Reforma, with the office buildings separated by the park where the Watchmaker was sitting at that moment. Across the street was the Jamaican consulate, protected by a series of concrete barriers — the bomb blast shields — and a gate. Rodolfo Luna and his team would be on the other side of those. Behind them were official vehicles parked in front of the embassy itself.

Then he frowned as he stared at the image of the barriers. To the left was a blast shield, perpendicular to the road. To the right were six others, parallel to it.

```
┌─────────────────────┐
│                     │
│      JAMAICAN       │
│      CONSULATE      │
│                     │
└─────────────────────┘

        |_ _ _ _ _ _
   _____

  Avenue Bosque de Reforma
   _____
```

The blast shields mimicked the letter I and the blank spaces from the package delivered to the Watchmaker at Mexico City Airport.

Gold letters . . .

Little blue booklet . . .

The mysterious numbers . . .

'Mel,' he said sharply. The tech's head snapped up at the urgency. 'Is there any passport that has the letters CC on the cover? Issued in blue?'

A moment later Cooper looked up from the State Department archive. 'Yes, as a matter of fact, there is. Navy blue with interlocking C's at the top. It's the Caribbean Community passport. There're about fifteen countries in — '

'Is Jamaica one?'

'Yes.'

He realized too they'd been thinking of the numbers as five hundred and seventy and three hundred seventy-nine. In fact, there was another way to refer to them. 'Quick. Look up Lexus

SUVs. Is there a model with a five seven zero or a three seven nine in the designation?'

This was even faster than the passport. 'Let's see . . . Yep, the LX five-seventy. It's a luxury — '

'Get me Luna on the phone. Now!' He didn't want to risk his own dialing, which would have taken some time and might have been inaccurate.

He felt the sweat again but ignored it.

'*Si?*'

'Rodolfo! It's Lincoln Rhyme.'

'Ah, Captain — '

'Listen to me! *You* are the target. The office building's a diversion! The package delivered to Logan? The rectangular images on the drawing? It was a diagram of the grounds of the Jamaican embassy, where you are right now. The rectangles are the blast barriers. And you drive a Lexus LX Five seventy?'

'Yes . . . You mean, *that* was the five hundred seventy?'

'I think so. And the Watchmaker was given a Jamaican passport to get into the compound. Is there a car parked nearby with three seven nine in the license plate?'

'I don't . . . Why, yes. It's a Mercedes with diplomatic plates.'

'Clear the area! Now. That's where the bomb is! The Mercedes.'

'A bomb?'

'Get away, Rodolfo!'

'Yes, yes!'

Rhyme heard shouting in Spanish, the sound of footfalls, hard breathing.

Then, a stunning explosion.

Rhyme blinked at the startling noise that rattled the speakers of the phone.

'Commander! Are you there? . . . Rodolfo?'

More shouting, static, screams.

'Rodolfo!'

After a long moment: 'Captain Rhyme? Hello?' The man was shouting — probably because he'd been partially deafened by the blast.

'Commander, are you all right?'

'Hello!'

A hissing noise, moans, gasping. Shouts.

Sirens and more shouting.

Cooper asked, 'Should we call — '

And then 'Qué? . . . Are you there, Captain?'

'Yes. Are you hurt, Rodolfo?'

'No, no. No bad injuries. Some cuts, stunned, you know.' The voice was gasping. 'We climbed over barriers and got down on the *other* side. I see people cut, bleeding. But no one is dead, I think. It would have killed me and the officers standing beside me. How did you know?'

'I'll go into that later, Commander. Where is the Watchmaker?'

'Wait a moment . . . All right. At the explosion he fled. Arturo's men were distracted by the blast — as he planned, of course. Arturo said a car drove into the park and he got inside. They're moving south now. We have officers following him . . . Thank you, Captain Rhyme. I cannot thank you enough. But now I must go. I will call as soon as we learn something.'

Inhaling deeply, ignoring the headache and the

426

sweat. Okay, Logan, Rhyme was thinking, we've stopped you. We've ruined your plan. But we still don't have you. Not yet.

Please, Rodolfo. Keep after him.

As he was thinking this, his eyes strayed over the evidence charts in the Galt case. Maybe this would be the conclusion of both of the operations. The Watchmaker would be apprehended in Mexico, and Ray Galt, in an abandoned school near Chinatown.

Then his eyes settled on one bit of evidence in particular.

Chinese herbs, ginseng and wolfberry.

And another listing, a substance that had been found in proximity to the herbs:

Diesel fuel.

Rhyme originally had thought that the fuel was from a possible site of an attack, a refinery perhaps. But it occurred to him now that diesel fuel would also run motors.

Like in an electric generator.

Then another thought occurred to him.

'Mel, the call — '

'Are you all right?'

'I'm fine,' Rhyme snapped.

'You look flushed.'

Ignoring the comment, he instructed, 'Find out the number of the cop who called in about Galt being in the school.'

The tech turned away and made a call. A few minutes later he looked up. 'Funny. I got the number from Patrol. But it's out of service.'

'Give it to me.'

Cooper did, slowly. Rhyme typed it into a

427

mobile phone database at the NYPD.

It was listed as prepaid.

'A cop with a prepaid mobile? And now out of service? No way.'

And the school was in Chinatown; that's where Galt had picked up the herbs. But it wasn't a staging area or where he was hiding out. It was a trap! Galt had run wires from a diesel-powered generator to kill whoever was searching for him and then, pretending to be a cop, he called in to report himself. Since the juice was off in the building, Sachs and the others wouldn't expect the electrocution danger.

There's no power. It's safe . . .

He had to warn them. He started to press 'Sachs' on the speed-dial panel on the computer. But just at that moment his nagging headache swelled to a blinding explosion in his head. Lights like electric sparks, a thousand electric sparks, flashed across his vision. Sweat poured from his skin, as the dysreflexia attack began in earnest.

Lincoln Rhyme whispered, 'Mel, you have to call — '

And then passed out.

60

They made it to the back of the school without being seen. Sachs and Pulaski were crouching, looking for entrances and exits, when they heard the first whimpers.

Pulaski turned an alarmed face toward the detective. She held up a finger and listened.

A woman's voice, it seemed. She was in pain, maybe held hostage, being tortured? The woman who'd spotted Galt? Someone else?

The sound faded. Then returned. They listened for a long ten seconds. Amelia Sachs gestured Ron Pulaski closer. They were in the back of the school, smelling urine, rotting plasterboard, mold.

The whimpering grew louder. What the hell was Galt doing? Maybe the victim had information he needed for his next attack. 'No, no, no.'

Or maybe Galt had slipped further from reality. Maybe he'd kidnapped an Algonquin worker and was torturing her, satisfying his lust for revenge. Maybe she was in charge of the long-distance transmission lines. Oh, no, Sachs thought. Could it be Andi Jessen herself? She sensed Pulaski staring at her with wide eyes.

'No . . . please,' the woman cried.

Sachs hit Transmit and radioed Emergency Service. 'Bo? It's Amelia, K?'

'Go ahead, K.'

'He's got a hostage here. Where are you?'

'Hostage? Who?'

'Female. Unknown.'

'Roger that. We'll be five minutes. K.'

'He's hurting her. I'm not going to wait. Ron and I're going in.'

'You have logistics?'

'Just what I told you before. Galt's in the middle of the building. Ground floor. Armed with a forty-five ACP. Nothing's electrified here. The power's off.'

'Well, that's the good news, I guess. Out.'

She disconnected and whispered to Pulaski, pointing, 'Now, move! We'll stage at the back door.'

The young officer said, 'Sure. Okay.' An uneasy glance into the shadows of the building, from which another moan floated out on the foul air.

Sachs surveyed their route to the back door and loading dock. The crumbling asphalt was littered with broken bottles and papers and cans. Noisy to traverse, but they didn't have a choice.

She gestured Pulaski forward. They began to pick their way over the ground, trying to be quiet, though they couldn't avoid crunching glass beneath their shoes.

But as they approached, they had some luck, which Sachs believed in, even if Lincoln Rhyme did not. Somewhere nearby a noisy diesel engine rattled to life, providing good covering sound.

Sometimes you do catch a break, Sachs thought. Lord knows we could use one now.

61

He wasn't going to lose Rhyme.

Thom Reston had his boss out of the Storm Arrow chair and into a near standing position, pinned against the wall. In autonomic dysreflexia attacks, the patient should be kept upright — the books say sitting, but Rhyme had been in his chair when the vessels tightened en masse and the aide wanted to get him even more elevated, to force the blood back toward the ground.

He'd planned for occurrences like this — even rehearsing when Rhyme wasn't around, since he knew his boss wouldn't have the patience for running mock emergencies. Now, without even looking, he grabbed a small vial of vasodilator medication, popped the cap with one thumb and slipped the delicate pill under Rhyme's tongue.

'Mel, help me here,' Thom said.

The rehearsals didn't include a real patient; Thom's unconscious boss was presently 180 pounds of deadweight.

Don't think about it that way, he thought.

Mel Cooper leapt forward, supporting Rhyme while Thom hit speed-dial button one on the phone he always made sure was charged and that had the best signal of any he'd tested. After two brief rings he was connected and in five long seconds he was speaking to a doctor in a private hospital. An SCI team was dispatched immediately. The hospital Rhyme went to regularly for specialized therapy and regular checkups had a large spinal cord injury department and two emergency response teams, for situations where it would take too long to get a disabled patient to the hospital.

Rhyme had had a dozen or so attacks over the years, but this was the worst Thom had ever seen. He couldn't support Rhyme and take his blood pressure simultaneously, but he knew it was dangerously high. His face was flushed, he was sweating. Thom could only imagine the pain of the excruciating headache as the body, tricked by the quadriplegia into believing it needed more blood and quickly, pumped hard and constricted the vessels.

The condition could cause death and, more troubling to Rhyme, a stroke, which could mean even more paralysis. In which case Rhyme might very well dust off his long-laid-to-rest idea of assisted suicide, which that damn Arlen Kopeski had brought up again.

'What can I do?' Cooper whispered, the normally placid face dark with worry, slick with sweat.

'We'll just keep him upright.'

Thom examined Rhyme's eyes. Blank.

The aide snagged a second vial and administered another dose of clonidine.

No response.

Thom stood helpless, both he and Cooper silent. He thought of the past years with Rhyme. They'd fought, sometimes bitterly, but Thom had been a caregiver all his working life and knew not to take the anger personally. Knew not to take it at all. He gave as much as he got.

He'd been fired by Rhyme and had quit in nearly equal measure.

But he'd never believed the separation between the two of them would last more than a day. And it never had.

Looking at Rhyme, wondering where the hell the medics were, he was considering: Was this my fault? Dysreflexia is frequently caused by the irritation that comes from a full bladder or bowel. Since Rhyme didn't know when he needed to relieve himself Thom noted the intake of food and liquid and judged the intervals. Had he gotten it wrong? He didn't think so, but maybe the stress of running the double case had exacerbated the irritation. He should have checked more often.

I should've exercised better judgment. I should've been firmer . . .

To lose Rhyme would be to lose the finest criminalist in the city, if not the world. And to lose countless victims because their killers would go undetected.

To lose Rhyme would be to lose one of his closest friends.

Yet he remained calm. Caregivers learn this early. Hard and fast decisions can't be made in panic.

Then the color of Rhyme's face stabilized and they got him into the wheelchair again. They couldn't have kept him up much longer anyway.

'Lincoln! Can you hear me?'

No response.

Then a moment later, the man's head lolled.

433

And he whispered something.

'Lincoln. You're going to be all right. Dr. Metz is sending a team.'

Another whisper.

'It's all right, Lincoln. You'll be all right.'

In a faint voice Rhyme said, 'You have to tell her . . . '

'Lincoln, stay still.'

'Sachs.'

Cooper said, 'She's at the scene. The school where you sent her. She's not back yet.'

'You have to tell Sachs . . . ' The voice faded.

'I will, Lincoln. I'll tell her. As soon as she calls in,' Thom said.

Cooper added, 'You don't want to disturb her now. She's moving in on Galt.'

'Tell her . . . '

Rhyme's eyes rolled back in his head and he went out again. Thom angrily looked out the window, as if that would speed the arrival of the ambulance. But all he saw were people strolling by on healthy legs, people jogging, people bicycling through the park, none of them with an apparent care in the world.

62

Ron Pulaski glanced at Sachs, who was peeking through a window at the back of the school.

She held up a finger, squinting and jockeying for position to try to get a better look at where Galt was. The whimpering was hard to hear from this vantage point since that diesel truck or engine was close, just on the other side of a fence.

Then came a louder moan.

Sachs turned back and, nodded at the door, whispering, 'We're going to get her. I want cross-fire coverage. Somebody up, somebody down. You want to go through here or up the fire escape?'

Pulaski glanced to their right, where a rusty metal ladder led up to a platform and an open window. He knew there was no chance they were electrified. Amelia had checked. But he really didn't want to go that way. Then he thought about his mistake at Galt's apartment. About Stanley Palmer, the man who might die. Who, even if he lived, might never be the same again.

He said, 'I'll go up.'

'You sure?'

'Yes.'

'Remember, we want him alive if at all possible. If he's set another trap, it might have a timer on it and we'll need him to tell us where it is and when it's going to activate.'

Pulaski nodded. Crouching, he made his way over the filthy asphalt strewn with all sort of garbage.

Concentrate, he told himself. You've got a job to do. You're not going to get spooked again. You're not going to make a mistake.

As he moved silently, he found he was, in fact, a lot less spooked than before. And then he wasn't spooked at all.

Ron Pulaski was angry.

Galt had gotten sick. Well, sorry. Well, too goddamn bad. Hell, Pulaski had had his head trauma, and he didn't blame anybody for it. Just like Lincoln Rhyme didn't sit around and mope. And Galt might very well be fine, all the new cancer treatments and techniques and everything. But here this whiny little shit was taking out his unhappiness on the innocent. And, Jesus Lord, what was he doing to that woman inside? She must've had information Galt needed. Or maybe she was a doctor who'd missed a diagnosis or something and he was getting revenge on her too.

At this thought he moved a little more quickly. He glanced back and saw Sachs waiting beside a half-open door, Glock drawn and pointed down, extended in a combat grip.

The anger growing, Pulaski came to a solid brick wall, where he couldn't be seen. He sped up further, heading toward the fire escape ladder. It was old and most of the paint had worn off, replaced by rust. He paused at the puddle of standing water surrounding the concrete around the base of the ladder. Water

. . . electricity. But there was no electricity. And, anyway, he couldn't avoid the water. He sloshed through it.

Ten feet away.

Looking up, picking the best window to go through. Hoping the stairs and platform wouldn't clank. Galt couldn't be more than forty feet from them.

Still, the sound of the diesel engine would cover up most squeaks.

Five feet.

Pulaski examined his heart and found its beat steady. He was going to make Lincoln Rhyme proud of him again.

Hell, he was going to collar this sick bastard himself.

He reached for the ladder.

And the next thing he knew he heard a snap and every muscle in his body contracted at once. In his mind he was looking at all the light of heaven, before his vision dissolved to yellow then black.

63

Standing together behind the school Amelia Sachs and Lon Sellitto watched the place being swept by ESU.

'A trap,' the lieutenant said.

'Right,' she replied grimly. 'Galt hooked up a big generator in a shed behind the school. He started it and then left. It was connected to the metal doors and the fire escape.'

'The fire escape. That's the way Pulaski was going.'

She nodded. 'Poor kid. He — '

An ESU officer, a tall African American, interrupted them. 'We've finished the sweep, Detective Lieutenant. It's clean. The whole place. We didn't touch anything inside, like you asked.'

'A digital recorder?' she asked. 'That's what I'm betting he used.'

'That's right, Detective. Sounded like a scene from a TV show or something. And a flashlight hanging by a cord. So it looked like somebody was holding it.'

No hostage. No Galt. Nobody at all.

'I'll run the scenes in a minute.'

The officer asked, 'There was no portable called it in?'

'Right,' Sellitto muttered. 'Was Galt. Probably on a prepaid mobile, I'd bet. I'll check it.'

'And he just did this — ' a wave at the school,

438

' — to kill some of us.'

'That's right,' Sachs said somberly.

The ESU officer grimaced and headed off to gather his team. Sachs had immediately called Rhyme to give him the news about the school. And about Ron Pulaski.

But, curiously, the phone went right to voice mail.

Maybe something had heated up in the case, or in the Watchmaker situation in Mexico.

A medic was walking toward her, head down, picking his way through the trash; the yard behind the school looked like a beach after a garbage spill. Sachs walked forward to meet him.

'You free now, Detective?' he asked her.

'Sure.'

She followed him around to the side of the building, where the ambulances waited.

There, sitting on a concrete stoop, was Ron Pulaski, head in his hands. She paused. Took a deep breath and walked up to him.

'I'm sorry, Ron.'

He was massaging his arm, flexing his fingers. 'No, ma'am.' He blinked at his own formality. Grinned. 'I should say, thank *you*.'

'If there'd been any other way, I would've done it. But I couldn't shout. I assumed Galt was still inside. And had his weapon.'

'I figured.'

Fifteen minutes earlier, as Sachs had waited at the door, she'd decided to use Sommers's current detector once more to double check that there was no electricity in the school.

To her horror she saw the metal door she was

inches away from contained 220 volts. And the concrete she was standing on was soaking wet. She realized that whether or not Galt was inside, he'd rigged wires to the metal infrastructure of the school. Probably from a diesel-powered generator; *that* was the racket they'd heard.

If Galt had rigged the door he would have rigged the fire escape as well. She'd leapt to her feet then and charged after Pulaski as he approached the ladder. She didn't dare call his name, even in a whisper, because if Galt was in the school, he'd hear and start shooting.

So she'd used Taser on Pulaski.

She carried an X26 model, which fired probes that delivered both high- and low-voltage charges. The X26 had a range of about thirty-five feet and when she saw that she couldn't tackle the officer in time, she'd hit him with the double probes. The neuromuscular incapacitation dropped him where he stood. He'd fallen hard on his shoulder, but, thank God, hadn't struck his head again. Sachs dragged him, gasping and quivering, to cover. She'd found and shut the generator off just as the ESU officers arrived, blowing open the chain on the front gate and storming the school.

'You look a little woozy.'

'Was quite a rush,' Pulaski said, breathing deeply.

She said, 'Take it easy.'

'I'm okay. I'm helping the scene.' He blinked like a drunk. 'I mean helping you search the scene.'

'You're up for it?'

440

'Long as I don't move too fast. But, listen, keep that thing of yours, that box that Charlie Sommers gave you? Keep it handy, okay? I'm not touching anything until you go over it.'

The first thing they did was walk the grid around the generator behind the school. Pulaski collected and bagged the wires that had carried the charge to the door and fire escapes. Sachs herself searched around the generator. It was a big unit several feet high and about three long. A placard on the side reported that its maximum output was 5,000 watts, producing 41 amps.

About four hundred times what was needed to kill you.

Nodding at the unit. 'Could you pack it up and get it to Rhyme's?' she asked the crime scene team from Queens, who'd just joined them. It weighed about two hundred pounds.

'You bet, Amelia. We'll get it there ASAP.'

She said to Pulaski, 'Let's walk the grid inside.'

They were heading into the school when Sachs's phone rang. 'Rhyme' popped up on caller ID.

'About time,' she said good naturedly as she answered. 'I've got some — '

'Amelia.' It was Thom's voice, but the tone was one she'd never heard before. 'You better come back here. You better come now.'

64

Breathing hard, Sachs hurried up the ramp and pushed open the door to Rhyme's townhouse.

Jogging across the foyer, boots slapping hard, she ran into the den, to the right, opposite the lab.

Thom looked toward her from where he was standing over Lincoln Rhyme in his wheelchair, eyes closed, face pale and damp. Between them was one of Rhyme's doctors, a solidly built African American, a former football star in college.

'Dr. Ralston,' she said, breathing hard.

He nodded. 'Amelia.'

Finally Rhyme's eyes opened. 'Ah, Sachs.' The voice was weak.

'How are you?'

'No, no, how are *you*?'

'I'm fine.'

'And the rookie?'

'He nearly had a problem, but it worked out okay.'

Rhyme said in a stiff voice, 'It was a generator, right?'

'Yes, how did you know? Did Crime Scene call?'

'No, I figured it out. Diesel fuel and herbs from Chinatown. The fact that there didn't seem to be any juice in the school. I figured out it was a trap. But had a little problem before I could call.'

'Didn't matter, Rhyme,' she said. 'I figured it out too.'

And didn't tell him how close Pulaski had come to getting electrocuted.

'Well, good. I . . . Good.'

She understood that he was thinking how he'd failed. How he'd nearly gotten one or both of them injured or killed. Normally he'd have been furious; a tantrum might have ensued. He'd want a drink, he'd insult people, he'd revel in sarcasm, all of which was directed toward himself, of course, as she and Thom knew very well.

But this was different. There was something about his eyes, something she didn't like one bit. Oddly, for someone with such a severe disability, there was rarely anything vulnerable about Lincoln Rhyme. Now, with this failure, he radiated weakness.

She found she had to look away and turned to the doctor, who said, 'He's out of danger. Blood pressure's down.' He then turned to Rhyme; even more than most patients, spinal cord injury victims hate being discussed in the third person. Which happens a lot. 'Stay in the chair and out of bed as much as you can, and make sure bladder and bowel are taken care of. Loose clothes and socks.'

Rhyme nodded. 'Why did it happen now?'

'Stress probably, combined with pressure somewhere. Internally, shoes, garments. You know how dysreflexia works. Mostly it's a mystery.'

'How long was I out?'

Thom said, 'Forty minutes, off and on.'

He rocked his head back in the chair. 'Forty,' he whispered. And Sachs understood he'd be replaying his failure. Which had nearly cost her and Pulaski their lives.

Now he was staring toward the lab. 'Where's the evidence?'

'I came here first. Ron's on his way. We needed some people from Queens to get the generator. It weighs a couple of hundred pounds.'

'Ron's coming?'

'That's right,' she confirmed, noting that she'd just told him this and wondering if the episode had made him disoriented. Maybe the doctor had given him a painkiller. Dysreflexia is accompanied by excruciating headaches.

'Good. He'll be here soon? Ron?'

A hesitant glance at Thom.

'Any minute now,' she said.

Dr. Ralston said, 'Lincoln, I'd rather you took it easy for the rest of the day.'

Rhyme was hesitating, looking down. Was he actually going to give in to a request like this?

But he said in a soft voice, 'I'm sorry, Doctor. I really can't. There's a case . . . it's important.'

'The grid thing? The terrorists?'

'Yes. I hope you don't mind.' His eyes were downcast. 'I'm sorry. I really have to work it.'

Sachs and Thom exchanged glances. Rhyme's apologetic mien was atypical, to put it mildly.

And, again, the vulnerability in his eyes.

'I know it's important, Lincoln. I can't force you to do anything. Just remember what I said: Stay upright and avoid any kinds of pressure on your body, inside and out. I guess it won't do any good to say avoid stress. Not with this madman on the loose.'

'Thank you. And thank you, Thom.'

The aide blinked and nodded uneasily.

Again, though, Rhyme was hesitating, staring down. Not driving into the parlor lab with all the speed the Storm Arrow could muster, which he'd be doing under other circumstances. And even when the front door to the townhouse opened and they could hear Pulaski and the other crime scene technicians hurrying in with the evidence, Rhyme remained where he was, staring down.

'Li — ' Sachs found herself saying and braking her words to a halt — their superstition again. 'Rhyme? You want to go into the lab?'

'Yes, sure.'

But *still* staring down. Not moving.

Alarmed, she wondered if he was having another attack.

Then he swallowed and moved the controller of the wheelchair. His face melted with relief and she understood what had been happening: Rhyme was worried — terrified — that the attack had caused yet more damage, that perhaps even the rudimentary mobility he'd achieved in his right hand and fingers had been erased.

That's what he'd been staring at: his hand. But apparently there'd been no damage.

'Come on, Sachs,' he said, though softly. 'We've got work to do.'

65

The pool parlor was looking like a crack house, R.C. decided.

He'd talk to his father about it.

The thirty-year-old pressed his pale hands around his beer bottle, watching the games at the pool tables. Snuck a cigarette and blew the smoke toward the exhaust vent. That smoking law was fucking stupid. His father said the socialists in Washington were to blame. They didn't mind sending kids to get killed in places with names you couldn't pronounce but they had to say, fuck you, no smoking.

Eyes on the pool tables. The fast one on the end might be trouble — there was serious money on it — but Stipp had the baseball bat behind the bar. And he liked to swing.

Speaking of which. Goddamn Mets. He grabbed the remote.

Boston didn't make him feel any better.

Then he put on the news about the crazy man screwing around with electricity. R.C.'s brother was handy and did a fair amount of electrical work, but wiring always scared him.

And now people around town were getting fried.

'You hear about that shit?' he asked Stipp.

'Yeah, which shit is that?' He had a cast eye, or one that didn't look right at you, if that's what a cast eye was.

'About the electricity thing? Some dude hooking up wires at that hotel? You touched the door handle and, *zzzzzzz*, you're dead.'

'Oh, *that* shit.' Stipp coughed a funky laugh. 'Like the electric chair.'

'Like that. Only it could be stairs or a puddle or those metal doors on the sidewalk. Elevators to the basements.'

'You walk on them and get zapped?'

'I guess. Fuck. And you push a 'walk' button in the crosswalks. They're metal. That's it. You're fucked.'

'What's he doing it for?'

'Fuck knows . . . The electric chair, you piss your pants and your hair catches fire. You know that? That's what kills you sometimes, the fire. Burns you to death.'

'Most states got injection.' Stipp frowned. 'You probably still piss your pants.'

R.C. was eyeing Janie in her tight blouse and trying to remember when his wife was coming by to pick up the grocery money, when the door opened and a couple of people came in. Two guys in delivery company uniforms, maybe early shifters, which was good, because they'd be spending money now that their day was over.

Then right behind them, a homeless guy pushed inside too.

Fuck.

The black guy, in filthy clothes, had abandoned a grocery cart of empties on the sidewalk and more or less run in here. He was now turning his back, staring out the window, scratching his leg. And then his head, under a disgusting cap.

R.C. caught the bartender's eye and shook his head no.

'Hey, mister,' Stipp called. 'Help you?'

'Something weird out there,' the man muttered. He talked to himself for a moment. Then louder: 'Something I saw. Something I don' like.' And he gave a high-pitched laugh that R.C. thought was pretty weird in itself.

'Yeah, well, take it outside, okay?'

'You see that?' the bum asked no one.

'Come on, buddy.'

But the man tottered to the bar, sat down. Spent a moment digging out some damp bills and a ton of change. He counted the coins carefully.

'Sorry, sir. I think you've had plenty.'

'I ain't had no drink. You see that guy? The guy with the wire?'

Wire?

R.C. and Stipp eyed each other.

'Crazy shit going down in this town.' He turned his mad eyes on R.C. 'Fucker was right outside. By that, you know, lamppost. He was doing something. Playing with the wires. You hear what's going down around here? Peoples gettin' their asses fried.'

R.C. wandered to the window past the guy, who stank so bad he felt like puking. But he looked out and saw the lamppost. Was that a wire attached? He couldn't tell. Was that terrorist around *here*? The Lower East Side?

Well, why not?

448

If he wanted to kill innocent citizens, this was as good a place as any.

R.C. said to the homeless guy, 'Listen, man, get outta here.'

'I wanna drink.'

'Well, you're not getting a drink.' Eyes outside again. R.C. was thinking he *did* see some cables or wires or shit. What was going on? Was somebody fucking with the bar itself? R.C. was thinking of all the metal in the place. The bar footrest, the sinks, the doorknobs, the register. Hell, the urinal was metal. If you peed, would the current run up the stream to your dick?

'You don't unnerstand, don't unnerstand!' the homeless guy was wailing, getting even weirder. 'It ain't safe out there. Look outside. Ain't safe. That asshole with the wires . . . I'ma staying in here till it safe.'

R.C., the bartender, Janie, the pool players and the delivery guys were all staring out the window now. The games had been suspended. R.C.'s interest in Janie had shriveled.

'Not safe, man. Gimmee a vodka and Coke.'

'Out. I'm not telling you again.'

'You don't think I can pay you. I got fucking money here. What you call this?'

The man's odor had wafted throughout the bar. It was repulsive.

Sometimes you burn to death . . .

'The wire man, the wire man . . . '

'Get the fuck out. Somebody's going to steal your fucking grocery cart.'

'I ain't going out there. You can't make me go. I ain't getting burnt up.'

'Out.'

'No!' The disgusting asshole slammed his fist down on the bar. 'You ain't service . . . you ain't *serving* me,' he corrected, ' 'cause I'm black.'

R.C. saw a flash on the street. He gasped. Then he relaxed. It was just a reflection off the windshield of a passing car. Getting spooked like that made him all the angrier. 'We ain't *servicing* you 'cause you stink and you're a prick. Out.'

The man had assembled all his wet bills and sticky coins. He must've had twenty dollars. He muttered, 'You the prick. You throwing me out and I'll go out there and get burnt up.'

'Just take your money and get out.' Stipp picked up the bat and displayed it.

The man didn't care. 'You throw me out I'ma tell ever'body what goes on here. I know what goes on here, you think I don't? I seen you looking at Miss Titty over there. An', shame on you, you got a wedding ring on. Whatta Mrs. Prick think 'bout — '

R.C. grabbed the guy's disgusting jacket with both hands.

The homeless guy winced and cried, 'No, no, man, don' hit me! You can' hit me! I'm a, you know, cop, I'm a agent!'

'Nice try, asshole. You're no fucking law.' R.C. gave a harsh laugh and drew back for a head butt.

Which didn't really get off the ground because an FBI ID card appeared in his face. The muzzle of a Glock wasn't far behind.

'Oh, fuck me,' R.C. muttered.

One of the two white guys who'd come into

the bar just before the homeless one said, 'Duly witnessed, Fred. He attempted to cause you bodily harm after you identified yourself as a law enforcement agent. We get back to work now?'

'Thanks, gentlemen. I'll take it from here.'

66

In the corner of the pool parlor, Fred Dellray sat on a wobbly chair, the back turned around, facing the youngster. It was a little less intimidating — the back of the chair in between them — but that was okay because the agent didn't need R.C. to be so afraid he couldn't think straight.

Though he needed him to be a *little* afraid.

'You know what I am, R.C.?'

The sigh shook the skinny kid's entire body. 'No, I mean, I know you're an FBI agent and you're undercover. But I don't know why you're hassling me.'

Dellray kept right on going, 'What I am is a walking lie detector. I been in the business so long I can look at a girl and hear her say, 'Let's go home and we can fuck,' and I know she's thinking he'll be so drunk by the time we get there I can just get some sleep.'

'I was just protecting myself. You were intimidating me.'

'Fuck, yes, I was intimidating you. And you can just close your lips and not say a word and wait for a lawyer to come by and hold your hand. You can even call the federal building and complain about me. But, either which way, word's going to get to your daddy in Sing-Sing that his kid hassled an FBI agent. And he's going to think that running this shit-hole bar, the *one* thing he left to you to keep an eye on while he's inside and hoped you didn't fuck up, you fucked up.'

Dellray watched him squirm. 'So, we all together on that?'

'Whatta you want?'

And just to make sure the back of the chair didn't make R.C. feel too much at ease, Dellray slapped his hand on the kid's thigh and squeezed hard.

'Ouch. Why'd you do that?'

'You ever been polygraphed, R.C.?'

'No, Dad's lawyer said never — '

'It's a rhe-tor-i-cal question,' Dellray said, even though it wasn't. It was just a way to burst a little intimidation over R.C.'s head like a tear gas grenade at a protest.

The agent gave another squeeze for good measure. He couldn't help thinking: Hey, McDaniel, can't do this while you're eavesdropping in the cloud zone, can you?

Which's too bad. 'Cause this is a lot more fun.

Fred Dellray was here thanks to one person: Serena. The favor that she'd asked had nothing to do with cleaning the basement. It was about getting off his ass. She'd led him downstairs into the messy storeroom, where he kept his outfits from his days as an undercover agent. She found one in particular, sealed up in the same kind of plastic bag that you used for wedding dresses. It was the Homeless Drunk costume, suitably perfumed with mold and sufficient human odor — and a little cat pee — to get a confession just by sitting down next to a suspect.

Serena had said, 'You lost your snitch. Quit feeling sorry for yourself and go pick up his trail. If you can't find him, then find out what *he* found.'

Dellray had smiled, hugged her and gone to change. As he left, Serena said, 'Whoa, you smell bad, son.' And gave him a playful swat on the butt. A gesture very, very few people had ever bestowed on Fred Dellray.

And he hit the street.

William Brent was good at hiding tracks, but Dellray was good at finding them. One thing he'd learned, encouragingly, was that maybe Brent had been on the job after all. Dellray found by tracing his movements that the CI *had* come up with a lead to Galt or to Justice For the Earth or something relevant to the attacks. The man had been working hard, tracking deep undercover. Finally he'd learned Brent had come here, to this dank pool parlor, where apparently the CI had sought, and ideally gotten, important information from the young man whose knee Dellray had just vice gripped.

Dellray now said, 'So. My cards. On the table. Are we havin' fun yet?'

'Jesus.' A fierce grimace that might've sent R.C.'s cheeks into a cramp. 'Just tell me what you want.'

'That's the spirit, son.' A picture of William Brent appeared.

Dellray watched his face closely and a flash of recognition popped into R.C.'s eyes before it dissolved. He asked the kid instantly, 'What'd he pay you?'

454

The blink of a pause told Dellray both that Brent had paid him and that the amount he was about to say would be considerably less than what really changed hands.

'One large.'

Damn. Brent was being pretty fucking generous with Dellray's money.

R.C. said, with a bit of whine, 'It wasn't drugs, man. I'm not into that.'

'Course you are. But I don't care. He was here about information. And now . . . now . . . now. I need to know what he asked and what you told him.' Dellray limbered up his lengthy fingers again.

'Okay, I'll tell you. Bill — he said his name was Bill.' R.C. pointed at the picture.

'Bill is as good as any. Keep going, friend.'

'He heard somebody was staying here in the hood. Some guy who'd come to town recent, was driving a white van, carrying a piece. A big fucking forty-five. He clipped somebody.'

Dellray gave nothing away. 'Who'd he kill? And why?'

'He didn't know.'

'Name?'

'Didn't have one.'

The agent didn't need a polygraph. R.C. was doing just fine with the dharmic quality of honesty.

'Come on, R.C., my friend, what else about him? White van, just came to town, big .45. Clipped somebody for reasons unknown.'

'Maybe kidnapped 'em before he killed 'em . . . Was somebody you didn't fuck with.'

That kind of went without saying.

R.C. continued, 'So this Bill or whoever heard I was connected, you know. Hooked into the wire, you know.'

'The wire.'

'Yeah. Not what that asshole's using to kill people. I mean the wire on the street.'

'Oh, *that's* what you mean,' Dellray said but R.C. floated below irony. 'And you are connected, aren't you, son? You know all 'bout the hood, right? You're the Ethel Mertz of the Lower East Side.'

'Who?'

'Keep going'

'Okay, well, like, I *had* heard something. I like to know who's around, what kind of shit could be going down. Anyway, I'd heard about this guy, was just like Bill said. And I sent him over to where he's staying. That's it. That's all.'

Dellray believed him. 'Gimme the address.'

He did, a decrepit street not far away. 'It's the basement apartment.'

'Okay, s'all I need for now.'

'You . . . '

'I won't tell Daddy anything. Don'tcha worry. 'Less you're fucking with me.'

'I'm not, no, Fred, really.'

When Dellray was at the door, R.C. called, 'It wasn't what you think.'

The agent turned.

'It really was 'cause you smelt bad. That's why we weren't going to serve you. Not because you're black.'

Five minutes later Dellray was approaching

456

the block R.C. had told him about. He'd debated calling in backup, but decided not to quite yet. Working the street required finesse, not sirens and takedown teams or Tucker McDaniel. Dellray loped through the streets, dodging the dense crowds. Thinking, as he often did, It's the middle of the day. What the hell do these people do for work? Then he turned two corners and eased into an alley, so he could approach the apartment in question from the back.

He looked quickly up the dim, rot-smelling canyon.

Not far away was a white guy in a cap and baggy shirt, sweeping cobblestones. Dellray counted addresses; he was directly behind the place where R.C. had sent William Brent.

Okay, this's weird, the agent thought. He started forward through the alley. The sweeper turned his mirrored sunglasses his way and then went back to sweeping. Dellray stopped near him, frowning and looking around. Trying to make sense of this.

Finally the sweeper asked gruffly, 'The fuck're you doing?'

'Well, I'll tell you,' Dellray offered. 'One thing I'm doing is looking at an NYPD undercover cop who, for some fucked-up reason, is trying to blend by sweeping cobblestones in a hood where they stopped sweeping cobblestones, oh, about a hundred and thirty years ago.' Dellray displayed his ID.

'Dellray? I heard of you.' Then defensively the cop said, 'I'm just doing what they told me. It's a stakeout.'

457

'Stakeout? Why? What *is* this place?'

'You don't know?'

Dellray rolled his eyes.

When the cop told him, Dellray froze. But only momentarily. A few seconds later he was ripping away his smelly undercover costume and dumping it in a waste bin. As he started sprinting for the subway, he noted the cop's startled reaction, and supposed it could have come from one of two things: the striptease act itself, or the fact that underneath the disgusting outfit he was wearing a kelly green velour tracksuit. He supposed it was a little of both.

67

'Rodolfo, tell me.'

'We may have good news soon, Lincoln. Arturo Diaz's men have followed Mr. Watchmaker into Gustavo Madero. It's a *delegación* in the north of the city — you would say borough, like your Bronx. Much of it is not so nice and Arturo believes that's where the associates helping him are.'

'But do you know where he is?'

'They think so. They've found the car he escaped in — they were no more than three or four minutes behind but could not get through the traffic to stop his car. He's been spotted in a large apartment building near the center of the *delegación*. It's being sealed off. We will do a complete search. I will call back with more information soon.'

Rhyme disconnected the call, and struggled to keep his impatience and concern at bay. He would believe that the Watchmaker had actually been arrested when he saw the man arraigned in a New York court.

He wasn't encouraged when he called Kathryn Dance to tell her the latest and she replied, 'Gustavo Madero? It's a lousy neighborhood, Lincoln,' she said. 'I was down in Mexico City for an extradition. We drove through the area. I was really glad the car didn't break down, even with two armed federal officers next to me. It's a

459

rabbit warren. Easy to hide in. But the good news is that the residents absolutely won't want the police there. If Luna moves a busload of riot cops in, the locals'll give up an American pretty fast.'

He said he'd keep her posted and disconnected. The fatigue and fogginess from the dysreflexia attack ebbed in once more and he rested his head on the back of the Storm Arrow.

Come on, stay sharp! he commanded, refusing to accept anything less than 110 percent from himself, just as he did from everybody else. But he wasn't feeling that measure, not at all.

Then he glanced up to see Ron Pulaski at the evidence table and thoughts of the Watchmaker faded. The young officer was moving pretty slowly. Rhyme regarded him with concern. The jolt of the Taser had been pretty powerful, apparently.

But that concern was accompanied by another emotion, one he'd been feeling for the past hour: guilt. It had been exclusively Rhyme's fault that Pulaski — and Sachs too — had come as close as they had to being electrocuted by Galt's trap at the school. Sachs had downplayed the incident. Pulaski too. Laughing, he'd said, 'She Tased me, bro,' which apparently was some kind of joke, drawing a smile from Mel Cooper, but Rhyme didn't get it. Nor was he in a mood that was at all humorous. He was confused and disoriented . . . and not just from the medical emergency. He was having trouble shaking his sense of failure from letting down Sachs and the rookie.

He forced himself to focus on the evidence that'd been collected from the school. Some bags of trace, some electronics. And most important, the generator. Lincoln Rhyme loved big, bulky pieces of equipment. To move them took a lot of physical contact and that meant such objects picked up significant prints, fibers, hair, sweat and skin cells, as well as other trace. The generator was attached to a wheeled cart, but it would still have taken some grappling to get it into place.

Ron Pulaski got a phone call. He glanced at Rhyme and then headed into the corner of the room to take it. Despite his groggy demeanor, his face began to brighten. He disconnected and stood for a moment, looking out the window. Though he didn't know the substance of the conversation, Rhyme wasn't surprised to see the young man walk toward him with a confessional cast to his eyes.

'I have to tell you something, Lincoln.' His glance took in Lon Sellitto too.

'Yeah?' Rhyme asked distractedly, offering a word that would have earned the young officer a glare, if he'd used it.

'I kind of wasn't honest with you earlier.'

'*Kind of?*'

'Okay, I wasn't.'

'What about?'

Scanning the evidence boards and the profile of Ray Galt, he said, 'The DNA results? I know I didn't need to get them. I used that as an excuse. I went to see Stan Palmer.'

'Who?'

'The man in the hospital, the one I ran into in the alley.'

Rhyme was impatient. The evidence beckoned. But this was important, it seemed; he nodded, then asked, 'He's okay?'

'They still don't know. But what I'm saying is, first, I'm sorry I didn't tell the truth. I was going to but it just seemed, I don't know, unprofessional.'

'It was.'

'But there's more. See, when I was at the hospital I asked the nurse for his social security number. And personal information. Guess what? He was a con. Did three years in Attica. Got a long sheet.'

'Really?' Sachs asked.

'Yep . . . I mean, yes. And there's active paper on him.'

'He's wanted,' Rhyme mused.

'Warrants for what?' Sellitto asked.

'Assault, receiving stolen, burglary.'

The rumpled cop barked a laugh. 'You backed into a collar. Like, literally.' He laughed again and looked at Rhyme, who didn't join in the fun.

The criminalist said, 'So that's why you're so chipper?'

'I'm not happy I hurt him. It was still a screwup.'

'But if you had to run over somebody, it's better him than a father of four.'

'Well, yeah,' Pulaski said.

Rhyme had more to say on the subject, but this wasn't the time or place. 'The important thing is you're not distracted anymore, right?'

462

'No.'

'Good. Now, if we've got the soap opera out of the way, maybe we can all get back to work.' He looked at the digital clock: 3 p.m. Rhyme felt the time pressure humming like, well, electricity in a high-tension wire. They had the perp's identity, they had his address. But they had no solid leads to his whereabouts.

It was then that the doorbell rang.

Thom appeared a moment later with Tucker McDaniel, minus his underling. Rhyme knew immediately what he was going to say. Everybody in the room probably did.

'Another demand?' Rhyme asked.

'Yes. And he's really upped the ante this time.'

68

'What's the deadline?' Sellitto asked.

'Six-thirty tonight.'

'Gives us a little over three hours. What's he want?'

'This demand's even crazier than the first two. Can I use a computer?'

Rhyme nodded toward it.

The ASAC typed and in a moment the letter appeared on the screen. Rhyme's vision was blurred. He blinked into clarity and leaned toward the monitor.

To Algonquin Consolidated Power and Light and CEO Andi Jessen:

At about 6 p.m. yesterday, a remote control switch routed current from a spot network distribution system at an office building at 235 W. 54th Street totaling 13,800 volts to the floor of the elevator which had a return line connected through the control panel in the car. When the car stopped before it got to the ground floor a passenger touched the panel to hit the alarm button, the circuit was closed and individuals inside died.

Twice I've asked you to show good faith by reducing output of supply. And twice you have refused. If you'd done what I reasonably requested you would never have brought such suffering into the lives of the people you call your customers.

464

You wantonly disregarded my requests and somebody else paid the price for that.

In 1931 when Thomas A. Edison died, his coworkers respectfully requested that all the power in the city be shut off for sixty seconds to mark the passing of the man who had created the grid and brought light to millions. The city declined.

I am now making the same request — not out of respect for the man who CREATED the grid but for the people who are being DESTROYED because of it — those who are made sick from the power lines and from the pollution from burning coal and from radiation, those who lose their houses from the earthquakes caused by geothermal drilling and damming our natural rivers, those cheated by companies like Enron, the list is endless.

Only unlike 1931 I am insisting you shut down the entire Northeastern Interconnection for one day. Beginning at 6:30 p.m. today.

If you do this people will see that they do not need to use as much power as they do. They will see that it is their greed and gluttony that motivates them, which you are happy to play into. Why? For PROFITS of course.

If you ignore me this time, the consequences will be far, far greater than the small incidents of yesterday and the day before, the loss of life far worse.

— R. Galt

McDaniel said, 'Absurd. There'll be civil chaos, riots, looting. The governor and President are adamant. No caving in.'

'Where's the letter?' Rhyme asked.

465

'What you're seeing there. It was an email.'

'Who'd he send it to?'

'Andi Jessen — personally. And the company itself. Their security office email account.'

'Traceable?'

'No. Used a proxy in Europe. He's going for a mass attack, it seems.' McDaniel looked up. 'Washington's involved now in a big way. Those senators — the ones working with the President on renewable energy — are coming to town early. They're going to meet with the mayor. The assistant director of the Bureau's coming in too. Gary Noble's coordinating everything. We've got even more agents and troops out on the streets. And the chief has mobilized a thousand more NYPD officers.' He rubbed his eyes. 'Lincoln, we've got the manpower and the firepower, but we need to know *some* idea of where to look for the next attack. What've you got? We need *something* concrete.'

McDaniel was reminding Rhyme he'd let the criminalist take the case with the assurance that his condition wouldn't slow the investigation.

From entrance to exit . . .

Rhyme had gotten what he wanted — the investigation. And yet he hadn't found the man. In fact, the very condition that he'd assured McDaniel wasn't a problem had nearly gotten Sachs and Pulaski killed, along with a dozen ESU officers.

He gazed back to the agent's smooth face and predator's eyes and said evenly, 'What I've got is more evidence to look at.'

McDaniel hesitated then waved his hand in an

466

ambiguous gesture. 'All right. Go ahead.'

Rhyme had already turned away to Cooper. A nod toward the digital recorder on which had been recorded the sounds of the 'victim' moaning. 'Audio analysis.'

With gloved hands, the tech plugged the unit into his computer and typed. A moment later, reading the sine curves on the screen, he said, 'The volume and signal quality suggest it was recorded from a TV program. Cable.'

'Brand of the recorder?'

'Sanoya. Chinese.' He typed some commands and then studied a new database. 'Sold in about ten thousand stores in the country. No serial number.'

'Anything more?'

'No prints on it or other trace, except more taramasalata.'

'The generator?'

Cooper and Sachs went over it carefully, while Tucker McDaniel made phone calls and fidgeted in the corner. The generator turned out to be a Power Plus model, made by the Williams-Jonas Manufacturing Company, in New Jersey.

'Where'd this one come from?' Rhyme asked.

'Let's find out,' Sachs said.

Two phone calls later — to the local sales office of the manufacturer and the general contractor that the company referred them to — revealed that it had been stolen from a job site in Manhattan. There were no leads in the theft, according to the local precinct. The construction project had no security cameras.

'Got some trace that's curious,' Cooper

announced. He ran it through the GC/MS. The machine hummed away.

'Getting something . . . ' Cooper was bending forward over the screen. 'Hmm.'

This would normally have drawn an acerbic 'what does that mean?' glance from Rhyme. But he still felt tired and shaken from the attack. He waited patiently for the tech to explain.

Finally: 'Don't think I've seen it before. A significant amount of quartz and some ammonium chloride. Ratio's about ten to one.'

Rhyme knew the answer instantly. 'Copper cleaner.'

'Copper wires?' Pulaski suggested. 'Galt is cleaning them?'

'Good idea, Rookie. But I'm not sure.' He didn't think electricians cleaned wires. Besides, he explained, 'Mostly it's used for cleaning copper on buildings. What else, Mel?'

'Some stone dust you don't usually see in Manhattan. Architectural terracotta.' Cooper was now looking into the eyepieces of a microscope. He added, 'And some granules that look like white marble.'

Rhyme blurted, 'The police riots of fifty-seven. That's *eighteen* fifty-seven.'

'What?' McDaniel asked.

'A few years ago. The *Delgado* case?'

'Oh, sure,' Sachs said.

Sellitto asked. 'Did we work it?'

Rhyme's grimace conveyed his message: It didn't matter who worked a case. Or when. Crime scene officers — hell, every officer on the force — had to be aware of all major cases in the city, present and past. The more you put into the brain, the more likely you were to make connections that solved your crime.

Homework . . .

He explained: A few years ago Steven Delgado, a paranoid schizophrenic, planned a series of murders to mimic deaths that occurred during the infamous New York City Police Riots of 1857. The madman picked the same locale as the carnage 150 years earlier: City Hall Park. He was captured after his first kill because Rhyme had traced him to an apartment on the Upper West Side, where he'd left trace that included copper cleaner, terracotta residue from the Woolworth building and white marble dust from the city courthouse, which was undergoing renovations, then as now.

'You think he's going to hit City Hall?' McDaniel asked urgently, the phone in his hand drooping.

'I think there's a connection. That's all I can say. Put it on the board and we'll think about it. What else do you have from the generator?'

'More hair,' Cooper announced, holding up a pair of tweezers. 'Blond, about nine inches long.' He slipped it under the microscope and slid the specimen tray up and down slowly. 'Not dyed. Natural blond. No color degradation and not desiccated. I'd say it's from somebody younger than fifty. Also refraction variation on one end. I could run it through the chromatograph, but I'm ninety percent sure it's — '

'Hair spray.'

'Right.'

'Woman probably. Anything else?'

'Another hair. Brown. Shorter. Crew cut. Also under fifty.'

'So,' Rhyme said. 'Not Galt's. Maybe we've got our Justice For the Earth connection. Or maybe some other players. Keep going.'

The other news wasn't so encouraging. 'The flashlight he could've bought in a thousand places. No trace or prints. The string was generic too. The cable he used to wire the doors at the school? Bennington, the same he's been using all along. Bolts are generic but similar to the others.'

Eye on the generator, Rhyme was aware his thoughts were spinning dizzily. Part of this was the attack he'd experienced a short time ago. But some of it had to do with the case itself. Something was wrong. Pieces of the puzzle were missing.

The answer had to be in the evidence. And just as important: what *wasn't* in the evidence. Rhyme now scanned the whiteboards, trying to stay calm. This wasn't to stave off another episode of dysreflexia, per doctor's orders; it was because nothing made you blind faster than desperation.

PROFILE

- Identified as Raymond Galt, 40, single, living in Manhattan, 227 Suffolk St.

- Terrorist connection? Relation to Justice For the Earth? Suspected ecoterror group. No profile in any U.S. or international database. New?

470

Underground? Individual named Rahman involved. Also Johnston. References to monetary disbursements, personnel movements and something 'big.'
— Algonquin security breach in Philadelphia might be related.
— SIGINT hits: code word reference to weapons, 'paper and supplies' (guns, explosives?).
— Personnel include man and woman.
— Galt's relationship unknown.
• Cancer patient; presence of vinblastine and prednisone in significant quantities, traces of etoposide. Leukemia.
• Galt is armed with military 1911 Colt .45.
• Masquerading as maintenance man in dark brown overalls. Dark green, as well?
• Wearing tan leather gloves.

CRIME SCENE: ALGONQUIN SUBSTATION MANHATTAN-10, WEST 57TH STREET

• Victim (deceased): Luis Martin, assistant manager in music store.
• No friction ridge prints on any surface.
• Shrapnel from molten metal, as a result of the arc flash.
• o-gauge insulated aluminum strand cable.
— Bennington Electrical Manufacturing, AM-MV-60, rated up to 60,000v.
— Cut by hand with hacksaw, new blade, broken tooth.
• Two 'split bolts,' 3/4 inch holes in them.
— Untraceable.
• Distinctive tool marks on bolts.
• Brass 'bus' bar, fixed to cable with two 1/4-inch bolts.

471

- — All untraceable.
- Boot prints.
  — Albertson-Fenwick Model E-20 for electrical work, size 11.
- Metal grating cut to allow access to substation, distinctive tool marks from bolt cutter.
- Access door and frame from basement.
  — DNA obtained. Sent out for testing.
  — Greek food, taramasalata.
- Blond hair, 1 inch long, natural, from someone 50 or under, discovered in coffee shop across the street from substation.
  — Sent out for tox-chem screening.
- Mineral trace: volcanic ash.
  — Not naturally found in New York

area.
  — Exhibits, museums, geology schools?
- Algonquin Control Center software accessed by internal codes, not outside hackers.

DEMAND NOTE

- Delivered to Andi Jessen at home.
  — No witnesses.
- Handwritten.
  — Sent to Parker Kincaid for analysis.
- Generic paper and ink.
  — Untraceable.
- No friction ridge prints, other than A. Jessen, doorman, messenger.
- No discernible trace discovered in paper.

CRIME SCENE: BATTERY PARK HOTEL AND SURROUNDINGS

- Victims (deceased):
  — Linda Kepler, Oklahoma City, tourist.
  — Morris Kepler, Oklahoma City, tourist.
  — Samuel Vetter,

Scottsdale, business-
man.
— Ali Mamoud, New
York City, waiter.
— Gerhart Schiller,
Frankfurt, Germany,
advertising executive.
- Remote control
switch for turning on
current.
— Components not
traceable.
- Bennington cable and
split bolts, identical
to first attack.
- Galt's Algonquin uni-
form, hard hat and
gear bag with his
friction ridge prints,
no others.
— Wrench with tool
marks that can be
associated with tool
marks on bolts at
first crime scene.
— Rat-tail file with
glass dust that can
be associated with
glass from bottle
found at substation
scene in Harlem.
— Probably working
alone.
- Trace from Algonquin
worker Joey Barzan,
assault victim of
Galt.
— Jet fuel and alter-
native jet fuel.
— Attack at military
base?

CRIME SCENE: GALT'S APARTMENT, 227 SUFFOLK ST., LOWER EAST SIDE

- Bic SoftFeel fine-
point pens, blue ink,
associated with ink
used in demand
letter.
- Generic 8½ × 11"
white computer
paper, associated
with demand letter.
- Generic No. 10 size
envelope, associated
with envelope con-
taining demand
letter.
- Bolt cutter, hacksaw
with tool marks
matching those at
initial scene.
- Computer printouts:
— Articles about
medical research on
cancer linked to
high-power electric
lines.

- Blog postings by Galt re: same.
- Albertson-Fenwick Model E-20 boots for electrical work, size 11, with treads the same as prints at initial scene.
- Additional traces of jet fuel and alternative jet fuel.
  - Attack at military base?
- No obvious leads as to where he might be hiding, or location of future attacks.

CRIME SCENE: ALGONQUIN SUBSTATION MH-7, E. 119TH STREET, HARLEM

- Molotov cocktail: 750-ml wine bottle, no source.
- BP gas used as accelerant.
- Cotton cloth strips, probably white T-shirt, used as fuse, no source determined.

SECOND DEMAND NOTE

- Delivered to Bernard Wahl, Algonquin security chief.
  - Assaulted by Galt.
  - No physical contact; no trace.
  - No indication of whereabouts or site of next attack.
- Paper and ink associated with those found in Galt's apartment.
- Additional traces of jet fuel and alternative jet fuel embedded in paper.
  - Attack on military base?

CRIME SCENE: OFFICE BUILDING AT 235 W. 54TH STREET

- Victims (deceased):
  - Larry Fishbein, New York City, accountant.
  - Robert Bodine, New York City, attorney.
  - Franklin Tucker,

Paramus, New Jersey, salesman.

- One friction ridge of Raymond Galt.
- Bennington cable and split bolts, same as at other scenes.
- Two hand-made remote relay switches:
  — One to shut off power to elevator.
  — One to complete circuit and electrify elevator car.
- Bolts and smaller wires connecting panel to elevator, not traceable.
- Victims had water on shoes.

- Trace:
  — Chinese herbs, ginseng and wolf-berry.
  — Hairspring (plan-ning on using timer, rather than remote for future attacks?).
  — Dark green cotton heavy-duty clothing fiber.
  — Containing trace of aviation jet fuel.
  — Dark brown cotton heavy duty clothing fiber.
  — Containing trace of diesel fuel.
  — Containing addi-tional Chinese herbs.

CRIME SCENE:
ABANDONED SCHOOL, CHINATOWN

- Bennington cable, identical to that at other scenes.
- Generator, Power Plus by Williams-Jonas Manufacturing, stolen from job site in Man-hattan.
- Digital voice recorder, Sanoya brand, on which was recorded segment from TV show or film. Cable TV.
  — Additional traces of taramasalata.
- Brite-Beam Flash-light.
  — Untraceable.
- Six-foot string hold-ing flashlight.
  — Untraceable.
- Trace evidence, asso-ciated with the area

around City Hall:
— Quartz and ammonium chloride copper cleaner.
— Terracotta dust, similar to building façades in area.
— White marble stone dust.
• Hair, 9 inches long, blond, sprayed, person under 50, probably woman's.
• Hair, $3/8$ inch long, brown, person under 50.

THIRD DEMAND

• Sent via email.
• Untraceable; used a proxy in Europe.

But it turned out that Rhyme was wrong.

It was true that, as he'd felt all along, the evidence — as much else in this case — just didn't add up. But he was wrong in that the key to unraveling the mystery wasn't to be found on the charts surrounding him. Rather, it came blustering into the lab just now, accompanied by Thom, in the form of a tall, lanky sweating man, skin black, clothing bright green.

Catching his breath, Fred Dellray nodded fast to everybody in the room, then proceeded to ignore them as he strode up to Rhyme. 'I need to throw something out, Lincoln. And you gotta tell me if it works or not.'

'Fred,' McDaniel began. 'What the hell — '

'Lincoln?' Dellray persisted.

'Sure, Fred. Go ahead.'

'What do you think of the theory that Ray Galt's a fall guy. He's dead, been dead for a couple of days, I think. It's somebody *else* who's put this whole thing together. From the beginning.'

Rhyme paused for a moment — the disorientation from the attack was slowing his analysis of Dellray's idea. But finally he offered a faint smile and said, 'What do I think? It's brilliant. That's what.'

69

Tucker McDaniel's response, however, was, 'Ridiculous. The whole investigation's based on Galt.'

Sellitto ignored him. 'What's your theory, Fred? I want to hear it.'

'My CI, a guy named William Brent. He was following up on a lead. He was on to somebody who was connected with — maybe behind — the grid attacks. But then he vanished. I found out that Brent was interested in somebody who'd just come to town, was armed with a forty-five and was driving a white van. He'd recently kidnapped and killed somebody. He'd been staying at an address on the Lower East Side for the past couple of days. I found out where. It turned out to be a crime scene.'

'Crime scene?' Rhyme asked.

'You betcha. It was Ray Galt's apartment.'

Sachs said, 'But Galt didn't just come to town. He's lived here all his adult life.'

'Ex-*actly*.'

'So what's this Brent have to say?' McDaniel asked skeptically.

'Oh, he ain't tellin' anybody anything. 'Cause yesterday he was in the alley behind Galt's and got himself run over by an NYPD patrolman. He's in the hospital, still unconscious.'

'Oh my God,' Ron Pulaski whispered. 'St. Vincent's?'

'Right.'

Pulaski said in a weak voice, 'That was me who hit him.'

'You?' Dellray asked, voice rising.

The officer said, 'But, no, it can't be. The guy I hit? His name's Stanley Palmer.'

'Yep, that's him. 'Palmer' was one of Brent's covers.'

'You mean, he didn't have warrants on him? He didn't do time for attempted murder, aggravated assault?'

Dellray shook his head. 'The rap sheet was fake, Ron. We put it into the system so anybody who checked'd find out he had a record. The worst we got him for was conspiracy and then I turned him. Brent's a stand-up guy. He snitched for the money mostly. One of the best in the business.'

'But what was he doing with groceries? In the alley?'

'Undercover technique a lot of us use. You cart around groceries or shopping bags, you look less suspicious. Baby carriage is the best. With a doll in it, course.'

'Oh,' Pulaski muttered. 'I . . . Oh.'

But Rhyme couldn't be concerned about his officer's psyche. Dellray had raised a credible theory that explained the inconsistencies that Rhyme had been sensing in the case all along.

He'd been looking for a wolf, when he should have been hunting a fox.

But could it be? Was somebody else behind the attacks and Galt just a fall guy?

479

McDaniel looked doubtful. 'But there've been witnesses . . . '

His brown eyes locked on his boss's blue ones, Dellray said, 'Are they reliable?'

'What do you mean, Fred?' An edge now in the slick ASAC's voice.

'Or were they people who *believed* it was Galt because *we* told the media that's who it was? And the media told the world?'

Rhyme added, 'You wear safety goggles, you wear a hard hat and a company uniform . . . If you're the same race and same build, and you've got a fake name badge with your *own* picture on it and Galt's name . . . sure, it could work.'

Sachs too was considering the evidence. 'The lineman in the tunnel, Joey Barzan, said he identified him because of the name badge. He'd never met Galt. And it was real dark down there.'

'And the security chief, Bernie Wahl,' Rhyme added, 'never saw him when he delivered the second demand note. The perp got him from behind.'

Rhyme said, 'And Galt was the one he kidnapped and killed. Like your CI found out.'

'That's right,' Dellray said.

'But the evidence?' McDaniel persisted.

Rhyme stared at the board, shaking his head. 'Shit. How could I've missed it?'

'What, Rhyme?'

'The boots in Galt's apartment? A pair of Albertson-Fenwicks.'

'But they matched,' Pulaski said.

'Of course they matched. But that's not the point, Rookie. The boots were *in* Galt's apartment. If they were his, they wouldn't've been there; he'd be *wearing* them! Workers wouldn't have two pairs of *new* boots. They're expensive and employees usually have to buy their own . . . No, the real perp found out what kind Galt wore and bought another pair. Same with the bolt cutter and hacksaw. The real perp left them in Galt's apartment to find. The rest of the evidence implicating Galt, like the hair in the coffee shop across from the substation on Fifty-seven Street? That was planted too.

'Look at the blog posting,' Rhyme continued, nodding at the documents Pulaski had wrestled from Galt's printer.

My story is typical of many. I was a lineman and later a troubleman (like a supervisor) for many years working for several power companies in direct contact with lines carrying over one hundred thousand volts. It was the electromagnetic fields created by the transmission lines, that are uninsulated, that led to my leukemia, I am convinced. In addition it has been proven that power lines attract aerosol particles that lead to lung cancer among others, but this is something that the media doesn't talk about.

We need to make all the power companies but more important the public aware of these dangers. Because the companies won't do anything voluntarily, why should they? if the people stopped using electricity by even half we could save thousands of lives a year and make them (the companies) more responsible. In turn they would

481

create safer ways to deliver electricity. And stop destroying the earth too.

People, you need to take matters into your own hands!

— Raymond Galt.

'Now look at the first couple of paragraphs of the first demand letter.'

At around 11:30 a.m. yesterday morning there was an arc flash incident at the MH-10 substation on W 57 Street in Manhattan, this happened by securing a Bennington cable and bus bar to a post-breaker line with two split bolts. By shutting down four substations and raising the breaker limit at MH-10 an overload of close to two hundred thousand volts caused the flash.

This incident was entirely your fault and due to your greed and selfishness. This is typical of the industry and it is reprehensable. Enron destroyed the financial lives of people, your company destroys our physical lives and the life of the earth. By exploiting electricity without regard for it's consequences you are destroying our world, you insideously work your way into our lives like a virus, until we are dependent on what is killing us.

'What's distinctive?' Rhyme asked.
Sachs shrugged.

482

Pulaski pointed out, 'No misspellings in the blog.'

'True, Rookie, but that's not my point. The computer's spell checker would have picked up any mistakes in the blog and corrected them. I'm talking about word choice.'

Sachs nodded vigorously. 'Sure. The blog language is a lot simpler.'

'Exactly. The blog was written by Galt himself. The letters were *transcribed* by him — it was his handwriting — but they were dictated by the real perp, the man who kidnapped Galt and forced him to write what he was saying. The perp used his own language, which Galt wasn't familiar with so he misspelled the big words. In the blog he never used any words like 'reprehensible' . . . And in the other letters there're similar misspellings. In the last letter — no misspellings because the perp wrote that himself in an email.'

Sellitto paced; the floor creaked. 'Remember what Parker Kincaid said? Our handwriting guy? That the letter was written by somebody who was emotional, upset — because he was being threatened to take the dictation. That'd make anybody upset. And he also forced Galt to handle the switches and hard hat so they'd have his prints on them.'

Rhyme nodded. 'In fact, I'll bet the blog postings were real. Hell, they were probably how the perp picked Galt in the first place. He'd read how angry Galt was about the power industry.'

A moment later his eyes took in the physical

483

evidence itself: the cables, the nuts and bolts.

And the generator. He gazed at it for a moment.

Then he called up word processing software on his computer and began to type. His neck and temple throbbed — this time, though, not as a prelude to an attack, but a sign that his heart was pounding hard with excitement.

Hunt lust.

Foxes, not wolves . . .

'Well,' McDaniel muttered, ignoring an incoming phone call. 'If that's right, I don't think it is, but if so, who the hell's behind it?'

Typing slowly, the criminalist continued, 'Let's think about the facts. We'll discount all the evidence specifically implicating Galt; for the moment let's assume it's been planted. So, the short blond hair is out, the tools are out, the boots are out, his uniform, gear bag, hard hat, friction ridges. All of those are out.

'Okay, so what else do we have left? We've got a Queens connection — the taramasalata. He tried to destroy the access door we found it on so we know that evidence is real. We've got the handgun. So the real perp has access to weapons. We've got a geographic connection to the City Hall area — the trace we found in the generator. We've got hair — long blond and short brown. That suggests two perps. One definitely male, rigging the attacks. The other unknown, but probably a woman. What else do we know?'

'He's from out of town,' Dellray pointed out.

Pulaski said, 'Knowledge of arc flashes and how to create the booby traps.'

'Good,' Rhyme said.

Sellitto said, 'One of them has access to Algonquin facilities.'

'Possibly, though they could have used Galt for that.'

Hums and clicks from the forensic instruments filled the parlor, coins jingled in somebody's pocket.

'A man and a woman,' McDaniel said. 'Just what we learned from T and C. Justice for the Earth.'

Rhyme exhaled a sigh. 'Tucker, I could buy that if we had any evidence about the group. But we don't. Not a single fiber, print, bit of trace.'

'It's all cloud zone.'

'But,' the criminalist snapped, 'if they exist they have a physical presence. Somewhere. I don't have any proof of that.'

'Well, then what do you think's going on?'

Rhyme smiled.

Almost simultaneously Amelia Sachs was shaking her head. 'Rhyme, you don't think it could be, do you?'

'You know what I say: when you've eliminated all the other possibilities, the remaining one, however outlandish it seems, has to be the answer.'

'I don't get it, Lincoln,' Pulaski said. McDaniel's expression echoed the same. 'What do you mean?'

'Well, Rookie, you might want to ask yourself a few questions: one, does Andi Jessen have blond hair about the length of what you found? Two, does she have a brother who's a former soldier who lives out of town and who might have access to weapons like a nineteen eleven Colt army forty-five? And, three, has Andi spent any time in City Hall in the last couple of days, oh, say, giving press conferences?'

70

'Andi Jessen?'

As he continued to type, Rhyme replied to McDaniel, 'And her brother's doing the legwork. Randall. He's the one who's actually staged the attacks. But they coordinated them together. That's why the transfer of evidence. She helped him move the generator out of the white van to the back of the school in Chinatown.'

Sachs crossed her arms as she considered this. 'Remember: Charlie Sommers said that the army teaches soldiers about arc flashes. Randall could've learned what he needed to know there.'

Cooper said, 'The fibers we found in Susan's wheelchair? The database said they might've come from a military uniform.'

Rhyme nodded at the evidence board. 'There was that report of an intrusion at a company substation in Philadelphia. We heard on TV that Randall Jessen lives in Pennsylvania.'

'That's right,' Sachs confirmed.

'He's got dark hair?' Pulaski asked.

'Yes, he does. Well, he did when he was a kid — from the pictures on Andi's desk. And Andi went out of her way to say he didn't live here. And there's something else. She told me she didn't come out of the technical side of the business. She said she got her father's talent — the business side of the energy industry. But remember that news story about her? Before the press conference?'

Cooper nodded. 'She was a lineman for a while before she moved into management and succeeded her father.' He pointed to the perp profile on the whiteboard. 'She was lying.'

Sachs said, 'And the Greek food — could have come from Andi herself. Or maybe she met her brother at a restaurant near the company.'

Eyes on what he was typing, Rhyme's brow furrowed as he considered something else. 'And why is Bernie Wahl still alive?'

'The security chief at Algonquin?' Sellitto mused. 'Fuck, I never thought about it. Sure, it would have made sense for Galt — well, the perp — to kill him.'

'Randall could've delivered the second demand letter a dozen different ways. The point was to make Wahl believe it was Galt. He never saw the perp's face.'

Dellray chimed in, 'No wonder nobody spotted the him, the *real* Galt, even after all the pictures on TV and the internet. It was a different goddamn perp altogether.'

McDaniel now looked less skeptical. 'So where's Randall Jessen now?'

'All we know is he's planning something big for six-thirty tonight.'

Eyeing the recent evidence, Rhyme was lost in thought for a moment, then continued to type — it was a list of instructions on how to proceed from here, one slow letter at a time.

Then the assistant special agent in charge's skeptical gaze returned. 'I'm sorry, time-out here. I can see what you're saying, but what's her motive? She's screwing up her own company. She's committing murder. That makes no sense.'

Rhyme corrected a typo and kept going.

Click, click . . .

Then he looked up and said softly, 'The victims.'

'What?'

Rhyme explained, 'If the perp was just making a statement, like it seemed, he could have rigged a timed device — and not risked being nearby. We know he could have done that; we found the timer spring at one of the crime scenes. But he didn't. He was using a remote control and he was nearby when the victims died. Why?'

Sellitto barked a laugh. 'Goddamn, Line. Andi and her brother were after somebody in particular. She was just making it look, you know, random. That's why the attacks happened before the deadlines.'

'Exactly! . . . Rookie, bring the whiteboards over here. Now!'

He did.

'The vices. Look at the vices.'

- *Luis Martin, assistant store manager.*
- *Linda Kepler, Oklahoma City, tourist.*
- *Morris Kepler, Oklahoma City, tourist.*
- *Samuel Vetter, Scottsdale, businessman.*
- *Ali Mamoud, New York City, waiter.*
- *Gerhart Schiller, Frankfurt, Germany, advertising executive.*
- *Larry Fishbein, New York City, accountant.*

489

- *Robert Bodine, New York City, attorney.*
- *Franklin Tucker, Paramus, New Jersey, salesman.*

'Do we know anything about the injured?'
Sachs said she didn't.
'Well, one of them might've been the intended victim too. We should find out. But what do we know about *them*, at least, the deceased?' Rhyme asked, staring at the names. 'Is there any reason Andi would want any of them dead?'
'The Keplers were tourists in town on a package tour,' Sachs said. 'Retired ten years ago. Vetter was the witness. Maybe that's why they killed him.'
'No, this was planned a month ago. What was the business?'
Sachs flipped through her notebook. 'President of Southwest Concrete.'
'Look 'em up, Mel.'
In a minute Cooper was saying, 'Well, listen to this. Based in Scottsdale. General construction, with a specialty in infrastructure projects. On the website it says that Vetter was attending an alternative energy financing seminar at the Battery Park Hotel.' He looked up. 'Recently they've been involved in constructing the foundations for photovoltaic arrays.'
'Solar power.' Rhyme's eyes continued to take in the evidence. He said, 'And the victims in the office building? Sachs, call Susan Stringer and see if she knows anything about them.'
Sachs pulled out her phone and had a conversation with the woman. When she hung up

she said, 'Okay, she doesn't know the lawyer or the man who got on at the sixth floor. But Larry Fishbein was an accountant she knew a little. She overheard him complaining that there was something odd about the books of a company where he'd just done an audit. Some money was disappearing. And wherever it was, the place was really hot. Too hot to golf.'

'Maybe Arizona. Call and find out.'

Sellitto got the number of the man's firm from Sachs and called. He spoke for a few minutes and then disconnected. 'Bingo. Fishbein was in Scottsdale. He got back Tuesday.'

'Ah, Scottsdale . . . Where Vetter had his company.'

McDaniel said, 'What is this, Lincoln? I still don't see the motive.'

After a moment Rhyme said, 'Andi Jessen's opposed to renewable energy, right?'

Sachs said, 'That's a little strong. But she's definitely not a fan.'

'What if she was bribing alternative energy companies to limit production or doing something else to sabotage them?'

'To keep demand for Algonquin's power high?' McDaniel asked. A motive in his pocket, he seemed more on board now.

'That's right. Vetter and Fishbein might've had information that would've sunk her. If they'd been murdered in separate incidents, just the two of them, the investigators might've wondered if there was a connection. But Andi arranged this whole thing to make it look like they were random victims so nobody'd put the pieces together. That's why the demands were impossible to comply with. She didn't *want* to comply with them. She needed the attacks to take place.'

Rhyme said to Sachs, 'And get the names of the injured and check out their histories. Maybe one of them was a target too.'

'Sure, Rhyme.'

'But,' Sellitto said with unusual urgency in his voice, 'there's the third demand letter, the email. That means she still needs to kill somebody else. Who's the next victim?'

Rhyme continued to type as quickly as he could on his keyboard. His eyes rose momentarily to the digital clock on the wall nearby. 'I don't know. And we've got less than two hours to figure it out.'

71

Despite the horror of Ray Galt's attacks, Charlie Sommers couldn't deny the exhilaration that now, well, electrified him.

He'd taken a coffee break, during which he'd spent the time jotting diagrams for a possible invention (on a napkin, of course): a way to deliver hydrogen gas to homes for fuel cells. He was now returning to the main floor of the New Energy Expo in the Manhattan convention center on the West Side, near the Hudson River. It was filled with thousands of the most innovative people in the world, inventors, scientists, professors, the all-important investors too, each devoted to one thing: alternative energy. Creating it, delivering it, storing it, using it. This was the biggest conference of its sort in the world, timed to coincide with Earth Day. It brought together those who knew the importance of energy but knew too the importance of making and using it in very different ways from what we'd been used to.

As Sommers made his way through the halls of the futuristic convention center — finished just a month or so ago — his heart was pounding like that of a schoolboy at his first science fair.

He felt dizzy, head swiveling back and forth as he took in the booths: those of companies operating wind farms, nonprofits seeking backers to create microgrids in remote parts of Third

World countries, solar power companies, geothermal exploration operations and smaller
outfits that made or installed photovoltaic arrays,
flywheel and liquid sodium storage systems,
batteries, superconductive transport systems,
smart grids . . . the list was endless.

And utterly enthralling.

He arrived at his company's ten-foot-wide
booth at the back end of the hall.

ALGONQUIN CONSOLIDATED POWER
SPECIAL PROJECTS DIVISION
THE SMARTER ALTERNATIVE

Although Algonquin was probably bigger than
the five largest exhibitors here put together, his
company had bought only the smallest booth
available for the New Energy Expo, and he was
the only one manning it.

Which was a pretty clear indication of how
CEO Andi Jessen felt about renewables.

Still, Sommers didn't care. Sure, he was here
as a company representative, but he'd also come
here to meet people and make contacts on his
own. Someday — soon, he hoped — he'd leave
Algonquin and spend all his time on his own
company. He was very up front with his
supervisors about his private work. Nobody at
Algonquin had ever had a problem with what he
did on his own time. They wouldn't be interested
in the inventions he created at home anyway,
things like the Sink-Rynicity water-saving system
for kitchens, or the Volt-Collector, a portable box
that used the motion of vehicles to create power

and store it in a battery you could plug into a fixture in your house or office, thus reducing demand from your local company.

The king of negawatts . . .

Already incorporated, Sommers Illuminating Innovations, Inc., was his company's name and it consisted of himself, his wife and her brother. The name was a play on Thomas Edison's corporation, Edison Illuminating Company, the first investor-owned utility and the operator of the first grid.

While he may have had a bit — a *tiny* bit — of Edison's gift, Sommers was no businessman. He was oblivious when it came to money. When he'd come up with the idea of creating regional grids so that smaller producers could sell excess electricity *to* Algonquin and other large power companies, a friend in the industry had laughed. 'And why would Algonquin want to *buy* electricity when they're in the business of *selling* it?'

'Well,' Sommers replied, blinking in surprise at his friend's naiveté, 'because it's more efficient. It'll be cheaper to customers and reduce the risk of outages.' This was obvious.

The laugh in response suggested that perhaps Sommers was the naïve one.

Sitting down at the booth, he flicked on light switches and removed the Be Back Soon sign. He poured more candy into a bowl. (Algonquin had vetoed hiring a model in a low-cut dress to stand in front of the booth and smile, like some of the exhibitors had.)

No, the smiling was up to him and he grinned

with a vengeance as he gestured people over and talked about power.

During a lull, he sat back and gazed around him, wondering what Thomas Edison would have thought walking through these halls. Sommers had a feeling that the man would have been fascinated and delighted, but not amazed. After all, electrical generation and the grid hadn't changed significantly for 125 years. The scale was bigger, the efficiency better, but every major system in use nowadays had been around then.

Edison would probably have gazed enviously at the halogen bulbs, knowing how hard it had been to find a filament that worked in his. And laughed to see the displays on micronuclear reactors, which could travel on barges to where they were needed (Edison had predicted in the 1800s that we would one day be using nuclear energy to power generators). He would also undoubtedly have been awed by the convention center building itself. The architect had made no attempt to hide the infrastructure; the beams, the walls, the ducts, even portions of the floor were gleaming copper and stainless steel.

It was, Sommers considered, like being inside a huge switchgear array.

The special project manager kept his guard up, though. There's a seamy side to invention. The creation of the lightbulb had been a fierce battle — not only technologically but legally. Dozens of people were involved in knock-down, drag-out battles for credit for — and the profit from — the lightbulb. Thomas Edison and

England's Joseph Wilson Swan emerged as the victors but from a field littered with lawsuits, anger, espionage and sabotage. And destroyed careers.

Sommers was thinking of this now because he'd seen a man in glasses and a cap not far from the Algonquin booth. He was suspicious because the guy had been lingering at two different booths nearby. One company made equipment for geothermal exploration, devices that would locate hot spots deep in the earth. The other built hybrid motors for small vehicles. But Sommers knew that someone interested in geothermal would likely have no interest in hybrids.

True, the man was paying little attention to Sommers or Algonquin, but he could easily have been taking pictures of some of the inventions and mockups on display at the booth. Spy cameras nowadays were extremely sophisticated.

Sommers turned away to answer a woman's question. When he looked back, the man — spy or businessman or just curious attendee — was gone.

Ten minutes later, another lull in visitors. He decided to use the restroom. He asked the man in the booth next to his to keep an eye on things and then headed down a nearly deserted corridor to the men's room. One advantage of being in the cheaper, small-booth area was that you had the toilets largely to yourself. He stepped into a corridor whose stylish steel floor was embossed with bumps, presumably to simulate the flooring of a space station or rocket.

When he was twenty feet away his cell phone started to ring.

He didn't recognize the number — from a local area code. He thought for a moment then hit the Ignore button.

Sommers continued toward the toilet, noticing the shiny copper handle on the door and thinking, They sure didn't spare any expense here. No wonder it's costing us so damn much for the booth.

72

'Please,' Sachs muttered out loud, hovering over the speakerphone. 'Charlie, pick up! Please!'

She'd called Sommers just a moment before but the phone rang only once and then went to voice mail.

She was trying again.

'Come on!' Rhyme too said.

Two rings . . . three . . .

And finally, in the speaker, a click. 'Hello?'

'Charlie, it's Amelia Sachs.'

'Oh, did you call a minute ago? I was on my way — '

'Charlie,' she broke in. 'You're in danger.'

'What?'

'Where are you?'

'In the convention center. About to . . . What do you mean, danger?'

'Are you near anything metal, anything that could produce an arc flash or something that could be rigged with a hot line?'

He gave an abrupt laugh. 'I'm standing on a metal floor. And I was just about to open a bathroom door with a metal handle.' Then the humor faded from his voice. 'Are you saying they might be booby-trapped?'

'It's possible. Get off the metal floor now.'

'I don't understand.'

'There's been another demand and a deadline. Six-thirty. But we think the attacks

499

— the hotel, the elevator — don't have anything to do with the threats or demands. They're cover-ups to target certain people. And you might be one of them.'

'Me? Why?'

'First of all, get someplace safe.'

'I'll go back to the main floor. It's concrete. Hold on.' A moment later he said, 'Okay. You know, I saw somebody here, watching me. But I don't think it was Galt.'

Rhyme said, 'Charlie, it's Lincoln. We think Ray Galt was set up. He's probably dead.'

'Somebody *else* is behind the attacks?'

'Yes.'

'Who?'

'Andi Jessen. The man you saw might've been her brother, Randall. The evidence shows that they're working together.'

'What? That's crazy. And why'm I in danger?'

Sachs continued, 'Some of the people killed in the other attacks were involved in alternative energy production. Like you. We think that she may have been bribing renewable power companies to cut back generation, to keep up demand for Algonquin's electricity.'

There was a pause. 'Well, it's true, one of my projects's been to consolidate regional grids so that they could be more self-sufficient — and start supplying juice to the big interconnections, like Algonquin. I guess that could be a problem for her.'

'Have you been to Scottsdale recently?'

'I'm working on some solar farm projects near

there, yes, among other places. California, it's wind farms and geothermal. Arizona is mostly solar farms.'

Sachs said, 'I was thinking back to something you said when I met you at Algonquin. Why did she ask *you* to help me with the investigation?'

He paused. 'You're right. She could've asked a dozen people.'

'I think she was setting you up.'

Then he gasped and said, 'Oh, Jesus.'

'What?' Rhyme asked.

'Maybe it's not just me who's at risk. Think about it: *Everybody* here at the convention's a threat to Algonquin. The whole event's about alternative energy, microgrids, decentralization. Andi could see every exhibitor here as a threat, if she's that obsessed with Algonquin being the number-one energy provider in North America.'

'Is there somebody at Algonquin we can trust? Somebody to shut off power there? And not let Andi know?'

'Algonquin doesn't run service here. Like some of the subway lines, the convention center makes its own juice. The plant's next to the building here. Should we evacuate the place?'

'Would people have to go over a metal floor to get outside?'

'Yes, most of them would. The front lobby and the loading docks are all steel. Not painted. Pure steel. And do you know how much electricity there is feeding in here? The load on a day like this is close to twenty million watts. Look, I can go downstairs, find the supply. Maybe I can pull the breakers. I could — '

'No, we need to find out exactly what they're doing. And how they're doing it. We'll call as soon as we know more. Stay put!'

73

Sweating, frantic, Charlie Sommers looked around him at the tens of thousands of visitors at the New Energy Expo, some hoping to make a fortune, some hoping to help, if not save, the planet, some here because it seemed like a fun idea to stop in for a while.

Some were young, teenagers who, like him years ago, would be inspired to take different courses in high school after seeing these exhibits. More science, less foreign language and history. And become the Edisons of their generations.

They were all at risk.

Stay put, the police had told him.

Crowds jostled, carting colorful bags — the exhibitors' giveaways, with the company logos printed boldly: Volt Storage Technologies, Next Generation Batteries, Geothermal Innovations.

Stay put . . .

Except his mind was in a place his wife called 'Charlie-think.' It was spinning on its own, like a dynamo, like an electricity storage flywheel. Ten thousand RPM. Thinking of the electricity usage here in the convention center. Twenty megawatts.

Twenty million watts.

Watts equals volts times amps . . .

Enough electricity, if channeled through this conductive superstructure, to electrocute thousands. Arc flashes, or just ground faults, the massive current surging through bodies, taking lives and leaving smoldering piles of flesh and clothing and hair.

Stay put . . .

Well, he couldn't.

And, like any inventor, Sommers considered the practical details. Randall Jessen and Andi would have somehow secured the power plant. They couldn't risk that the police would call the maintenance staff and simply cut the supply. But there'd be a main line coming into this building. Probably like an area transmission line it would be carrying 138,000v. They would have cut into the line to electrify floors or stairways or doorknobs. The elevators again maybe.

Sommers reflected:

The attendees here couldn't avoid the juice.

They couldn't protect themselves against it.

So he'd have to cut its head off.

There was no *staying put.*

If he could find the incoming line before Randall Jessen ran the splice, Sommers could short it out. He'd run a cable from the hot line directly to a return. The resulting short circuit, accompanied by an arc flash as powerful as the one at the bus station the other morning, would pop breakers in the convention center power plant, eliminating the danger. The emergency lighting system would kick on but that was low voltage — probably from 12-volt lead-calcium batteries. There'd be no risk of electrocution with that small supply. A few people would be stuck in the elevators, maybe there'd be some panic. But injuries would be minimal.

But then reality came home to him. The only way to short out the system was to do the most dangerous procedure in the utility business: bare hand work on an energized line carrying 138,000 volts. Only the top linemen ever attempted this. Working from insulated buckets or helicopters to avoid any risk of ground contact and wearing faraday suits — actual metal clothing — the linemen connected themselves directly to the high-voltage wire itself. In effect, they became part of it, and hundreds of thousands of volts streamed over their bodies.

Charlie Sommers had never tried bare hand work with high voltage, but he knew how to perform it — in theory.

Like a bird on a wire . . .

At the Algonquin booth he now grabbed his pathetically sparse tool kit and borrowed a length of lightweight high-tension wire from a nearby exhibitor. He ran into the dim hallway to find a service door. He glanced at the copper doorknob, hesitated only a moment then yanked it open and plunged into the dimness of the center's several basements.

Stay put?

I don't think so.

74

He sat in the front seat of his white van, hot because the air conditioner was off. He didn't want to run the engine and draw attention to himself. A parked vehicle is one thing. A parked vehicle with an engine running exponentially increased suspicion.

Sweat tickled the side of his cheek. He hardly noticed it. He pressed the headset more firmly against his ear. Still nothing. He turned the volume higher. Static. A clunk or two. A snap.

He was thinking of the words he'd sent via email earlier today.

If you ignore me this time, the consequences will be far, far greater than the small incidents of yesterday and the day before, the loss of life far worse . . .

Yes and no.

He tilted his head, listening for more words to flow through the microphone he'd hidden in the generator he'd planted at the school near Chinatown. A Trojan horse, one that the Crime Scene Unit had courteously carted right into Lincoln Rhyme's townhouse. He'd already gotten the low-down on the cast of characters helping Rhyme and their whereabouts. Lon Sellitto, the NYPD detective, and Tucker McDaniel, ASAC of the FBI, were gone, headed downtown to City Hall, where they would coordinate the defense of the convention center.

Amelia Sachs and Ron Pulaski were speeding there now, to see if they could shut the power off.

Waste of time, he reflected.

Then he stiffened, hearing the voice of Lincoln Rhyme.

'Okay, Mel, I need you to get that cable to the lab in Queens.'

'The — ?'

'The cable!'

'Which one?'

'How the hell many cables are there?'

'About four.'

'Well, the one Sachs and Pulaski found at the school in Chinatown. I want the trace between the insulation and the wire itself dug out and run through their SEM.'

Then came the sound of plastic and paper. A moment later, footsteps. 'I'll be back in forty minutes, an hour.'

'I don't care when you get back. I care when you call me with the results.'

Footsteps, thudding.

The microphone was very sensitive.

A door slammed. Silence. The tapping of computer keys, nothing else.

Then Rhyme, shouting: 'Goddamn it, Thom! . . . Thom!'

'What, Lincoln? Are you — '

'Is Mel gone?'

'Hold on.'

After a moment the voice called, 'Yes, his car

just left. You want me to call him?'

'No, don't bother. Look, I need a piece of wire. I want to see if I can duplicate something Randall did . . . A long piece of wire. Do we have anything like that here?'

'Extension cord?'

'No, bigger. Twenty, thirty feet.'

'Why would I have any wire that long here?'

'I just thought maybe you would. Well, go find some. Now.'

'Where am I supposed to find wire?'

'A fucking wire store. I don't know. A hardware store. There's that one on Broadway, right? There used to be.'

'It's still there. So you need thirty feet?'

'That should do it . . . What?'

'It's just, you're not looking well, Lincoln. I'm not sure I should leave you.'

'Yes, you should. You should do what I'm asking. The sooner you leave, the sooner you'll be back and you can mother-hen me to your heart's content. But for now: Go!'

There was no sound for a moment.

'All right. But I'm checking your blood pressure first.'

Another pause.

'Go ahead.'

Muffled sounds, a faint hiss, the rasp of Velcro. 'It's not bad. But I want to make sure it stays that way . . . How are you feeling?'

'I'm just tired.'

'I'll be back in a half hour.'

Faint steps sounded on the floor. The door opened again then closed.

He listened for a moment more and then rose. He pulled on a cable TV repairman's uniform. He slipped the 1911 Colt into a gear bag, which he slung over his shoulder.

He checked the front windows and mirrors of the van and, noting that the alley was empty, climbed out. He verified there were no security cameras and walked to the back door of Lincoln Rhyme's townhouse. In three minutes he'd made sure the alarm was off and had picked the lock, slipping into the basement.

He found the electrical service panel and silently went to work, rigging another of his remote control switchgear units to the incoming service line, 400 amps, which was double that of most other residences in the area.

This was interesting to note but not particularly significant, of course, since he knew that all he needed to cause virtually instant death was a tiny portion of that.

One tenth of one amp . . .

75

Rhyme was looking over the evidence boards when the electricity went off in his townhouse. The computer screen turned black, machinery sighed to silence. The red, green and yellow eyes of the LEDs on the equipment surrounding him vanished.

He swiveled his head from side to side.

From the basement, the creak of a door. Then he heard footsteps. Not the footfalls themselves, but the faint protest of human weight on old, dry wood.

'Hello?' he shouted. 'Thom? Is that you? The power. There's something wrong with the power.'

The creaking grew closer. Then it vanished. Rhyme turned his chair in a circle. He scanned the room, eyes darting the way they used to dart at crime scenes upon first arrival, taking in all the relevant evidence, getting the impression of the scene. Looking for the dangers too: the places where the perp might still be hiding, maybe injured, maybe panicked, maybe coolly waiting for a chance to kill a police officer.

Another creak.

He spun the wheelchair around again, three-sixty, but saw nothing. Then he spotted, on one of the examination tables at the far end of the room, a cell phone. Although the power was off in the rest of the town-house, of course, the mobile would be working.

Batteries . . .

Rhyme pushed the controller touchpad forward and the chair responded quickly. He sped to the table and stopped, his back to the doorway, and stared down at the phone. It was no more than eighteen inches from his face.

Its LCD indicator glowed green. Plenty of juice, ready to take or send a call.

'Thom?' he called again.

Nothing.

Rhyme felt the pounding of his heart through the telegraph of his temples and the throbbing veins in his neck.

Alone in the room, virtually immobile. Less than two feet away from the phone, staring. Rhyme turned the chair slightly sideways and then back, quickly, knocking into the table, rocking the phone. But it remained exactly where it was.

Then he was aware of a change in the acoustics of the room, and he knew the intruder had entered. He banged into the table once again. But before the phone skidded closer to him, he heard footsteps pound across the floor behind him. A gloved hand reached over his shoulder and seized the phone.

'Is that you?' Rhyme demanded of the person behind him. 'Randall? Randall Jessen?'

No answer.

Only faint sounds behind him, clicks. Then jostling, which he felt in his shoulders. The wheelchair's battery indicator light on the touchpad went black. The intruder disengaged the brake manually and wheeled the chair to an area illuminated by a band of pale sunlight falling through the window.

The man then slowly turned the chair around.

Rhyme opened his mouth to speak but then his eyes narrowed as he studied the face before him carefully. He said nothing for a moment. Then, in a whisper: 'It can't be.'

The cosmetic surgery had been very good. Still, there were familiar landmarks in the man's face. Besides, how could Rhyme possibly fail to recognize Richard Logan, the Watchmaker, the man who was supposedly hiding out at that very moment in an unsavory part of Mexico City?

76

Logan shut off the cell phone that Lincoln Rhyme had apparently been trying in his desperation to knock into service.

'I don't understand,' the criminalist said.

Logan sloughed a gear bag off his shoulder and set it on the floor, crouching and opening it. His quick fingers dug into the bag and he extracted a laptop computer and two wireless video cameras. One he took into the kitchen and pointed into the alley. The other he set in a front window. He booted up the computer and placed it on a nearby table. He typed in some commands. Immediately images of the alley and sidewalk approaches to Rhyme's townhouse came on the screen. It was the same system he'd used at the Battery Park Hotel to spy on Vetter and determine the exact moment to hit the switch: when flesh met metal.

Then Logan looked up and gave a faint laugh. He walked to the dark oak mantelpiece where a pocketwatch sat on a stand.

'You still have my present,' he whispered. 'You have it . . . have it *out*, on display.' He was shocked. He'd assumed the ancient Breguet had been dismantled and every piece examined to determine where Logan lived.

Though they were enemies, and Logan would soon kill him, he admired Rhyme a great deal and was oddly pleased that the man had kept the timepiece intact.

When he thought about it, however, he decided that, of course, the criminalist had indeed ordered it taken apart, down to the last hairspring and jewel, for the forensics team but then had it reassembled perfectly.

Making Rhyme a bit of a watchmaker too.

Next to the pocketwatch was the note that had accompanied the timepiece. It was both an appreciation of Rhyme, and an ominous promise that they'd meet again.

A promise now fulfilled.

The criminalist was recovering from his shock. He said, 'People'll be back here any minute.'

'No, Lincoln. They won't.' Logan recited the whereabouts of everyone who'd been in the room fifteen minutes ago.

Rhyme frowned, 'How did you . . . ? Oh, no. Of course, the generator. You have a bug in it.' He closed his eyes in disgust.

'That's right. And I know how much time I have.'

Richard Logan reflected that whatever else occurred in his life, he *always* knew exactly how much time he had.

The dismay on Rhyme's face then faded into confusion. 'So it wasn't Randall Jessen masquerading as Ray Galt. It was you.'

Logan fondly studied the Breguet. Compared the time to a watch on his own wrist. 'You keep it wound.' Then he replaced it. 'That's right. I've been Raymond Galt, master electrician and troubleman, for the past week.'

'But I saw you in the airport security video . . . You were hired to kill Rodolfo Luna in Mexico.'

'Not exactly. His colleague Arturo Diaz was on the payroll of one of the big drug cartels out of Puerto Vallarta. Luna is one of the few honest cops left in Mexico. Diaz *wanted* to hire me to kill him. But I was too busy. For a fee, though, I did agree to *pretend* I was behind it, to keep suspicion off him. It served *my* purposes too. I needed everyone — especially you — to believe I was someplace other than New York City.'

'But at the airport . . .' Rhyme's voice fell to a confused whisper. 'You were on the plane. The security tape. We *saw* you get in that truck, hide under the tarp. And you were spotted in Mexico City and on the road there from the airport. You were seen in Gustavo Madero an hour ago. Your fingerprints and . . . 'The words dissolved. The criminalist shook his head and gave a resigned smile. 'My God. You never left the airport at all.'

'No, I didn't.'

'You picked up that package and got onto the truck in front of the security camera — you knew it was there. But then it just drove out of view and you got out. You handed the package off to somebody else and got onto a flight headed to the East Coast. Diaz's men just lied. They kept reporting you in Mexico City — to make everybody think you were there. How many of Diaz's people were on the take?'

'About two dozen.'

'There was no car fleeing to Gustavo Madero?'

'No.' Pity was an emotion that to Logan was inefficient and therefore pointless. Still, he could recognize, without being moved personally, that there was something pitiable about Lincoln Rhyme at the moment. He also looked smaller than when last they met. Nearly frail. Perhaps he'd been sick. Which was good, Logan decided; the electricity coursing through his body would take its toll more quickly. He certainly didn't want Rhyme to suffer.

He added, as if in consolation, 'You anticipated the attack on Luna. You stopped Diaz from killing him. I never thought you'd figure it out in time. But, on reflection, I shouldn't have been surprised.'

'But I didn't stop *you*.'

Logan had killed a number of people in his lengthy career as a professional. Most of them, if they were aware they were about to die, grew calm, as they understood the inevitability of what was about to happen. But Rhyme went even further. The criminalist now almost looked relieved. Perhaps that was what Logan saw in Rhyme's face: the symptoms of a terminal illness. Or maybe he'd just lost the will to live, given his condition. A fast death would be a blessing.

'Where's Galt's body?'

'The Burn — the boiler furnace at Algonquin Power. There's nothing left.' Logan glanced at the laptop. Still all clear. He took out a length of Bennington medium-voltage cable and attached one end to the hot line in a nearby 220-volt outlet. He'd spent months learning all about juice. He felt as comfortable with it now as with the fine gears and springs of clocks and watches.

Logan felt in his pocket the weight of the remote control that would turn the power back on and send sufficient amperage into the criminalist to kill him instantly.

As he wound part of the cable around Rhyme's arm, the man said, 'But if you bugged the generator you must've heard what we were saying before. We know Raymond Galt isn't the real perp, that he was set up. And we know that Andi Jessen wanted to kill Sam Vetter and Larry Fishbein. Whether or not it was her brother who rigged the traps or you, she'll still get collared and . . .'

Logan did no more than glance at Rhyme, on whose face appeared a look of both understanding and complete resignation. 'But that's not what this is about, is it? That's not what this is about at all.'

'No, Lincoln. It's not.'

77

A bird not on, but above, a wire.

Dangling in the air in the deepest subbasement of the convention center, Charlie Sommers was in an improvised sling exactly two feet away from a line carrying 138,000 volts, swathed in red insulation.

If electricity were water, the pressure in the cable in front of him would be like that at the bottom of the sea, millions of pounds per square inch, just waiting for any excuse to crush the submarine into a flat, bloody strip of metal.

The main line, suspended on insulated glass supports, was ten feet off the ground running from the wall across the basement to the convention center's own substation, at the far end of the dim space.

Because he couldn't touch both the bare wire and anything connected to the ground at the same time, he'd improvised a sling from fire hose, which he'd tied to a catwalk above the high-voltage cable. Using all his strength, he'd shimmied down the hose and had managed to slide into the crux of the sling. He fervently hoped that fire hoses were made exclusively of rubber and canvas; if the hose was, for some reason, reinforced with metal strands, then in a few minutes he would become a major player in a phase-to-ground fault and would turn into vapor.

Around his neck was a length of 1/0-gauge cable — what he'd borrowed from the booth next to Algonquin's. With his Swiss army knife Sommers was slowly stripping away the dark red insulation on it. When he was finished he would similarly strip away the protective coating from the high-voltage line, exposing the aluminum strands. And, with his unprotected hands, he'd join the two wires.

Then one of two things would happen. Either: Nothing.

Or, a phase-to-ground fault . . . and vapor.

If the case of the former, he would then carefully extend the exposed end of the wire and touch it to a nearby return source — some iron girders connected to the convention center's foundation. The result would be a spectacular short that would blow the breakers in the center's power plant.

As for him, well, Charlie Sommers himself wouldn't be grounded, but voltage that high would produce a huge arc flash, which could easily burn him to death.

Knowing now that the deadline was meaningless and that Randall and Andi Jessen might trip the switchgear at any moment, he worked feverishly, slicing the blood red insulation off the cable. The curled strips of dielectric fell to the floor beneath him and Sommers couldn't help but think they were like petals falling from dying roses in a funeral home after the mourners had returned home.

78

Richard Logan watched Lincoln Rhyme gazing out one of the large windows of the townhouse — in the direction of the East River. Somewhere out there the gray and red towers of Algonquin Consolidated Power presided over the grim riverfront. The smokestacks weren't visible from here but Logan supposed that on a cold day Rhyme could see the billowing exhaust rising over the skyline.

Shaking his head, the criminalist whispered, 'Andi Jessen didn't hire you at all.'

'No.'

'She's the *target*, isn't she? You're setting her up.'

'That's right.'

Rhyme nodded at the gear bag at Logan's feet. 'There's evidence in there implicating her and her brother. You're going to plant it here, as if Andi and Randall had killed me too. Just like you've been planting evidence all along. The trace from City Hall, the blond hair, the Greek food. You were hired by somebody to make it look like Andi was using Ray Galt to kill Sam Vetter and Larry Fishbein . . . Why them?'

'It wasn't them particularly. The victims could have been anybody from the seminar at the Battery Park Hotel or from Fishbein's accounting firm. Anybody who might have information about some scam or another Andi Jessen wanted to cover up.'

'Even though they didn't have any information.'

'No. Nothing to do with Algonquin or Andi Jessen at all.'

'Who's behind it?' Rhyme's brow was furrowed, the eyes now darting over the evidence boards, as if he needed to know the answer to the puzzle before he died. 'I can't figure that out.'

Logan looked down at the man's gaunt face.

Pity . . .

He extracted a second wire and rigged it too to Rhyme. He'd connect this to the closest ground, the radiator.

Richard Logan never cared, on a moral level, why his clients wanted the victims dead, but he made a point of learning the motive because it helped him to plan his job and to get away afterward. So he'd listened with interest when it was explained to him why Andi Jessen had to be discredited and go to jail for a long, long time. He now said, 'Andi is a threat to the new order. Her view — her very *vocal* view, apparently — is that oil and gas and coal and nuke are the only significant sources for energy and will be for the next hundred years. Renewables are a kid's toy.'

'She's pointing out the emperor's new clothes.'

'Exactly.'

'So some ecoterror group *is* behind this, then?'

Logan grimaced. 'Ecoterrorists? Oh, please. Bearded unwashed idiots who can't even burn down a ski resort construction site without

521

getting caught in the act?' Logan laughed. 'No, Lincoln. It's about money.'

Rhyme seemed to understand. 'Ah, sure . . . It doesn't matter that clean energy and renewables don't add up to much in the great scheme of things yet; there's still lots of profit to be made building wind and solar farms and regional grids and the transmission equipment.'

'Exactly. Government subsidies and tax breaks too. Not to mention consumers who'll pay whatever they're billed for green power because they think they're saving the earth.'

Rhyme said, 'When we found Galt's apartment, his emails about the cancer, we were thinking that revenge never sits well as a motive.'

'No, but greed's perennial.'

The criminalist apparently couldn't help but laugh. 'So a green cartel's behind this. What a thought.' His eyes took in the whiteboards. 'I think I can deduce one of the players . . . Bob Cavanaugh?'

'Good. Yes. He's the principal, in fact. How did you know?'

'He gave us information implicating Randall Jessen.' Rhyme squinted. 'And he helped us at the hotel in Battery Park. We might've saved Vetter . . . But, sure, it didn't matter if you actually killed him or Fishbein, or anyone else for that matter.'

'No. What was important was that Andi Jessen get arrested for the attacks. Discredited and sent to jail. And there was another motive: Cavanaugh was an associate of Andi's father, and never very happy he'd been passed over for the president and CEO spot by daddy's little girl.'

'He can't be the only one.'

'No. The cartel has CEOs from a half dozen alternative-energy equipment suppliers around the world, mostly in the U.S., China and Switzerland.'

'A green cartel.' Rhyme shook his head.

'Times change,' Logan said.

'But why not just kill her, Andi?'

'My very question,' Logan said. 'But there was an economic component. Cavanaugh and the others needed Andi out but also needed to have Algonquin's share price drop. The cartel is going to snap up the company.'

'And the attack on the bus?'

'Needed to get everybody's attention.' Logan felt a ping of regret. And he was comfortable confessing to Rhyme, 'I didn't want anyone to die there. That passenger would have been okay if he'd gotten onto the bus instead of hesitating. But I couldn't wait anymore.'

'I can see why you'd set up Vetter and Fishbein to make it look like Andi wanted them dead — they were involved in alternative energy projects in Arizona. They'd be logical victims. But why would the cartel want to kill Charlie Sommers? Wasn't his job *developing* alternative energy?'

'Sommers?' A nod at the generator. 'I heard you mention him. And Bernie Wahl dimed him out when I delivered the second note. Wahl snitched on you too, by the way . . . '

'Because you threatened to, what? Electrocute his family?'

'Yes.'

'I hardly blame him.'

Logan continued, 'But whoever this Sommers is, he's not part of the plan.'

'But you sent Algonquin a third demand letter. That meant you had to kill somebody else. You don't have a trap at the convention center?' Rhyme looked confused.

'No.'

Then he nodded with understanding. 'Of course . . . me. I'm the next victim.'

Logan paused, the wire taut in his hands. 'That's right.'

'You took on this whole assignment because of me.'

'I get a lot of calls. But I've been waiting for a job that would bring me back to New York.' Logan lowered his head. 'You nearly caught me when I was here a few years ago — and you ruined that assignment. It was the first time that anyone's ever stopped me from fulfilling a contract. I had to return the fee . . . It wasn't the cash; it was the embarrassment. Shameful. And then you nearly caught me in England too. Next time . . . you might get lucky. That's why I took the job when Cavanaugh called me. I needed to get close to you.'

Logan wondered why he'd chosen those words. He pushed the thought away, finished affixing the ground wire. He rose. 'Sorry. But I have to do this,' he apologized. Then poured water onto Rhyme's chest, soaking his shirt. It

524

was undignified but he didn't have a choice. 'Conductivity.'

'And Justice For the Earth? Nothing to do with you either?'

'No. I never heard of them.'

Rhyme was watching him. 'So that remote control switch you've made? It's rigged downstairs in my circuit breaker panel?'

'Yes.'

Rhyme mused, 'Electricity . . . I've learned a lot about it in the past few days.'

'I've been studying it for months.'

'Galt taught you the Algonquin computer controls?'

'No, that was Cavanaugh. He got me the pass codes to the system.'

'Ah, sure.'

Logan said, 'But I also took a course in SCADA and the Algonquin system in particular.'

'Of course, you would have.'

Logan continued, 'I was surprised how fascinated I've become. I always belittled electricity.'

'Because of your watchmaking?'

'Exactly. A battery and a mass-produced chip can equal the capability of the finest hand-made watches.'

Rhyme nodded with understanding. 'Electrical clocks seemed cheap to you. Somehow using battery power lessened the beauty of a watch. Lessened the art.'

Logan felt excitement coursing through him. To engage in a conversation like this was enthralling; there were so few people who were his equal. And the criminalist actually knew what he was feeling! 'Yes, yes, exactly. But then, working on this job, my opinion changed. Why is a watch that tells time by an oscillator regulated by a quartz crystal any less astonishing than one run by gears and levers and springs? In the end, it all comes down to physics. As a man of science, you'd appreciate that ... Oh, and complications? You know what complications are.'

Rhyme said, 'All the bells and whistles they build into watches. The date, the phases of the moon, the equinox, chimes.'

Logan was surprised. Rhyme added, 'Oh, I've studied watchmaking too.'

Close to you ...

'Electronic watches duplicate all of those functions and a hundred more. The Timex DataLink. You know it?'

'No,' Rhyme said.

'They're classics now — wristwatches that link to your computer. Telling the time is only one of a hundred things they can do. Astronauts have worn them to the moon.'

Another look at the computer screen. No one was approaching the townhouse.

'And all this change, this modernity doesn't bother you?' Rhyme asked.

'No, it simply proves how integrated in our lives is the subject of time. We forget that the watchmakers were the Silicon Valley innovators of their day. Why, look at this project. What an impressive weapon — electricity. I shut down the entire city for a few days, thanks just to

526

electricity. It's part of our nature now, part of our being. We couldn't live without it . . . Times change. We have to change too. Whatever the risks. Whatever we have to leave behind.'

Rhyme said, 'I have a favor.'

'I've adjusted the circuit breakers in your service panel. They'll carry three times the load. It'll be fast. You won't feel anything.'

'I never feel very much in any event,' Rhyme said.

'I . . . ' Logan felt as if he had committed a shameful faux pas. 'I apologize. I wasn't thinking.'

A demurring nod. 'What I'm asking has to do with Amelia.'

'Sachs?'

'There's no reason to go after her.'

Logan had considered this and he now told Rhyme his conclusion. 'No, I have no intention to. She'll have the drive to find me. The tenacity. But she's no match for me. She'll be safe.'

And now Rhyme's smile was faint. 'Thank you . . . I was going to say, Richard. You *are* Richard Logan, right? Or is that fake?'

'That's my real name.' Logan glanced at the screen again. The sidewalk outside was empty. No police. None of Rhyme's associates returning. He and the criminalist were completely alone. It was time. 'You're remarkably calm.'

Rhyme replied, 'Why shouldn't I be? I've been living on borrowed time for years. Every day it's a bit of surprise when I wake up.'

Logan dug into his gear bag and tossed another coil of wire, containing Randall Jessen's fingerprints, onto the floor. He then opened a Baggie and upended it, letting some of Randall's hairs flutter to the ground nearby. He used one of the brother's shoes to leave an impression in the spilled water. Then he planted more of Andi Jessen's blond hairs, along with some fibers from one of her suits, which he'd gotten from her closet at work.

He looked up and checked the electrical connections again. Why was he hesitating? Perhaps it was that Rhyme's death represented for him the end of an era. Killing the criminalist would be a vast relief. But it would also be a loss he'd feel forever. He supposed what he was experiencing now was what one felt making the decision to take a loved one off life support.

Close to you . . .

He slipped the remote control from his pocket, stood back from the wheelchair.

Lincoln Rhyme was studying him calmly. He sighed and said, 'I guess that's about it, then.'

Logan hesitated and his eyes narrowed, staring at Rhyme. There was something very different about the criminalist's tone, as he'd spoken those words. His facial expression too. And the eyes . . . the eyes were suddenly a predator's.

Richard Logan actually shivered as he suddenly understood that that incongruous sentence, delivered so incongruously, was not directed toward him at all.

It was a message. To somebody else.

'What've you done?' Logan whispered, heart pounding. He stared at the small computer monitor. There was no sign that anybody was

528

returning to the townhouse.

But . . . but what if they'd never left in the first place?

Oh, no . . .

Logan stared at Rhyme and then jammed his finger onto the two buttons of the remote control switch.

Nothing happened.

Rhyme said matter-of-factly, 'As soon as you came upstairs one of our officers disconnected it.'

'No,' Logan gasped.

A creak sounded on the floor behind him. He spun around.

'Richard Logan, do not move!' It was that police detective they'd just been talking about, Amelia Sachs. 'Keep your hands in view. If you move your hands you will be shot.'

Behind her were two other men. Logan took them to be police too. One was heavy and wearing a wrinkled blue suit. The other, skinnier, was in shirtsleeves, wearing black-framed glasses.

All three officers trained weapons on him.

But Logan's eyes were on Amelia Sachs, who seemed the most eager to shoot. He realized that Rhyme had asked the question about Sachs to alert them that he was ready to say the magic words and spring the trap.

I guess that's about it then . . .

But the consequence was that she would have heard Logan's comment about her, her inferior skills.

Still, when she stepped forward to cuff him, it

was with utmost professionalism, gently almost. Then she eased him to the floor with minimal discomfort.

The heavy officer stepped forward and reached for the wires coiled around Rhyme.

'Gloves, please,' said the criminalist calmly.

The big cop hesitated. Then pulled on latex gloves and removed the cables. He said into his radio, 'It's clear up here. You can put the power back on.'

A moment later lights filled the room and, surrounded by the clicks of the equipment returning to life and the diodes flickering red, green and white, Richard Logan, the Watchmaker, was read his rights.

79

It was time for the heroics.

Not generally the bailiwick of inventors.

Charlie Sommers decided he had removed enough insulation from the lightweight cable so that he was ready to try for the short circuit.

In theory this should work.

The risk was that, in its desperation to get to the ground, the instant he moved it closer to the return, the massive voltage in the feeder line would arc to the cable then consume his body in a plasma spark. He was only ten feet above the concrete; Sommers had seen videos of arc flashes that were fifty feet in length.

But he'd waited long enough.

First step: Connect the cable to the main line.

Thinking of his wife, thinking of his children — and his *other* children: the inventions he'd fathered over the years — he leaned toward the hot wire and with a deep breath touched the lightweight cable to it, using his hands.

Nothing happened. So far, so good. His body and the wires were now at the same potential. In effect, Charlie Sommers was simply a portion of a 138,000v line.

He worked the bare section of the cable around the far side of the energized line and caught the end underneath. He twisted it so there was tight contact.

Gripping the insulated part of the lightweight cable, he eased back, in his unsure fire-hose swing, and stared at the place he'd decided to close the connection: a girder that rose to the ceiling but, more important for his purposes, descended deep into the earth.

To which all juice had a primal instinct to return.

The girder was about six feet away.

Charlie Sommers gave a faint laugh.

This was fucking ridiculous. The minute the exposed end of the other wire neared the metal beam, the current would anticipate the contact and lunge outward in a huge explosion of arc flash. Plasma, flame, molten metal flying at three thousand feet per second . . .

But he saw no other choice.

Now!

Cut its head off . . .

He began to feed the cable to the metal bar.

Six feet, five, four . . .

'Hey there! Charlie? Charlie Sommers?'

He gasped. The end of the cable swung wildly but he reeled it in fast.

'Who's there?' Sommers blurted before realizing that it might be Andi Jessen's brother, who'd come to shoot him.

'It's Ron Pulaski. I'm that officer works with Detective Sachs.'

'Yes, what?' Sommers gasped. 'What're you doing here?'

'We've been trying to call you for a half hour.'

'Get out of here, Officer. It's dangerous!'

'We couldn't get through. We called you right

after you hung up speaking to Amelia and Lincoln.'

Sommers steadied his voice. 'I don't have my goddamn phone. Look, I'm shutting down the power here, in the whole area. It's the only way to stop him. There's going to be a huge — '

'He's already stopped.'

'What?'

'Yessir, they sent me here to find you. To tell you that what they were saying on the phone was fake. They knew the killer was listening in and they couldn't tell you what they were really planning. We had to make him think we believed the attack was happening here. As soon as I left Lincoln's, I tried to call you. But we couldn't get through. Somebody said they saw you coming down here.'

Jesus Lord in heaven.

Sommers stared at the cable dangling below him. The juice in the feeder cable could decide at any moment that it wanted to take a shortcut to get back home and Sommers would simply disappear.

Pulaski called, 'Say, what exactly're you doing up there?'

Killing myself.

Sommers retracted the cable slowly and then he reached into the enclosure and began undoing the connection with the main line, expecting — no, positive — that at any moment he would hear, very, very briefly, the arc flash hum and bang as he died.

The process of unraveling the beast seemed to take forever.

'Anything I can do sir?'

Yes, shut the hell up.

'Um, just stay back and give me a minute, Officer.'

'Sure.'

Finally, the cable came away from the feeder line and Sommers dropped it to the floor.

He eased out of the fire hose sling, hung for a moment, then tumbled to the ground on top of the cable. He collapsed in pain from the fall but stood and tested for broken bones. He sensed there were none.

'What's that you were saying, sir?' Pulaski asked.

He'd been repeating a frantic mantra: *stay put, stay put, stay put* . . .

But he told the cop, 'Nothing.' Then he dusted off his slacks and looked around. He asked, 'Hey, Officer?'

'Yessir?'

'By any chance you pass a restroom on your way down here?'

80

'Charlie Sommers's okay,' Sachs called, slipping away her cell phone. 'Ron just called.'

Rhyme frowned. 'I didn't know he *wasn't* okay.'

'Seems he tried to play hero. He was going to shut down the power at the convention center. Ron found him in the basement with a wire and some tools. He was hanging from the ceiling.'

'Doing what?'

'I don't know.'

'What part of 'stay put' did he have trouble with?'

Sachs shrugged.

'You couldn't've just called him?'

'Didn't have his phone on him. Something about a hundred thousand volts.'

Andi Jessen's brother was fine too, though filthy and hungry and furious. He'd been recovered from the back of Logan's white van parked in the alley behind Rhyme's townhouse. Logan had shared nothing with him and had kept him in the dark — in both senses. Randall Jessen had assumed he'd been kidnapped in some scheme to extort money from his wealthy CEO sister. Randall'd heard nothing of the attacks, and Logan's plan was apparently to electrocute him in Rhyme's besement, as if he'd accidentally touched a hot wire dismantling the switch he'd installed in the service panel to kill

535

the criminalist. He'd been reunited with his sister, who'd been briefed by Gary Noble about the situation.

Rhyme wondered if she'd respond to the fact that the target of her attacks in the press — the alternative energy world — had been behind the scheme.

Rhyme asked, 'And Bob Cavanaugh? The operations man?'

'McDaniel's guys got him. He was in his office. No resistance. Tons of business records on start-up alternative energy companies the conspirators planned to do deals with after they'd taken over Algonquin. The Bureau'll get the other names from his computer and phone records — if he doesn't cooperate.'

A green cartel . . .

Rhyme now realized that Richard Logan, sitting cuffed and shackled in a chair between two uniformed patrolmen, was speaking to him. In a cool, eerily analytical voice, the killer repeated, 'A setup? All fake. You knew all along.'

'I knew.' Rhyme regarded him carefully. Though he'd confirmed the name Richard Logan, it was impossible to think of him as that. To Rhyme he would always be the Watchmaker. The face was different, yes, after the plastic surgery, but the eyes were those of the same man who'd proved every bit as smart as Rhyme himself. Smarter even, on occasion. And unbridled by the trivia of law and conscience.

The shackles were sturdy and the cuffs tight but Lon Sellitto sat nearby anyway, keeping an eye on the man, as if the cop thought that Logan was using his considerable mental prowess to plan an escape.

But Rhyme believed not. The prisoner's darting eyes had taken in the room and the other officers and had concluded that there was nothing to be gained by resisting.

'So,' Logan said evenly, 'how did you do it?' He seemed genuinely curious.

As Sachs and Cooper logged and bagged the new evidence, Rhyme, with no small ego himself, was pleased to indulge him. 'When our FBI agent told me that it was somebody else, not Galt, that jarred me out of my rut. You know the risk of making assumptions . . . I'd been assuming all along that Galt was the perp. But once that idea got turned upside down, I started thinking about the whole — ' Rhyme smiled at the fortuitous word that popped into his mind, ' — the whole *arc* of the crimes. Take the trap at the school: What was the point of trying to hurt only two or three officers? And with a noisy generator? It occurred to me that that'd be a good way to get some planted evidence inside the lab — and big enough to hide a microphone.

'I took the chance it was that the generator was wired and that you were listening. So I started rambling about new theories involving Andi Jessen and her brother, which is where the evidence was obviously leading us. But at the same time I was typing out instructions for everybody in the lab. They were all reading over my shoulder. I had Mel — my associate — scan the generator for a bug . . . and there it was. Well, if you wanted the generator to be found, that meant that any evidence in it was planted. So whoever it pointed to was *not* involved in the crimes: Andi Jessen and her brother were innocent.'

Logan was frowning. 'But you *never* suspected her?'

'I did, yes. We thought Andi'd lied to us. You heard that on the microphone?'

'Yes, though I wasn't sure what you meant.'

'She told Sachs that she got her skills from her father. As if she was hiding the fact that she'd been a lineman and could rig arc flashes. But if you think about what she said, she wasn't denying that she'd worked in the field but that she was simply saying her talent was mostly on the business side of the operation . . . Well, if it wasn't Andi or her brother, then who? I kept going back over the evidence.' A glance at the charts. 'There were some items unaccounted for. The one that stuck in my mind was the spring.'

'Spring? Yes, you mentioned that.'

'We found a tiny hairspring at one of the scenes. Nearly invisible. We thought it could have been from a timer in some switchgear. But I decided if it could come from a timer, it could also be used in watch-making. That put me in mind of you, of course.'

'A hairspring?' Logan's face fell. 'I always use a roller on my clothes — ' He nodded to a rack of pet-hair rollers near an examination table. ' — to make sure I pick up any trace before I go out on a job. That must've fallen into my cuff. And you want to know something funny, Lincoln? It probably got there because I was putting away a lot of my old supplies and tools. What I told you before ... I'd become fascinated with the idea of electronic timekeeping. That's what I was going to try next. I wanted to make the most perfect clock in the world. Even better than the government's atomic clock. But an electronic one.'

Rhyme continued, 'And then all the other pieces fell into place. My conclusion about the letters — that they were written by Galt under threat — worked if you were the one dictating them. The alternative jet fuel? It was being tested *mostly* in military jets — but that means it was also being tested at least in some private and commercial flights. I decided it wouldn't make sense for anybody to plan an attack at an airport or a military base; the security around the electrical systems would be too high. So where did that trace come from? The only aviation scenario that had come up recently didn't involve this case at all; it involved you — in Mexico. And we found a green fiber at one of the scenes ... it was the exact shade of Mexican police uniforms. And it had aviation fuel in it.'

'I left a fiber?' Angry with himself now. Furious.

'I supposed you picked it up from meeting with Arturo Diaz at the airport before you flew back to Philadelphia to kidnap Randall Jessen and drive to New York.'

Logan could only sigh, confirming Rhyme's theory.

'Well, that was my theory, that you were involved. But it was purely speculation — until I realized I had the answer right in front of me.

The definitive answer.'

'What do you mean?'

'The DNA. We had the analysis of the blood we found on the access door near the first substation attack. But I never ran it through CODIS — the DNA database. Why should we? We *knew* Galt's identity.'

This was the final check. Not long ago Rhyme had typed instructions to Cooper — he couldn't tell him orally because of the bug in the generator — to have the DNA lab send a copy of the sample to CODIS. 'We had a sample of your DNA from your assignment in New York a few years ago. I was reading the confirmation that they were the same when you showed up. I scrambled to switch screens pretty quickly.'

Logan's face tightened with anger at himself. 'Yes, yes . . . in the substation, at the access door, I cut my finger on a burr of metal. I wiped the blood off as best I could but I was worried that you'd find it. It's why I rigged the battery to blow and burn off the DNA.'

'Locard's principle,' Rhyme said, citing the early-twentieth-century criminologist. He quoted, ''In every crime there is an exchange —''

Logan finished, ' — 'between criminal and victim or criminal and the site of the crime. It may be very difficult to find, but the connection exists. And it is the obligation of every crime scene professional to find that one common bit of evidence that will lead to the perpetrator's identity, if not his doorstep.''

Rhyme couldn't help but laugh. That particular quotation was his own, a paraphrase of

540

Locard's. It had appeared in an article about forensics he'd written only two or three months ago. Richard Logan had apparently been doing his homework too.

Or was it more than research?

That's why I took the job . . . I needed to get close to you . . .

Logan said, 'You're not only a good criminalist, you're a good actor. You had me fooled.'

'You've done some of that yourself now, haven't you?'

The men's eyes met and their gaze held steady. Then Sellitto's phone rang and he answered, had a brief conversation and hung up. 'Transport's here.'

Three officers arrived in the doorway, two uniforms and a brown-haired detective in blue jeans, blue shirt and tan sports coat. He had an easy-going smile, which was tempered by the fact he wore two very large automatic pistols, one on each hip.

'Hey, Roland,' Amelia Sachs said, smiling.

Rhyme offered, 'Haven't seen you for a while.'

'Howdy. Well, you got yourself some catch here.' Roland Bell was a transplant from a sheriff's office in North Carolina. He'd been a detective on the NYPD for some years but had yet to lose the southern Mid-Atlantic twang. His specialty was protecting witnesses and making sure suspects didn't escape. There was nobody better at the job. Rhyme was pleased that he'd be the one shepherding the Watchmaker down to detention. 'He'll be in good hands.'

At a nod from Bell, the patrolmen helped Logan to his feet. Bell checked the shackles and cuffs and then searched the man himself. He nodded and they headed for the door. The Watchmaker turned back, saying coyly, 'I'll see you again, Lincoln.'

'I know you will. I'm looking forward to it.'

The suspect's smile was replaced by a perplexed look.

Rhyme continued, 'I'll be the expert forensic witness at your trial.'

'Maybe there. Maybe someplace else.' The man glanced at the Breguet. 'Don't forget to keep it wound.'

And with that he was gone.

81

'I'm sorry to tell you, Rodolfo.'

The boisterous voice was absent completely. 'Arturo? No. I can hardly believe it.'

Rhyme continued, explaining about the plot that Diaz had engineered — to kill his boss and make it seem like a by-product of an assassination mission to Mexico City.

In the ensuing silence, Rhyme asked, 'He was a friend?'

'Ah, friendship . . . I would say, when it comes to betrayals, the wife who sleeps with a man and returns home to care for your children and to make you a hot meal is less of a sinner than the friend who betrays you for greed. What do you say to that, Captain Rhyme?'

'Betrayal is a symptom of the truth.'

'Ah, Captain Rhyme, you are a Buddhist? You are a Hindu?'

Rhyme had to laugh. 'No.'

'But you wax philosophical. I think the answer is that Arturo Diaz was a Mexican law enforcer and that is reason enough for him to do what he did. Life is impossible down here.'

'Yet you persist. You continue to fight.'

'I do. But I'm a fool. Much like you, my friend. Could you not be making millions by writing security reports for corporations?'

The criminalist replied, 'But what's the fun of that?'

The laugh was genuine and rich. The Mexican asked, 'What will happen to him now?'

'Logan? He'll be convicted of murder for these crimes. And for crimes here several years ago.'

'Will he get the death penalty?'

'He could but he won't be executed.'

'Why not? Those liberals in America that I hear so much about?'

'It's more complicated than that. The question is one of momentary politics. Right now, the governor here doesn't want to execute any prisoners, whatever they've done, because it would be awkward.'

'Especially so for the prisoner.'

'His opinion doesn't much enter into the matter.'

'I suppose not. Well, despite such leniency, Captain, I think I would like America. Perhaps I'll sneak across the border and become an illegal immigrant. I could work in McDonald's and solve crimes at night.'

'I'll sponsor you, Rodolfo.'

'Ha. My traveling there is about as likely as you coming to Mexico City for mole chicken and tequila.'

'Yes, that's true too. Though I would like the tequila.'

'Now, I'm afraid I must go clean out the rats' nest that my department has become. I may . . . '

The voice faded.

'What's that, Commander?'

'I may have some questions of evidence. I know it's presumptuous of me, but perhaps I could impose upon you.'

'I'd be delighted to help, however I can.'

'Very good.' Another chuckle. 'Perhaps in a few years, if I am lucky, I can add those magic letters to my name too.'

'Magic letters?'

'R.E.T.'

'You? Retire, Commander?'

'I am making a joke, Captain. Retirement is not for people like us. We will die on the job. Let's pray that it's a long time from now. Now, my friend, good-bye.'

They disconnected. Rhyme then ordered his phone to call Kathryn Dance in California. He gave her the news about the apprehension of Richard Logan. The conversation was brief. Not because he was feeling antisocial — just the contrary: He was thrilled at his victory.

But the aftermath of the dysreflexia attack was settling on him like cold dew. He let Sachs take over the phone call, girl talk, and Rhyme asked Thom to bring him some Glenmorangie.

'The eighteen year, if you would be so kind. Please and thank you.'

Thom poured a generous slug into the tumbler and propped it in the cup holder near his boss's mouth. Rhyme sipped through the straw. He savored the smoky scotch and then swallowed it. He felt the warmth, the comfort, though it also accentuated that damn fatigue plaguing him the past week or so. He forced himself not to think about it.

When Sachs disconnected her call, he asked, 'You'll join me, Sachs?'

'You bet I will.'

'I feel like music,' he said.

'Jazz?'

'Sure.'

He picked Dave Brubeck, a recording from a live concert in the sixties. The signature tune, 'Take Five,' came on and, in with its distinctive five-four beat, the music cantered from speakers, scratchy and infectious.

As Sachs poured the liquor and sat beside him, her eyes strayed to the evidence boards. 'There's one thing we forgot about, Rhyme.'

'What?'

'That supposed terrorist group? Justice For the Earth.'

'That's McDaniel's case now. If we'd found any evidence I'd be more concerned. But . . . nothing.' Rhyme sipped more liquor and felt another wave of the persistent fatigue nestle around him. Still he managed a small joke: 'Personally I think it was just a wrong number from the cloud zone.'

82

The Earth Day festivities in Central Park were in full swing.

At 6:20 on this pleasant, though cool and overcast evening, an FBI agent was on the edge of the Sheep Meadow, scanning the crowd, most of which were protesting something or another. Some picnickers and some tourists. But the crowd of fifty thousand mostly just seemed pissed off about one thing or another: global warming, oil, big business, carbon dioxide, greenhouse gasses.

And methane.

Special Agent Timothy Conradt blinked as he looked at a group of people protesting bovine flatulence. Methane from livestock apparently burned holes in the ozone layer too.

Cow farts.

What a crazy world.

Conradt was sporting an undercover mustache and wore jeans and a baggy shirt, concealing his radio and weapon. His wife had ironed the wrinkles into his garments that morning, vetoing his idea that he sleep in his clothes to get that 'lived-in' look.

He was no fan of knee-jerk liberals and people who'd sell the country out in the name of . . . well, who knew what? Complacency, Europe, Globalism, Socialism . . . Cowardice.

But one thing he had in common with *these*

547

people was the environment. Conradt lived for the outdoors. Hunting, fishing, hiking. So he sympathized.

He was scanning the crowds carefully because even though the perp known as the Watchmaker had been collared, ASAC Tucker McDaniel still was sure that that group Justice For the Earth was going to try something. The SIGINT hits were compelling, even non-tech Conradt had to admit. Justice For the Earth. Or, as the agents were referring to it now, per McDaniel's instruction, JFTE, pronounced 'Juf-tee.'

Teams of agents and NYPD cops were deployed throughout the city, covering the convention center near the Hudson River, a parade downtown in Battery Park and this gathering in Central Park.

McDaniel's theory was that they'd misread the connection among Richard Logan, Algonquin Consolidated Power and JFTE, but it was likely that the group could have formed an alliance with, possibly, an Islamic fundamentalist cell.

A symbiotic construct.

A phrase that would give the agents plenty of ammunition for the next few months when they were out for drinks.

Conradt's own feeling, from years on the street, was that JFTE may have existed but it was just a bunch of cranks, of no threat to anybody. He strolled around casually, but all the while he was looking for people who fit the profile. Watching where their arms were in relation to their bodies, watching for certain types of backpacks, watching for a gait that might reveal

548

if they were carrying a weapon or an IED. Watching for pale jaws that suggested a newly shaved beard, or a woman's absent touch to her hair, possibly indicating her ill ease at being in public without a *hijab* for the first time since adolescence.

And always: watching the eyes.

So far Conradt had seen some devout eyes and oblivious eyes and curious eyes.

But none that suggested they were in the head of a man or woman who wanted to murder a large number of people in the name of a deity. Or in the name of whales or trees or spotted owls. He circulated for a while and finally eased up beside his partner, an unsmiling thirty-five-year-old, dressed in a long peasant skirt and a blouse as baggy and concealing as Conradt's shirt.

'Anything?'

A pointless question because she would have called him — and every other of the multitude of law enforcers here tonight — if she'd spotted 'anything.'

A shake of the head.

Pointless questions weren't worth answering aloud, in Barb's opinion.

Bar-bar-a, he corrected himself. As she'd corrected him when they first started working together.

'Are they here yet?' Conradt nodded at the stage set up at the south end of the Sheep Meadow, referring to the speakers scheduled to begin at 6:30: the two senators who'd flown into the city from Washington. They'd been working with the President on environmental issues, sponsoring legislation that made the green libbers happy but half the corporations in America mad enough to wring their necks.

A concert would follow. He couldn't decide if most people were here for the music or the speeches. With this crowd, it was probably evenly divided.

'Just got here,' Barbara said.

They both scanned for a while. Then Conradt said, 'That acronym's weird. Juf-tee. They should just call it 'JFTE.''

'Juf-tee's not an acronym.'

'What do you mean?'

Barbara explained, 'By definition, to be an acronym, the letters themselves have to spell an actual word.'

'In English?'

She gave what he thought was a condescending sigh. 'Well, in an English-speaking country. Obviously.'

'So NFL isn't an acronym?'

'No, that's initials. ARC — American Resource Council. That's an acronym.'

Conradt thought: Barbara is a . . .

'How about BIC?' he asked.

'I suppose. I don't know about brand names. What does it stand for?'

'I forget.'

Their radios clattered simultaneously and they cocked their heads. 'Be advised, the visitors are at the stage. Repeat, the visitors are at the stage.'

The visitors — a euphemism for the senators.

The command post agent ordered Conradt

and Barbara to move into position on the west side of the stage. They made their way forward.

'You know, this actually *was* a sheep meadow,' Conradt told BIC. 'The city fathers let them graze here until the thirties. Then they got moved to Prospect Park. Brooklyn. The sheep, I mean.'

Barbara looked at him blankly. Meaning: What does that have to do with anything?

Conradt let her precede him up a narrow path.

There was a burst of applause. And shouts.

Then the two senators were up on the podium. The first one to speak leaned forward into the microphone and began talking in low, resonant tones, his voice echoing across the Sheep Meadow. The crowd was soon hoarse from shouting their mad approval every two minutes or so as the senator fed them platitudes.

Preaching to the converted.

It was then that Conradt saw something off to the side of the stage, moving steadily to the front, where the senators were standing, He stiffened then leapt forward.

'What?' Barbara called, reaching for her weapon.

'Juf-tee,' he whispered. And grabbed his radio.

83

At 7 p.m. Fred Dellray returned to the Manhattan Federal Building from visiting William Brent, AKA Stanley Palmer, AKA a lot of other names, in the hospital. The man was badly injured but had regained consciousness. He'd be discharged in three or four days.

Brent had already been contacted by the city lawyers about a settlement for the accident. Being hit by an NYPD police officer who fucks up with a squad car was pretty much a no-brainer. The figure being offered was about $50,000, plus medical bills.

So William Brent was having a pretty good couple of days, financially at least, being the recipient of both the settlement, tax-free, as a personal injury award, and the hundred Gs Dellray had paid him — tax free, too, though solely because the IRS and NY Department of Revenue would never hear a whisper about it.

Dellray was in his office, savoring the news that Richard Logan, the Watchmaker, was in custody, when his assistant, a sharp African-American woman in her twenties, said, 'You hear about that Earth Day thing?'

'What's that?'

'I don't know the details. But that group, Juf-tee — '

'What?'

'JFTE. Justice For the Earth. Whatever it is.

The ecoterror group?'

Dellray set down his coffee, his heart pounding. 'It's real?'

'Yep.'

'What happened?' he asked urgently.

'All I heard is they got into Central Park, right near those two senators — the ones the President sent down to speak at the rally. The SAC wants you in his office. Now.'

'Anybody hurt, killed?' Dellray whispered in dismay.

'I don't know.'

Grim-faced, the lanky agent stood. He started down the hallway quickly. His variation of lope, the way he usually walked. The gait came, of course, from the street.

Which he was now about to say goodbye to. He'd tracked down an important clue to help catch the Watchmaker. But he'd failed in the primary mission: to find the terror group.

And that's what McDaniel would use to crucify him . . . in his bright-eyed yet somber, energetic yet subtle way. Apparently he already had, if the SAC wanted him.

Well, keep at it, Fred. You're doing a good job . . .

As he walked he glanced into offices, to find somebody to ask about the incident. But they were empty. It was after hours but more likely, he guessed, everybody'd sped to Central Park after Justice For the Earth was spotted. That was perhaps the best indicator that his career was over: nobody had even called to request his presence in the operation.

Of course, there was another possible reason for that too — and for the summons to the SAC's office: the stolen $100K.

What the hell had he been thinking of? He'd done it for the city he loved, for the citizens he was sworn to protect. But did he actually believe he'd get away with it? Especially with an ASAC who wanted him out and who pored over his agents' paperwork like a crossword-puzzle addict.

Could he negotiate his way out of jail time?

He wasn't sure. With the fuckup over Justice For the Earth, his stock was real low.

Down one corridor of the nondescript office building. Down another.

Finally he came to the den of the Special Agent in Charge. His assistant announced Dellray and the agent walked inside the large corner office.

'Fred.'

'Jon.'

The SAC, Jonathan Phelps, mid-fifties, brushed at his gray swept-back hair, pushing it a little further back, and motioned the agent into a chair across from his cluttered desk.

No, Dellray thought, cluttered wasn't the right word. It was ordered and organized; it was just layered in three inches of files. This was, after all, New York. There was a lot that could go wrong and needed mending by people like the SAC

Dellray tried to read the man but could find no clues. He too had worked undercover earlier in his career. But that wouldn't buy Dellray any sympathy, that wisp of common past. That was one thing about the Bureau; federal law and the regulations promulgated thereunder trumped everything. The SAC was the only person in the room, which didn't surprise Dellray. Tucker McDaniel would be reading rights to terrorists in Central Park.

'So, Fred. I'll get right to it.'

'Sure.'

'About this Juf-tee thing.'

'Justice For the Earth.'

'Right.' Another sweep through the opulent hair. It was as ordered after the fingers left as when they arrived.

'I just want to understand. You didn't find anything about the group, right?'

Dellray hadn't gotten this far by poking at the truth. 'No, Jon. I blew it. I hit up all my usual sources and a half dozen new ones. Everybody I'm running now and a dozen I've retired. Two dozen. I didn't come up with squat. I'm sorry.'

'And yet Tucker McDaniel's surveillance team's had ten clear hits.'

The cloud zone . . .

Dellray wasn't going to trash McDaniel either, not even wing him a bit. 'That's what I understand. His teams came up with a bucketful of good details. The personnel — this Rahman, Johnston. And code words about weapons.' He sighed. 'I heard there was an incident, Jon. What happened?'

'Oh, yeah. Juf-Tee made a move.'

'Casualties?'

'We've got a video. You want to see it?'

Dellray thought: No, sir, you betcha I don't.

The last thing I want to see is footage of people hurt because I screwed up. Or of Tucker McDaniel leading in a takedown team to save the day. But he said, 'Sure. Roll it.'

The SAC leaned over his laptop and hit some keys, then spun the unit around for Dellray to look at. He expected to see one of the typical Bureau surveillance videos, shot with a wide-angle lens, low contrast to pick up all the details, information at the bottom: location and by-the-second time stamp.

Instead, he was looking at a CNN newscast.

CNN?

A smiling, coiffed woman reporter, holding a sheaf of notes, was talking to a man in his thirties, wearing a mismatched suit jacket and slacks. He was dark-complexioned and his hair was cropped short. He was smiling uneasily, eyes shifting between the reporter and the camera. A young redheaded boy with freckles, about eight years old, stood next to him.

The reporter was saying to the man, 'Now, I understand your students have been preparing for Earth Day for the past several months.'

'That's right,' the man answered, awkward but proud.

'There are a lot of different groups here in Central Park tonight, supporting one issue or another. Do your students have a particular environmental cause?'

'Not really. They have a lot of different interests: renewable energy, risks to the rain forest, global warming and carbon dioxide, protecting the ozone layer, recycling.'

'And who's your young assistant here?'

'This is a student of mine, Tony Johnston.'

Johnston?

'Hello, Tony. Can you tell our viewers at home the name of your environmental club at school?'

'Uhm, yeah. It's Just Us Kids for the Earth.'

'And those are quite some posters. Did you and your classmates make them yourself?'

'Uhm. Yeah. But, you know, our teacher, Mr. Rahman — ' He glanced up at the man beside him. ' — he helped us some.'

'Well, good for you, Tony. And thanks to you and all your fellow students in Peter Rahman's third-grade class at Ralph Waldo Emerson elementary school in Queens, who believe you're never too young to start making a difference when it comes to the environment . . . This is Kathy Brigham reporting from — '

Under the SAC's stabbing finger, the screen went blank. He sat back. Dellray couldn't tell if he was going to laugh or utter some obscenity. 'Justice,' he said, enunciating carefully. 'Just Us . . . Kids.' He sighed. 'Want to guess how much shit this office is in, Fred?'

Dellray cocked a bushy eyebrow.

'We begged Washington for an extra five million dollars, on top of the expense of mobilizing four hundred agents. Two dozen warrants were ramrodded through magistrates' offices in New York, Westchester, Phillie, Baltimore and Boston . . . We had absolutely rock solid SIGINT that an ecoterror group, worse than Timothy McVeigh, worse than Bin Laden, was going to bring America to its knees with the attack of all time.

'And they turned out to be a bunch of eight- and nine-year-olds. The code words for the weapons, 'paper and supplies'? They meant paper and supplies. The communication wasn't going on in the cloud zone; it went on face-to-face when they woke up from nap time at school. The woman working with Rahman? It was probably little Tony because his goddamn voice hasn't changed yet . . . It's a good thing we didn't get SIGINT hits about somebody, quote 'releasing doves' in Central Park at the rally because we might've called in a fucking surface-to-air missile strike.'

There was silence for a moment.

'You're not gloating, Fred.'

A shrug of the lanky shoulders.

'You want Tucker's job?'

'And where will he — ?'

'Elsewhere. Washington. Does it matter? . . . So? The ASAC spot? You want it, you can move in tonight.'

Dellray didn't hesitate. 'No, Jon. Thanks, but no.'

'You're one of the most respected agents in this office. People look up to you. I'll ask you to reconsider.'

'I want to be on the street. That's all I've ever wanted. It's important to me.' Sounding as un-Street as any human being possibly could.

'You cowboys.' The SAC chuckled. 'Now you might wanta get back to your office. McDaniel's on his way here for a conversation. I'm assuming you don't want to meet him.'

'Probably not.'

As Dellray was at the door, the SAC said, 'Oh, Fred, there's one other thing.'

The agent stopped in mid-lope.

'You worked the Gonzalez case, didn't you?'

Dellray had faced down some of the most dangerous assholes in the city without his pulse speeding up a single beat. He now was sure his neck was throbbing visibly as the blood pumped. 'The drug collar, Staten Island. Right.'

'There was a little mix-up somewhere, it seems.'

'Mix-up?'

'Yeah, with the evidence.'

'Really?'

The SAC rubbed his eyes. 'At the bust your teams scored thirty ki's of smack, a couple dozen guns and some big bricks of money.'

'That's right.'

'The press release said the cash recovered was one point one million. But we were getting the case ready for the grand jury and it looks like there's only one million even in the evidence locker.'

'Mislogging a hundred K?'

The SAC cocked his head. 'Naw, it's something else. Not mislogging.'

'Uh-huh.' Dellray breathed deeply. Oh man . . . this is it.

'I looked over the paperwork and, it was funny, the second zero on the chain of custody card, the zero after the one million, was real skinny. You look at it fast, you could think it was a one. Somebody glanced at it and wrote the

559

press release wrong. They wrote, 'one point one.''

'I see.'

'Just wanted to tell you, if the question comes up: It was a typo. The exact amount the Bureau collected in the Gonzalez bust was one million even. That's official.'

'Sure. Thanks, Jon.'

A frown. 'For what?'

'Clarifying.'

A nod. It was a nod with a message and that message had been delivered. The SAC added, 'By the way, you did a good job helping nail Richard Logan. He had that plan a few years ago to take out dozens of soldiers and Pentagon people. Some of our folks too. Glad he's going away forever.'

Dellray turned and left the office. As he returned to his own, he allowed himself a single nervous laugh.

Third graders?

Then pulled out his mobile to text Serena and to tell her that he'd be home soon.

84

Lincoln Rhyme glanced up to see Pulaski in the doorway.

'Rookie, what're you doing here? I thought you were logging in evidence in Queens.'

'I was. Just . . . ' His voice slowed like a car hitting a patch of soupy fog.

'Just?'

It was close to 9 p.m., and they were alone in Rhyme's parlor. Comforting domestic sounds in the kitchen. Sachs and Thom were getting dinner ready. It was, Rhyme noticed, well past cocktail hour and he was a bit piqued that nobody had filled up his plastic tumbler of scotch again.

A failing he now told Pulaski to remedy, which the young cop did.

'That's not a double,' Rhyme muttered. But Pulaski seemed not to hear. He'd walked to the window, eyes outside.

Shaping up to be a dramatic scene from a slow-moving Brit drama, Rhyme deduced, and sipped the smoky liquor through the straw.

'I've kind of made a decision. I wanted to tell you first.'

'Kind of?' Rhyme chided once again.

'I mean, I *have* made a decision.'

Rhyme raised his eyebrow. He didn't want to be too encouraging. What was coming next? he wondered, though he believed he had an idea. Rhyme's life might have been devoted to science but he'd also been in charge of hundreds of employees and cops. And despite his impatience, his gruffness, his fits of temper, he'd been a reasonable and fair boss.

As long as you didn't screw up.

'Go on, Rookie.'

'I'm leaving.'

'The area?'

'The force.'

'Ah.'

Rhyme had become aware of body language since he'd known Kathryn Dance. He sensed that Pulaski was now delivering lines he'd rehearsed. Many times.

The cop rubbed his hand through his short blond hair. 'William Brent.'

'Dellray's CI?'

'Right, yessir.'

Rhyme thought once more about reminding the young man that he didn't need to use such deferential appellations. But he said only, 'Go on, Pulaski.'

His face grim, eyes turbulent, Pulaski sat down in the creaking wicker chair near Rhyme's Storm Arrow. 'At Galt's place, I was spooked. I panicked. I didn't exercise good judgment. I wasn't aware enough of procedures.' As if in summary, he added, 'I didn't assess the situation properly and adjust my behavior accordingly.'

Like a schoolboy who wasn't sure of the test answers and was rattling off as many as he could think of, hoping one would stick.

'He's out of his coma.'

'But he might've died.'

'And that's why you're quitting?'

'I made a mistake. It nearly cost somebody his life . . . I just don't feel I can keep functioning at full capacity.'

Jesus, where did he get these lines?

'It was an accident, Rookie.'

'And one that shouldn't've happened.'

'Are there any other kinds of accidents?'

'You know what I mean, Lincoln. It's not like I haven't thought this through.'

'I can prove that you have to stay, that it'd be wrong for you to quit.'

'What, say that I'm talented, I have a lot to contribute?' The cop's face was skeptical. He was young but he looked a lot older than when Rhyme had met him. Policing will do that.

So will working with Lincoln Rhyme.

'You know why you can't quit? You'd be a hypocrite.'

Pulaski blinked.

Rhyme continued, an edge to his voice. 'You missed your window of opportunity.'

'What's that mean?'

'Okay, you fucked up and somebody was injured badly. But then when it looked like Brent was a perp with outstanding paper, you thought you'd been given a reprieve, right?'

'Well . . . I guess.'

'You suddenly didn't care that you'd hit him. Since he was, what, less than human?'

'No, I just — '

'Let me finish. The minute after you backed into that guy, you had a choice to make: Either you should've decided that the risk of collateral damage and accidents isn't acceptable to you and quit on the spot. Or you should've put the whole thing behind you and learned to live with what happened. It doesn't make any difference if that guy was a serial killer or a deacon at his church. And it's intellectually dishonest for you to whine about it now.'

The rookie's eyes narrowed with anger and he was about to offer a defense of some sort, but Rhyme said, 'You made a mistake. You didn't commit a crime . . . Mistakes happen in this business. The problem is that when they do it's not like accounting or making shoes. When we fuck up, there's a chance somebody's going to get killed. But if we stopped and worried about that, we'd never get anything done. We'd be looking over our shoulders all the time and that would mean more people would die because we weren't doing our jobs.'

'Easy for you to say,' Pulaski snapped angrily.

Good for him, Rhyme thought, but kept his face solemn.

'Have you ever been in a situation like this?' Pulaski muttered.

Of course he had. Rhyme had made mistakes. Dozens, if not hundreds, of them. It was a mistake years ago, one that indeed resulted in the deaths of innocent people, that led to the case that brought Rhyme and Sachs together for the first time. But he didn't want a band-of-brothers argument at the moment. 'That's not the point, Pulaski. The point is you've already made your decision. Coming back here with the evidence from Galt's, after you'd run over Brent,

564

you lost the right to quit. So it's a nonissue.'

'This is eating me up.'

'Well, it's time to tell it — whatever the hell *it* is — to stop eating. Part of being a cop is putting that wall up.'

'Lincoln, you're not listening to me.'

'I did listen. I considered your arguments and I rejected them. They're invalid.'

'They're valid to me.'

'No, they're not. And I'll tell you why.' Rhyme hesitated. 'Because they're not valid to *me* . . . and you and I are a lot alike, Pulaski. I myself hate to goddamn admit it, but it's true.'

This brought the young man up short.

'Now, forget all this crap you've been boring me with. I'm glad you're here because I need you to do some follow-up work. At the — '

Pulaski stared at the criminalist and gave a cold laugh. 'I'm not doing *anything*. I'm quitting. I'm not listening to you.'

'Well, you're not going to quit now. You can do it in a few days. I need you. The case — your case as much as mine — isn't over with yet. We have to make absolutely sure Logan's convicted. You agree?'

A sigh. 'I agree.'

'Before McDaniel got removed from command and sent to the cloud zone, or wherever he went, he had his men search Bob Cavanaugh's office. He didn't call us to do it. The Bureau's Evidence Response Team is good — I helped set it up. But we should've walked the grid too. I want you to do that now. Logan was saying there's a cartel involved and I want to make sure every one of them gets nailed.'

A resigned grimace. 'I'll do it. But that's my last assignment.' Shaking his head, the young man stormed from the room.

Lincoln Rhyme struggled to keep the smile from his face as he sought the straw sprouting from his tumbler of whisky.

85

Lincoln Rhyme was now alone.

Ron Pulaski was walking the grid at Algonquin Consolidated. Mel Cooper and Lon Sellitto were back in their respective homes. Roland Bell had reported that Richard Logan was tucked away safely in a special high-security wing of downtown detention.

Amelia Sachs had been downtown too, helping with the paperwork, but was now back in Brooklyn. Rhyme hoped she might be taking a little time to herself, maybe to sneak a drive in her Cobra Torino. She occasionally took Pammy out on the road. The girl reported that the drives were 'untotallybelievable,' which he interpreted as meaning 'exhilarating.'

He knew, though, that the girl was never in any danger. Unlike when Sachs was by herself, she knew the right moment to pull back when her nature tried to assert itself.

Thom was out too, with his partner, a reporter for *The New York Times*. He'd wanted to stay at home and keep an eye on his boss, watching for horrific side effects from the dysreflexia or for . . . who knew what? But the criminalist had insisted he go out for the night.

'You've got a curfew,' he'd snapped. 'Midnight.'

'Lincoln, I'll be back before — '

'No. You'll be back *after* midnight. It's a negative curfew.'

'That's crazy. I'm not leaving — '

'I'll fucking fire you if you come back before then.'

The aide examined him carefully and said, 'Okay. Thanks.'

Rhyme had no patience for the gratitude and proceeded to ignore the aide as he busied himself on the computer, organizing the lists of evidence that would be turned over to the prosecutor for the trial, at the end of which the Watchmaker would go to jail for an impressive assortment of crimes, including capital murder. He would surely be convicted but New York, unlike California and Texas, treated the death penalty like an embarrassing birthmark in the middle of its forehead. As he'd told Rodolfo Luna, he doubted the man would die.

Other jurisdictions would be vying for him too. But he'd been caught in New York; they'd have to wait in line.

Rhyme secretly was not troubled by a life sentence for the man. Had Logan been killed during the confrontation here — say, going after a gun to hurt Sachs or Sellitto — that would have been a fair end, an honest end. That Rhyme had captured him and that he'd spend the rest of his life in prison was justice enough. Lethal injection seemed cheap. Insulting. And Rhyme wouldn't want to be part of the case that sent the man on that final stroll to the gurney.

Enjoying the solitude, Rhyme now dictated several pages of crime scene reports. Some forensic officers wrote lyrical ones, dramatic or poetic. This wasn't Rhyme's way. The language was lean and hard — cast metal, not carved wood. He reviewed it and was pleased, though irritated at the gaps. He was waiting for some analytical results to come in. Still, he reminded himself that impatience was a sin too, even if not as grave as carelessness, and that the case would not suffer if the final report were delayed for a day or two.

Good, he allowed. More to do — always more to do — but good.

Rhyme looked over the lab, left in pristine shape by Mel Cooper, presently at his mother's home in Queens, where he lived, or perhaps, after a quick check-in on mom, with his Scandinavian girlfriend; they might be dancing up a storm by now in some ballroom in Midtown.

Aware of a slight headache, like the one he'd experienced earlier, he glanced at a nearby shelf of his medications. And noticed a bottle of clonidine, the vasodilator, that had possibly saved his life earlier. It occurred to him that if he had an attack at this moment he might very well not survive. The bottle was inches away from his hands. But it might as well have been miles.

Rhyme looked over the familiar evidence boards, filled with Sachs's and Mel Cooper's writing. There were smears and cross-outs, erasures of false starts, misspellings and down-right errors.

An emblem for the way criminal cases always unfolded.

He then gazed at the equipment: the density gradient device, the forceps and vials, the gloves, the flasks, the collection gear and the battleships of the line: the scanning electron microscope and the chromatograph/mass spectrometer, silent and bulky. He thought back on the many, many hours he'd spent on these machines and their predecessors, recalled the sound of the units, the smell as he sacrificed a sample in the fiery heart of the chromatograph to learn what a mysterious compound really was. Often, the debate: If you destroyed your sole sample to find the identity and whereabouts of the perp, you risked jeopardizing the case at trial because the sample had disappeared.

Lincoln Rhyme always voted to burn.

He recalled the rumble of the machine under his hand when his hand could still feel rumbles.

He now looked too at the snaky wires crisscrossing the parquet floor, remembered feeling — in his jaw and head only, of course — the bumps as the wheelchair thumped over them on the way from one examining table to another or to the computer monitor.

Wires . . .

He then wheeled into the den, looking at family pictures. Thinking of his cousin Arthur. His uncle Henry. Thinking too of his parents.

And of Amelia Sachs, of course. Always of Amelia.

Then the good memories faded and he couldn't help thinking about how his failings had nearly cost her her life today. Because his rebellious body had betrayed them all. Rhyme and Sachs and Ron Pulaski. And who knew how many ESU officers who might have been electrocuted storming the rigged school in Chinatown?

From there his thoughts continued to spiral and he realized that the incident was a symbol of their relationship. The love was there, of course, but he couldn't deny that he was holding her back. That she was only partly the person she could be, if she were with somebody else, or even on her own.

This wasn't self-pity, and, in fact, Rhyme was feeling oddly exhilarated by where his thoughts were going.

He considered what would happen if she were to go on in life alone. Dispassionately he pictured the scenario. And he concluded that Amelia Sachs would be just fine. Once again he had this image of Ron Pulaski and Sachs running the Crime Scene in a couple of years.

Now, in the quiet den across from the lab, surrounded by pictures of his family, Rhyme glanced down at something that sat on the table nearby. Colorful and glossy. It was the brochure that the assisted-suicide advocate Arlen Kopeski had left.

Choices . . .

Rhyme was amused to note that the brochure had been designed, cleverly, with the disabled in mind. You didn't need to pick it up and flip through it. The phone number of the euthanasia organization was printed on the front and in large type — in the event that the condition spurring someone to kill himself involved deteriorating vision.

As he gazed at the brochure, his mind spun. The plan that was formulating itself would take some organizing.

It would take some secrecy.

It would take some conspiracy. And bribery.

But such was the life of a quadriplegic, a life where thinking was free and easy but where acting required complicity.

The plan would take some time too. But nothing that was important in life ever happened quickly. Rhyme was filled with the thrill that comes with making a firm decision.

His big concern was making sure that his testimony against the Watchmaker regarding the evidence could be heard by the jury without Rhyme's presence. There's a procedure for this: sworn depositions. Besides, Sachs and Mel Cooper were seasoned witnesses for the prosecution. He believed that Ron Pulaski would be too.

He'd talk to the prosecutor tomorrow, a private conversation, and have a court reporter come to the townhouse and take his testimony. Thom would think nothing of it.

Smiling, Lincoln Rhyme wheeled back into the empty lab with its electronics and software and — ah, yes — the wires that would allow him to make the phone call he'd been thinking of, no, *obsessing* over, from virtually the moment the Watchmaker was arrested.

IV

THE LAST CASE

TEN DAYS AFTER
EARTH DAY

'Most of the exercise I get is from standing
and walking all day from one laboratory table
to another. I derive more benefit and
entertainment from this than some of my
friends and competitors get from playing
games like golf.'

— THOMAS ALVA EDISON

86

Amelia Sachs and Thom Reston hurried through the door of the hospital. Neither spoke.

The lobby and hallways were calm, odd for places like this on a Saturday evening in New York City. Usually chaos ruled in the houses of healing, chaos from accidents, alcohol poisoning, overdoses and, of course, the occasional gunshot or knife wound.

Here, though, the atmosphere was oddly, eerily, sedate.

Grim-faced, Sachs paused and regarded signs. She pointed and they started down an even dimmer corridor in the basement of the hospital.

They paused again.

'That way?' Sachs whispered.

'It's not well marked. It should be better marked.'

Sachs heard the exasperation in Thom's voice but she knew the tone was grounded mostly in dismay.

'There.'

They continued on, past a station where nurses sat, leisurely chatting behind the high counter. There were plenty of official accoutrements of the job, papers and files, but also coffee cups, some makeup and a book of puzzles. A lot of Sudoku, Sachs noted, wondering why the game had caught on. She didn't have the patience.

She supposed that down here, in this department, the staff weren't required to leap into action very often, a la TV medics in emergency rooms.

At a second counter Sachs approached a solitary nurse, a middle-aged woman, and said one word. 'Rhyme.'

'Ah, yes,' the nurse said, looking up. Not needing to consult a chart or any other document. 'And you are?'

'His partner,' she said. She'd used the term a number of times regarding the man in both the professional and personal sense, but had never realized until now how completely inadequate it was. She didn't like it. Hated it.

Thom identified himself as 'caregiver.'

Which also clunked like plastic.

'I'm afraid I don't know any details,' the nurse said, echoing what would have been Sachs's question. 'Come with me.'

The staunch woman led them down another corridor, even more grim than the first. Spotless, pleasingly designed, ordered. And abhorrent.

What better word to describe hospitals anyway?

As they approached a room with an open door, the nurse said not unsympathetically, 'Wait in there, please. Somebody will be in soon.'

The woman was instantly gone, as if afraid one of them might shove her into a chair and interrogate her. Which Sachs was half inclined to do.

She and Thom turned the corner and stepped

into the waiting room. It was empty. Lon Sellitto and Rhyme's cousin Arthur and his wife, Judy, were on their way. Sachs's mother too, Rose. The woman had been going to take the subway here; Sachs had insisted on a car service.

They sat in silence. Sachs picked up yet another Sudoku book, looked through it. Thom glanced toward her. He squeezed her arm and slumped back. It was curious to see him abdicate his usually perfect posture.

The man said, 'He never said anything. Not a word.'

'That surprises you?'

He began to say that it did. But then he slumped even more. 'No.'

A man in a business suit, tie askew, came into the room, looked at the faces of the two already there and decided to wait elsewhere. Sachs could hardly blame him.

At times like this, you don't want to share a public space with strangers.

Sachs leaned her head against Thom, who hugged her hard. She'd forgotten how strong the man was.

This evening was the culmination of perhaps the strangest, and most tense, twelve hours in all the years she'd known Rhyme. That morning, when she'd arrived from spending the night in Brooklyn, she'd found Thom gazing at the door expectantly. The aide had then glanced behind her and frowned.

'What?' she'd asked, also glancing back.

'Wasn't he with you?'

'Who?'

'Lincoln.'

'No.'

'Goddamn it. He's disappeared.'

Thanks to the speedy and reliable Storm Arrow wheelchair, Rhyme was as mobile as any quad and it was not unheard of for him to drive out to Central Park on his own. Though it was also true that the out-of-doors held little interest to him, Rhyme preferring to be in the lab, surrounded by his equipment and mentally wrestling with a case.

The aide had gotten him up early today, as Rhyme had instructed, dressed and deposited him into the wheelchair. The criminalist had then said, 'I'm meeting somebody for breakfast.'

'Where are we going?' Thom had asked.

'"I" is singular first person, Thom. 'We' is plural. Also first person and a pronoun, but other than that they have very little in common. You're not invited and it's for your own sake. You'd be bored.'

'It's never boring around you, Lincoln.'

'Ha. I'll be back soon.'

The criminalist had been in such a good mood that Thom had agreed.

But then Rhyme simply hadn't returned.

Another hour had gone by after Sachs had arrived. And curiosity became concern. But at that very instant they'd both received an email, dinging on computers and BlackBerrys. It was as clipped and functional as one would expect from Lincoln Rhyme.

Thom, Sachs —

After a great deal of deliberation I've concluded
that I don't want to continue to live in my current
condition.

'No,' Thom had gasped.
'Keep reading.'

Recent events have made clear that certain inabili-
ties are no longer acceptable to me. I've been
motivated to act by two things. The visit by Kopeski, which told me that while I would never kill
myself, nonetheless there are times when the risk
of death should not deter one from making a decision.

The second was meeting Susan Stringer. She said
there were no coincidences and that she felt she
was fated to tell me about Pembroke Spinal Cord
Center. (You know how much I believe in THAT
— and if this is the point where I'm supposed to
type 'LOL,' it's not going to happen.)

I've been in regular discussions with the center
and have made four appointments for various procedures over the next eight months. The first of
these is about to begin.

Of course, there's the possibility that I might not
make the other three appointments, but one can
only wait and see. If things turn out as I hope I'll
be giving you all the gory details of the surgery in
a day or two. If not, Thom, you know where all

the paperwork is kept. Oh, and one thing I forgot to put into the will, give all my scotch to my cousin Arthur. He'll appreciate it.

Sachs, there's another letter for you. Thom will hand it over.

Sorry I handled it this way, but you both have better things to do on this fine day than shepherd a bad patient like me to a hospital and waste time. Besides, you know me. Some things I'd just rather do on my own. Haven't had much of a chance to do that in the past few years.

Somebody will call with information late this afternoon or early evening.

As for our last case, Sachs, I expect to testify at the Watchmaker's trial in person. But if things don't go quite right, I've filed my depositions with the attorney general. You and Mel and Ron can take up the slack. Make sure Mr. Logan spends the rest of his life in jail.

This thought, from someone I've been close to, describes what I'm feeling perfectly: 'Times change. We have to change too. Whatever the risks. Whatever we have to leave behind.'

-LR

And now, in the abhorrent hospital, they waited.

Finally, an official. A tall man in green scrubs, with graying hair, slim, walked into the room.

'You're Amelia Sachs.'

'That's right.'

'And Thom?'

A nod.

The man turned out to be the chief surgeon of the Pembroke Spinal Cord Center. He said, 'He's come through the surgery, but he's still unconscious.'

He continued, explaining technical things to them. Sachs nodded, taking in the details. Some seemed good, some seemed less so. But mostly she noted that he wasn't answering the one question that mattered — not about the success of the surgery in technical terms, but when, or if, Lincoln Rhyme would swim back to consciousness.

When she bluntly posed that question, the best the doctor could say was: 'We just don't know. We'll have to wait.'

87

The 3D swirls of fingerprints evolved not to help forensic scientists identify and convict criminals but simply to give our digits sure purchase, so that whatever we were holding that was precious or necessary or unrecognized wouldn't slip from our frail human grasp.

We are, after all, bereft of claws, and our muscle tone — sorry, ardent health club devotees — is truly pathetic compared with that of any wild animal of comparable weight.

The official title of the patterns on the fingers (feet too) is, in fact, *friction* ridge, revealing their true purpose.

Lincoln Rhyme glanced briefly at Amelia Sachs, who was ten feet away, curled up, sleeping in a chair, in an oddly content and demure pose. Her red hair fell straight and thick, bisecting her face.

Nearly midnight.

He returned to his contemplation of friction ridges. They occur on digits, which word includes both fingers and toes, and on the palms and soles of the feet. You can be convicted as easily by an incriminating sole print as by a fingerprint, though the circumstances of the crime in which one was involved would surely be a bit unusual.

People have known about the individuality of friction rides for a long time — they were used to mark official documents eight hundred years ago

— but it wasn't until the 1890s that prints became recognized as a way to link criminal and crime. The world's first fingerprint department within a law enforcement agency was in Calcutta, India, formed under the direction of Sir Edward Richard Henry, who gave his name to the classification system of fingerprinting used by police for the next century.

The reason for Rhyme's meditation on fingerprints was that he was presently looking at his own. For the first time in years.

For the first time since the accident in the subway.

His right arm was raised, flexed at the elbow, the wrist and palm twisted so that it was facing him and he was gazing intently at the patterns. He was thoroughly exhilarated, filled with the same sensation as when he'd find the tiny fiber, the bit of trace evidence, the faint impression in the mud that allowed him to make a connection between suspect and crime scene.

The surgery had worked: the implantation of the wires, the computer, controlled by movements of his head and shoulders above the site of his injury. He'd begun tightening muscles in his neck and shoulder to levitate the arm carefully and rotate the wrist. Seeing his own fingerprints had long been a dream of his, and he'd decided that if he could ever regain arm movement, gazing at the whorls and ridges would be the first thing he'd do.

There'd be much therapy ahead of him, of course. And he'd have the other operations too. Nerve rerouting, which would have little effect on mobility but might improve some bodily functions. Then stem cell therapy. And physical rehabilitation too: the treadmill and bicycle and range-of-motion exercises.

There would be limitations too, of course — Thom's job wasn't in any danger. Even if his arms and hands moved, even if his lungs were working better than ever and the business below the waist was approaching that of the nondisabled, he still had no sensation, was still subject to sepsis, would not walk — probably never would, or at least not for many years. But this didn't bother Lincoln Rhyme. He'd learned from his work in forensics that you rarely got one hundred percent of what you sought. But usually, with hard work and the alignment of circumstance — never, in Rhyme's view, 'luck,' of course — what you did achieve was enough . . . for the identification, the arrest, the conviction. Besides, Lincoln Rhyme was a man who needed goals. He lived to fill gaps, to — as Sachs knew well — scratch the itch. His life would be useless without having someplace to go, constantly someplace to go.

Now, carefully, using faint movements of the muscles in his neck, he rotated his palm and lowered it to the bed, with all the coordination of a newborn foal finding its legs.

Then exhaustion and the residue of the drugs were all over him. Rhyme was certainly prepared to sleep. Still he managed to postpone oblivion for a few minutes, choosing instead to rest his eyes on Amelia Sachs's face, pale and half visible through her hair, like the midpoint of a lunar eclipse.

Acknowledgments

Warm thanks to *Crimespree* magazine, the Muskego, Wisconsin library and all those who attended the Murder and Mayhem get-together there last November and who won this product placement for their enthusiastic participation at the event, and for their love of reading!

And to Julie, Madelyn, Will, Tina, Ralph, Kay, Adriano and Lisa . . .

THE SLEEPING DOLL

Jeffery Deaver

Daniel Pell is a contemporary Charles Manson. Obsessed with controlling people, he had formed a quasi cult with a group of women in central California. Eight years ago, he slaughtered a family, though the three women in his own 'Family' were absolved of any part in the deaths. Now, Pell has escaped and Kathryn Dance, interrogator and kinesic analyst, must work with her team to find him. She brings together the three women, now leading normal lives, to help her find out what Pell is up to. Dance must also find the 'Sleeping Doll', the one surviving daughter of the original murder eight years ago. Meanwhile, Pell, with a young woman he has manipulated to help him, tries to fulfil his mission . . .

THE COLD MOON

Jeffery Deaver

On a freezing December night, with a full moon hovering in the black skies over New York City, two people are brutally murdered. Their prolonged deaths are marked by eerie calling cards: moon-faced clocks ticking away the victims' last minutes on earth. Lincoln Rhyme and his team have only hours to stop the icy-cold, brilliant Watchmaker, whose obsession with time drives him to plan his carnage with the precision of a fine timepiece. Amelia is not only Lincoln's eyes and ears on the Watchmaker investigation. She's now, for the first time, lead detective on a homicide — a case that sets into motion clockwork gears of its own. A case with consequences which will endanger many lives, as well as Lincoln and Amelia's future together . . .

THE TWELFTH CARD

Jeffery Deaver

Geneva Settle is working on her research project into her slave ancestor Charles Singleton when she is suddenly the target of a professional assassin. A man who will kill anyone in his way unless top criminalist Lincoln Rhyme can piece together the deadly puzzle . . . Trapped inside a paralysed body, Rhyme's brilliant mind is channelled through his partner, policewoman Amelia Sachs. Rhyme and Sachs find that the only way to stop the killer is to discover the secret Charles Singleton took to his grave over 140 years ago — a secret that threatens to destroy the future of human rights itself . . .

GARDEN OF BEASTS

Jeffery Deaver

Paul Schumann is a mobster hitman known equally for his brilliant tactics and for taking only 'righteous' jobs. When a hit goes wrong and Schumann is nabbed, he's offered a stark choice. He can travel to Berlin and kill the man behind Hitler's rearmament scheme, and walk free forever, or be sent to the electric chair. The instant Paul sets foot in Berlin his mission goes awry. For forty-eight hours, as the city prepares for the coming Olympics, Schumann stalks Reinhardt Ernst, while a dogged criminal police officer and the entire Third Reich apparatus search frantically for the American. It's a cat-and-mouse chase, with Schumann both cat and mouse, and a man who thinks he has nothing to lose . . .